~ DREAM WITH ~

JENNY COLGAN

JENNY COLGAN

The Bookshop on the Corner

Corner

sphere

SPHERE

First published in Great Britain in 2016 by Sphere as
The Little Shop of Happy Ever After
Reissued in 2021 by Sphere

1 3 5 7 9 10 8 6 4 2

A CIP catalogue record for this book
is available from the British Library.

ISBN 978-0-7515-8404-2

Typeset in Caslon by M Rules
Printed and bound in Great Britain by
Clays Ltd, Elcograf S.p.A.

Papers used by Sphere are from well-managed forests
and other responsible sources.

MIX
Paper from
responsible sources
FSC® C104740

Sphere
An imprint of
Little, Brown Book Group
Carmelite House
50 Victoria Embankment
London EC4Y 0DZ

An Hachette UK Company
www.hachette.co.uk

www.littlebrown.co.uk

Let us read, and let us dance; these two amusements will never do any harm to the world.

VOLTAIRE

A Message to Readers

There is no dedication in this book because the entire book is dedicated to you: the reader. To all readers.

Because this book is about reading and books, and how these things can change your life, always, I would argue, for the better. It's also about what it feels like to move and start over (something I've done quite a lot in my life), and the effect that where we choose to live has on how we feel; and can falling in love in real life be like falling in love in stories, and also there's some stuff about cheese, because I have just moved somewhere they make lots of cheese and I can't stop eating it. And a dog called Parsley.

But it has a lot about books in it, because Nina Redmond, the heroine, dreams of opening a bookshop.

So here are some useful tips about where you read, because I want you to be as comfortable as possible. If I have missed out a really obvious one, or you do something completely different, please drop me a line via Facebook or @jennycolgan on Twitter, because I am of the old-fashioned conviction that reading is a pleasure to be carefully guarded at all times, and I truly hope you find this book as pleasing to read as I did to write, wherever you do so.

Bath

9.45 p.m. is my chosen wind-down time for a bath, which drives my husband crazy, as he has to sort the thermostat out if it's not the correct temperature (only very slightly cooler than the surface of the sun), and keep the water constantly topped up. It is a true luxury. Except I don't like bath oil. It's disgusting, isn't it? It just coats everything. Anyway, not the point. Book in bath. Paperbacks are ideal, obviously, and the worst that can happen is you have to dry it out on the radiator (all my children's handed-down Harry Potters are utterly warped), but I read a lot on my e-reader and I will let you into a secret: I turn the pages with my nose. You may not have been blessed with a magnificent Scots-Italian Peter Capaldi nose like me, but with a bit of practice you should soon find it's perfectly possible to keep one of your hands in the water and turn the pages at the same time. If there is anyone in your house with a habit of bursting into the bathroom, make sure you lock the door, as in my experience people do find the sight slightly hilarious.

Alternatively, my friend Sez uses both hands but wraps her e-reader in a plastic bag. Sensible.

Bed

The only problem with bed reading is its brevity: two to three pages and you're out like a light. If it's been a particularly long day, you may swim in and out a bit before you actually doze off, and then you'll pick up the book the next evening thinking, was there a pink unicorn running through an examination hall whilst I chased after it in my pyjamas in this book? and I will have to say to you, no. There is nothing like that in this book. You were dropping off and I'm afraid you have to go back a couple of pages. However, I have helpfully given all the characters very different names from one another. There's nothing worse than reading about a Cathy and a Katie late at night, and I don't want to make anyone's life harder than it needs to be.

Sunbed

On holiday on a sunbed is supposed to be perfect for reading, and in fact in my life I have measured out my sunburn in terms of how brilliant the books I was reading at the time were. Where to hold the book is a problem, though. Hold it up and your arm gets tired and you get a big book-shaped tan mark (which I believe in some circles is quite the cool signifier). Read into the sun and you squint in an unattractive fashion. Sitting cross-legged with it on the towel is not the most flattering of poses (if you're me; I droop somewhat). Lie on your front and you sweat on to it and the plastic bits of the sunbed cut into you. The best thing if you can find one is one of those terrific old-lady sunbeds with the fabric protecting bits on them that you can pull over your head. Yes, they look totally stupid. But hey, you're reading in comfort and nobody else is, so you still win.

Walking down the street

It used to be quite acceptable to walk down the street carrying a book in front of your nose. People would smile indulgently and step out of your way, because they knew what it was like to need to read something so desperately (I once saw a girl hanging on a strap on the London tube dislocate her wrist trying to change at Bank and finish *A Suitable Boy* at the same time).

However, these days everyone holds their stupid smartphone in front of them the entire time in case somebody likes a dog picture on Facebook and they miss it by two seconds, and therefore simply walking down the street has become far more of an obstacle course even without holding up a paperback. Proceed with caution.

Book group

If you're reading this for a book group, I can only apologise and assume it's 2.15 a.m. the night before the evening. Something about being forced to read a book, I find, makes you feel like you're still at school, and hey, if we wanted to do homework, we'd go and take that evening class we keep promising we'll do when we get the time. Mostly if you have to read in a rush it's in case someone says, 'Well, what did you think of that ending?' and you have to nod along, desperately hoping it wasn't a trick ending where they reversed everything (I will tell you, this has happened to me). Therefore, let me reassure you: there is no twist ending in this book. Except I would say that, wouldn't I, if there actually was.

Hammock

Once upon a time when I was young, I had a lovely boyfriend who bought me a hammock and hooked it up on my tiny and highly perilous roof terrace, where I spent many happy hours just rocking and reading, eating Quavers and reflecting on my lovely handsome boyfriend.

Then (reader), I married him and we had a bunch of children and a dog and moved somewhere where it rains all the time, and I think the hammock is in storage. This, my friends, is apparently what's known as 'happy ever after'.

Stolen book time

Ah, the best time. I often turn up ten minutes early to pick the children up from swimming, or steal a quarter of an hour after I've done the supermarket shop, and sit in the car and grab some time back from the world for me and my book. We deserve it, and it is all the sweeter.

Commuting

Commuting reading is great, if you can get the hang of it. Because commuting is so regimented – just watch the glazed looks of people who trace that infinitely complicated, beautiful dance through stations every day – your brain instantly complies with the order to remove you from all this for exactly the right amount of time. Put your phone away; all that fussy crud can wait till you get into work. This is your reward for having to commute.

Travelling

Travelling is not the same as commuting. I am, as you might expect, very much against Wi-Fi coming to cars and aeroplanes, although of course it absolutely is. Even so, pre-book a window seat so you can curl up; put your headphones on and something soothing on the in-flight radio, and dive in for several hours. Except for that bit when they're bringing drinks down the aisle and you think they're going to miss you and you get a bit antsy and can't concentrate. Put the book down at that point and glance at a magazine, pretending to be really casual and utterly unfussed as to whether you get served or not. I have also tried to eat, drink, listen to music and read in an economy airline seat all at the same time. Don't do this unless you have plenty of spare cash handy for someone else's dry-cleaning bill.

Trains are built for reading. I find a good pair of headphones less troublesome than sitting in the quiet carriage and having to police it for noisy idiots. I'm not saying they should get a prison sentence. But I'm not saying they shouldn't, either.

In front of the fire
If you haven't got a fire, a candle will do. The one thing I really look forward to as the nights draw in is a big cosy fire and a good book – the longer the better. I love a really, really long novel, a large cup of tea, or glass of wine depending on how close to the weekend we are (or how much I am in the mood to stretch the definition of what constitutes the weekend), and a bit of peace and quiet. A dog helps too. Dogs are tremendously good at showing you you don't have to check your phone every two seconds to have a happy life.

Hospital
I have spent a lot of time in hospitals for one reason or another: I worked in one, I had a bunch of children in one, and those children have subsequently spent a bunch of times falling out of trees and breaking limbs, etc. etc.

Hospital time doesn't move like other time. It's a hell of a lot slower, for one thing. It doesn't stop at night. And there is always that slight sense of wonder at everything that is going on, for all the real dramas most of us will know – loss and new life, happiness and the deepest mourning – are happening all around, on every floor of a sterile, overheated building, terror and pain and joy in every clipped professional footstep on highly polished linoleum.

I find it hard to read in hospital; it is like being in a great ship pushing through difficult waters, whilst outside are people on land, walking about and carrying on with normal lives, oblivious to the choppy waters being navigated so very close to them.

Poetry works well in hospital, I find. Short things, from which you can look up and feel not quite so fragile, not quite so disconnected; for we are all there, or have been, or will be.

It is also a very kind place, a place to sit and read quietly to somebody else.

This is why I don't feel any moral outrage when people complain about hospital shops selling cakes and ice cream. Hospitals should always have cakes. At the very, very least.

Under a shady tree in a sunny park
But of course. Mr Whippy ice cream, please, not the solid stuff.

Misc
Some of my proudest achievements have been figuring out how to read whilst breastfeeding (use a pillow UNDER the baby's head); drying my hair (I have awful hair); brushing my

teeth (I have good teeth, probably because I brush for well over the official time); waiting for roadworks traffic lights to turn from red to green; locked in the bathroom at a very boring wedding (not my own); at soft play (I once read an entire novel on a wet afternoon whilst my kids frolicked in a ball pool; I think we all had the best day ever); having a pedicure (I never have manis, can't read through 'em); standing in a queue; in a convertible (tricky); in church (a sin, and one for which I was righteously punished); on business trips where I had to eat alone in restaurants (you're never alone with a book); and, all the way back to where this started, for about a million hours in the right-hand back seat of my dad's old green Saab 99, the weight of my youngest brother's curly head fast asleep in my lap and a Fab lolly to accompany me. So do let me know where you read. Because every day with a book is slightly better with one than without, and I wish you nothing but the happiest of days.

Now, come and meet Nina . . .

Jenny xxx

Chapter One

The problem with good things that happen is that very often they disguise themselves as awful things. It would be lovely, wouldn't it, whenever you're going through something difficult, if someone could just tap you on the shoulder and say, 'Don't worry, it's completely worth it. It seems like absolutely horrible crap now, but I promise it will all come good in the end,' and you could say, 'Thank you, Fairy Godmother.' You might also say, 'Will I also lose that half-stone?' and they would say, 'But of course, my child!'

That would be useful, but it isn't how it is, which is why we sometimes plough on too long with things that aren't making us happy, or give up too quickly on something that might yet work itself out, and it is often difficult to tell precisely which is which.

A life lived forwards can be a really irritating thing. So Nina thought, at any rate.

Nina Redmond, twenty-nine, was telling herself not to cry in public. If you have ever tried giving yourself a good talking-to, you'll know it doesn't work terribly well. She was at work, for goodness' sake. You weren't meant to cry at work.

She wondered if anyone else ever did. Then she wondered if maybe everyone did, even Cathy Neeson, with her stiff too-blonde hair, and her thin mouth and her spreadsheets, who was right at this moment standing in a corner, watching the room with folded arms and a grim expression, after delivering to the small team Nina was a member of a speech filled with jargon about how there were cutbacks all over, and Birmingham couldn't afford to maintain all its libraries, and how austerity was something they just had to get used to.

Nina reckoned probably not. Some people just didn't have a tear in them.

(What Nina didn't know was that Cathy Neeson cried on the way to work, on the way home from work – post eight o'clock most nights – every time she made someone redundant, every time she was asked to shave another few per cent off an already skeleton budget, every time she was ordered to produce some new quality relevant paperwork, and every time her boss dumped a load of admin on her at four o'clock on a Friday afternoon on his way to a skiing holiday, of which he took many.

Eventually she ditched the entire thing and went and worked in a National Trust gift shop for a fifth of the salary and half the hours and none of the tears. But this story is not about Cathy Neeson.)

It was just, Nina thought, trying to squash down the lump

in her throat … it was just that they had been such a *little* library.

Children's story time Tuesday and Thursday mornings. Early closing Wednesday afternoon. A shabby old-fashioned building with tatty linoleum floors. A little musty sometimes, it was true. The big dripping radiators could take a while to get going of a morning and then would become instantly too warm, with a bit of a fug, particularly off old Charlie Evans, who came in to keep warm and read the *Morning Star* cover to cover, very slowly. She wondered where the Charlie Evanses of the world would go now.

Cathy Neeson had explained that they were going to compress the library services into the centre of town, where they would become a 'hub', with a 'multimedia experience zone' and a coffee shop and an 'inter-sensory experience', whatever that was, even though town was at least two bus trips too far for most of their elderly or buggied-up clientele.

Their lovely tatty old pitched-roof premises were being sold off to become executive apartments that would be well beyond the reach of a librarian's salary.

And Nina Redmond, twenty-nine, bookworm, with her long tangle of auburn hair, her pale skin with freckles dotted here and there, and a shyness that made her blush – or want to burst into tears – at the most inopportune moments, was, she got the feeling, going to be thrown out into the cold winds of a world that was getting a lot of unemployed librarians on the market at the same time.

'So,' Cathy Neeson had concluded, 'you can pretty much get started on packing up the "books" right away.'

She said 'books' like it was a word she found distasteful in

3

her shiny new vision of Mediatech Services. All those grubby, awkward books.

Nina dragged herself into the back room with a heavy heart and a slight redness around her eyes. Fortunately, everyone else looked more or less the same way. Old Rita O'Leary, who should probably have retired about a decade ago but was so kind to their clientele that everyone overlooked the fact that she couldn't see the numbers on the Dewey Decimal System any more and filed more or less at random, had burst into floods, and Nina had been able to cover up her own sadness comforting her.

'You know who else did this?' hissed her colleague Griffin through his straggly beard as she made her way through. Griffin was casting a wary look at Cathy Neeson still out in the main area as he spoke. 'The Nazis. They packed up all the books and threw them on to bonfires.'

'They're not throwing them on to bonfires!' said Nina. 'They're not actually Nazis.'

'That's what everyone thinks. Then before you know it, you've got Nazis.'

With breathtaking speed, there'd been a sale, of sorts, with most of their clientele leafing through old familiar favourites in the 10p box and leaving the shinier newer stock behind.

Now, as the days went on, they were meant to be packing up the rest of the books to ship them to the central library, but Griffin's normally sullen face was looking even darker

4

than usual. He had a long, unpleasantly scrawny beard, and a scornful attitude towards people who didn't read the books he liked. As the only books he liked were obscure 1950s out-of-print stories about frustrated young men who drank too much in Fitzrovia, that gave him a lot of time to hone his attitude. He was still talking about book burners.

'They won't get burned! They'll go to the big place in town.'

Nina couldn't bring herself to even say Mediatech.

Griffin snorted. 'Have you seen the plans? Coffee, computers, DVDs, plants, admin offices, and people doing cost–benefit analysis and harassing the unemployed – sorry, running "mindfulness workshops". There isn't room for a book in the whole damn place.' He gestured at the dozens of boxes. 'This will be landfill. They'll use it to make roads.'

'They won't!'

'They will! That's what they do with dead books, didn't you know? Turn them into underlay for roads. So great big cars can roll over the top of centuries of thought and ideas and scholarship, metaphorically stamping a love of learning into the dust with their stupid big tyres and blustering *Top Gear* idiots killing the planet.'

'You're not in the best of moods this morning, are you, Griffin?'

'Could you two hurry it along a bit over there?' said Cathy Neeson, bustling in, sounding anxious. They only had the budget for the collection trucks for one afternoon; if they didn't manage to load everything up in time, she'd be in serious trouble.

'Yes, Commandant Über-Führer,' said Griffin under his

breath as she bustled out again, her blonde bob still rigid. 'God, that woman is so evil it's unbelievable.'

But Nina wasn't listening. She was looking instead in despair at the thousands of volumes around her, so hopeful with their beautiful covers and optimistic blurbs. To condemn any of them to the waste disposal seemed heartbreaking: these were books! To Nina it was like closing down a dogs' home. And there was no way they were going to get it all done today, no matter what Cathy Neeson thought.

Which was how, six hours later, when Nina's Mini Metro pulled up in front of the front door of her tiny shared house, it was completely and utterly stuffed with volumes.

'Oh no,' said Surinder, coming to the door and folding her arms over her rather impressive bosom. She had a grim expression on her face. Nina had met her mother, who was a police superintendent. Surinder had inherited the expression. She used it on Nina quite a lot. 'You're not bringing them in here. Absolutely not.'

'It's just . . . I mean, they're in perfect condition.'

'It's not that,' said Surinder. 'And don't give me that look, like I'm turning away orphans.'

'Well, in a way . . . ' said Nina, trying not to look too pleading.

'The joists of the house won't take it, Nina! I've told you before.'

Nina and Surinder had shared the tiny terraced house very happily for four years, ever since Nina had arrived in Edgbaston by way of Chester. They hadn't known each other beforehand, and had thus been in the happy position of being able to become housemate friends, rather than friends who moved in together and then fell out.

Nina lived in some worry about Surinder finding a serious boyfriend and moving out or moving him in, but despite a large number of suitors, it hadn't happened yet, which was useful. Surinder would point out that there was no reason to think she was the only person this might happen to. But Nina's crippling shyness and solitary habit of reading all the time meant they both felt reasonably sure that Surinder was going to get lucky first. Nina had always been the quiet one, on the sidelines, observing things through the medium of the novels she loved to read.

Plus, she thought, after another awkward evening chatting to the clumsy friends of Surinder's latest paramour, she just hadn't met anyone who compared to the heroes of the books she loved. A Mr Darcy, or a Heathcliff, or even, in the right mood, a Christian Grey . . . the nervous, clammy-handed boys to whom she could never think of anything funny or witty to say really couldn't compare. They didn't stride over Yorkshire moors looking swarthy and furious. They didn't refuse to dance with you at the Pump Room whilst secretly harbouring a deep lifelong passion for you. They just got drunk at the Christmas party, as Griffin had, and tried to stick their tongue down your throat whilst bleating on for hours about how their relationship with their girlfriend wasn't actually that serious really. Anyway. Surinder was looking furious, and worst of all, she was right. When it came to books, there simply wasn't the space. There were books everywhere. Books on the landing, books on the stairs, books filling Nina's room completely,

7

books carefully filed in the sitting room, books in the loo, just in case. Nina always liked to feel that *Little Women* was close by in a crisis.

'But I can't leave them out in the cold,' she pleaded.

'Nina, it's a load of DEAD WOOD! Some of which smells!'

'But . . .'

Surinder's expression didn't change as she looked severely at Nina. 'Nina, I'm calling it. This is getting totally out of hand. You're packing up the library all week. It will just get worse and worse.'

She stepped forward and grabbed a huge romance Nina adored from the top of the pile.

'Look at this! You already have it.'

'Yes, I know, but this is the hardback first edition. Look! It's beautiful! Never been read!'

'And it won't be read either, because your reading pile is taller than I am!'

The two girls were standing out on the street now, Surinder so cross she'd piled out of the front door.

'No!' said Surinder, raising her voice. 'No. This time I am absolutely putting my foot down.'

Nina felt herself starting to shake. She realised they were on the verge of having a falling-out, and she couldn't bear confrontation or any form of argument at all. Surinder knew this as well.

'Please,' she said.

Surinder threw up her hands. 'God, it's like kicking a puppy. You're not dealing with this job change, are you? You're not dealing with it at all. You just roll over and play dead.'

'Also,' Nina whispered, staring at the pavement as the door

swung shut behind them, 'I forgot my keys this morning. I think we're locked out.'

Surinder had stared at her furiously, then, thank God, after making the police commissioner face, had finally burst out laughing. They had gone down to the corner of their street, to a nice little gastro pub, which was normally overrun but tonight wasn't too jammed, and found a cosy corner.

Surinder had bought a bottle of wine, which Nina looked at warily. This was normally a bad sign, the start of the 'what's wrong with Nina' conversation that generally began after the second glass.

After all, it was okay, wasn't it? To love books and love your job and live life like that? Nice, cosy. Routine. Or it had been.

'No,' said Surinder, putting down her second glass with a sigh.

Nina composed her face into a long-suffering listening look. Surinder worked in a jewellery-importing office, running the books and the diamond traders. She was great at it. They were all terrified of her. Both her admin and her absenteeism skills were legendary.

'It's not enough, is it, Neens?'

Nina concentrated on her glass, wishing the attention was anywhere else.

'What did the resettlement officer say?'

'He said ... he said there weren't a lot of jobs left in libraries, not after the cuts. They're going to staff them with volunteers.'

Surinder made a snorting noise. 'Those lovely old ladies?'

Nina nodded.

'But they can't set people up with the right novels! They don't know what a nine-year-old needs to read after Harry Potter.'

'*The Knife of Never Letting Go*,' said Nina automatically.

'That's exactly what I mean! That expertise! Can they work the ordering system? The filing? The back office?'

Nina shook her head. 'Not really.'

'So where are you meant to go?'

Nina shrugged. 'There might be facilitation roles in the new media hub, but I'd have to take a team-building course and reapply.'

'A team-building course?'

'Yes.'

'*You?*' Surinder laughed. 'Did you sign up?'

Nina shook her head. 'Griffin did.'

'Well, you have to.'

Nina heaved a sigh. 'I suppose so.'

'You're losing your job, Nina! You're losing it! Mooning around reading Georgette Heyer all afternoon isn't going to change that, is it?'

Nina shook her head.

'Get it together!'

'If I do, can I bring the books into the house?'

'No!'

Chapter Two

Nina turned up to the team-building course nervously. She wasn't sure what to expect at all. Also, she still had a car full of books. Griffin was there, his leg casually placed on his opposite knee, as if he was trying to give the impression of being the most laid-back person of all time. It didn't work terribly well. His ponytail hung lankly down the back of his slightly grey T-shirt, and his glasses were smeared.

'Trainee tossers,' he whispered to Nina, to make her feel better. She didn't; she felt worse, and fussed with her floral shirt. Outside, spring was tossing itself about like a small boat, one moment drenched, the next bathed in sunlight.

Surinder had been right: it absolutely was time to buck herself up.

But sometimes she felt the world wasn't built for people like her. Confident, big-personality people like Surinder simply didn't understand. If you weren't an extrovert, if you weren't shoving yourself out into the open all the time, posting selfies everywhere, demanding attention, talking constantly, people just gazed straight past you. You got over-looked. And normally she didn't mind.

But now Nina could see she was in danger of overlooking herself. However many books she tried to save, whatever she tried to do, the branch library was closing. Her job was going, and it wasn't just a case of finding another one. Librarians were unemployed everywhere. Thirty would apply for every job going. It was like being a typewriter repair man, or some-one who made fax machines. She felt, at twenty-nine, oddly surplus to life's requirements.

A young man bounded up on to the little dais at the front of the back room of the library where they'd all gathered along with the groups from the other two libraries also closing in the region. There was a lot of muttering and complaining when they met, about the bloody government and how crap everything was, and didn't they know – didn't they *know* – what libraries did for their communities?

Nina thought they did know: they simply didn't care.

'Hey!' said the young man, who was dressed in jeans and a pink open-necked shirt.

'I wonder what he's paid for doing this,' whispered Griffin. 'More than us, I bet.'

Nina blinked. She'd never been in it for the money.

'Hey, everyone!' said the young man, who had one of those voices that went up at the end and made everything sound like a question. 'Now, I know this isn't an ideal situation?'

'You reckon?' snorted Griffin.

'But I'm sure we're going to all get on great by the end of the day ... do a bit of bonding, a bit of confidence-building, yeah?'

Griffin snorted again. But Nina leaned forward a little. Confidence-building? Couldn't hurt.

It came an hour into the morning. They were playing 'trust games' to restore faith in something or other, despite the fact that they were all going to have to compete against one another for the few remaining jobs. Nina had walked blind-folded across the room, guided only by the others' voices. And now here she was standing on a table, again with her eyes shut, waiting to fall backwards. She felt nervous and irritated all at once. This wasn't for her, the shouting, the showing-off.

Mungo, the young man, had been encouraging, however. 'Don't think there isn't anything you can't do!' he'd shouted. 'Yeah?'

Griffin had sighed. Nina, though, had looked at him. Could there be something in it after all?

'There's nothing you can't do if you try.'

'Oh good, I think I'll join the Olympic diving squad,' Griffin had commented.

Mungo's smile hadn't dropped for a moment. Then he'd lifted his trouser leg and the room had gasped. Underneath, his leg was smooth plastic.

'I'd still give it a go,' he said. 'Come on. What do you really want to do?'

'Run a Mediatech department,' said Griffin quickly. He was convinced, Nina knew, that Mungo was a corporate spy.

Mungo merely nodded. 'Let's go round the room,' he said. 'Be honest. There are no spies here.'

Nina shrank back in her seat. She couldn't bear speaking in public.

A gruff man she didn't know spoke up from the back of the room.

'I always wanted to work with animals,' he said. 'Out in the wild. Spotting them, tracking their numbers, you know what I mean?'

'That sounds amazing,' said Mungo, and he sounded like he meant it. 'Great! Come up to the front!'

Nina shrivelled inside as they all had to gather around the table, and the man stood up on it and fell back, letting the crowd catch him.

'I always wanted to do make-up for movies,' said a young receptionist from central services. 'Make up the big stars and that.'

Mungo nodded, and she came forward and fell too. Nina couldn't believe how casually everyone got into it.

'I just want to work with books,' said Rita. 'That's all I ever wanted to do.'

More ideas came in from around the room, with lots of nodding from everyone and the occasional round of applause. They didn't make Rita do the fall backwards, though, not with her hips. Even Griffin modified his original answer, muttering that actually he'd really wanted to be a comic-book artist. Nina didn't speak. She was thinking furiously. Finally she saw that Mungo was staring at her.

'Yes?'

'Come on. You're last. You have to say what you want to do. And be honest.'

Very reluctantly, Nina edged towards the table.

14

'I haven't really thought about it.'

'Course you have,' said Mungo. 'Everybody has.'

'Well, it'll sound silly. Especially these days.'

'Nothing sounds silly in here,' he said. 'We've all been falling backwards off tables.'

Nina climbed up on to the table. The rest of the group looked at her expectantly. Her throat went dry and her mind went blank.

'Well,' she said, feeling herself colour in that awful way. She swallowed painfully. 'Well . . . I mean. Well. I always . . . I always dreamed that one day I might have my own bookshop. Just a very little one.'

There was a silence. And then, around the room, 'Me too!' 'Oh, yes!' 'That sounds LOVELY.'

'Close your eyes,' said Mungo, gently.

And with that, she leaned backwards, eyes tight shut, and fell into the waiting arms, which held her, then gently returned her to the floor.

And by the time she opened her eyes again, she wondered . . .

'A SHOP?' Griffin, of course, pooh-poohed it. 'A BOOKSHOP? Are you NUTS?'

Nina shrugged. 'I don't know,' she said. 'I could sell your comics in it.'

She was still feeling oddly inspired. Mungo had taken her aside at the break and they'd discussed it. She'd expressed her inability to deal with overheads or stock or staff or all the huge and paralysing commitments that running a shop would entail that she didn't feel she could deal with. He'd nodded gently. Finally she'd confessed that she had a whole shop's worth of stock in her car, and he'd laughed and then held up his hand.

'You know,' he'd said, 'there are mobile versions of this kind of thing.'

'What do you mean?'

'Well, instead of a shop with running costs and so on, you could do something different.'

He showed her a picture on a website of a woman who ran a bookshop from a barge. Nina had seen her before and sighed with envy.

'It doesn't have to be a barge,' he said. Mungo pulled up a few more sites on his computer. 'I knew a woman in Cornwall who ran a bakery from a van.'

'A whole bakery?'

'A whole bakery. People used to come for miles.'

Nina blinked. 'A van?'

'Why not? Can you drive?'

'Yes.'

'You could kit it out quite nicely, couldn't you?'

Nina didn't tell him it had taken her forever to learn how to reverse around corners. Mungo's bouncy enthusiasm was so all-encompassing, it somehow felt easier just to agree with him.

She showed Griffin an ad in the paper she'd found during the break, helped by an admiring Mungo. 'Look at this.'

'What is that?'

'It's a van.'

'A smelly old food van?'

'A smelly old food van,' agreed Nina reluctantly. 'Okay, that one probably won't work. But look at this one.'

'You think vans are the answer to everything,' grumbled Griffin. 'They'll have bugs.'

'I just said, no food vans!' Nina's faintly irritated voice caused Griffin to look up from his pint in surprise, as if a mouse had roared. 'Be sensible. Look at this.'

'It's a van,' said Griffin with exaggerated sarcasm. 'I don't know what you expect me to say about it.'

'I expect you to say, wow, Nina, that's amazing, imagine you taking charge of your life and thinking of something like that.'

'Have you gone soft on that Mungo?'

'No, Griffin, he's a child. But I like his attitude.'

'I don't get it,' said Griffin. 'A van. I thought you said you wanted to run a bookshop?'

'I do!' said Nina. 'But I can't afford premises, can I?'

'No,' said Griffin. 'You're a terrible risk for a bank to lend money to. You don't know anything about running a shop.'

'I know,' said Nina. 'But I do know about books, don't I?'

Griffin looked at her. 'Yes,' he admitted grudgingly. 'You're pretty good at books.'

'And I'd get redundancy money,' said Nina. 'And I could sell the Mini Metro. I mean, I could ... I could afford a van ... just about. And I've got all the stock from the library. And my life. And everywhere, really. I mean, I could start with that, pretty much fill it and see where I go from there.'

'You do have too many books,' said Griffin. 'And I never thought I'd say that about anybody.'

17

'Well,' said Nina, 'if I have the stock ... and I have a van ...'

'What?'

'I mean, I don't see what's stopping me just travelling about selling books.'

She was feeling genuinely excited now, something buzzing in her chest. Why not her? Why should everyone else get to have dreams and not her?

'What, in Edgbaston?'

'No,' said Nina. 'It will have to be somewhere without parking restrictions.'

'I think that's, like, nowhere.'

'Somewhere they don't mind. Somewhere I'm allowed to just sell books.'

'I don't think it works like that.'

'Well, like a farmers' market, where they turn up once a week to sell stuff.'

'So you'll work one day a week and spend the rest of the time tending your book crops?'

'Stop pouring cold water on everything.'

'I'm not, I'm just being realistic. What kind of a friend would I be if I sat here saying, yes, Nina, drop everything in your life before you even know if you have a job or not, toss it all away for a pipe dream when you're nearly thirty?'

'Mm,' said Nina, feeling flattened.

'I mean,' said Griffin, 'you can't say it's in your nature to take daredevil risks. You've never been late back from a lunch break in the six years I've known you; you've never made a staff suggestion or complained about anything or stayed out to have an extra cup of coffee during a fire alarm – nothing.

Little Miss Perfect Corporate Person. Little Miss Ultimate Librarian . . . and now you're going to buy a van and sell books out in the wild? For a job?'

'Does that sound crazy?' said Nina.

'Yes,' said Griffin.

'Mmmm,' said Nina. 'What are *you* going to do? Are you going to apply to comic shops and illustrators and stuff?'

Griffin looked embarrassed for a moment. 'Oh,' he said. 'God, no, not really. No. I'll probably just apply for one of the new jobs. You know? For safety? As a knowledge facilitator.'

Nina nodded sadly. 'Yes, me too.'

'I'll never get it against you,' said Griffin.

'Don't be daft, of course you will,' said Nina, glancing down at the paper again, feeling an awkward flush pass through her. She focused on the ad. 'This van is miles away, probably.'

Griffin leaned over her to look at the ad, then shook with laughter.

'Nina, you can't have that van!'

'Why not? That's the one I want!'

She modified what she was saying.

'That's the one I would have wanted.'

The van was white, boxy, old-fashioned, with big head-lamps. It had a door towards the back of one of the sides, with a little set of metal steps that folded out. It looked retro and rather lovely, and best of all, there was plenty of space for shelving inside, a leftover from the bread van it had once been. It was gorgeous.

'Well good luck,' said Griffin, pointing at the small print. 'Look! It's in Scotland.'

Chapter Three

Cathy Neeson had everyone in individually to look at 'core skills development'. It wasn't an interview. Of course it wasn't. What it was, truly, was cold-blooded torture, but of course nobody could say that. Nina was quivering with nerves by the time she got into the room.

Cathy looked up as if she didn't recognise her (which she didn't, as she had a child with whooping cough whom she'd settled at 3 a.m.), which didn't fill Nina with confidence. She glanced quickly at her notes.

'Ah, Nina,' she said. 'Nice to see you.'

She looked again at her paperwork and frowned slightly.

'So, you've enjoyed working at the library, yes?'

Nina nodded. 'Yes, very much.'

'But you must be excited by our new direction, no?'

'I found the team-building course really helpful,' Nina said. To be honest, she had thought of little else since. Of how the van might look, parked up, inviting and sparkling, and what she might put inside, and how big a collection she would need to have a good chance of stocking the kinds of things people might like, and where she could source other second-hand books when the library had been totally cleared, and ...

She realised she'd drifted off and that Cathy Neeson was staring at her intently.

(Cathy Neeson hated this part of her job so much she wanted to stab it. The idea was to gently dissuade unsuitable candidates from applying and save the interview process some time. But the truth was, Cathy wasn't sure the noisy *Apprentice*-style kids who seemed to get all the jobs these days were what they really needed. A nice manner and a level head would surely get you much further. But that didn't cut much ice with the big cheeses, who liked flashy mission statements and loud, confident remarks.)

'So are you still thinking of applying?'

'Why?' said Nina, a look of panic crossing her face. 'Shouldn't I?'

Cathy Neeson sighed. 'Just have a think about how your core skill set would fit in,' she said blandly. 'And ... good luck.'

What the hell does that mean? thought Nina, stumbling up to go.

Nina was still obsessing over the small ads for vans when she ought to have been preparing for the interview, but couldn't find anything even vaguely as nice as this one elsewhere. It just felt right, with its funny little nose and its curved roof. There was nothing for it. She was going to have to go to Scotland.

Griffin came up behind her, squinting.

'You cannot be serious,' he said.

'I just want to have a look,' she protested. 'It's just a thought.'

'Time's running a bit short for thoughts,' said Griffin. 'Uh, could I ask you something?'

'What?' said Nina, instantly wary.

'Could you look over this application for me?' He looked shamefaced.

'Griffin, you know I'm going for the same job!'

'Uh huh. But you're so much better at this stuff than me.'

'Well why wouldn't I totally just tell you all the wrong things to write and make you put in a really terrible application?'

'Because you're too nice to do that.'

'Maybe I've just been lulling you into a false sense of security.'

'For four years?'

'Maybe!'

'Neh,' said Griffin, with a complacent look that made Nina want to spill her coffee on him. 'You're too sweet. Too sweet not to help me, and too sweet to drive a truck.'

'You reckon?' said Nina.

'Yup.'

He pushed over the forms. 'Could you just take a look at it? Let me know? Come on, they're interviewing us both anyway. Might as well help out your illiterate chum.'

Nina looked at him. She knew her session with Cathy had not gone well. It was almost like she was sabotaging herself by helping Griffin. On the other hand, he needed help . . .

With a sigh, she took the application, and plunged deep into impenetrable paragraphs about multimedia, moving forward, and crowd-sourcing content. The more she read, the more depressed she felt. Was this what the world wanted now? Because if it was, she didn't know if she had it. She tried to help Griffin with some of his more incomprehensible sentence structures, but she couldn't help comparing all this stuff about paradigms and envelope-pushing and sustainability targets with her own application, which had short, neatly typed paragraphs about libraries being the centre of their communities and how reading helped children fulfil their potential. This had, she could see, much grander ambitions.

She sighed and looked at the ad again.

The van was long, not unlike an ice cream truck, with an old-fashioned frontage. The pictures of the interior revealed it to be completely empty, with enough space – she'd actually drawn a model of it on some paper – for plenty of high shelving down each side, plus a little corner seating area where she could have a sofa, and maybe the children's books . . . a couple of bean bags . . . She found herself staring dreamily out of the open window into the noisy Birmingham evening.

Outside, two men were having a loud discussion about how someone had stitched them up about a car; a clutch of adolescents were screaming with laughter on their way down the road; there were four buses honking at the crossroads for some reason; and there was the endless roar of traffic from the nearby flyover. But Nina didn't hear any of it.

She could see it perfectly. She could. She could imagine the entire thing. Some petrol, her stock – so many of the books she'd picked up were absolutely brand new, in perfect order. And with all the libraries closing . . . was it possible she could bring something good out of something so awful?

She glanced at the address again. Kirrinfief. She looked up ways of getting there. The fast ones weren't cheap, and the cheap ones . . .

She had weeks of holiday entitlement that she'd never taken. If she didn't get a new job, she was going to lose it all anyway, right? She might as well take advantage of some of the last free days she'd ever get paid for.

Before she knew it, she'd finished Griffin's grandiose application form – and booked herself a coach ticket.

Chapter Four

Nina let her book fall into her lap, conscious that she was getting drowsy.

It was late in the evening and she'd been on the bus all day, with only the shortest of stops to stretch her legs and wander about at motorway service stations – not normally great places to relax. The day was nearly over but the sun was still high in the sky – it stayed light here far later than it did down in Birmingham – and it was glowing strongly through the left-hand window she was leaning against as they crossed the Forth Road Bridge. The glow off the quiet Firth was shining pink, making it feel for an instant as though the bus was flying through the white wires of the great structure.

Nina had never been to Scotland before. In fact, as she'd booked her ticket, for less than the price of an evening in the pub, she'd realised that at the age of twenty-nine, there were lots of places she'd never been. Of course she had been to Narnia and the Little House on the Prairie, and Wonderland, but to actually smell the deep, rich, yeasty smell of the old grey streets as they'd approached Edinburgh, the ancient cobbles almost making her dismount then and there as the iron sky was reflected in the windows of the tall houses, the oldest skyscrapers on earth – that had made her sit up, entranced by the higgledy-piggledy little streets that wandered here and there, tangling over the great wide ones, and the austere castle on a cliff that appeared to have been parachuted into the middle of the bustling city.

And still they went on: north, ever north, the sky growing even larger as they crossed the great bridge, the iron railway bridge to the right of her, the traffic thinning out as they drove through rolling farmland and harsh craggy landscapes and long moors under the wide clouded sky.

There were fewer people on the bus, too. There had been plenty of comings and goings at Newcastle and Berwick and Edinburgh, but now it was only her and a few elderly people and what looked like oil workers, sitting patiently; tough-looking men on their own, grunting at each other, their faces set to whatever lay ahead of them.

One moment she would look up from her book to see a great brown plain, the golden light playing through the heather; the next, she was in time to see an osprey dive across the road towards a loch, which made her start; then, as they crested the next mountain, a ray of sunshine came out and she put her book down altogether.

Perhaps if it had been rainy that spring weekend, everything would have been very different.

Nina would have sat reading, huddled up in her duffle coat; she would have exchanged a few words with the sellers of the van, thanked them politely, gone home to think again.

Had the wind been coming off the sea; had the bridge been closed to high-sided traffic because of strong winds. Had a million different tiny things happened.

Because life is like that, isn't it? If you thought of all the tiny things that divert your path one way or another, some good, some bad, you'd never do anything ever again.

And some people don't. Some people go through life not really deciding to do much, not wanting to, always too fearful of the consequences to try something new. Of course, that in itself is also a decision. You'll get somewhere whether you put any effort into it or not. But doing something new is so hard. And a few things can help.

That evening, as Nina arrived in Scotland for the very first time, it was not stormy and wet and overcast, with clouds so low they seemed to clip the trees. Instead it was as if the entire country was showing off for her. The evening was golden; the northern light strange and beautiful. Everywhere she looked, it seemed, were grey stone castles and long bright vistas, lambs gambolling in the fields and deer scattering away in distant woods as the coach rolled past. Two old men who'd got on in Edinburgh started speaking gently to one another in Gaelic, and she tuned her ear in, feeling as she did so that it was not so much talking as singing, and thrilled and astonished that whilst she was technically still in the UK, where she'd spent her entire life, it could still be so strange, so foreign.

The road coasted higher, but never seemed to end in the untouched landscape, instead floating above the heathery fields, and Nina found herself urging the bus on and on, to where there were no cars, and even fewer towns and people.

She had a guilty moment when she felt as if she was betraying her beloved Birmingham, with its ring roads and tower blocks and police sirens and jostling pubs and noisy parties and dense traffic. Normally she loved that. Well, she liked it. Well, she tolerated it.

But up here, it wasn't hard at all to understand why the Scots thought of themselves as different and apart. She'd travelled in the UK – to London, of course, to Manchester, on holiday in tended, manicured Dorset and Devon. But this: this was a completely different proposition, a far wilder land unfolding in front of her, so much larger than she'd ever thought of it, had she thought of it at all. Towns and villages appeared at a leisurely rate, with the strangest of names – Auchterdub, Balwearie, Donibristle – all of it unfolding in a strange tongue. It was startling.

Just after 9 p.m., but with the sky still light, even though it was only April, the bus finally arrived in Kirrinfief.

Nina was the only one getting off here, feeling odd and crushed and so very far from home. She looked around. There were two narrow streets winding down from the side of the hills that surrounded the town; a little pub, a grey-painted restaurant with scrubbed wooden tables, a small grocer's shop, a bakery, a tiny post office and a shop selling fishing rods. There wasn't a single soul to be seen anywhere, nobody on the road.

Nina felt nervous. In novels, this usually meant that the next person you met was going to try and kill you and the rest of the community was going to cover it up, or everyone would turn into a werewolf. She told herself not to be ridiculous. Griffin and Surinder knew where she was. She was going to look at a van, an insurance policy if everything kept going so horribly at work. That was all. This was just business. Normal people did it all the time. She took out her phone regardless and checked it. No signal. She bit her lip, then told herself to get on with it.

The pub was called the Rob Roy and was covered in pretty hanging baskets. There was no one sitting outside; the evening had taken on a chill, even though a weak sun was still making its slow way down over the horizon. Nina took a deep breath and pushed open the door.

Inside, the old wooden tables were highly polished, and there was a great stone fireplace surrounded by horse brasses and filled with dried flowers. The room was almost empty, but at the bar, two old men turned round and regarded her carefully above the pints they were clearly nursing. Nina had to grab her courage with both hands to smile nicely and walk forward. After all, the bus had gone, and there wasn't another until tomorrow, so it wasn't like she had a lot of choice in the matter.

'Uh, hello,' she said, conscious suddenly of how English she sounded. 'Is, er . . . Is the landlord in?'

'Hesjustawainnit.'

Nina couldn't remember feeling more embarrassed in her entire life. A hot flush rose up around her neck; she genuinely hadn't understood a word the man had said. She put her hand to her throat.

'Uh, sorry?' she said. It felt like the more she tried to make herself comprehensible, the more she sounded like the Queen. Suddenly she wished herself very, very far away from here; almost anywhere, in fact.

29

Both men sniggered, then, thank heavens, the door burst open and a ruddy-faced man came in carrying a barrel of beer as if it weighed nothing.

'The lass!' he said cheerfully. 'Hello there! I was wondering if the bus had been through.'

'It has.' She nodded, relieved beyond words. If she concentrated, she could follow him.

'I'm Alasdair. So what brings you here this time of year? The snow's barely melted off the peak land.'

Nina smiled. 'I know. It's beautiful.'

His face softened at that. 'Aye, it is. Can I get you a drink?'

Nina didn't recognise any of the beers on tap. She asked for a mineral water, then saw the men shake their heads sadly and changed her order to half a pint of the local beer, which tasted like fizzy treacle.

'Get some of that down you, lass,' Alasdair said.

'Are you still doing food?' asked Nina. They all laughed.

'Naw, not at this time of night,' said Alasdair. He looked up, his eyes very blue under his sandy hair. 'I can probably make you a sandwich if you like.'

Nina was starving; the food in the service stations hadn't looked particularly nice and cost a fortune, and she was conscious that she might well be out of work very soon. She'd hoped for a hotpot or a pie or something warm and filling – in fact if she was totally honest, she'd fantasised about a friendly farmer's wife and home-baked apple pie and cream, then realised that she was thinking about an Enid Blyton novel, not a real place she was actually visiting.

'Um, yes please,' she said, and the man disappeared through the back into what looked like a tiny kitchen space while Nina stared hard at her phone as if that might make it work, and wondered if she could just take her book out again.

One of the men asked her a question, which she didn't quite understand but guessed to be 'What are you doing up here?', and she mentioned that she'd come to look at a van.

At this they both burst out laughing and ushered her outside. In the little town square, the fading light picking out the names on the war memorial – MacAindra, MacGhie, MacIngliss – they led her across the cobbles to a side street completely blocked by the van from the advert.

Nina stared at it. It was pretty grubby, but she could see that underneath the dirt, and some rust on the front grille, was the lovely curved roof and friendly nose that had so attracted her in the advert. The main thing that struck her, though, was that it was far, far larger than she'd expected, worryingly large, in fact. Could she really handle it?

Seeing the van in the flesh, as it were, rather than in a fantasy or just as an idea, made her suddenly anxious. Her idea of a future doing something where she wasn't protected by a salary and sick pay and holiday pay and someone else doing all the planning and organisation ... if it was to start anywhere, it would start in this little grey stone square, with the last weak rays of evening sunshine coming over the hills, the smell of sharp pine and sweet gorse in her nostrils, a chill wind blowing down the valley and the air so clear she could see for miles.

'Finally getting rid of that eyesore!' said one of the men, laughing, as the other one sized her up. Nina's ear was beginning to getting attuned to their way of speaking.

'You're no' really going to buy Findhorn's van?' said the

other in disbelief. 'That thing's been rusting out there since the year dot.'

'Are you sure you can handle it, a wee thing like you?' said the first man, unfortunately echoing exactly what Nina had been thinking herself. The van had looked pretty normal in the photograph, but here it seemed absolutely gigantic, old-fashioned and terrifying.

'What are you going to do with it?' said the older man, wonderingly.

'Um . . . not sure,' said Nina, unwilling to give herself away in case she got committed. Now that she'd actually made her way here, everything felt so terribly real. The men exchanged glances.

'Well, Wullie'll be in soon enough.'

They headed back to the pub, Nina shooting anxious glances behind her. It was truly, terribly big. Doubt gripped her. After all, this was completely out of character. She'd seen it now. It wasn't appropriate. She'd go back and write a CV like Griffin's and promise Cathy Neeson that she'd do anything, sacrifice anything, perform motivational handstands, if she could just hold on to her job. Yes, that was what she'd do. And she could go back to working all day and reading all evening and occasionally going for drinks with Surinder, because her life wasn't bad, was it? It was absolutely fine. It was okay. Whereas doing something like this – nobody would believe it. It would be a crazy huge mistake and she'd just quietly go home and never mention it again and nobody would even notice.

The landlord looked up with a broad grin when she re-entered.

'Ah, there you are,' he said, pushing across a loaded plate. There was a huge doorstop sandwich on fresh white bread with a thick crackling crust; in between were slathers of butter and some ripe, crumbly local cheese Nina had never tasted before, smothered in home-made pickle, with a crisp pickled onion on the side. She smiled to see it; she really was starving, and Alasdair's face was friendly and kind.

Suddenly, together with the smooth beer, the meal made perfect sense, and she consumed it all sitting at the bar, her book propped in front of her.

Alasdair beamed approvingly. 'I like a girl who enjoys her food,' he said. 'That's our cheese, you know. Got some goats up on the moor.'

'Well it's lovely,' said Nina appreciatively.

The door creaked open behind her and she turned around. Another old man, heavy-set, with deep wrinkles around his blue eyes and an old hat entered the bar. He sounded gruff.

'Has that bus been through?' he said.

'Aye, Wullie!' said one of the other men. 'Here's your latest van buyer!'

Wullie looked at Nina and his cheery face turned suddenly grave.

'Youse are having me on?' he said to his jubilant companions.

'Uh, hello?' said Nina nervously. 'Are you Mr Findhorn?'

'Mmm,' said Wullie. 'Aye.'

'I answered your ad.'

'I know ... I didn't realise you were a young lass, though.'

Nina bit her lip crossly. 'Well I'm a young lass with a driver's licence,' she said.

'Aye, I'm sure, but …' His brow furrowed. 'I'm not … I mean, I was expecting someone a bit older, like. Maybe from a trucking company.'

'How do you know I'm not from a trucking company?'

There was a pause in the quiet bar. On the other side, underneath the taps, there was a kind of squirming, groaning noise, and Nina realised there must be a dog back there.

Wullie thought it over.

'Are you from a trucking company?' he said finally.

'No,' said Nina. 'I'm a librarian.'

The two old men cackled like Statler and Waldorf, until Nina had to give them her special 'silence in the library' look. She was starting to lose patience. Ten minutes ago she'd been all ready to call it off and go home. Now she wanted to show this stupid man she was perfectly capable of whatever he didn't think she was capable of.

'Is this van for sale or not?' she said loudly.

Wullie took his hat off and nodded at Alasdair, who poured him a pint of something called 80 Shilling.

'Aye,' he said in a resigned voice. 'I can let you have a test drive in the morning.'

Nina felt suddenly exhausted as Alasdair showed her up to a small, basic, but very clean and tidy whitewashed room with bare floorboards. It looked out over the back of the pub, away from the village and across the great dipping hills beyond, the sun only now making its way below the horizon.

There were loads of birds chattering around the window, but apart from that there was absolutely no noise; a distant car, maybe, but no traffic, no sirens, no bin lorries or people shouting out on the street or neighbours having a party.

She sniffed the air. It was so fresh and clean it made her head spin. She swallowed a glass of tap water; it was freezing cold, and utterly refreshing.

She had thought she would lie awake in the comfortable white-linened bed and draw up a list of pros and cons and things that might help her decide what she should do next. Instead, with the birds still singing outside the window, she was fast asleep by the time her head hit the pillow.

'What kind of sausage do you want?'

Nina shrugged. She didn't know how many kinds of sausages they had.

'Whichever's best.'

The landlord smiled. 'Okay then. We'll give you some Lorne sausage off Wullie's pigs. That'll be fitting.'

Nina had slept like the dead until something had woken her like an alarm clock at 7 a.m. Peering blearily out of the little dormer window, she had realised it appeared to be a rooster. She had dressed and gone downstairs, ready to try out the van for appearance's sake before hitting the bus again and forgetting all about her little Scottish adventure. There must be bookshops and places that needed staff. Maybe she'd start there. The money wouldn't be as good as she'd been on, but she had never met a bookseller she didn't like, and as long as she could still be around books, still be close by, surely that would be enough.

Breakfast, when it arrived, was a serious affair, a meal to

be treated with respect. She sat at the polished table by the window, where she could see all the comings and goings of the village – schoolchildren running along in a free and easy manner in their bright red jumpers; tractors pulling trailers full of mysterious machinery; horses out for their morning exercise, and plenty of Land Rovers off and about their business.

Alasdair set down a huge bowl of porridge with honey and thick fresh cream, still slightly warm. This was followed by a plate of Lorne sausage, which turned out to be square and crispy and utterly delicious; golden-yolked eggs that tasted better than any Nina had ever had – she assumed they came courtesy of the chickens out the back; crispy bacon, black pudding, and triangular things that she thought were toast but turned out to be some kind of thin potato cake. After just a sandwich for supper, she realised she was ravenous, and polished off the entire thing. It was completely and utterly delicious.

'Get that down you,' said the landlord happily, refilling her coffee cup. 'Wullie'll be busy up the farm till eleven, so there's no rush.'

'This is amazing,' said Nina happily.

'You look like you could do with a feed,' said Alasdair. 'A feed and a bit of fresh air.'

Nina had been told regularly since she was a child that she needed more fresh air, at which she would take her book and clamber up the apple tree at the bottom of their tatty garden, away from the car her father was always tinkering with but had never driven in all the years of her childhood – she wondered what had happened to it – and hide there, braced against the trunk, her feet swinging, burying herself in Enid Blyton or Roald Dahl until she was allowed back inside again. It was a good place to be because, she had learned, when people were looking for you, they never looked up, which meant that her two brothers couldn't track her down to either rope her into one of their stupid war games or, when she refused, tease her for liking books so much and sometimes grab whatever she was reading and throw it to each other over her head until she cried. So she simply smiled politely at Alasdair.

Nina really loved wet and cold winter days; she liked to sit with her back to the radiator, listening to the rain hurl itself against the window panes as if it could breach them; she liked knowing she had nothing to do that afternoon, that there was bread to toast and cream cheese to spread and gentle music playing, and she could curl up cosy and warm and lose herself in Victorian London, or a zombie-laden future, or wherever else she felt like. For most of her life, the outdoors had simply been something to shelter from whilst she got on with her reading.

Now she stood at the threshold of the pub door. The air outside was bracing, the sun bright, the breeze cold and fresh. She took a deep breath. Then she did, for Nina, a very unusual thing.

'Can I just leave this here?' she said to the landlord, and when he nodded, she placed the huge hardback down on top of the table.

'I'll be back soon,' she said as he waved her away, and she stepped outside, book-free for the first time in a very long time.

Chapter Five

It was another splendid day outside, not at all what Nina had been expecting. It looked like the sky had been freshly laundered: a bright TV-studio blue, with fluffy clouds passing across. It was ridiculous, she mused, how little time she spent in the countryside, considering how much Britain had of it. There was always concrete under her feet – she rarely stepped off the pavement – and the sky was hemmed in by street lamps and the high-rises that were popping up in Birmingham city centre at the rate of about one a week, it felt like.

She looked around. Sunlight rippled through the trees, puddled down the furrows of the fields. Across the road were great lakes of shimmering yellow rape. A tractor happily trundled across a field with birds flying in front of it, like something out of an old Ladybird book about life on a farm. Reflecting the clouds above, a little cohort of lambs were charging around, hopping up and down and nipping at one another's tails in a field so green it looked Technicolor. Nina watched them, unable to stop herself smiling.

This was so unlike her, she took a selfie of herself with the lambs behind her and sent it to Griffin and Surinder. Her housemate immediately replied enquiring whether she'd been kidnapped by aliens, and did she need help? Two seconds later, Griffin texted back asking if she knew what 'interfacing methodologies in library connectivity' was, but she ignored that and tried to damp down the anxiety it sparked in her.

After exploring the village, she noticed there was no library. She walked on up a hill track, from where she could see the sea, closer than she'd expected, with a little rocky cove one could clamber down to. She shook her head. It was paradise, this place. Where was everyone? Why were they all crammed into the same corner of England, honking at each other in traffic jams, breathing each other's fumes and food smells and squeezing in and out of pubs and clubs? She saw a huge black rain cloud building up in the far distance. It couldn't just be that, could it?

Apart from the distant putt of the tractor, she could hear nothing at all. She felt suddenly as if she hadn't been breathing, not properly, for a long time. It was as if her entire body was exhaling. Standing on top of the hill, she surveyed the landscape. She could see for miles. There were several other villages dotted about, all looking quite similar, in ancient soft grey stone and slate, and in front of her the valley unfolded, green and yellow and brown, rolling onwards all the way down to the white-crested sea.

It was a most peculiar feeling. Nina breathed in suddenly, all the way in, and felt her shoulders uncurl, as if they'd been jammed up around her ears.

Maybe they had been, she thought. After all, it had been a year since they'd first heard rumours about the library. Seven months before they knew it was the subject of a consultation paper. Two months since they knew it was definitely happening, and three weeks since she'd known for certain she was out of a job if she didn't pass the interview. But she'd been living with that uncertainty, that inability to plan the next stage of her life, for much longer than that.

She stared into the distance and tried to think, honestly and properly, about her life: up here where it was clearer, and she could breathe, and she wasn't surrounded by a million people in a tearing hurry dashing or grabbing or shouting or achieving things in their lives that they plastered all over Facebook and Instagram, making you feel inadequate.

Some people buried their fears in food, she knew, and some in booze, and some in planning elaborate engagements and weddings and other life events that took up every spare moment of their time, in case unpleasant thoughts intruded. But for Nina, whenever reality, or the grimmer side of reality, threatened to invade, she always turned to a book. Books had been her solace when she was sad; her friends when she was lonely. They had mended her heart when it was broken, and encouraged her to hope when she was down.

Yet much as she disputed the fact, it was time to admit that books were not real life. She'd managed to hold reality at bay for the best part of thirty years, but now it was approaching at an incredibly speedy rate, and she was absolutely going to have to do something – anything – about it. That was what Surinder had said when Nina had asked her honestly what she thought about the van idea. 'Just do something. You might make a mistake, then you can fix it. But if you do nothing, you can't fix anything. And your life might turn out full of regrets.'

Suddenly that seemed to make sense. Suddenly everything she'd thought on the way up – I can't do this, I'm not assertive enough, I couldn't possibly run my own business, I won't be any good at it, I can't drive that van, I can't make this happen, I have to hold on to my safe job – sounded feeble and pathetic.

Here, looking down on the valley, at the tiny villages full of people getting on with their own lives in their own way, unbothered by trends, or fashions, or the pace of the city, or some kind of odd concept of getting ahead, Nina had the oddest sense of things she had ever experienced. She'd been raised in a city, educated in a city, had worked and lived in that world. Yet somehow, deep within herself, she felt that she had come home.

A cloud passed over the sun, and Nina shivered. It turned cold quickly here, and she headed back down the hill towards the pub, lost in thought. The two old men who'd been there yesterday were propped up against the bar again. One of them was holding her book and looked to be deeply into it already.

'Are you enjoying that?' she asked with a smile. It was an Arctic thriller, set at the very ends of the earth, just one man against the elements, the polar bears and a mysterious presence beyond the ice.

The man glanced up guiltily. 'Oh, sorry, lass,' he said. 'I just picked it up to have a look at it and ... I don't know. It kind of sucked me in.'

'It's great,' said Nina, adding, 'I'll leave it for you after I'm done with it, if you like.'

'Oh no, no, lass, don't be silly, big expensive book like this . . . ' His watery eyes looked sad suddenly. 'We used to have a library and a bookshop, you know. Both gone now.'

His friend nodded. 'Used to be a nice wee trip out, that, if you wanted to go to the big library. Get the bus. Go choose a book. Have a cup of tea.'

The men looked at one another.

'Ah well, you know, things change, Hugh.'

'They do, Edwin. They do.'

The double doors of the old pub creaked open and Wullie stood there, squinting in the darkness of the bar. He glanced over to where Nina was standing, then looked around, just in case there was anyone else there he hadn't noticed the first time, putting off the moment when he was actually going to have to interact with her. Eventually his eyes came back to settle on her, and his face took on a look of disappointment.

'Hi, Wullie,' said Alasdair, already setting a foaming pint of brown ale on top of the counter. 'How's it going this morning?'

Wullie looked downcast as he headed towards the bar to sit down.

'Aye so . . . ' he began.

'The young lady's ready for her test drive!' announced the landlord cheerily. 'She's only a little thing, but . . . '

'Aye so,' Wullie said again. The room fell silent. 'Aw,' said Wullie finally, taking off a very battered-looking hat. 'Only this time I really thought I'd sold her, I swear to God.'

'Um, hello?' said Nina, stepping forward. 'I'm Nina, remember? Here to look at your van?'

'Aye so,' said Wullie. 'But it's a big van, ye ken?'

He took a long sup of his pint.

'I really thought we'd got it sold this time,' he repeated. He shook his head. 'I don't understand why nobody wants it.'

'I might want it,' said Nina impatiently.

'It's not really a wee lassie's van,' said Wullie.

'Well I'm not really a wee lassie, whatever that is,' said Nina. 'I'm perfectly capable of driving that van, and I've come all this way to try it out.'

Edwin and Hugh were snickering now. Nina didn't think they'd had such a spectacle round the village in years.

'It's a big van,' said Wullie again.

Nina sighed in exasperation. 'Can I have the keys, please? I did email you about this.'

'Yes, but I had no idea you were a lassie.'

'My name is Nina.'

'Yeah, but that's a foreign name, isn't it? I mean, it could be . . . '

'Wullie,' said Alasdair, his normally twinkly face suddenly turning stern, 'this lassie's come a long way to see your van. You've put it up for sale. I don't see what the problem is.'

'I don't want her crashing it is the problem,' said Wullie. 'She dies and I have even more problems than I have now, which is a lot.'

'I'm not going to crash it!' said Nina.

'How many vans have you driven?'

'Well, not many, but—'

'What do you drive now?'

'A Mini Metro . . .'

Wullie harrumphed.

'Wullie, if you don't stop being rude to the lady, you're no' getting a pint.'

'Oh come on, man, I've been up for seven hours.'

The landlord held the beer up threateningly. Wullie scowled and rifled in his pockets, which were deep and many. Finally he took out a large set of keys and threw them on a nearby table.

'I'll need security,' he scowled.

Nina took out her passport. 'Can I leave this with you?'

He frowned. 'You don't actually need one of those to get into Scotland. Yet.'

The men at the bar cackled appreciatively.

Nina was desperate to throw her hands up in surrender – she hated conflict in any form – but she couldn't, wouldn't forget how she'd felt that morning. She would be as kick-ass as Katniss Everdeen, as uncompromising as Elizabeth Bennet, as brave as Hero. She told herself she only needed to drive it across the square, then she could leave. Turn around. Go home. Hope for the best at the library. Her bravado had been shaken by this man, but she wasn't entirely deterred.

She picked up the keys. 'I'll be back shortly,' she said.

She stepped out of the pub and into the square. She felt wobbly inside. She was used to dealing with the occasional rowdy child, or people unhappy that she was charging them for late returns, but those weren't personal attacks. This was different; it was someone making a very clear point that she was annoying them.

The men had followed her outside the pub and she could feel their eyes on her – where were all the women around these parts? she wondered as she crossed the cobbles and moved over to the side street where the big white behemoth was parked. She paused for a moment and looked at its old-fashioned headlamps.

'Listen, Van,' she said, 'I don't really know what I'm doing here. But neither do you, right? You've been abandoned on this street for years. You're lonely. So you help me and I'll help you, okay?'

She unlocked the door, which was a start, at least.

The next thing was getting into the cab. There were a couple of steps, but even they were high. She pulled her skirt above her knees and hoisted herself up. It wasn't graceful, but it was effective. She wobbled a little opening the door and thought for a second she was going to fall off the step, but she didn't, and in a moment she was sitting in a big cracked leather seat patched with gaffer tape.

The inside of the cab smelled – not unpleasantly – of faded straw and distant grass. Nina turned round. It seemed huge to her, but she reminded herself yet again that it wasn't a lorry. She didn't need an HGV licence; anyone could drive this thing. People did it all the time.

It felt a lot like a bus, though. And it was parked in such a very narrow street, the little stone cottages either side of her almost touching the vehicle.

She swallowed, then turned back again and inspected the controls. It looked like a normal car, except everything was much further away. She fumbled under the seat for the release, and moved a little closer to the huge steering wheel.

The gearstick too was massive and unwieldy. There wasn't a rear-view mirror, and the side mirrors just scared her sick.

She sat there for a moment in silence. Then she glanced towards the pub, where the men were standing staring at her, and felt a new wellspring of iron in her heart. Leaning forward, adjusting the mirrors and making sure at least five times that she was in neutral, she put the key in the ignition and turned it.

The noise it made was a huge growl, an awful lot louder than the Mini Metro. An awful lot louder than anything. Nina saw a flock of birds rise up over the houses and spiral into the air. Holding her breath and saying a silent prayer, she moved into first, put her foot very carefully on the accelerator and pushed down the heavy handbrake.

The van jumped forward and immediately stalled and stuttered to a halt. Nina thought she saw the men laughing outside the pub and narrowed her eyes. She turned the key back and tried again. This time it moved smoothly into gear and she took off into the square, bouncing on the cobbles.

Not knowing exactly where she was going, she turned left down the first wide street she came to, and within moments found herself rumbling up the hill towards the moors. The van was a lot nippier than it had first appeared. Nina changed down into second and held on for the ride. She'd never driven so high up before. She could see right out to sea over the crest of the hill; there were great tankers arriving – from the Netherlands and Scandinavia and China, she imagined, bringing in toys and furniture and paper, and taking oil and whisky back the other way.

A huge red truck drove past her and honked loudly. Nina

jumped in her seat before realising it was just a friendly greeting between trucks. As she rounded an unusually sharp bend, a tiny zippy sports car nipped in front of her and raced off, which also gave her a fright. Shaken, she parked up in the first lay-by she came to and gripped the steering wheel tightly. She noticed that her hands were shaking.

She wound down the window and gulped in several breaths of bracing fresh air until she felt a little better. Then she jumped out of the cab, scrambled down to the ground and took a proper look around.

The problem was, Nina thought, kicking the tyres, she didn't really know enough about vans to know if this one was any good. She wasn't even sure you were meant to kick the tyres, although there was a certain satisfaction to it, especially when the tyres were as big as these ones. They didn't seem bald, though. And she managed to open the bonnet, even though she didn't know what she was looking for. Nothing was rusty, and there was oil in it; even she could check oil.

Inside, the back needed a bit of a clean-up, mostly straw removed, but that was fine. It was easy to see how the shelving would go in, and how the little seating area could work at the back; and the side door opened perfectly, with the set of steps unfolding smoothly.

In fact, as Nina carried on with her inspection, she started to get excited again. Suddenly she could see it all in her mind's eye. Parking up somewhere like this beautiful lay-by. Well, maybe not a lay-by. Somewhere in town, where people could get to her. Painting the insides colourfully; filling the shelves with the very best of everything she knew. Helping to match people to the book that would change their life, or make them fall in love, or get over a love affair gone wrong.

And for the children, she could show them where to dive into a crocodile-infested river, or fly through the stars, or open the door of a wardrobe . . .

She sat gazing at her fantasy, imagining it bustling and filled with life and people coming up to her saying, 'Nina, thank goodness you're here; I need a book that will save my life!'

She slammed the door shut excitedly.

Yes! She could do it! She thought back to how she'd felt that morning. She would show that old guy in the pub! She would buy this blooming van and make a success of it, and everything would be absolutely fine. She was so excited that she only stalled four times on the way back to the village, got lost once, and spooked a horse, which made the posh-sounding woman riding it curse her in an extremely non-posh fashion that rang in her ears all the way back down to Kirrinfief and, she was pretty sure, would traumatise the horse far more than the van would have done.

'I've changed my mind,' said Wullie when she parked up carefully outside the pub. 'It's not for sale.'

Nina stared at him, aghast. 'But I managed to reverse it and everything!'

This wasn't strictly true, but she'd looked at where the reverse lever would go and reckoned she could handle it, as long as nobody was yelling horse abuse at her.

'I don't want to sell it.'

'That's just sexist!'

'It's my van, and I don't care.'

Wullie turned and looked to stomp off out of the pub.

'Please,' said Nina. 'I have plans for it, and there aren't any others I can find for sale that are just what I need, and I've come all this way and I'm really going to look after it.'

Wullie turned round and Nina's heart leapt briefly.

'Naw,' he said. And he let the door bang behind him on the way out.

Chapter Six

Nina snuck a glance at Cathy Neeson, who was sitting on the end of the interview panel with her arms folded and her face giving absolutely nothing away. Would it really hurt her to smile? thought Nina. She was doing her best, in her new black tights she'd splurged on, trying to make her hands look calm and relaxed rather than squirming them on her lap. Just a little glimmer of recognition? Although she hadn't studied that hard for the interview, nobody knew the ins and outs of the books better than she; the ordering and filing systems and everything that went into making the library work properly.

(She couldn't know that Cathy Neeson had forty-six interviews to sit in on this week, for only two jobs, both of which she was under instruction to give to lively young people who could shout a lot, looked nice in the literature and would work for next to nothing, and although she'd argued about it at the top level till she was blue in the face, she could do absolutely nothing about it. Top management was completely safe. New

50

young cheap hires who would do anything were coming in. It was the middle ranks, the professional, clever book people, who were simply no longer required.)

'So I feel that a library meeting and anticipating the needs of its readers is absolutely my top priority,' went on Nina, feeling as she did so the sense of her words going into space, of simply tumbling unheard from her mouth. She had a ridiculous, nervous urge to say something utterly absurd just to see if they kept nodding or not.

'Yes,' said a different humourless-looking woman with a trouser suit and very pink lipstick, leaning forward. 'But what about anticipating the needs of your *non*-readers?'

'I'm sorry?' said Nina, not sure she'd understood. 'What do you mean?'

'Well, you're trying to satisfy the needs of all your consumer base, yes?'

'Uh, yes?' said Nina, conscious that she was on unsteady ground.

'So what do you propose for the non-readers?'

'Well, we have children's story time twice a week – I'd love to make that three times; it's so nice for the mums to have a place to get together and chat. And I know our children's literature section back to front, so I've always got something to recommend to those who are a bit more reluctant – there are loads more terrific books coming along for boys, who we all know are a little hard to persuade ... Plus we have adult literacy classes at the town hall, and we're always directing people there; if you can improve literacy, you're doing the best thing you can.'

'No, no, you're not hearing me: what do you propose for

the *non*-readers? Not the people who *can't* read. Your adult clientele who simply don't *like* to read?'

Nina paused. She could hear the heavy traffic going round the roundabout outside. A rubbish truck was reversing with a loud beeping sound. There was a huge crash as it emptied one of the bottle recycling bins from round the back of the library.

'Um,' she said finally, blushing furiously under the gaze of the four interviewers, one of whom – Cathy Neeson, of course – was already checking her phone for the name of the next person. 'I could recommend them a REALLY good book ...'

The pink-lipsticked lady looked disappointed rather than angry. 'I don't think you're seeing what we're getting at, at all.'

Nina couldn't disagree. She absolutely didn't.

'You should have talked about interfaces!' hissed Griffin, as they hid round the corner sipping their consolatory frappuccinos, a justifiable extravagance under the circumstances.

Outside, it was raining, a heavy, joyless spring shower that rendered the city colourless and made the cars splash and thunder through the streets, catching passers-by with sprays of water. People were looking furious, their brows as heavy as the low clouds above. Birmingham was not at its loveliest.

The coffee shop was absolutely heaving with shopping bags and damp coats and buggies and people wearing big earphones and glowering at other people trying to share their table or getting in their way and young kids sharing muffins and sniggering and slagging each other off. She and Griffin were sitting at a crumb-strewn table next to the toilets, beside a lawyer and his client deep in the throes of discussing her imminent divorce. It was hard not to listen in, but Nina felt she had enough problems of her own right now.

'What kind of interfaces?' she said. The interview had not gone much further after that question.

'It doesn't matter: computer, or peer-to-peer, or integrated confluence,' hissed Griffin. 'They really don't care as long as you use a buzzword that they can tick off on their sheet. And if they tick off enough, then it's like bingo and you win your old job back, except at a reduced salary.'

He took a suck of his frappuccino and looked glum.

'God, I should just tell them all to piss off. Illiterate paper-pushers.'

'Why don't you?' said Nina suddenly, interested. People had given her enough advice; she might as well pass it on. 'You're smart. You've got a degree. You're not tied down. You could do anything. You could travel the world. Write a novel. Go teach English in China. Hang out on a surf beach in California. I mean, you're not old, you're not married. The world's your oyster. Why not tell them to stuff it, if you hate it all so much?'

'I still might do all of those things,' said Griffin sullenly. 'I won't be stuck here for ever. Anyway, you're the one off on wild goose chases to look at crazy buses. I'd say you're closer to it than I am.'

Nina had known he'd been secretly pleased when she'd come back from Scotland empty-handed. She'd resented the implication of that: that he was worried that if she could get away, pathetic as she was, what did it say about him?

'I know,' she sighed. 'It was a ridiculous dream.' She

53

looked around. 'I just don't know … I mean, after that …'
She shivered, remembering Cathy Neeson's smile, which
hadn't reached her eyes as she'd stood up to leave, before the
end of the allotted interview time but after the entire thing
had clearly come to a close.

Nina hadn't slept well since she'd returned from Scotland.
The atmosphere had been muggy and grey, pressing down on
her relentlessly. Things she'd once liked – the buzz, the city
noise – now made her feel like she didn't have enough space
to catch her breath. She'd read lots of books about people
finding new lives, which hadn't helped her mood either; had
made her feel more and more trapped and stuck where she
was, as if everyone except her was managing to get away and
do interesting things.

She'd trawled the job websites, but it seemed there was no
place for librarians any more. Information officers, yes. Play
advisers and local council PRs and marketing consultants, but
nothing that seemed to have anything to do with what she'd
done her entire life, the only job she wanted: finding the right
book for the right person.

She found herself missing the fresh air, the long views, the
clear sunlight bouncing off yellow fields, lush green rolling
hills and the sparkling, dancing, beguiling North Sea. It felt
very odd that somewhere she'd spent such a small amount of
time – and which had ended up so badly – had had such a
profound effect on her.

She stared at her coffee again. A large woman barged past
her, almost clubbing her in the face with her gigantic, expensive, directional handbag.

'I don't know,' Nina said again.

'Oh, I'm sure you'll have got the job,' said Griffin, incredibly insincerely. Nina realised for the first time that he'd cut off his ponytail.

Her phone rang. They both looked at each other and froze.

'They'll be calling the successful people first,' said Griffin immediately. 'Well done. It'll definitely be you. Congratulations. Maybe they wanted a way back to the old-fashioned style all along.'

'I don't recognise the number,' said Nina, looking at the phone as though it was a live snake. 'But it's not Birmingham.'

'No, it won't be,' said Griffin. 'It'll be centralised in some Swindon office or something.'

Nina picked up the phone and carefully pressed the green button.

'Nina Redmond?'

The line was crackly and unclear, and at first it was hard to hear anything in the noisy coffee shop.

'Hello? Hello?'

'Aye, hello there,' came the voice. 'Is that Nina?'

'Yes, it's me.'

'Aye, listen. It's Alasdair McRae.'

The name meant nothing to Nina, but the Scottish accent was familiar. Her brow furrowed.

'Hello?'

'Aye, the landlord, you know. Of the Rob Roy.'

Nina couldn't help smiling. 'Hello! Did I leave something behind? You can keep the book.' She hadn't had the heart to take it away in the end.

'Oh, it was brilliant, that book. Edwin passed it on to me when he was done with it.'

'I'm glad to hear it.'

'Then I passed it on to Wullie.'

'Oh.'

'Aye, well, he was in, looking glum.'

'Well, books are for everyone,' said Nina, trying to be charitable.

'Anyway, listen. Me and the lads were thinking.'

It took Nina a moment to realise that by 'the lads' he meant the two old duffers who sat by the bar.

'Oh yes?'

'Listen, that Wullie, he doesn't know what he's talking about. He's had a sad life, you know.'

Well I'm having one right now, Nina found herself thinking, quite shocked that the thought had flickered across her mind.

'Mmm?' she said.

'Well, we reckon the three of us . . . we can buy it off him, then sell it on to you. You know, if you like.'

There was a pause. Nina didn't know what to say. It was so unexpected.

'Not to make a profit, like. I mean, I reckon we'd probably get it cheaper off him than you would. Just to get him to change his mind about selling it to a lass.'

'Well that's . . . ' Nina was still speechless.

'We just thought you looked like a lassie who needed a hand. And we really liked that book you left us. I mean, we'd quite like more books. Nina had told Alasdair the plan and he had not stopped badgering her since. And that van is an eyesore in the village. And he was wrong not to sell it to you when you wanted it.'

This was clearly a long speech for the landlord, who sounded embarrassed. Nina rushed in to reassure him.

'Are you sure? That would be really—'

'I mean, only if you haven't found another one you like . . .'

'I haven't, no. I haven't found another one.'

Nina looked up. The rain was belting against the windows of the coffee shop now; every time the door opened, the wind howled in. The place was absolutely packed, a huge noisy queue at the counter, children crying, people looking cross and getting in each other's way. She looked at Griffin, who was checking his phone. Suddenly he jumped up, full of delight, and punched the air.

Nina blinked. 'Listen, Alasdair, that's so kind of you. I'll need to think about it. Can I call you back?'

'Aye, of course.'

He told her the price he thought he could get the van for, which was way below what she'd expected, and she put the phone down.

'I got it!' said Griffin, his face pink with emotion. 'YAY!'

Gradually he lowered his arms, looking at Nina. 'I mean,' he stuttered. 'I mean, I'm sorry. I mean, they've probably made a mistake. You'd have been masses better.'

Nina glanced down at her phone. A new email was blinking. She didn't even have to open it. 'I regret to inform you . . .' was the first line that came across in the preview screen.

'Well done,' she said to Griffin, almost entirely meaning it. 'I've got to head up a "dynamic young multi-functional team",' read Griffin excitedly. 'Of course it will probably be absolutely awful ... I'm really sorry,' he said as he saw her face.

'It's okay,' said Nina. 'Really. Someone had to get it. I'm glad it was you. I would have been hopeless heading up a multi-whatever.'

'Yeah,' said Griffin. 'You would have hated it. I'm sure I'll hate it too.'

His fingers moved furiously, and Nina realised he had already put it up on Facebook. She could hear the 'like' button starting to ping.

'Listen, I'd better go,' she said quietly.

'No, don't,' said Griffin. 'Come on, please. I'll buy you a drink somewhere.'

'No thanks,' said Nina. 'Honestly, I'm all right. I'm fine.'

Griffin glanced down at his phone again. 'Come on, a bunch of my mates are just round the corner. Join us for a pint. We'll plan your next move. I must know someone who can help.'

He was more energised than Nina had seen him in months. She desperately wanted a cup of tea and a quiet sit-down to think things over.

'Really, I have to get back,' she said. 'Well done again, though.'

He stood up as she put her coat on and moved to leave. She gave him a half-smile as they stood waiting for a parade of buggies to squeeze past them.

'Nina,' said Griffin, suddenly emboldened as she finally moved forward.

She turned. 'Yes?'

'Now we're not working together ... now we're no longer colleagues and I broke up with my girlfriend ... will you come for a drink with me? You know. Just a drink? Please?'

She looked at his pale, anxious face and felt suddenly awkward, and slightly more determined. For just a second she hovered, thinking. Then she decided.

'I'm sorry,' she said. 'I have to ... I have to call a man about a thing.'

She walked past the buggies and the shopping bags and the steamed-up windows and the schoolchildren throwing things at one another and the crumpled bags of sugar and discarded plates and greasy cups, and she pushed open the door and walked into the wet street. Then, pulling up her hood, she pulled out her phone, knowing that if she didn't do it now, she never would.

'Alasdair,' she said as he picked up. 'Thank you for your incredibly kind offer. Yes please.'

Chapter Seven

Even Surinder's enthusiasm for the plan had started to evaporate now that Nina had called around the authorities and been told that to get a licence to sell from the van would be difficult bordering on impossible. Apparently it would be much easier if she just wanted to flog burgers and cups of tea and dodgy hot dogs.

She had pointed out to the man at the council that surely it would be much easier to accidentally kill a member of the public with a dodgy burger than with a book, and he had replied with no little snippiness in his voice that she obviously hadn't read *Das Kapital*. She had to admit that she hadn't and they didn't get much further than that.

But still, here she was on the coach again, armed with the *Lark Rise to Candleford* trilogy as well as the entire *Outlander* series to sink into on the journey.

It turned cooler the further north they went, but it was still clear, that astonishing eastern light making Edinburgh glimmer like Moscow as they passed through. The great bridge felt once more like an astonishing gateway into the unknown; then further north and north again, the cities and towns and traffic and people falling away, leaving long lazy red trains swaying alongside the twisting roads; tiny villages, endless birds soaring through valleys, and sheep everywhere in the lush green grass, under the long rays of the late-setting sun.

She ate cherry Bakewells from the service station as she lost herself in the pages of her book, and when she finally alighted at Kirrinfief, she felt like she was coming home, something absolutely reinforced by Edwin and Alasdair's smiling faces when she pushed open the door of the pub.

'The book girl!' they said, pleased, and Alasdair poured her half a lager without waiting for her order. He must have noticed her struggling with the local beer last time. 'What have you brought us?'

Nina had, of course, come well prepared, and unzipped her case to bring out a selection of thrillers and crime novels, which the men fell upon happily.

'So,' said Edwin finally. 'You're really going to fill this truck full of books?'

Alasdair was happily rootling around for the keys to the van. Nina had handed over the cheque that, when cashed, would represent, more or less, her entire redundancy payment.

'That's the idea.'

It hadn't been too bad going to work now that she had a plan. She had a few weeks' notice to work out, but nobody was going to care very much if she took long lunches, or came in late, or carted home trunkfuls of books every night, which she was doing. She felt as though she was rescuing orphans from destruction.

Griffin had started wearing a shirt and tie. The beard was gone too. He came in early and spent a lot of time in meetings, and was beginning to wear a harassed expression instead of his bored and annoyed one. One night he stopped her and said she needed a requisition form for all the books she was taking, and she'd said, 'Seriously?' and he'd looked pained, and Nina had been happier than ever that she was going.

'Oh, it's going to be great,' said Edwin. 'You'll have to go down to Carnie village. And over to Bonnie Banks. And Windygates. My sister lives there. They used to have a library bus, but of course that shut down. So you'll be better than nothing. You can't run it as a library?'

'Afraid not,' said Nina. 'I have to eat.' She turned to face them. 'You do know I'm not keeping the van here? I'm driving it back to Birmingham.'

The men's faces looked confused.

'But it's for here!' said Edwin. 'That's why we bought it!'

'No, I'm taking it down south,' explained Nina patiently. 'That's where I live.'

'But they don't need books down south in a city,' said Alasdair. 'They're falling over themselves for bookshops and libraries and universities and all the rest of it. They've got as much as they need! It's us that needs them.'

'Yes, but I live down there,' repeated Nina. 'It's my home. I have to go back.'

There was a silence.

'You could make a home up here,' said Alasdair. 'Could do with some new blood around the place.'

'I couldn't move here!' said Nina. 'I've never lived in the country.'

'Yes, but you've never run a book bus either,' said Edwin with stubborn logic.

'Aw, I thought we were helping you out so that you could stay around,' said Alasdair. 'I've told all my regulars.'

'I thought Edwin and Hugh were all your regulars,' said Nina.

'Aye well, shows what you know. Everyone was delighted.'

'I'd love to,' said Nina. 'But truly, I can't. I have to get back and set up and start earning a living.'

There was a silence in the bar. Nina felt terrible for having misled them; she genuinely hadn't meant to.

'But—' said Edwin.

'I'm sorry,' said Nina firmly. Her plan was to pick up the van and drive back to Birmingham that night. She couldn't really afford to stay, even somewhere as cheap and cheerful as the pub. Plus Surinder had been very clear that if she didn't find a home for the books without delay, either the floor was going to collapse or Nina was. So that was that organised.

'I have to go,' she said sadly. They all looked at the keys lying on the bar.

'It was very kind what you did for me,' she said again. 'Thank you.'

The two men grunted and turned away.

Outside, it had finally got dark, the final rays of pink fading away over the western hills. As soon as the sun went, it turned instantly cold, and Nina shivered as she stepped towards the van. She pulled her coat around her and looked up at it, huge now in the quiet little cobbled square. She took a deep breath. She couldn't remember feeling lonelier. Still, this was what she had to do. She was committed now. She was going to find a way.

She glanced down at her phone. She had obviously managed to pick up some kind of a signal whilst she was in the pub, and her email had come through. At the top was one from the district council.

```
Dear Ms Redmond

We wish to inform you that your
application for a parking permit Class
2(b) (Vending and Trading, Non-Catering)
has been turned down, due to height
restrictions in the area. There is no
appeal to this decision.
```

Nina swore. Loudly.

There was more in an official vein, but she couldn't read it through her tears. It seemed that whatever she did, she couldn't get a break. The one thing she had never thought there would be a problem with was parking the van outside her house. Now, looking at it in the rapidly fading light of day, she realised how enormous it was. It would block out the light from the downstairs windows, and their neighbours' too. What had she been thinking?

She'd spent all her redundancy money – she couldn't imagine for a second going back to the men in the pub and saying she'd changed her mind. She was out of a job, and she knew she hadn't prepared as well as she might have done for the interview because she'd been so distracted thinking about other possibilities. And now she'd failed at the most basic, obvious hurdle.

She'd have to move. Somewhere she could park the van. She'd have to tell Surinder. But what if she couldn't afford to move? Who'd let her rent a property without a job? Oh my God, she'd end up living in the van.

Her tears dripped down and she felt very panicky. She glanced around. Nobody there, of course. The village was completely deserted, and very cold. Nina felt completely and utterly alone.

She tried to think of what Nancy Drew would do. Or Elizabeth Bennet, or Moll Flanders. But none of them seemed quite prepared for such a moment. No heroine she could think of had ever found herself crouching beside a gigantic unsaleable van in the middle of nowhere, not knowing where she was going to live, shivering in the bitter cold.

She straightened up carefully and painfully. Her hands were shaking. She simply didn't know where to go. She tried to think of places where she could park the van, and wondered if she'd be safe there or whether she could just abandon it.

In the absence of a better idea, she got into the cab and turned the key.

There are plenty of warnings about driving when you are tired, and Nina was normally a careful driver who paid attention to all of them. Normally.

But now, shocked and worried to the core, and driving

a huge vehicle she wasn't used to, she felt very frightened indeed. She knew she should come off the road, but where? She couldn't afford to waste money on a hotel, even if she knew where there was one up here in this wilderness.

She didn't have sat nav and her phone wasn't getting a signal and in any case was running out of charge. She put her headlights on full beam and carried on along endless country roads, none of which seemed to be taking her anywhere useful. She had fuel in the tank, which for now seemed to be enough, as she wiped the tears from her cheeks with her right hand and tried not to panic. She'd find somewhere. She'd find somewhere.

She spotted the lights of the level crossing ahead but drove on; the barriers weren't coming down yet so she'd have plenty of time to get through. She didn't see the deer until it was too late. It was hopping and bouncing away from the red lights and ran straight into her path. She saw the huge black eyes flash in front of her face, startled, beautiful and terrified, and without even thinking, she slammed on the brakes. The van skidded and juddered to an immediate halt on the crossing, at a sideways angle to the road.

The deer jumped away from the vehicle, its hooves tapping on the side, then vanished into the trees, unscathed. As Nina caught her breath, she heard the dinging of a bell and looked up, horrified, to see the barrier coming down across the road in front of her.

Unable to think straight, she turned the key in the ignition, panicking, forgetting to put her foot on the clutch, unable to understand why she couldn't start the engine.

The lights of the train were clearly visible, looming closer and closer and stronger and stronger. She knew she should get out, but somehow, although she tried, the door seemed to be locked. She scrabbled around with the ignition, trying to start the van again, and again she failed.

The radio wouldn't stop playing. Her hands wouldn't work. Her fight-or-flight instinct had let her down completely. She stared at the train again as a great screeching noise filled the air, and was struck by the oddest, most ridiculous thought: how embarrassed her mother would be having to tell people that her university-educated daughter had done something as stupid as getting herself trapped on a level crossing and killed by a train.

By a train.

Her mouth slowly opened in what she realised was a scream, and as the ground shook and the train thundered and shrieked towards her, she closed her eyes and awaited the awful inevitable.

Chapter Eight

There was a dark and deathly silence. The radio had some-how turned itself off; she didn't know how. The lights had gone out too. Nina blinked. Was this the afterlife? She hadn't felt anything; no impact, no pain. Maybe this was it and it was all over. The blackness was all-encompassing.

But no: she was still in the van. She could see the handle, and she reached and pulled it. The door was unlocked. It had been unlocked the entire time. What on earth had happened?

Carefully she stepped down on to the ground. Then she stumbled over to the side of the track, her legs refusing to obey her, and was promptly sick in a hedge.

She found a half-empty bottle of mineral water in her bag and drank some of it, then stopped in case she threw up again. She couldn't stop trembling. Gradually, after trying hard to sort out her breathing, she dared to look up.

Mere inches away from the untouched van on the crossing was the engine of a huge goods train, heaving like a living thing. Nina thought she was going to throw up again.

A man was leaning against the side of the engine, also breathing heavily. When he saw her, he started to move forward.

'What ...' he said. His voice was so trembly he could hardly speak. 'What the f ...' He made a huge effort to stop himself swearing. 'What ... what the bloody hell ...' His throat wheezed. 'WHAT the BLOODY HELL!?'

'I ...' Nina heard her voice break. 'There was a deer ... and I braked ...'

'A DEER! You nearly killed the bloody lot of us for a DEER? You STUPID BLOODY ... What were you THINKING?!'

'I couldn't ... I couldn't think ...'

'No, that's right, isn't it? Not bloody thinking at all! LOOK, there's ten bloody metres ...'

Suddenly there were running footsteps up the side of the track. Another man appeared, out of breath, the smoke from the train brakes rolling around him like a fog.

'What has happened?' he said. He had an accent – European of some kind, Nina thought vaguely.

'This STUPID wee LASSIE here nearly killed you, me, herself, and half the local population if the fuel had gone up!' shouted the first man, puce in the face with fury.

The second man looked at Nina.

'Are you all right?' he asked.

'Is she all right? She nearly killed—'

'Yes, Jim. Yes. I understand.'

Jim shook his head, still trembling. 'This is a bad business. A bad business.'

The lights of the level crossing were dinging again, and the barriers were coming up.

'They shouldn't do that,' said the second man. 'We're not through. Are you all right?' he asked Nina again, who realised she couldn't stand up and slumped suddenly against the van.

'I'm going to talk to control,' the first man said.

When the second man reached Nina, she saw that he had curly black hair, rather too long, and tired-looking black eyes with long eyelashes. His skin was olive, with taut high cheek-bones. He was of medium height, thickset.

'You are all right, yes?'

Nina blinked. She was too shocked to speak.

'Breathe,' he said. 'Drink more water, yes?'

She tried a little more water, and spluttered as she did so. She put her hands on her knees until she could get her breath back.

'I thought,' she said, her teeth chattering uncontrollably, 'I thought I was dead.'

'Nobody is dead,' said the man. 'Nobody is dead. We have me and we have Jim and we have wool, whisky, oil and gin. No one is to be dead.'

He looked at her.

'You are freezing. Come, come.' He bundled her towards the train.

The first man had hopped up into the cab and was talking into a radio. He popped his head back out.

'I don't know what to tell them.'

'There is nothing to tell them! Everyone is fine. Gin, oil, wool is fine. Nobody is hurt.'

'If I tell them, there'll be a huge investigation. Police. It'll go on for months.' He regarded Nina sternly. 'She'll be in big trouble.'

'Ha. Yes. Don't tell them,' said the second man.

'I didn't . . . I didn't . . . ' Nina could hardly speak. Jim's face up in the cab softened.

'I have to tell them; they've called through already. Nobody's going anywhere.' He looked at her. 'Oh for God's sake,' he said. 'You might as well come up and have a cup of tea.'

'Yes, tea,' said the other man, propelling her gently forward. 'Tea is answer to everything. Come up into cab! Right now! Be in warm, not cold.'

Nina, not knowing what else to do, stumbled towards the cab, then found she couldn't swing herself up. Her arms had turned to jelly.

The man leapt up nimbly, then turned and held out a hand.

'Come,' he said. He had wiry black stubble, and his arm was hairy and muscular and covered in oil. He grabbed Nina's small hand and swung her up into the cab as if she weighed nothing.

The tiny space was warm and cosy. Jim was sitting in front of a large grey moulded plastic control panel, and the second man indicated that Nina should sit there too, but instead she slid to the ground and burst into tears.

The two men exchanged glances.

'Have tea?' said the second man eventually. Jim leaned

over and brought out a flask. He poured a cup and handed it to Nina, who accepted it gratefully.

'Don't cry, lassie,' he said. 'Drink that.'

The tea was hot and very sweet, and Nina started to feel better.

'I'm so sorry,' she sobbed. 'So, so sorry.'

'Oh God,' said Jim again. 'The paperwork. The police will be on their way right now. There'll be filing and investigations up the wazoo.'

'But nobody hurt,' said the second man. 'You hero, Jim.'

There was a long pause. The driver didn't say anything. Then he said, 'I didn't think of it like that.'

'You are,' said Nina, feeling livened up. 'You absolutely are. I thought I was dead. I owe you my life. You're amazing. You stopped just in time.'

The driver's anger seemed to have almost completely disappeared as he drank his own cup of tea.

'It was just instinct taking over really,' he said modestly.

'You'll be in paper,' said the second man, smiling and winking at Nina. 'You have photograph in paper.'

'Do you think so?'

'You saved my life,' said Nina again, just glad that he wasn't angry any more. 'You saved me.'

Jim took another slug of tea, then smiled.

'Well,' he said. 'Well. Accidents happen.'

The police did arrive, and took long statements from everyone: the driver, Jim, who was quite recovered and pumped up about the entire incident, describing his rapid, life-saving

72

use of the brake to anyone who wanted to listen; the second man, the engineer, whose name was Marek, trying to move everything on; and Nina, who was utterly horrified to learn that she might face criminal charges.

Marek stepped in and smoothly explained that it really ought to be the deer that faced criminal charges, and after they'd breathalysed her and called in some paramedics to check both her and Jim over, they agreed there was nothing to be done except move the van off the crossing and let everyone carry on, thank God.

The night sleeper from Inverness was backed up behind them and getting rather grumpy about it, and there wasn't a replacement driver available from here to Darlington, so Marek offered to take the shift.

There was one big problem, though: Nina was in absolutely no fit state to drive the van, and nobody else was insured. One of the policemen had kindly moved it into a lay-by next to a field and put a warning sticker on it saying *Police Aware* so nobody else would touch it, but there was still the problem of now.

The police offered to run her back to the pub – they were taking a still-shaken Jim there. But it was 2 a.m., and Nina didn't have a friendly railway employer who would put her up somewhere and couldn't afford a hotel room. She blinked a lot, hoping she wouldn't burst into tears again, wishing desperately she knew what to do. Eventually Marek leaned forward.

'You know, we go to Birmingham,' he said quietly. She looked at him. The policemen looked at each other, not knowing whether this was allowed, but aware that it would be a massive problem off their hands. Jim was already waving goodbye.

'Fine,' said one of the policemen finally, handing her an incident report. 'Don't go driving on to any more level crossings, okay?'

Nina nodded. 'Never again,' she said.

And then everyone left and the blue lights vanished and suddenly they were up in the cab by themselves. Marek spoke to control and the level-crossing gates came down once more, and this time, without anyone in the way, the train moved off smoothly.

Marek had insisted on wrapping Nina up in a blanket and putting her on the seat. After everything they'd been through, she felt almost sleepy, but she couldn't fall asleep. She had never sat in the front of a train before, if you didn't count the Docklands Light Railway once when she was little. The windows were big and wide with – she was surprised, although she realised she shouldn't have been – perfectly normal windscreen wipers on them. As the great tender started gradually to move, and then to pick up speed, she leaned forward eagerly to watch. The night sky wasn't, in fact, all black as they passed through the woods and out into open hills; the black was in the great curve of the land, but the sky itself was an array of dark velvety colours, spotted with stars, the moon almost full. In the bushes besides the train, watchful eyes lit up; there was a scurry of movement in the hedgerows; here and there across the track, little rabbits hopped so quickly Nina gasped, but they were never caught.

'Like you, heh?' said Marek, his voice deep, standing carefully at the handle as the train rattled its way across the night.

'They gave me a fright,' said Nina.

'I think you nearly killed Jim,' said Marek. 'With the fright.'

'I really didn't mean to.'

'I know, I know,' said Marek. The cab was dark, for better visibility outside; Nina could only make out his profile, his stubbly chin against the moon shining through the window as they sped on through towns and villages shut down tight against the night.

'So what are you doing out like this at night, huh?' said Marek. 'You're not Scottish, no?'

Nina shook her head.

'Birmingham.'

'I'm from Chester, but I live in Birmingham. Yes. Where are you from?' she asked out of curiosity.

'Latvia,' he grunted.

'So we're both far from home,' said Nina. Marek didn't answer.

'I was ... I was bringing the van home,' she said. 'For work.'

'What is your work? You drive van?'

'Not very well,' said Nina. 'I was ... I wanted to open a bookshop.'

Marek turned briefly to look at her. 'Ah,' he said. 'Bookshops. Very good. People like bookshops.'

Nina nodded. 'I hope so. I wanted to ... you know. Bring books to people. Find the right kind of thing for them to read.'

Marek smiled. 'And where is your shop? Birmingham?'

Nina shook her head. 'No. I thought I'd have it ... in the van.'

'Inside the van? A shop inside a van?'

'I know,' said Nina. 'Maybe it's a terrible idea. I'm not having much luck with it so far.'

'So you drive and look for people who need books?'

'Yes.'

'What book do I need, huh? No Russians.'

She looked at him and smiled. 'Well,' she said, 'I would recommend something about people who work nights. There's *Ovian Falls*. It's about a man in a war who stands watch all night before the signal to advance in the morning, and about what goes through his head before they have to go over the top and fight. He thinks about his family and when he was a child, and it's funny and sad, and there's a sniper who he thinks is trying to kill him. And the sniper *is* trying to kill him. It's good and sad and exciting and it feels like all of life in a night. '

Marek nodded his head. 'That is what it is like for me sometimes,' he said. 'Only the clock is the sniper. Not real sniper. That sounds like just the book for me. I will buy. Very good.'

Nina smiled. 'Really?'

'Yes. I think so. You have convinced me. Perhaps we should turn this train to books, huh? Have a book train?'

'I love that idea!' said Nina. 'But, uh, maybe best start small.'

'But you will be in Birmingham and your van will be in Scotland.'

'Yes, I know,' said Nina. 'I'm going to figure it out soon.'

'That does not seem to me very good way to run a bookshop.'

Nina looked at him to see if he was teasing her, but his face was inscrutable.

'No, not particularly.' She sighed. 'But I can't park it in Birmingham. I don't really know where I'm going. My life is just full of problems.'

Marek smiled sadly in the darkness, and she could see his white teeth gleaming.

'Oh, you think you have problems?' he said.

'Well, I don't have a job, all my assets are parked in a lay-by in a place I don't even know, my housemate is going to evict me in case I bring the ceiling down and I just nearly got run over by a train. So, yes, I think I've got problems.'

He shrugged.

'What, you think I've spent all my savings on a van I can't drive for fun?' She huddled more tightly into her blanket. 'How can you not think I have problems?'

Marek shrugged again. 'You are young. You are healthy. You have van. Many people from my country would think you were very lucky.'

'I suppose,' said Nina quietly.

They racketed across a bridge, startling a group of herons that had been crowding round a lake. They took off in flight, silhouetted across the moon.

'Wow,' said Nina. 'Look at that.'

'You see many things on the night train,' said Marek. 'Look.'

He indicated a tiny village, all in darkness except for one light on in a bedroom. 'Most nights – not every night – that light is on. Who is there? Can they not sleep? Is there a baby? Every time I wonder. Who are these lives all here one after another; and how kind of them to let us peer in, how generous of them.'

'I don't think people really like living on the railway line,' said Nina, smiling.

'Oh, then they are even kinder,' said Marek, and they fell into silence.

When they pulled in to Newcastle, Marek told her to sit down out of sight, she shouldn't really be here. There was a great thundering and clanging in the goods yard, which was lit up like a Christmas tree, so bright it looked like day; men shouting and attaching cranes and pulleys to the containers on the train: wool, Marek had said, for the Netherlands and Belgium; whisky, of course; oil; gin. And coming on, goods from China, destined for pound shops and kitchen shops: toys, salt and pepper shakers, picture frames; bananas and yoghurt and post and anything you could think of, swinging off the great docks at Gateshead and being loaded on to lorries and trains to spread throughout the country overnight, like a network of blood in its veins; a dark midnight world Nina rarely gave a second thought to as she picked up a coffee stirrer or a jar of honey or a nailbrush. The clanging and shouting went on and on, and she dozed off in the corner of the cab. It had been an exceedingly long day and night.

She woke with a start as they were flying through the Peak District. She was disorientated and thirsty. Marek smiled.

'Ah, I thought you were gone for the whole time,' he said. 'Maybe you are not good for night work, huh? A night library is not for you.'

'It's a nice idea, though,' said Nina, dreamily. She hadn't been fast asleep, but rather untethered, feeling the train as if it were on rails through the sky. 'You could swap children's

78

books for them at night when they were asleep. They could wake up with a new story.' She rubbed the sleep out of her eyes and looked around. 'Sorry, I'm talking nonsense.'

The tea in the flask was cold, but Marek offered it and she drank it anyway.

'What is your dream?' said Marek as they flew along, the noisy engine rattling, the radio occasionally stuttering into life.

'Oh, I wasn't really asleep,' she said.

'No, I mean for what you are doing. What do you want to do? For ever. What is it your dream to do?'

Nina sat up. 'Well,' she said. 'I suppose … I want to be with books, have them all around me. And recommend them to other people: books for the broken-hearted and the happy, and people excited to be going on holiday, and people who need to know they aren't alone in the universe, and books for children who really like monkeys, and, well, everything really. And to go places where I'm needed.'

'You're not needed up there? Where we were? In Scotland?'

'Well, yes, maybe, but I've never lived there, and …'

'It will be better in Birmingham?'

'No, not really. I mean, not at all. It's really congested there and there's nowhere to stop and they kind of have libraries and bookshops and things … not as many as they did, but they do still have some.'

'Mmm,' said Marek. 'And you don't like Scotland?'

Nina thought back to standing on top of the hill, looking out over the fields, the ancient stone walls, the sun layering down, flickering in and out of the darker clouds, drawing tremendous stripes across the huge long empty land.

'I do,' she said. 'I like it a lot. But I don't know anyone there.'

'You'd have your books,' said Marek. 'And you'd know me. Well, I am in Scotland for a little bit. Most nights.'

The first hints of dawn – dimming stars, a tiny line of summer gold – were appearing as the train came further south. Now the towns were bigger and longer and went on and on and on, with only the depot names to differentiate them one from another; there was more traffic as the country very gradually started to wake itself and stretch his legs.

'Where do you live, Marek?' said Nina.

'Oh, the same place as you,' he said. 'Birmingham innit.'

The way he said *innit* was so English that she found herself smiling.

'I can tell,' she teased, while marvelling at the coincidence that they had both ended up in the same city.

'I do not like it,' he said. 'Is expensive to me and too busy and too fast. I like it where is quiet and free and you can think and breathe proper air, like home. I like Scotland. Scotland reminds me of home. Is beautiful and not too hot.'

'So why don't you move there?'

He smiled. 'I not know anyone there either.'

At Birmingham, he helped her down and pointed her towards the exit. It was 5 a.m., but quite light, and absolutely bitterly cold.

Nina looked at him. 'Thank you so much.'

'Thank Jim,' said Marek simply. 'That he not run you down and turn you to jam on the tracks. And you must be careful here. If you are jam on the tracks here, well, it will all have been in vain and no good.'

Nina smiled. 'I'll be careful, I promise.'

They looked at one another.

'Well,' said Nina. His bristles were more pronounced in the morning, almost a beard, and he ran his hand over them carefully, as if reading her thoughts. His dark eyes were twinkling in his high-cheekboned face.

'Good luck, book girl,' he said.

She was feeling in need of a hot shower and a long nap. The sun glinted off the steel of the train. Nina noticed she had a name: *The Lady of Argyll*. She turned and went to circumnavigate the end of the tracks; it came quite suddenly at the terminus, just a wooden barrier telling you not to go any further.

'Wait, book girl!' came a voice suddenly behind her. She turned round. It was Marek, waving a piece of paper. Her brow furrowed. He looked rather red; like a big clumsy bear. He glanced down, shy.

'Well,' he said, 'if you would like . . . I can maybe take you back to van. One night. We are not always two people on. Often just one. And I know where is van.'

Nina widened her eyes. 'You're allowed to do that?'

'Completely and absolutely not,' he said.

'Oh,' said Nina. 'Well, probably . . . I mean, thanks for the offer, amazing, but I'll probably . . . I mean, it'll . . . I don't want to get you into trouble.'

'Not to worry,' said Marek, blushing more furiously than

ever, and handed her the piece of paper. It had a completely incomprehensible email address on it. 'But, you know.'

Nina smiled and took it. 'Thank you,' she said.

There was a loud honking noise from one of the other trains, and quickly, lightly, she ran round the edge of the railway track – the very end of the line, she found herself thinking – and out through a link-fence doorway into a non-descript street in a part of Birmingham she had never visited before. To her joy, there was a little workman's café right there on the corner, condensation steaming up the windows, and she spent her last five pounds on a bacon sandwich and a steaming mug of tea as she watched *The Lady of Argyll*, now less heavily laden, back slowly out of the depot and make its great journey onwards to London.

Chapter Nine

Surinder was not wearing her friendliest smile when she drowsily answered the door.

'Have a good trip?' she said. 'How come you're back so early?'

Nina considered telling her, then decided against it.

'Long story,' she said.

'Come on then,' said Surinder. 'I've given up the entire day to move these damn books out. Can we get started?'

'Well,' said Nina, wondering if there was time to go and make a cup of coffee before they got stuck into this. 'There's a thing. A kind of . . . Well. Here's the thing. I can't park here.'

'What do you mean?'

'I had my parking permit turned down. The van's too big for Edgbaston, it appears.'

'Oh, that's why you're back so quickly. You flew!'

'Not exactly.'

'Well at least you didn't buy the van. But Nina!' Surinder put her empty coffee cup down on a quivering pile of Regency romances, which promptly collapsed on the floor in a fainting fit. 'What are you going to do with all of this?'

At the exact same moment, Nina said, with a vision of blinding clarity, 'But I did buy it.'

'You didn't ... You what?!' Confused, Surinder looked around, scattering a mint-condition collection of Orwell in the process.

Nina winced. 'Watch George!'

'Watch George?! Nina, what the HELL is wrong with you? What were you thinking? Why didn't you wait to find out about parking before you bought the damn thing?'

'I don't know. I just assumed it was going to be okay.'

'Why did you hand over money for it not knowing what you were doing?'

'I don't know that either. I just ... I thought I wouldn't go through with it if I waited too long.'

'Nina ...'

Nina had never seen Surinder so furious. She wished she wasn't exhausted, as she could feel the tears already building behind her eyes.

'Nina, I have tried to be patient. I have tried to help when things go wrong and you buy a book and things go well and you buy a book and it rains so you bring home some books and it's sunny so you get some books. But ...'

It might, Nina thought later (more in hope than expectation), have been Surinder's high-pitched voice that set the whole thing off. It might not have been purely Nina's fault.

That, however, was not how she felt just then, as Surinder gestured again in frustration and knocked the rather wobbly banister, which immediately started to wobble even more and dislodged a pile of books at the top of the stairs. And inevitably, as though in a terrible slow-motion film, they then knocked into the next pile, and the next, and sent the whole lot tumbling over and down the stairs, where they hit a large ornamental vase, which banged on to the hall floor so hard that a small crack appeared in the hall ceiling and a puff of dust came down.

Everything seemed to happen so slowly. Nina watched the spiral of dust tremble its way from the ceiling, wavering in the light, a tiny cloud of white, nothing more. But it was, she knew, enough. She looked at Surinder.

It was the last straw. The very final one. They'd both known it was coming.

'Okay,' said Nina. 'Okay. I'm out of here.'

Once it was decided – or rather once Nina had announced it and they had both calmed down – Surinder was genuinely sad. They had been housemates for four years, and good ones on the whole. She took the rest of the month's rent in lieu of Nina paying for fixing the crack in the ceiling and immediately spunked some of it on a couple of bottles of Prosecco and a gigantic bag of Haribo, and they sat in the sitting room the following evening talking it all through.

'Where will you live?' said Surinder.

'I don't know,' said Nina. 'I don't think it's that expensive up there. Cheaper than here, anyway. Which is useful, seeing as I won't actually have any money.'

'What are you going to charge for the books?' said Surinder.

'It depends,' said Nina. 'I think I might just make up prices when I see people.'

'I don't think you're allowed to do that,' said Surinder. 'Are you sure you won't forget you're a librarian and start just handing books out to people?'

'Only until I miss my first two meals,' said Nina, taking another handful of Haribo.

'Have you told your mum?'

Nina made a face. Her mum worried a lot about everything. Usually her younger brother Ant, which was useful.

'I'll email her as soon as I've got a change of address.'

'You're not going to tell her you're leaving the country?'

'It sounds bad when you put it like that.'

'Uh huh,' said Surinder, who went round to see her mother pretty much every day and rarely came home without a Tupperware box filled with something delicious, and who thought Nina's relationship with her mother was suspicious in the extreme.

'Okay, okay, I'll tell her,' said Nina. 'Just give me five minutes to get settled. This is all happening awfully fast.'

Surinder leaned forward on the sofa and topped up their glasses.

'You know,' she said conspiratorially, 'the kind of people who are going to be up there?'

'Old geezers,' said Nina promptly. 'I know, I've met them.'

'No!' said Surinder. 'No, no no no. I don't mean that at all. Up there, it's all chaps, you know.'

'Really?'

'Of course! Middle of nowhere. Who's there? Farmers. Vets. Probably a military base nearby. Hikers. Mountain bikers.'

'I'm not sure I'd get on very well with a mountain biker. Bit too much cagoule action. Also, I don't like being outside.'

'It's just a concept. Geologists. Agricultural students. Tree surgeons. Men men men men men! You'll be hopelessly outnumbered.'

'Do you think so?'

There had only been two men – Griffin and old Mo Singh – at the library, and eight women. And in the media centre there were about forty women, mostly young, Nina had learned in the course of a very excitable email from Griffin.

'Course! And there's none here.'

'You do all right.'

Surinder rolled her eyes. She got asked out constantly, and was interested in almost none of them, complaining that they were all too metropolitan and she didn't like beards.

'Whatever,' she said, waving her hand. 'You'll see. Boys everywhere.'

'I'm not going for the boys,' said Nina. 'I'm going for the books.'

'But surely if a boy or two turns up you're not going to be too disappointed?'

'I told you,' said Nina. 'They're all a hundred and two and live in a bar. And stop whistling "Over the Sea to Skye".'

Chapter Ten

It was raining. Living in Birmingham, Nina had thought she knew a bit about rain. Turned out she was wrong. Very wrong. In Birmingham when it rained you popped into a café or stayed inside your cosy centrally heated house or went to the Bullring so you could wander around in comfort.

Here in the Highlands, it rained and it rained and it rained until it felt as if the clouds were coming down and getting in your face; rolling their big black way towards you and unleashing their relentless showers on top of you.

Nina wouldn't have minded, but she absolutely had to get back to the van; it had been sitting out there for five days as it was. She'd packed as much as she could into her largest suitcase, crammed boxes of books into the back of the Mini Metro until she could hardly see out of the rear windscreen – it still made barely a dent in the piles in the house, but Surinder was hung-over and in a generous mood – then slipped away with many hugs and kisses and a final Tupperware for the road and a promise to visit as soon as she was fixed up, i.e., had finally sold the car and found a place to live.

But first she needed to collect the van. As soon as she'd arrived, she'd asked Alasdair in the bar, ridiculously, if there was a taxi service, and he'd looked confused and asked her if she wanted Hugh to give her a lift on his tractor and she'd said not to worry. He then, kindly, offered to lend her an old bicycle that was out back.

It was incredibly old, in fact, a great big heavy metal bone-shaker with a solid frame, three gears and a withered brown basket on the front. The one thing in its favour was that riding it was so incredibly difficult that she soon ceased to feel the cold as she pedalled ferociously through the rain in the direction of where she thought the van was.

As she approached the crest of the hill, panting, she saw a small crack in the clouds that raced across the sky. Suddenly, and only for an instant, a great beam of golden sunshine flooded through it and she raised her head towards it, craning like a sunflower. At the very top of the hill, she stopped and gazed at the clouds. She never saw them back home, for glass and steel tended to obscure the top end of the weather; you kept your eyes on the pavement, or your phone, and you carried on. Clearing the drops out of her eyes and shaking her hair behind her – it would frizz like crazy, she thought, but who was there to mind or care? – she was rewarded suddenly by the rain stopping, as if on her command, and the golden sunlight splashed down again, illuminating every crystal raindrop, every damp leaf and shiny field of rapeseed all the way down to the little cove, an enormous rainbow cracking through the gaps. The clouds continued to race by as if speeding up, making a patchwork of the field below.

Nina took a deep breath of the incredibly fresh air, then looked to her right, where a red train was running parallel to the road. She knew it wouldn't have Marek in it – it was a passenger train – but she hopped back on her bike nevertheless and coasted down the other side of the hill, racing the train, watching as it sped on its way: Perth, Dundee ... maybe Edinburgh, Glasgow and beyond, Britain for once not feeling like the small, cramped country she had always thought it to be, hugger-mugger, that corner of London and the south-east continuously sending out its fingers into more and more of the world around it, trying to swallow it whole; concreting over the entire land into a dark, grimy urban sprawl, with a coffee shop in every street and everyone shut away in highly priced boxy little flats, attached to their Wi-Fi, living through a screen even as another nine skyscrapers were thrown up right next door, blocking out more of the light and the clouds and the air and the view and nobody seeming to care, everyone thinking of it as progress.

She let her feet fly off the pedals and freewheeled faster and faster, watching the train speed ahead, knowing that even though she had no job, no pension, no partner, nothing at all except a rackety old van, somehow, more than ever in her life, she felt free.

Not at all where she remembered it being – and rather further away; she was starving by the time she reached it – she came upon the level crossing. In the lay-by next to it, completely untouched apart from the police sticker, which, had she still been in Birmingham, she'd have been tempted not to peel off in case it got her free parking, was the big van, looking a lot less daunting in the sunshine than it had the last time she'd seen it, in the middle of the night.

As she dismounted the bicycle, she saw the red lights begin to flash and the striped barriers making their descent. Immediately she felt tense; how awful that she'd been so nearly caught there, so nearly trapped. That feeling of panicky powerlessness when she'd fumbled for the door came over her again, and she forced herself to watch the train – a small local service, but even that felt huge and noisy – thunder across. She shivered as a cloud passed once more across the sun and she leaned against a nearby tree. It was okay. It was okay. It was fine. She had to tell herself that and not let her imagination run away with her. It was a freak accident, the train had stopped; it would not happen again.

She wondered if there was an alternative road that avoided the level crossing. There had to be. She would always take it from now on, just in case. Then she told herself no: she couldn't. She would have to face it and deal with it, and that was an end to it.

The gates hadn't gone up. She glanced up the line cautiously. Sure enough, dramatically slower than the passenger train – thank goodness, thank goodness – a large goods train was coming down the line. She wondered if it was slowing because of what had happened before.

Suddenly, on impulse, she moved closer to the barrier. She hadn't emailed Marek – she couldn't decipher the strange hieroglyphs in the address – although she had thought about him. He had been kind to her when by rights he should have been extremely cross, and had given her a lift, but he was obviously just being nice. He was quite a lot older than her and doubtless had a wife and family, either here or in Latvia. But even so, as Nina had been reading a novel with a dark-eyed romantic hero, she had allowed her thoughts to stray – briefly, very briefly – to his dark, kind, saggy eyes.

She leaned on the top of the gate so she could see up into the cab. It was true, the train was slowing right down. They must have been given new instructions. Craning her neck, she made out a bald head and a sturdy figure in a pale blue boiler suit. To her surprise, she saw it was Jim; he must be on day shift. Raising her hand, she waved and waved.

The train slowed down even further and Jim leaned his head out of the window, smiling, Nina was very relieved to note. She could barely make out what he was shouting over the noise of the engine, but it sounded something like: 'We have to slow down because of the likes of you!' Nonetheless, he was still smiling as he shouted, and as the many loading decks of the train began to make their rattling way past her, he blew the whistle three sharp times.

Nina waited for the entire train to pass – fifty-five trucks, she counted – but there was no sign of Marek. He'd said there weren't always two members of crew; it just depended on what they carried. Still, she realised, she'd had a thought that he might be on the back, waving just a little. The final truck had a ledge on the outside like a balcony. You could have stood there if you wanted to watch the world go by. But he wasn't.

Nina opened up the van. She had found an old cardboard estate agent's sign, complete with nail still in it, in a ditch and decided to keep it. On impulse, she felt in her bag for a pen – she always had a pen; she bought stationery the way other women bought lipsticks – and wrote on the sign, in thick black letters, HELLO JIM AND MAREK! THANK YOU ALWAYS. Nina xxxx

She knew the colour would run the second it started to rain again – probably in the next five minutes. But she drove the nail into the tree nevertheless. Then, delving into her bag once more, she found the book she'd set aside – an enthralling out-of-print history of the Baltic states written by an English gentleman adventurer – wrapped it in a plastic bag and hung that from the nail too. Finally, she tapped the van sharply on the side, said a small but fervent prayer, and took out her keys.

Chapter Eleven

As luck would have it – and Nina was definitely, she felt, way beyond the point where she was due some luck – the person who bought the Mini Metro, after she'd removed all the boxes from it and put them in the van (where they instantly disappeared and looked tiny; she'd need a *lot* more stock), was a very smartly dressed farmer's wife in need of a runaround, who also recommended that Nina go and look at a place to rent that apparently wouldn't mind a monstrous van parked outside.

Nina was undeniably worried. The amount she could pay in rent was negligible; even Surinder had been charging below market prices because they'd become such good mates (when Nina wasn't knocking down her house). She had a bit from the car, and the very last dregs of her redundancy, and she'd tried to be careful with her salary, which usually lasted as long as her next foray past a bookshop, but she'd still have to manage month to month based on what she could sell.

She'd phoned the local council, who'd sounded absolutely relaxed about her parking up one morning a week here and there, and, even better, had promised to email her a list of farmers' markets and car-boot sales where she could rent a pitch. That seemed a pretty good idea. But first she needed to get everything ready, and to do that, she needed a place to stay.

Lennox Farm was just outside the village, set back a little from the road; a gorgeous farmhouse, painted a deep orange, which should have stood out but in fact was enhanced by the country hills around it, even in spring; Nina expected it must be absolutely glorious in the autumn.

According to the woman who'd bought the Mini Metro, the farmer's wife had planned to turn a cottage near the farmhouse into a holiday rental, but apparently she wasn't around any more – quite the scandal, the woman had said, without elaborating – so it was up for rent longer-term instead. 'Standing derelict, more like,' she added. Something had obviously gone very wrong somewhere, Nina figured, and hoped the place wasn't in too decrepit a state. But what choice did she have?

No one was around as she drove up, following quite tenuous directions. She'd thought people would be all too ready to notice the van, as a) it tended to cast a shadow over everything it passed, and b) she had taken to driving at twenty miles an hour, just in case. But as she pulled in to the courtyard of the farm, all she could see was a lone chicken pecking its way cheerfully across the forecourt, eyeing her beadily as she parked up and stepped down.

'Hello?' she shouted, feeling suddenly terribly self-conscious. She'd tried to google the place, but had found only a faded-looking website, where the photos had come down and most of the links weren't working. A dead website was a sad thing, she thought. Full of hope when it had been set up, and now floating away down the Google plughole, gently decaying. Like the cottage itself, she thought glumly. An idea half executed then left to rot. On the other hand, she couldn't sleep in the van.

'Hello?' she called again, then went and knocked on the door. There was absolutely nobody there, she could tell straight away. She sighed and peered through the kitchen window. It was neat and tidy and very, very bare. There were no pictures on the walls or piles of post or dirty cups. It looked like this was the holiday cottage, but it was clearly the farmhouse. Across the cobbles and past the hen was a garage. She couldn't see anything that resembled a cottage. She sighed and checked the address. This was it all right.

She glanced about. She didn't know anything about farms. She thought that she must have been on a school trip once. That was about it. She knew about closing gates, that there was manure everywhere, that you shouldn't let your dog in and that there were electric fences. All of those things conspired to make her think that perhaps farms were fairly scary places to be. On the other hand, she didn't know what she'd do otherwise in terms of finding a place to stay. She couldn't even afford the pub for much longer.

The mountains opposite were gleaming with sunshine, even though the day was chilly. Nina had sought out her winter anorak before she'd come up, and she was glad of it now, even though it was technically spring. She pulled it closer around her and tried to figure out what to do.

Half an hour later, she was utterly engrossed in *Fair Stood the Wind for France* in the front of the van, with the radio on, when a violent banging on the driver's window made her start. She looked up blinking, as she often did when she was immersed in a book, not quite knowing where she was.

Standing next to the van was a rather gruff-looking man wearing a flat cap on curly brown hair. He wasn't smiling. Nina wound down the window.

'Um, hello,' she said, suddenly totally shy.

'You can't park here! It's not a campsite,' barked the man.

Nina stared back at him, slightly shocked. 'Yes, I know that,' she said. She pulled the handle to open the door, and the man, reluctantly, stepped back. When she jumped down, she realised he was extremely tall and was holding a big stick. He was rather imposing, in fact.

'And I'm not expecting any deliveries. Are you lost?'

Nina was about to say he didn't know what a deep question that was for this particular time in her life, but instead set her chin forward.

'I was told to come and look at the cottage,' she said. 'I thought you knew.'

There was a moment's quiet. Then his hand went to his forehead.

'Oh,' he said gruffly. 'Right. I'd forgotten all about that.'

There was another silence as Nina waited for him to apologise, which he didn't.

'Do people often try and camp here?' she asked, kicking a stone with her toe.

'Aye,' he said. 'I don't mind normally, if they ask first. Well. It depends.'

'On whether you like the look of them?' said Nina, trying to raise a smile.

The man didn't answer, just sighed briefly.

'Do you want to see the place then?'

'Um, yes please.' She stuck out her hand. 'Nina Redmond.'

The man looked at her, then took it. His hand was strong, large and weather-beaten; a working hand. He was, she realised, younger than she'd thought at first.

'Lennox,' he said shortly.

'Like Lewis?' Nina said before she could help herself. He frowned even more deeply, if that were possible.

'If you like,' he said in a thick, melodious accent, and Nina regretted saying it instantly.

'Right,' he said. 'Follow me.' And he set off across the farmyard with a broad stride, scattering the chickens that had come out to see him.

About twenty yards from the house, tucked away at the end of a beaten track that Nina eyed carefully but figured she could probably get the van up, was a stone building.

'You're sure you don't mind me parking the van here?' she asked nervously.

'What on earth have you got a van for?' said Lennox. 'You're only little.'

'Why can't short people drive vans?' said Nina crossly. 'Anyway, I'm a perfectly normal size. You're too tall.'

'Well at least I don't need a ladder to get into my van.'

'Well at least I don't need to wear a pillow on my head to get through a door frame,' said Nina. It was, she found, oddly liberating to be rude to someone who was rude first. She wasn't normally nearly so cheeky.

'Hmm,' he grunted. 'You can park it there. If you can manoeuvre it.'

'I hope you weren't about to be sexist?' said Nina.

'No,' said Lennox. 'Um. Not sure. It's difficult to tell these days.'

Nina looked at the muddy slope next to the building. 'I'm sure it'll be totally fine,' she said, trying to sound blithely confident.

'Well, maybe leave it in gear. Which you knew already, as you are totally competent about everything,' said Lennox quickly.

Nina stepped forward to inspect the building. It just looked like a barn.

'Have you got the key?' she said.

'Oh. Yes. Key,' said Lennox vaguely. 'I didn't think of that. Don't lock up much around here.'

'Because you know, if I rent it, I'll probably need a key.'

Lennox squinted against the sun. 'I'm sure I know where it is . . . It's definitely somewhere.'

The barn door was made of heavy wood. The entire place looked very forbidding. Nina worried suddenly that it wasn't actually converted; that it would just be an old barn filled with straw, with eaves open to the sky and one set of cutlery. Which had always sounded like utter heaven when it happened in *Heidi*, but she wasn't at all sure what it would be like now. She took a deep breath as Lennox pushed the door open and groped around inside for the lights, which turned on.

'Oh thank goodness,' he said. 'I couldnae remember if we'd wired it up or not. Obviously we did.'

Nina followed him into the space. It smelled a little musty

and dank, like a place that hadn't been lived in, and there was a chill to the air. But she didn't notice that. She didn't notice it at all.

Instead, as she stepped forward, she stared straight ahead. Someone had installed, at what must have been vast expense, big picture windows on the south side of the barn, the side facing away from where they'd come in, so you couldn't see the farmhouse or the road behind or the mountains to the north; simply what looked like an advertisement for bread: miles of gently rolling hills carved up by lazy stone walls; blobs of sheep, wild-flower meadows, and a long, low river with a humpback bridge over it.

All that could be heard through the double glazing was a little lowing, while a chicken scratched about on the small lawn space that had been formed out the front.

'Oh my God!' she said. 'This is amazing!'

Then she remembered she didn't have a lot of money to pay for rent.

'I mean, it's quite ... It must have been a lot of work,' she said more stiffly. She moved forward into the room. The lights weren't needed; the sun, currently out, flooded the place, making her feel like lounging in it, like a cat, without the biting wind of outside.

It wasn't a large space. There was a cosy-looking wood-burning stove down at one end, and a set of swish kitchen units along the back wall. A little spiral staircase led up to a small mezzanine with a vast double bed and a bath-room, which both had huge windows of their own looking over the hillside. Bookshelves lined the far wall against the original grey stone.

It was stunning. As perfect a sanctuary as she could ever have imagined. Nina had never wanted to live somewhere as much in her entire life. Someone had designed and made this barn with the utmost care and attention. She wouldn't have marked Lennox down as an interior-design type on their short acquaintance.

'Um,' she said carefully, scampering back down the spiral wooden staircase. 'Do you rent this out a lot?'

Lennox looked around as if he hadn't been in the building for a year (as indeed he hadn't).

'Oh, no,' he said. 'No, I ... I never have. Don't really have the time for all that nonsense. No, it was ...' He went quiet for a second. 'Well. My wife did all that stuff. My soon to be ex-wife.'

His pain in simply pronouncing the words made Nina wary about saying more.

'Right,' she said quietly. 'Okay.'

Lennox turned away from the beautiful little apartment.

'Well,' he said, gesturing with a large arm that nearly knocked a lamp off a side table. 'Anyway. This is it if you want it.'

'Um,' said Nina. 'How much ...'

Lennox sighed. 'Oh God, I don't know,' he said, then named a sum that was less than Nina could have hoped for.

She could barely conceal her delight, and suddenly felt guilty that she was getting the property for so much less than it was worth. It wouldn't have paid for a room in a shared student house in Birmingham. Then she looked around and realised that he had about forty thousand sheep and so many chickens he didn't even check where they were around the place, and he was probably doing all right for himself. What was he going to buy, a new flat cap?

'Um, that should be fine,' she said carefully, suddenly flashing back to the last time she'd gone flat-hunting in Birmingham: absolutely loads of horrid places with damp patches on the walls going for a fortune, and weird people until she'd finally been lucky enough to team up with Surinder. 'Yes please,' she said, more vehemently.

'Okay.' Lennox shrugged. 'I'll give you the keys when I find them.'

'I will need keys,' said Nina.

'And turn on the water and whatnot . . . ' He waved his hand vaguely. 'And anything else you need. Do you need sheets and stuff? We have an absolute ton of those too. Kate . . . She was going to do up all the outbuildings just like this. Had a real fire of enthusiasm for it.' He swallowed hard. 'Fell for the interior designer. I didn't even know he liked girls. Anyway.'

Nina noticed a beautiful picture on the wall. It was dark and gloomy, a heavy canvas, quite out of keeping with the rest of the delicate room. She looked at it.

'I'm sorry to hear that,' she said, wondering about it.

'Oh well,' said Lennox. 'Time to get over it, apparently. Bloody Marilyn Frears from the village seems to think so anyway. Bleating about it over the phone, talking about moving on, getting someone in . . . '

He remembered himself.

'Which would be you, of course.'

'Thanks,' said Nina. 'I promise I'll look after it.'

Lennox squinted out through the door suddenly and raised his hand to his forehead.

'Is that your van rolling down the hill?'

'What?' shouted Nina. 'No, I left the handbrake on. I did! I'm sure I definitely did!'

'It'd better not run over any of my bloody chickens.'

'My VAN!' Nina was shouting and charging down the hill as fast as her wellies would take her.

'Get back from there!' shouted Lennox, pounding down behind her and overtaking her easily with his long legs. 'Get away from it!'

The van was just picking up speed, heading towards a ditch at the edge of the field. Quickly, and without fuss, Lennox swung himself up into the cab – thank goodness she hadn't locked it, Nina thought – gracefully dropped in and pulled on the handbrake so hard Nina could smell the burning across the farmyard. There was a pause, as a chicken hopped sharply to the side. Nobody said anything.

Then Nina walked forward.

'I think my van has a death wish,' she said miserably. 'It's trying to kill itself. Sometimes with me in it, sometimes on its own. Maybe it's haunted.'

Lennox clambered down, frowning. 'You're going to have to look after it properly. Which means putting the handbrake on.'

Nina went bright red. 'Sorry,' she said. 'I had an accident – or nearly an accident – when I couldn't get the handbrake off, and that's why I don't really like putting it on.'

'I'm not sure your aversion to handbrakes has much to do with it,' said Lennox. 'You want to park that thing here, you park it properly.'

'Okay. Yes. Sorry.'

Lennox glanced back into the cab. 'What's back there ...
books?'

'Uh huh.'

'You've got a van full of books?'

'Not quite full yet,' said Nina. 'But I'm planning on heading that way, yes. Do you read?'

Lennox shrugged. 'Don't see the point.'

Nina's eyebrows lifted. 'Really?'

'Well, I get *Farmers Weekly* and I read that. I *can* read,' he said, as if she'd accused him of being illiterate.

'I assumed you could,' said Nina. 'But you never read for fun?'

He looked at her. His eyes, creased at the edges, were blue against his sun-tanned face; his expression was bleak. Nina wondered if showing her the house, built with such loving care in happier times, had caused him pain. He didn't look like a man who did anything for fun.

'I never understand,' he said, shaking his head, 'why anyone would go to the trouble of making up new people in this world when there's already billions of the buggers I don't give a shit about.'

Nina spent the rest of the day moving in, having paid Lennox a month's rent. He had taken the envelope gruffly, then gone back to work, disappearing over the horizon even as Nina wondered just how far the farm actually extended.

She unpacked her meagre possessions into the smart built-in wardrobes – far too smart, now she thought about it, for a humble holiday cottage. They couldn't have hoped to recoup this investment in a hundred years. She wondered if the mysterious ex-Mrs Lennox was simply looking for excuses to call back the interior designer.

She touched the heavy lined curtains and gazed out across the beautiful fields, wondering what Lennox's wife had been like. Perhaps she had longed for the city, just as Nina, sitting in her tiny bedroom in Edgbaston looking out on to the long street of terraced houses opposite, had begun to dream of wide-open spaces and fresh air. Perhaps they had had the wrong lives all along. It was a strange thing to think. She looked at the quality of the pale oak flooring, the tongue and groove in the bathroom, the claw-footed bath and the huge bed, almost as wide as it was long, and smiled wryly to herself. Yes, she and Mrs Lennox were almost certainly quite, quite different. But for once, Nina had had her stroke of luck.

Chapter Twelve

After she'd unpacked her few possessions, Nina wasn't quite sure what to do with herself. Then she looked at the van, and realised it would need a massive scrub-down. The problem, she realised, having been used to zipping around in a tiny Mini Metro, was that if she ever wanted to go anywhere, the van had to come too, like a huge lumbering elephant too wide for half the streets of the town. She gave it a severe look and considered extending her rental on Edwin's bicycle.

She steeled herself, though, and trundled down to the village at ten miles an hour – she wasn't entirely sure she and the van trusted each other at this point. As she drove, she pondered the further problem of how she was going to get the rest of the books up from Birmingham. In reality she should simply drive down and fetch them, but it was such an incredibly long way, and she wasn't a hundred per cent sure yet she had the nerve, especially following her near-death experience the last time she had set out for Birmingham.

The village had a small grocer's shop, painted a pretty

pale blue. A woman said a curt hello as she went in, the bell dinging overhead. Although the shop was tiny, it appeared to sell absolutely everything.

Nina looked at the paper-wrapped lamb chops. They were marked 'Lennox Farm'. Back in Birmingham, meat generally came from the supermarket, encased in plastic. This was kind of new. There was chicken, too. She thought of the jolly little hen scratching outside her new window. Of course it was having a much better life than any chicken she normally bought, she told herself. Even so, she found herself choosing some cauliflower to make cauliflower cheese instead. There was also a plethora of local cheeses she'd never seen before. The woman noticed her looking.

'Do you need any help?' she said. 'I know it's a bit confusing.'

'I'm new here,' said Nina, smiling.

'Oh, I know that!' said the woman. 'I'm Lesley. You bought Wullie's van, for some crazy reason, and you can't drive it, and you've moved into Lennox's mystery palace.' She gave a rather pleased-with-herself smile. She was small and neat, with weather-beaten cheeks and a tight look about her face.

'Mystery palace?' said Nina.

'Oh yes, nobody's seen that place since Kate left. What's it like? I heard she spent a fortune, got people up from Edinburgh; even Inverness wasn't good enough!'

'Right,' said Nina.

'Well?' Lesley folded her arms. Obviously gossip was something you paid for together with whatever you were actually buying.

'It's very nice,' said Nina. 'Kind of all glass at the front, with a little balcony for sleeping, and a good view.'

Lesley sighed. 'That sounds nice. Is it insulated?'

'I didn't ask.'

Lesley stared at her. 'You rented a house without finding out if it was insulated? You can tell you're foreign.'

Nina had never thought of herself as foreign before.

'There's a wood-burning stove,' she said hopefully.

Lesley looked at her. 'Okay then,' and she laughed in a way that made Nina feel slightly uncomfortable.

Nina picked out as many scrubbing and cleaning products as she could carry.

'What's all that for?'

She had absolutely vowed to support the local shop and the people who worked in the area, but found she was quickly going off the idea.

'It's for the van.'

'What are you going to do with a van anyway? You don't look as though you could do house removals.'

'Actually,' began Nina, feeling timid and trying to force herself to speak a little louder. This was her life now; she was going to have to own it, even though she felt as you often do when you've had to do absolutely everything by yourself: rather like a grumpy child. She took a breath. 'Actually, I'm going to run a mobile bookshop. Go around to the towns where they don't have one, like here.'

Lesley's eyebrows lifted. 'Really?'

'Uh, yes,' said Nina, glancing round anxiously just in case Lesley was already hiding a full bookshop in the back of the little blue shop and wouldn't appreciate her competition in the slightest.

'Have you got the new E. L. James?'

'I'm afraid not,' said Nina apologetically. 'But I can get it! Also, I have something I think you might like even more.'

Lesley looked suspicious. 'I doubt it.'

'You should trust me on this.'

'I know what I like,' said the woman.

Nina looked down and fumbled in her wallet. 'Well, um, hopefully see you down there anyway.'

Outside, she found a cluster of people around the van, who peered inside as she unlocked the back. The books were still in their boxes on the floor, but people reached out their hands to pick them up and look at them.

'Um, hi everyone,' said Nina shyly, her own hands full of cleaning bottles.

'Is this the new library?' said an older woman with a pull-along trolley. 'We need a new library.'

Lots of other old ladies nodded approvingly.

'I'm afraid not,' said Nina. 'It's going to be a shop.'

'It's a van.'

'I know. A bookshop in a van.'

'I miss that library.'

'So do I.'

Nina winced. 'Well, once we're ready, we'll have lots of lovely books for you.'

A young woman with a buggy stopped beside the van.

'Hello! Are you selling books?' she said cheerfully. 'Got any for children?'

'Of course!' said Nina, leaning into the buggy. 'Hello there.'

'This is Aonghus,' said the woman. She squinted. 'I know you're meant to read to them, but he gets really bored and wobbles off or tries to bite something. Mostly the biting thing.'

Aonghus grinned, showing gummy teeth.

'All our books are ripped to shreds,' the mother went on. 'Someone asked me if we had a dog and I nearly said yes.'

'Have you tried cloth books?'

'Yes,' she said glumly. 'He actually swallowed those ones. So we're back to board. At least they've got some fibre.'

Nina smiled. 'Hang on,' she said. 'Someone else had exactly that problem.' She hopped up into the van and came out with a near-pristine copy of *Don't Bite Me*. It was an incredibly successful board book about various animals with teeth that encouraged children to point at their own teeth rather than use them.

'What's that?'

'Well, it's got a lot of pointing. Maybe if he's pointing at it, he won't bite it so much.'

'Or he'll bite his own finger,' said the woman hopefully. 'Good training. Thanks! I'll take it! I'm Moira, by the way.'

'Nice to meet you, Moira and Aonghus,' said Nina, realising that she would have to get prices marked up in the front of the books. 'And also your invisible dog.'

Moira paid her, looking cheerful as she handed the book to Aonghus, who stuffed it in his mouth hungrily.

'Maybe keep it in your bag till you can practise the pointing,' suggested Nina.

She watched Moira go, smiling, then, as if the floodgates had opened, sold her entire stock of Georgette Heyer and

Norah Lofts to a cluster of old ladies, who buzzed around her still complaining about how awful it was that the library had gone. By the time she'd driven back to the barn to make cauliflower cheese (swiftly followed by a reminder to herself that until either she'd got a separate kitchen or it was warm enough to have all the doors and windows open, she shouldn't cook cauliflower again) and start scrubbing the van, she realised she'd have to figure out some way of getting the rest of the books up here, and sharpish. Because this might just work.

Nina turned round and looked out of the window of the barn the following day, over the fields, where moorhens and even the occasional kestrel were swooping down. The place was full of birds. And there was just so much sky. A grey bank of clouds was hanging over the sea, approaching fast, racing one another. A piercing shaft of sunlight pushed in between them. There was rain, far away, the mist coming off it as some other farmer's field was watered, and the faintest pink line on the horizon, later in the evening, illuminating the end of the multicoloured fields. Every time she crested the top of Kirrin Hill, she saw the shining fields of rapeseed pop up, almost too bright a yellow against the blue patches of sky. It felt like weather was being made in front of her eyes; the sky a huge screen of flowing and whorling movement.

Which meant you generally needed an extra jumper, she realised. And a jacket. But it was worth it.

It was time to drive over the level crossing again. Surinder had been very clear about this during their final wine-fuelled chat: she needed to conquer her fears and get on with everything anew; she'd had a shock, but she couldn't let it beat her. But also, Nina was curious – no more than that, she told herself – as to whether Marek and Jim had picked up her bag from the tree.

It was a daft idea, and she shouldn't dwell on it. Anyone could have taken it. And they shouldn't be leaning out of trains anyway. She'd caused enough damage. Nonetheless, she slowed down carefully, and parked in the lay-by just before the crossing. The bag was gone. But that didn't mean anything. There was, however, she noticed suddenly, another bag there, hanging quite far out on a branch, bright yellow.

Smiling to herself, she shinned up the side of the tree, remembering those days of hiding in the apple tree to read in peace. She inched her way up the trunk until she could grab a lower bough, then lightly raised herself and crawled towards the bag. As she got closer, she could see that it very clearly said *Nina* in big square letters. She leaned over with excitement blooming in her chest and untied it.

Inside was a little book of poetry, in Russian and English, by a writer Nina had never heard of called Fyodor Tyutchev. She smiled in delight. It was an old cloth hardback, evidently well-worn. There was no inscription.

Tucked into the front of it was a little note from Jim that said, gruffly, *Hope you're okay after everything. Sorry again I shouted. Got a fright. Marek says maybe we can make it up to you by bringing some stuff up. Let us know.* And underneath, an email address.

Suddenly the sun came out from behind a fast-moving cloud and hit the tree trunk dead on. The warmth felt absolutely glorious on Nina's back. She wriggled backwards with the book and got comfortable against the tree trunk – she was an expert at getting comfortable in trees – then began to read.

> *Be silent, hide away and let*
> *your thoughts and longings rise and set*
> *in the deep places of your heart.*
> *Let dreams move silently as stars,*
> *in wonder more than you can tell.*
> *Let them fulfil you – and be still.*

She looked at the first poem for a long time, idly rubbing a leaf between her fingers. How very strange that someone she had met so briefly, under such extraordinary circumstances, should turn out to be able to pinpoint exactly what she was feeling, and how. Or, rather, take what she was feeling and make her feel so very much better about it.

The verse in the original Russian looked equally beguiling, if completely incomprehensible.

> Молчи, скрывайся и таи
> И чувства и мечты свои –
> Пускай в душевной глубине
> Встают и заходят оне
> Безмолвно, как звезды в ночи –
> Любуйся ими – и молчи.

She read the poem again, feeling herself sinking slightly in the warm, cosy haven of the great oak tree. She warned herself not to fall asleep and topple off, but it was so quiet, merely the hum of the bees in the bluebells below, the occasional call of a tern high above the trees, and she felt the most remarkable sense of inner peace.

HONK!

The sound of a car horn startled Nina and very nearly did make her topple off the branch.

HONK!

Below her was a big, arrogant-looking Land Rover taking up more than half the road. She'd left enough space for it to get through, hadn't she? So what was the problem?

'It's fine!' she yelled down, to no avail. The Land Rover honked again. Furious now, Nina was tempted to throw something down on top of it – an acorn, perhaps, although it wasn't the right season. The birds stuttered and flew away at the ugly noise of the horn, the utter peace and calm of the setting disrupted because some stupid driver thought she might clip their expensive wing mirror.

She shinned down, crossly.

'It's fine,' she repeated loudly to the open window. 'Just drive past it! It's not that big!'

The face greeting her was stern.

'Well, firstly, it *is* that big. It's huge.'

Nina realised belatedly that it was Lennox the farmer – her new landlord – in the Land Rover, which paradoxically made her angrier. This was his countryside, after all; why was he determined to ruin it?

'And secondly, that branch you were so languidly relaxing on is actually rotten right through, couldn't you see?'

Nina glanced upwards to where there were flaking bits of bark and green spores blooming in the bare wood beneath the branch.

'It's dying,' said Lennox, his face still set.

'Oh,' she said. 'I didn't realise.'

'Obviously,' sniffed Lennox. 'If you fall off that and land on the railway line again, you get special marks for carelessness. What the hell were you doing up there anyway?'

Nina shrugged and held the book close. 'No reason,' she said.

'I mean, there's no shortage of trees.'

'Well maybe this was just the one I liked.'

There was a short silence and Lennox looked awkward. He rubbed the back of his neck with his hand.

'So, you settling in all right?'

Nina looked down at the book in her hand. 'Oh,' she said awkwardly. 'I should be working harder. I mean, I can afford my rent!'

'That's not what I meant,' said Lennox, going pink at the tops of his ears. 'I heard the women in the village are all a-flutter about you coming. It's just me that thinks it's a stupid idea.'

'Do you think reading is only for girls, then?' said Nina, still cross. 'You know, women find men who read really frightfully attractive.'

She instantly worried that she'd gone too far, as he got out of the Land Rover and stood beside her, not looking at her. Then he heaved a sigh, and clicked his fingers. Instantly, a black and white dog leapt out of the back of the Land Rover and whizzed to his side, and he put his hand down and automatically caressed its ears. Nina found herself thinking how useful that would be, to have an automatic comforting device. The dog looked nice.

'Do they?' said Lennox gruffly.

'I like your dog,' said Nina. 'He's very cute.'

The dog wandered up to her and sniffed her hand.

'And clever,' she said. 'Oh you're a lovely boy, aren't you! You're a lovely boy.'

'He's a working dog,' said Lennox shortly. 'He isn't a lovely boy. And he and I have to get back to work.'

Nina watched the Land Rover take off, mud splattering from under its tyres as it made its way into the distance. She sighed. Pissing off her landlord hadn't exactly been top of her to-do list. She glanced back down at the book and the scrap of paper she was still holding. On the other hand, the day had hardly been a write-off.

As she drove back to the farm, she sank into a reverie: the handsome, sad-eyed foreign gentleman with the deeply romantic heart racing through the night on a dashing charger – well, a big train. She knew she shouldn't think this way, but she couldn't help it. It was just how she was built. And now she had an email address she could actually read.

Chapter Thirteen

It was exciting staying up until midnight to go and meet the night train.

Jim had pointed out in an email several times that what they were doing was completely against regulations and also illegal to boot, so she couldn't tell anyone about it, and she had promised faithfully, feeling rather thrillingly that she was inside a spy novel as she did so.

She was to be at the level crossing at 12.10 precisely. Jim was going to drive too fast – which he never did, he had said solemnly – to begin with, then tell signal control that they needed to stop to delay the timetable. But she would have to be quick.

Feeling the part, Nina dressed entirely in black, including a high scarf, and tweeted a picture of herself to Surinder, feeling slightly regretful that her friend wasn't there to share the adventure. Surinder didn't even get back to her, which she found rather hurtful. Plus, Griffin's Facebook had been absolutely chock-full of what a jolly time he was having at his amazing new media centre; Nina wasn't sure whether this was actually true or in fact meant that his new bosses monitored all his social media accounts, so it was pretty difficult to figure out what he was trying to say. And her other friends said hi, of course, but that was about their limit. Everyone was busy, she told herself. Everyone's life went on. And this was definitely something new.

She marched to the door and turned out the lights. In the farmhouse, which she could see down the slope, a lamp was still burning. Nina didn't think farmers stayed up late in general. Perhaps Lennox was the exception. Maybe that was why he was so grumpy all the time. Maybe he was looking through his wedding album, getting maudlin with a glass of whisky. A shot of pity went through her. She didn't want to think of him like that; think of anyone like that. It was hard. She crept past the farmhouse quietly, even though of course as soon as she started the van, it made enough noise to wake the dead.

As she pulled up at the now familiar level crossing and turned off the van's headlights, she felt like the only human being for miles around. Then, realising that she *was* the only human being for miles around, she pulled up her scarf and stepped out of the vehicle.

It was cold outside. Owls hooted in the trees, the flapping of wings merging with the noise of the leaves rustling in the wind. Oddly, even though it was right in the middle of the night, it didn't feel quite black. The moon and stars were bright against the patchwork landscape in a way they never could be in the city sky, with its fiercely delineated halogen lights. The chill air caught sharply in her throat, and the world felt very strange.

Suddenly, from far off, she heard it: a tremble, then the

slight rattling of wheels on the rails, slowing down; then, coming round the bend, a shockingly bright light. It gave her a quick, unnerving flashback to being trapped, and she found herself glancing instinctively back at the van to make sure it was still there, safely on the other side of the barrier.

The train was huge in the night, utterly vast and dark, a great metal dragon. No wonder people used to be so scared of them. It slowed and slowed but still made a dark and sinister outline against the grey fields, until a light went on in the cabin and she saw Jim's cheery face, someone else by his side.

Down beside the track she heard footsteps, and she wondered who the second person in the cabin was; for there, suddenly, was Marek, beaming, his white teeth visible above his stubble in the headlamp of the train. She flushed at the sight of him, as she always did when, as so often, she had excitedly built up a book-fuelled idea of someone in her head, someone who would match up to her romantic fantasies. She felt foolish immediately. But his smile was genuine; he was truly pleased to see her. And his curly black hair still fell over his heavy-lidded eyes.

'Come!' he said. 'Come unpack!'

Nina grinned so widely it almost split her face. 'I will!'

'AND!' he shouted, excited, moving more quickly. 'Come see!'

Jim jumped down from the front of the train.

'Hurry up, hurry up!' he said. 'We can't dawdle. The sleeper will have our guts for garters.'

'The sleeper stop too early anyway,' grumbled Marek. 'They should be pleased of a few more minutes in their beds. And also, look!'

119

Behind Jim, the figure Nina had glimpsed in the cab jumped down. To her amazement, it was none other than Surinder.

'SOORS!' she screamed, running to her friend and flinging her arms around her. 'You're here! Why are you here?! I've missed you so much.'

Surinder grinned. 'It was Marek's idea. When they came to pick up the books. By the way, can you let me know how you managed to persuade these two gigantic hunks to do all your dirty work for you?'

'It's Scotland's new-found proud confidence as a nation,' said Nina, amazed by how delighted she was, even after just a week, to see a friendly face – or rather, it seemed, three friendly faces. She realised suddenly that despite all the new exciting feelings – of autonomy, of freedom – that she'd felt since she arrived, she'd been missing the simple familiarity that came with ... well, someone you understood, she supposed.

'Come on!' said Marek. 'Move!'

They all scurried to the first truck, and Jim loosened the pegs, first glancing round furtively. Fortunately there wasn't a soul in sight. Underneath the tarpaulin were what Nina knew were over 70 boxes of books. She eyed them guiltily.

'I had no idea there were that many,' she lied.

'Really?' said Surinder, hoisting two at once. 'No, how could you have done, with only all the many, many warnings from me to move the damn things?'

Nina felt awful. 'I must have been the worst housemate in the world.'

Surinder rolled her eyes. 'Actually, I moved someone else

in too fast. She cries in the bath a lot. Then when I ask her if she's all right, she says, "I'm fine, but why are all these books in here?"'

Nina frowned. 'That sounds awful,' she said. 'She's probably depressed. I have a couple of excellent books I could recommend.'

Surinder dumped the boxes in the back of the van.

'Okay,' she said. 'I'll pay you on the way out.'

'No you won't,' said Nina, as the two men lifted large boxes off the truck. 'Oh, I am so thrilled to see you! How did you meet up with them?'

'Flew to Inverness and hitched a lift. It was quite exciting, actually. And I have a clutch of annual leave left over. The office can fall apart. Which it will. I need a break from that place.'

Surinder watched Marek bend over and load a large pile of boxes effortlessly and tidily into the van.

'Good view here, though,' she said.

'Surinder!' said Nina, shocked. She'd had more romantic thoughts.

Surinder looked at her. 'Come on, don't say you hadn't noticed,' she said slyly.

Nina thought of the poem suddenly, and caught herself blushing.

'Don't be daft,' she said. 'He's a very nice man doing us both a favour.'

'It's a hell of a favour, risking their jobs.' Surinder glanced back. 'Do you think he looks a bit like Mark Ruffalo?'

'Stop it.'

'I'm just asking.'

'Do I think a Latvian train driver looks like Mark Ruffalo?'

'A little bit.'

'Hey, you two, hurry up, huh? I do not want to get sacked for deeply illegal move on Britain's railways.'

The girls straightened up and giggled.

'Also, I have tea,' added Jim helpfully, holding up his flask. 'So unload the boxes before it gets cold.'

They scurried back to the train to fetch more books.

'Is there not loads of this going on?' Nina asked suddenly as the thought occurred to her. 'Lots of illegal naughty things travelling up and down the railway? Smuggling and stuff?'

Jim and Marek smiled.

'Not with us,' said Jim. 'I've seen what drugs have done to the place I grew up in. Won't have nothing to do with anything like that. No way. This. This is different.'

Marek frowned. 'You know,' he said, 'when my parents were little, books were banned in my language. That is why, alas, I read in Russian first and then in the beautiful music of my homeland. So. Anything that spreads books and brings about more books, I would say it is good. Good medicine, not bad.'

They sat on the stoop, talking about books in the moonlight, passing around the hot, very sweet tea, and Nina could easily have stayed there until the dawn; but there was a telephone sound in the cab, and simultaneously a loud honk from behind them somewhere – the impatient sleeper, Nina deduced – and it was time for the boys to go.

Jim hopped into the cabin and fired up the engine, which made a deep throbbing sound that shook the ground. Surinder declared herself absolutely bloody freezing and went and sat in the van to warm herself up. Then Marek jumped lightly on to the plate, and Nina smiled up at him.

'I can't thank you enough,' she said.

'You can,' he said gently. 'Leave me book every now and again. Whenever you think of us.'

'I shall think of you every day,' said Nina, colouring a little.

'Well, every day it shall also be good,' said Marek, blushing slightly too.

'I liked your book of poems,' said Nina. 'I liked it very much.'

'Poetry is good for people who are in strange lands,' said Marek.

'Yes,' said Nina. 'Yes, it is.'

The train gave out a long honk and then slowly, gracefully began to move away beneath the starry sky.

Nina turned round and saw that Surinder, obviously exhausted from her long day, had curled up in the front of the van and fallen fast asleep. Nina herself stayed by the track as the noise from the train faded away, followed in short order by the long and beautiful burgundy and navy-blue sleeper, with its busy bar full of strangers meeting and passing by; its hard recliner seats where the cash-strapped and the shift workers tried to get some shut-eye; and the mysterious, dimly lit windows of the first-class compartments. As the train slowed, then slid smoothly through the level crossing, nobody aboard was the least bit aware of a girl standing alone in the dark, staring straight ahead.

And then at last the track stopped humming and all was silence once again, and the wide dark highland valley belonged once more to the owls and the scurrying squirrels and the gentle deer and the wind rustling in the branches and the bright moon overhead and the sense of a world completely and utterly at peace, and Nina, even though she felt chilled, also felt profoundly touched and grateful for her good fortune; and she could not have said how long it had been since she had felt that way.

Chapter Fourteen

Surinder slept all the way back to the farm, waking briefly as they went into the barn to squeak, 'Seriously? You get this? It's all yours? There's nobody in the bath or anything? How is this fair?', then immediately falling on the sofa and passing out again.

Nina, however, felt wide awake, even though it was well after one o'clock in the morning. She looked out of the small back window and noticed the light still on over in the farmhouse. Someone else wasn't sleeping. As she watched, she saw another light come on, and another, then the door banged hard as Lennox stalked out of the house. He appeared to be swearing. Nina jumped up. She pulled her coat and wellies back on and slipped out of the door.

'Jesus CHRIST!'

She hadn't meant to creep up on Lennox as quietly as she did and scare him out of his wits, but it was too late. He whirled round as if she was holding a spade poised to whack him on the head.

'Sorry! Sorry!'

'What … what the hell are you doing out here? It's the middle of the bloody night!'

'I know! I know! I'm sorry! I wondered what you were doing.'

'What the ruddy hell do you think I'm doing?'

Nina thought this might be a rhetorical question, because she absolutely didn't have a clue.

'Um. I don't know. I thought maybe you might have heard an intruder.'

'I did,' said Lennox shortly. 'It turned out to be you.'

'Oh,' said Nina.

Lennox sighed. 'You're a townie, aren't you? What do you think: that farming is a nine-to-five job? Well, it's not. If you must know, Ruaridh thinks we've a lambing gone wrong in the upper field, and I'm going to check it out and see if we need to call Kyle out. He's the vet. Vets are like doctors for sick animals.'

'Yeah, yeah, all right, I've got it,' said Nina. Lennox had stopped by the Land Rover.

'Are you still here?' he said.

Nina didn't know what to say, but she felt emboldened by her night's adventure, and not at all ready for sleep. She simply shrugged.

Lennox paused.

'Do you want tae come? We might be able to use a small pair of hands.'

'Sure,' she found herself saying, barely able to recognise herself.

As she jumped into the Land Rover, she was surprised, but then not really surprised, to find the dog in there too. He licked her hand.

'What's your doggie's name?'

Lennox looked appalled. 'He's a dog, not a doggie. He's a professional working farm dog. Very valuable, too.'

'So does he have a name, or just a bar code?'

Lennox's hand strayed to the dog's head, as it often did, seemingly unconsciously.

'Parsley.'

This was so unexpected – she had assumed it would be Bob or Rex or something equally to the point – that Nina grinned.

'Hello, Parsley,' she said. 'What a lovely name!'

Parsley snuffled a little and licked her hand.

'It's a silly name,' said Lennox.

'Well *I* think it's lovely,' said Nina. 'A lovely name for a lovely doggie. Dog, I mean.'

For once, as the Land Rover bumped over the muddy track up the hill, Nina didn't care about saying the wrong thing, didn't feel embarrassed. There was something quite liberating in Lennox being so rude. She could tell he was like this with everyone, and it gave her licence to be slightly bolder than she might have been otherwise. She turned in her seat to look at him. He had a solid jaw, blue eyes creased from squinting across the fields, a strong nose and chin, a sprinkling of wiry stubble across his cheeks, and thick hair poking out from under his cap. He didn't look like a man who had ever been inside; even the car seemed too confining for him. He was made to stride across the moors on long legs, the wind behind him. There wasn't a soft edge to him anywhere; he was all lean angles.

Suddenly, seemingly in the middle of nowhere – there wasn't a light to be seen – Lennox stopped the Land Rover. He got a hurricane light from the back seat and turned it up to full.

'Ruaridh?' he whispered into the night.

'Aye, here, boss,' came a voice behind him.

'Where are you?'

'In the lean-to. She's not having a good time in there. Twins by the feel of it. It's like a jigsaw puzzle.'

Lennox swore and strode forwards, Nina stumbling behind him.

'Did you call Kyle?'

'Aye, he's at a calving the other side of the brae.'

'Well that's terrific,' said Lennox, putting down his lantern.

The lean-to, attached to the side of a barn, wasn't cosy, but it was out of the full force of the wind, which made a lot of difference. A ewe was lying on her side, looking very distressed, bleating pitifully.

'I know, I know, old girl,' he said. It was the first time Nina had heard anything like softness in his voice. 'There, there.'

There was a large jar of a Vaseline-style concoction on the floor, and Lennox started rolling up his sleeves and scrubbing up in a bucket. Suddenly Nina got a massive James Herriot flashback.

'You're not ...' she said, nervously, 'you're not going to stick your arm up that animal's fanny? This isn't *All Creatures Great and Small*.'

The carrot-topped Ruaridh shot a glance in Nina's direction.

'Don't mind her,' said Lennox.

'What is she, work experience?' said Ruaridh, in an accent Nina could barely understand. Then he said something else in Gaelic that she one hundred per cent absolutely couldn't understand, but it made Lennox laugh, which Nina thought was profoundly unfair in the circumstances. Lennox shook his head.

'Nah, let's have a shot at it.'

Ruaridh held the ewe's legs to stop her struggling, and Nina found she couldn't help but look away as Lennox stuck his arm inside the animal.

'Oh for goodness' sake,' said Lennox, cross but amused by her reaction. 'Honestly, there's being a townie and there's living in complete and utter denial. Do you want this ewe to have her lambs or not?'

'I know,' said Nina. 'I've just never seen anything like it before.'

'Won't get this in your books,' he teased. Then he frowned. 'Ah, I can't grip it. My damn hands are too big. Come on. Come on, little one.'

The sheep bleated painfully again.

'I know, I know. Sorry,' said Lennox, wrestling around. 'Dammit. What about you?' he said to Ruaridh.

'Mine are the same,' said the younger man, showing his large rough hands. 'Couldn't get my hand and the legs out at the same time.'

'No. I know.'

There was a pause. Then Lennox fixed Nina with a look. 'I was going to see if you could help us, but you seem far too squeamish for all of this.'

Nina swallowed. She had read plenty of animal stories, not from preference but simply because she had read nearly everything as a child. Calligraphy, code-breaking, ventriloquism; there was absolutely nothing in the little children's library she hadn't devoured, nothing she'd missed at all.

But as for dealing with real animals, in the wild, that was something she hadn't considered. She'd never got closer to a lamb than eating one on Easter Sunday, or briefly looking up from her book whilst passing a field of them on a train. This big, smelly, panicking creature in front of her, this was something different altogether, and she wasn't at all sure how to cope with it.

She nervously advanced a little bit. She felt Lennox's eyes on her, and realised he totally expected her not to be able to cope. This steeled her a little. He already thought she was a useless townie; she wasn't going to confirm his suspicion.

'I could . . . I could have a shot,' she said carefully. Lennox's eyebrow moved ever so slightly.

'Are you sure?'

'Could I make things worse?'

'Maybe. Any news from Kyle?'

Ruaridh looked up from his phone. 'Still at the calving.'

Lennox sighed in exasperation, then looked at Nina again.

'Hmm,' he said.

'Do you want me to have a shot or don't you?' said Nina, cross and anxious.

'Well, that sheep is worth a bit more than you, that's all,' said Lennox.

The ewe gave a noise of keening pain that made them all wince.

'Oh God, okay. Get in there,' he said, and knelt down by the animal's side. 'And try not to make things worse.'

Nina washed thoroughly in a basin of soapy water, then lathered up her hands with the Vaseline and tried to get used to the smell. Then tentatively she touched the sheep.

Lennox laughed. 'It's only a sheep. It's not going to bite you.'

'There's a live animal in there,' pointed out Nina. 'It totally might bite me.'

'Well it won't be alive for much longer if you don't get a move on,' said Lennox, as the poor sheep strained and twisted in distress.

Nina took a deep breath and plunged her hand in. She was left-handed, so Lennox jumped up and came around her other side.

'Right,' he said. 'What can you feel?'

'A whole load of squidge,' said Nina, panicking slightly. She could feel her hand and arm getting crushed. 'I can't . . .'

'Okay, okay. Just relax, get used to it. It's not every day you stick your hand up a sheep.'

'It isn't,' agreed Nina.

'Try shutting your eyes,' suggested Lennox. 'You'll feel more of what you're looking for that way.'

Nina closed her eyes briefly and it made a lot of difference. Under her fingers, the baby sheep started to become clear: a little nose, ears, and a great tangle of legs.

'He's all mixed up!' she said. 'He's got too many legs! Oh no!'

'Okay,' said Lennox, his mouth twitching.

'Why has he got too many legs?' Nina was becoming slightly hysterical. It felt like some kind of alien spider being.

'Well, let's just assume for a moment that there's more than one lamb in there.'

'Oh yes,' said Nina, relieved. 'Twins. Of course. You said. That makes more sense.'

Ruaridh snorted in the corner, and Lennox shot him a look. He went off to fetch some fresh water, still looking very sceptical.

'Now,' said Lennox. 'I need you to get four legs together that all belong to the same animal. Do you understand?'

Nina nodded. She could feel them now, all mixed up like a jigsaw puzzle, as Ruaridh had said, and quickly and carefully she set about unfolding the legs from under each lamb, until triumphantly, she had four hooves in one hand. It felt oddly like changing a duvet.

'I've got one!' she said.

'That's great,' said Lennox. 'Now, pull it a little. Gently. Not too much.'

The little animal moved forward, then stopped.

'It's stuck,' said Nina, as the sheep gave another great wail of distress. 'It's stuck! I can't get him any more!'

'Don't worry,' said Lennox, pulling out a piece of rope. 'Here. Get your hand out and then loop this round the hooves.'

Nina stared at him. 'You're going to pull out a lamb with a rope?'

'Unless you'd rather perform a Caesarean section?' grunted Lennox, speedily tying a slip knot and passing her the rope.

Her hands were absolutely disgusting now, and although it was horribly warm inside the sheep, it was still completely freezing in the lean-to, and she'd had to take her jacket off and roll her sleeves up, which she wasn't enjoying in the slightest. She was trembling slightly as she took the rope and put her hand back inside the ewe, but after a few false starts she managed somehow to get it around the hooves.

'Okay,' said Lennox. 'Are you ready? Because I'm going to pull, but if it's not ready, we'll have to start all over again.'

'Farming is very different to how I thought it was,' said Nina, looking anxiously at the coiled rope in Lennox's hands.

'There are things you can't read about in books, you know,' grunted Lennox. 'Are we ready or not?'

'Please do it now,' said Nina. 'I'm freezing to death.'

'Okay,' said Lennox. 'One . . . two . . . three . . .'

Nina removed her hand, then, gently, without straining or tugging, Lennox pulled on the rope just so – slowly at first, then faster – and suddenly out plopped a blinking, brand-new, soaking-wet little lamb.

'OH!' said Nina. 'OH my goodness!'

Lennox looked at her with narrowed eyes. 'What on earth did you think was going to come out?' he said. 'Something shrink-wrapped at the Co-op?'

And then, with a happy surge, the sheep heaved strongly and the second little lamb came rushing out on to the hay and looked up and around with a blind-eyed, confused stare, and Nina gasped.

'Oh, WOW!'

Nina scrubbed her hands clean as Lennox rubbed the new lambs down with fresh hay, checking their mouths and nostrils, and the mother delivered the afterbirth. Then, astonishingly, as if they hadn't been through a great traumatic entrance to the world, the tiny creatures found their wobbly feet and stumbled up blindly, making little bleating noises. They were utterly and hopelessly enchanting, and Nina couldn't take her eyes off them.

'Oh my goodness,' she said. 'Look at them! That's amazing! That's AMAZING!'

She gazed, fascinated, as the newborn lambs somehow, instinctively, made their way to their mother, who was now lying exhausted on her side, and found exactly the place to go to start sucking milk. She found to her amazement that she was rather tearful. The ewe, who had been in such awful pain, then utterly exhausted, somehow recovered herself enough to sit up in a rather ungainly fashion and start licking clean her new babies.

'Well done you,' said Nina. 'Well done, Mum.'

Lennox smiled.

'I don't care if you're laughing at me,' said Nina. 'This is totally awesome, actually.'

'I'm not laughing at you,' said Lennox. 'I'm agreeing with you. Just because I see a lot of lambs being born doesn't mean I don't think it's pretty incredible. Every time. Lovely little buggers they are too.'

He petted them roughly.

'Come on,' he said. 'Tea.'

When Nina stood up she realised she was still frozen to the bone. Outside, she was amazed to see the first rays of dawn in the corner of the sky.

'We weren't in there for that long,' she said. 'Were we?'

Lennox nodded 'Aye, it was a pretty gnarly one. It's gone three.'

'It's just after three and getting light?' said Nina. 'This is ridiculous. You basically live above the Arctic circle. It's the land of the midnight sun.'

Down at the farmhouse, the log burner had been banked and was smouldering happily; the room was cosy, and Lennox stoked the fire and went to boil the kettle for tea. Nina took the opportunity to wash up more thoroughly, even though she was resigning herself to the fact that she would obviously smell of sheep for ever.

She was intrigued by the farmhouse bathroom; it was absolutely cutting-edge brand new, all polished marble and walk-in showers and jacuzzi baths. It was like a really, really posh hotel, with thick white towels hanging everywhere.

'Nice bathroom,' she said as she came out. Lennox nodded briefly, and it occurred to Nina – and would have occurred to her earlier, except she was so very tired – that of course Kate must have done it. Of course she must.

The main room too didn't look in the slightest like a farmhouse; it was all plain minimalist Scandinavian wood and floors. It didn't really suit Lennox, Nina thought, whose clothes, whilst clean, were so old and faded they looked as if he'd inherited them. He looked too big, too sharply cut for this decor – it was austere, yes, but so carefully designed to look austere, with its piles of artistic twigs and ironic antlers, that it actually ended up looking overdone.

She looked for a bookshelf, but she didn't see one. Instead there was a magazine basket – in white, of course – overflowing with copies of *Farmers Weekly* and, deep underneath all of those, a few old issues of *Interiors* magazine. She wondered if Lennox had kept them by mistake, or if he really didn't notice.

She moved closer to the fire. Parsley was already ensconced in front of it, cosy and stretched out. Nina budged him up and sat next to him, staring into the flames. Lennox handed her a cup of tea with, she soon discovered, coughing, whisky in it.

'What's this?' she said.

'Hot toddy,' said Lennox. 'Warm you up.'

She took another sip and let the gentle peaty warmth flood through her.

'Oh yes,' she said. 'That is very nice.'

'You look pleased with yourself.'

She glanced up at him. 'I am pleased with myself,' she said. 'I saved those lambs, and now I'm lovely and cosy in front of a fire, drinking whisky with a nice dog. I consider this to be a very good night!'

She set the cup down. Lennox smiled broadly.

'Okay, fair enough,' he said. 'Don't fall asleep in front of the fire, though.'

But it was too late. Nina's head had already nodded down on to her chest, and before she knew it, she was fast asleep.

'Well done tonight,' Lennox added, but she didn't hear him.

Chapter Fifteen

Nina ended up sleeping till nearly lunchtime in Lennox's house.

She woke up on the modish cream cord sofa, covered in a cream cashmere blanket, the sun streaming in through the windows, and at first she had absolutely no idea where she was. Gradually the night before came back to her, and although she still felt groggy, she realised she had to get up before Surinder stomped out hollering her name.

There was no sign of Lennox or Parsley. Nina wondered if they'd slept at all. She smiled a little, thinking of grumpy Lennox putting a blanket over her. Then she felt a bit embarrassed about it too: one sip of whisky and she was out as if she'd been felled. Obviously not built for country living, he must be thinking.

The sun beaming in so strongly through the window made it feel like she was somewhere hot, like Spain, until she opened the door and the cold wind rushed right through her, the clouds scudding across the sky as if they had somewhere more important to be. She smiled.

'Morning, Scotland,' she said out loud.

She'd left her wellingtons at the back door, and she put them on and crossed the yard, saying hello to the chickens pecking here and there, and wondering how her lambs were getting on. She also wondered if she'd be allowed to name them, until she remembered what they were for – what farms were for – and told herself off for being so naïve and sentimental.

At the door to the barn was a little basket. She bent down. It was full of eggs, still warm. Some of them had funny crumped shapes; not at all like you'd find in the shops. She smiled unconsciously and picked them up. Lennox must have left them.

Surinder was half dozing on the sofa, which felt like a bit of a waste of the lovely mezzanine bed, as well as the lovely day. Nina put the coffee on.

'Have you been out already?' said Surinder sleepily. 'This isn't like you. Normally on the weekends you need to get three hours' reading in before you can even go to the corner shop for a packet of bacon.'

'Um,' said Nina. 'Firstly, it's after eleven. And secondly, actually I didn't come home last night.'

Surinder sat bolt upright.

'TELL ME,' she said. 'You ran after the train and caught up with it in Edinburgh?'

Nina shook her head, pushed down the cafetière and cut some bread. She was completely and utterly ravenous.

'Scrambled eggs?' she said happily, surprised she didn't feel more tired. 'From the chooks in the farmyard.'

Surinder narrowed her eyes and looked at a particularly

plump specimen who was marching up and down outside the picture window.

'You want me to eat something that just came out of that hen's butt?' she asked.

'You eat eggs! You eat them all the time!'

'But this one is warm! From a hen's butt!'

'It doesn't come out of its butt. It comes out of its—'

'Foofoo,' said Surinder gloomily. 'Man, that's even worse.'

Nina burst out laughing. 'Seriously! You are so weird. Where did you think they made them, a cake shop?'

'No,' said Surinder.

'How about I take the shells off them?' said Nina. 'So they don't have any foofoo stuff on them.'

'Yes. Do that.' Surinder shut her eyes again. 'And don't make me watch you cook them.'

Nina threw a couple of rashers of the local bacon into the frying pan – it smelled absolutely amazing – put some bread into the expensive designer toaster, and finally brought two groaning plates of breakfast over to the scrubbed wooden table. Surinder, forgetting her horror of fresh eggs, started burrowing into her plate.

'Oh my God,' she said suddenly, stopping. 'What have I been eating all these years?'

Nina added some more creamy local milk to her coffee. 'What do you mean?'

'These eggs! That bacon! I mean, this is awesome! You don't get this down the newsagent's!'

'Yeah,' said Nina. She looked regretfully down at her plate. She'd been so furiously hungry, she'd basically inhaled breakfast without tasting it. 'Yes. It's good.'

'It's better than good! They'd charge about a million quid for it down the organic café! Is it all from round here?'

'Of course,' said Nina. 'This is what they do "round here".'

Surinder blinked at her. 'You know,' she said faintly. 'Everyone thought you were a complete and utter lunatic for coming up here.'

'You tell me that now?' said Nina. 'Really? Everyone? I thought everyone said I was awesome for being so brave and heading off and changing my life and all that.'

Surinder rolled her eyes. 'Yeah, well, they've got to say something. Remember when Kelly married that French bloke she met down the market.'

'Oh, yeah,' said Nina. 'Yeah, we totally pretended we thought he was awesome.'

'We did.'

They chewed in silence for a moment.

'You know, he wasn't even really French,' said Surinder.

Nina grinned. 'Oh GOD, I forgot about that bit.'

Surinder grabbed another piece of toast and waved her hand at the big windows.

'But now . . . look at this. I mean, I think you might actually be a genius.'

'It's sunny today,' said Nina. 'But it's not sunny very often. Well, every ten minutes. Then it rains, then it snows, then it hails, then it's sunny again.'

'Stunning,' said Surinder. 'Now tell me what you did last night, under pain of death.'

Nina smiled. 'I delivered two lambs! Well, I helped. No, I totally did it. With help.' And she explained.

'Oh, ffs,' said Surinder. 'I knew it. Not a sniff of a bloke

140

around you for four years, then you move up here and five seconds later it's men central. I KNEW it! So you went back to the farmhouse ... Is the farmer hunky, by the way? In my head they've all got round red cheeks and wellingtons and crooks and jolly expressions.'

'You're thinking about a picture of a farmer. In a children's book,' said Nina.

'Oh yeah,' said Surinder. 'Okay, surprise me. Topknot? Dreads? Sandals?'

'No,' said Nina. 'No, you're right, nothing like that. He's grumpy. Getting a divorce. He's kind of tall and wiry and pointy-looking. Bit sad.'

'Oh, right,' said Surinder. She thought for a moment. 'Is he like that farmer in *Babe*?'

'No!' said Nina. 'You've got to stop thinking about farmers you've seen on television! He's a real bloke. Young. Who just happens to be a farmer.'

'Well he's not *that* much of a real bloke,' said Surinder. 'All the real blokes I know are obsessed with cars and have started doing cycling at the weekend and being really, really boring about it and banging on about their Fitbits and growing stupid beards and talking about being on Tinder. That's what all the real men are like these days.'

She lowered her voice.

'They're rubbish.'

'You seem to like them.'

Surinder ignored this.

'Also, you fell asleep on his sofa and he didn't even vaguely try it on with you. That doesn't sound much like the blokes I know either.'

She sighed.

'Right. What are we doing today? If it's unpacking books, you can sod off. I helped Marek pack them all up.'

'Fine,' said Nina. 'What I will totally not do is get on with work really, really loudly, giving big sighs every so often, whilst you recline on the sofa.'

'I don't give a toss,' said Surinder. 'This is the most comfortable sofa I have ever sat on in my entire life. I don't think this is a sofa that gets advertised on television as costing very, very small amounts of money on bank holiday weekends.'

'Neither do I,' said Nina. 'I don't think this is a sofa that advertises at all. I think this is a sofa you have to beg to come and live with you in exchange for lots of money and blood sacrifice.'

'And if the sofa doesn't think you're worth it, it won't bother,' said Surinder. 'It just keeps sitting in its palace. Whoops.'

'Did you just spill coffee on it?'

'Your furniture makes me really nervous.'

'Me too,' said Nina, looking around. 'Shall we head out?'

'But I'm staying and lying on the sofa!' said Surinder. 'I took holiday for this!'

Nina didn't say anything, just put on her wellingtons with a martyred expression, refilled her coffee cup, went out into the cool sunlight and started work on the van.

She'd managed to put up the shelves she'd ordered from Inverness – there were useful grooves in the walls for exactly that – without too much trouble, so she turned the radio up loud and went to work with a will, scrubbing down the walls and floors until it was utterly spotless, then starting on the happy task of dusting down the books and figuring out what went where.

Fiction to the right, she decided, as you came in, seeing as that was what most people would be looking for; non-fiction to the left, and children's at the far end, so they could get right inside the van and up close. She had bought several cheap colourful bean bags for the children to jump on for story hour. Her Right to Trade certificate was proudly displayed on the inside of the window. What had caused a lot of teeth-sucking and head-shaking in Birmingham had been granted with a ready smile up here.

She sang along to the radio, making everything just so, and although it took all afternoon, it still didn't feel long before she was opening her very last box and gasping with surprise. It wasn't books at all, but all the little things she'd collected over the years to go with the books and show them off. She had always wondered why she had picked up these bits and pieces of bric-a-brac (or junk, as Surinder called them). But now, as she surveyed the clean, bare walls of the van, she realised exactly why she had been stockpiling all this time, without even knowing herself what she'd been doing.

She strung garlands of fairy-light blossoms here and there; added funny bookends: a lighthouse, a Gruffalo for the little ones. A set of huge cut-out bronze letters with light bulbs in them, spelling out B-O-O-K-S, which could be placed outside the van whenever she parked up on her rounds. Beautifully ornate notebooks she could use as book ledgers. Framed Mother Goose prints to make an old-fashioned A–Z around the children's section. Some bunting printed with pages of a vintage book.

'This van is going to rattle like anything,' observed Surinder, slopping the tea a little as she crossed the farmyard, slightly wary of the chickens.

'It won't,' said Nina. 'It's not going faster than twenty miles an hour. Ever. I don't care who's behind me. They're just going to have to wait.'

She pulled out a tin of blue paint.

'Okay,' she said. 'Something for you to do.'

'Nooo,' said Surinder. 'I'm still sleepy. I'll muck it up.'

'Then we'll paint over it,' said Nina. 'Come on, you're so good at it.'

Surinder stuck out her bottom lip, but Nina knew how beautiful her handwriting was. She was always being prevailed upon to do people's wedding invitations. She moaned about it non-stop, but she always did it in the end.

'Really?'

'I'll make you breakfast again tomorrow,' said Nina. 'Wait till you taste the sausages they do round here.'

Surinder groaned. 'Seriously?'

'Better than anything you've ever eaten in your life. Oh, and I think I have some local biscuits in.'

'What are they like?'

'A surprise,' said Nina, who hadn't tasted the round red and silver striped Tunnock's tea cakes herself. 'You get started, I'll go and find them.'

Surinder frowned. 'You know, the last wedding I did, they gave me champagne and everything.'

'Biscuits and sausages,' said Nina. 'Basically I'm spoiling you.' She strode towards the barn.

'Hang on!' shouted Surinder behind her. 'What on earth is it called?'

Nina turned round. 'Oh,' she said. 'I hadn't thought. Can you just put Book Bus?'

'No,' said Surinder. 'That sounds like a library.'

'Hmm. Bookshop?'

'That sounds like a delivery van. For books that are going somewhere else.'

'Buy Your Books Here?'

'That's your name for your shop?'

'Nina's Book Bus?'

'You're not a children's educational television programme. Although you do dress like you're in one.'

Nina sighed.

'What?' said Surinder. 'Come on, you've obviously dreamed about this for ages. I mean, look at all the crap you stashed away for it. I absolutely don't believe that someone as obsessed as you with books and words hasn't thought about a name.'

'Well,' said Nina, looking embarrassed and staring at her feet. She'd never said this out loud to anyone before. Barely even admitted it to herself.

'I knew it,' said Surinder. 'I KNEW it! Go on! Tell your auntyji.'

Nina shrugged. 'You'll think it's stupid ...'

'You've moved an entire country away with a big bunch of books and a van,' said Surinder. 'I already think you are totally stupid.'

'Oh yeah,' said Nina. 'I suppose.'

She kicked her heels a little.

'Well,' she said. 'I always thought if I ever had a little shop – and I only wanted a very little one – I might call it ... the Little Shop of Happy-Ever-After.'

Surinder stared at her for a moment. Nina felt her face grow very red. There was a long pause.

Surinder stepped forward and peered inside the van. Nina had even managed to fix up a light in the corner; a rug, stuck down with suckers; a table with a comfortable chair beside it, so it made a little reading corner. Surinder smiled and turned round.

'Yeah,' she said. 'Yes. I like it. I really like it. I can do that.'

'Really?' said Nina.

'Yes,' said Surinder. 'Look at that table and chair. That is just so cute. It's a cutesy name. But I think it's all right. I think it'll be okay.'

She picked up the paint and a brush, and Nina's face broke into a huge grin.

'Mind you, it does look like you could just sit there all day. What if someone just sits there all day?'

'Then they obviously need to,' said Nina. 'But we won't be staying anywhere all day. We'll be like the lands above the Magic Faraway Tree, arriving and leaving without notice.'

Surinder smiled. 'Well just don't crash it,' she said, rolling up her sleeves. 'Again.'

'Hmm,' said Nina, who was a little worried she'd overdone the fairy lights. 'Right now, I'm most worried about fusing it.'

She fetched a couple of beers, then stood back and watched as Surinder first chalked a rough outline then, with clear, precise strokes, and a lovely hand, wrote *The Little Shop of Happy-Ever-After* on the side. Nina thought she'd never been so happy.

Finally Surinder pronounced herself satisfied. They both stood back, and Nina, rather self-consciously, chinked her beer against Surinder's.

'We should have had a ribbon,' Surinder pointed out. 'To chop.'

146

Nina gazed at the little shop. It was beautiful, far bigger inside than it seemed, with the tidy rows of books, the bean bags and even a little set of library steps that Nina had liberated when the new head of development had asked what use they could possibly be in the new media centre.

They threw the back doors open wide, counted to three and turned the ignition.

The fairy lights and the big bronze letters lit up as if it was Christmas, the bunting flapping in the wind.

'HOORAY!' said Surinder, and clapped despite herself. Nina stared, amazed. It was as if her dream had come to life and was standing in front of her, with the fields behind them, the meadow butterflies flittering amongst the daisies and an owl hooting somewhere in the distance. She could barely believe it and couldn't stop smiling.

'Let's go sell some books!' she said. 'Where shall we start?'

At that exact moment, a Land Rover turned in at the gate, honking loudly. Nina glanced at her watch. It was nearly 6 p.m. Still bright daylight, of course. She turned round. Normally people didn't honk their horns on the farm; it made the chickens crazy. Shading her eyes, she saw a bunch of young men, mostly ruddy and cheery-looking.

'LENNOX!' one of them was shouting. They looked surprised to see Nina and Surinder there as they drove in and came to a halt. Nina was shocked to see they were all wearing kilts.

'Whoa!' said Surinder. 'Look at you lot.'

'Look at you,' said one man instantly, in that local musical brogue. 'We're the ones looking smart. You're all covered in paint.'

'What's this?' said another. 'It looks cool.'

'It's our book bus,' said Surinder instantly. The young guy jumped down.

'What've you got, like?'

The others laughed and made catcalls.

'Aye, have you got any Noddy for him?'

'Shut up. At least I can read. All you can do is look at pictures of nuddie ladies on the internet, you big fanny.'

'Quite,' said Nina. 'Um, do you want to come in?'

There was more catcalling behind them, but the young chap jumped up happily and started to browse the shelves, and eventually curiosity drew the others forward to have a look too.

'It's nice,' said the one who'd been rude before, shuffling his feet.

Nina was embarrassed to ask them if they were going somewhere special, in case they always dressed like that. Some of them were in black tie from the waist up, though, so surely they were. The kilts looked lovely all together. She knew that the tartans indicated families and clans; she liked the older, worsted ones in faded reds and greens, although the rich purples and blacks were also smart, together with cream socks on well-shaped calves. All the men had a solid, healthy look about them, and as they spoke more, it was obvious that they were farmers.

'Knock up Lennox, for God's sake. What's he doing?'

'He was up all night lambing,' said Nina in his defence. They all burst out laughing.

'Och aye, as opposed to the full night's slumber the rest of us get this time of year,' said one.

'Where are you all going?' asked Surinder.

'Young Farmers' dance,' said another, who had bright red hair and green eyes. 'Are youse no' coming to that? I thought that's why you were here. They're always short of lasses.'

'The Young Farmers' what?' said Surinder. 'What is this, 1932?'

Nina was distracted for a second; coming out of the house, looking slightly embarrassed to be all togged up, was Lennox, to a chorus of good-natured approval and some hoots.

He was wearing a pale green tweed jacket, over a plain cream shirt. His kilt was pale green too, with a fine red line, and he had matching flashes in his socks, and stout brogues. His hair had been flattened, none too successfully as it happened, as errant curls were already popping back up here and there.

'Hurry up, man!'

Nina felt a little put out that Lennox hadn't mentioned the dance to her. No, he was right, she thought. It was nothing to do with her. He was her landlord, she was his tenant. The last thing he was going to do was start asking her to dances. This was somebody else's social life after all. She was new here. She'd have to find her own.

'Did you no' invite the lasses?' came a voice.

'I didn't realise there were two lasses,' said Lennox, moving to shake Surinder's hand. 'Nice to meet you.'

'Ooh!' said Surinder, casting a look at Nina. She was obviously quite impressed. 'I've never met anyone in a kilt before. Nice to meet you too. Uh, sir.'

Nina stifled a giggle and Surinder gave her a dirty look.

Lennox raised his eyebrows. Then he spotted the van, where Nina lingered shyly.

'Wow,' he said, standing back to inspect it. 'Look at that.' He appeared genuinely impressed.

The young man who'd been inside came out triumphantly waving three books on the Second World War.

'Look at these! I'm taking them.'

'He'd always rather read than dance with a girl,' said one of the lads.

'Not sure I blame him, some of the lasses coming,' said one, instantly hushed by his fellows. 'Oh. They're all lovely and charming is what I mean,' he said, colouring thickly.

Nina happily took the money for the books – splendid brand-new hardbacks too, glossy and fresh. She thought he would enjoy them.

'Right then,' said the red-headed chap, whose name was Hamish. 'We'd better get a move on. You know what a crush it gets. Youse up for it?' He nodded at Nina and Surinder. Nina instinctively glanced at Lennox.

'You . . . you could come if you liked,' he said, as if it didn't bother him one way or the other. 'There's never enough girls at these things.'

'You should come to Birmingham,' said Surinder. 'It's crawling with girls. Far too many.'

There was an awkward silence. They all stood around the courtyard nervously.

'Yes, of course we're coming,' said Surinder eventually.

'Really?' said Nina, nervous. The idea of a big noisy dance where she didn't know anyone made her profoundly uncomfortable. She would be much happier kicking back with a beer with Surinder, then spending the night reading a Regency romance, if that was all right with everyone.

'Come on, Nina, you big nerd!' said Surinder. 'I've not come all this way to sit in and watch you read all evening.'

Hamish glanced at his watch. 'Can youse be ready quickly?'

'Two hours, three tops,' said Surinder. 'Oh, I'm KIDDING.'

'Woo hoo!' said Surinder. 'What would you do without me?' They were putting lipstick on side by side in the bathroom.

'I don't know,' said Nina. 'Keep my dignity?'

Surinder ignored her. 'I wonder how sex-starved they really are?'

'Surinder!'

'Come on! It's just men up here. All those lovely hunky farm boys ... I mean, it's nuts. I don't think I've seen another woman since I got here. Certainly no one as hot as us.'

'Surinder, please ... I've just moved here.'

'Yes, but *I'm* on my holidays. I wonder if they serve pina coladas.'

'I very much doubt it.'

The one thing Nina had never thought to pack was a party dress. It had come very low down the list of things she'd expected to need.

Instead she found a pretty floral shift. It wasn't in the least dressy and she didn't have any jewellery at all. But she did find, somewhat to her surprise, that her legs were brown from being out and about in the sun, so the dress would do.

She curled her hair back off her face in a slightly Second

World War style, added a bright red lipstick at Surinder's suggestion, and figured she would just have to manage as best she could.

Surinder, on the other hand, was always prepared for every eventuality, and slipped on a diamanté top as if she'd expected to go to a major social event all along.

The boys were very complimentary as they emerged twenty minutes later, and budged up on the shelf seating of the Land Rover.

Lennox said very little, and Nina suspected he slightly regretted asking them. Well, that was tough luck. The sun was still high in the sky, the fields golden, the wind fresh rather than biting, and everything seemed well with the world. She turned her head for one last look at the Little Shop of Happy-Ever-After, and couldn't help smiling in satisfaction.

'You're proud of that, aren't you?' he said, seeing her glance at it.

'Well don't sound so surprised.'

'No, no,' he said, then lapsed into silence again.

They twisted through country lanes, occasionally cresting amazing hills, lit up all the way to the sea, a patchwork of light and shade that stretched for miles and miles. Great armies of wind farms marched across the hills like sentinels.

'I can't believe you didn't remind me to bring a jacket,' said Surinder. 'It's not like it's not signposted by the MILES OF WIND TURBINES.'

'You're right,' said Nina, almost smugly. 'It's so much worse than miles and miles of identical terraced houses and discount outlets.'

They heard the dance before they saw it. Down a steep

little mud track, tractors were parked up in rows, along with dirt-spattered Land Rovers, in front of a huge barn decorated with flowers. People were spilling out from it, sitting around on hay bales; young men, all in kilts of course, were drinking pints and letting off steam.

'Once a quarter,' said Hamish, his green eyes twinkling, 'it's where you're meant to meet your wife.'

'Seriously?' said Surinder, leaning forward.

'Of course, it's not like that any more, not a cattle market at all.'

'So nobody meets their partners there these days?'

There was some nervous shuffling around the Land Rover.

'Aye, yeah, well. Most folk, like.'

'I think I'm going to like 1932,' said Surinder cheerfully.

Inside the barn, it was incredibly hot, simply from the crush of bodies, and didn't smell of cow at all; instead it smelled of deodorant, aftershave and heavily applied perfume; beer and pipe tobacco.

It was also incredibly noisy. In the corner was a four-piece band – a violin, a bodhrán, a whistle and an accordion – playing music at a thousand miles an hour. On one side was a roughly set-up bar made of wooden barrels and trestle tables, where teenage bar staff dispensed pints of the local 80 Shilling Ale at lightning speed and hurled huge gin and tonics and glasses of wine across the counter with abandon. All the cash was simply dumped in a large pot. The queue at the bar was thick. In the other half of the room, people were ... well, at first Nina wasn't exactly sure what they were doing. It didn't seem to make sense until she started concentrating. The men were hurling the women around at breakneck speed, and it took her a moment to realise that they were dancing. It looked absolutely brutal.

'Wow,' she said. It was a lot to take in. There were obviously far more men than women, but when she looked at the women who were there, she immediately realised she was notably underdressed. They had high hairstyles and proper evening gowns, some stiff and long; lots of black lace pulled tightly over muscular upper bodies, and make-up applied with a heavy hand. They were all in high heels.

In comparison, Nina wasn't dressed for a party at all. But in fact, knowing that she wasn't trying to make an impression (which could sometimes make her feel very anxious at events), she felt light and easy in the hot perfumed room, and didn't mind even when Surinder glanced at her and said, 'Wow, you look like a proper country girl,' which Nina realised was obviously a compliment of some kind.

They supped their drinks and chatted to the boys, even though their eyes were on stalks and their heads swivelling as the girls in their scented finery pranced past. Nina was perfectly happy just to listen and take in their discussion of fertiliser brands, tractor parts, meat to market and a clutch of other concepts she didn't understand.

After a couple of drinks, the boys were ready to dance. Nina and Surinder declined several times, partly because they weren't out on the pull like the boys were (well, Nina wasn't; Surinder was feeling torn), and partly because they didn't have the first clue what to do.

From a distance, the dancing still looked fearsome. The

girls were being flung about by the boys, and every so often somebody would crash into a trestle table or topple to the floor. It was all good-natured fun, though, and nobody did anything but laugh, as the noise levels continued to rise and the amount of floor space taken up by the wildly reeling dancers got larger and larger. High heels were starting to be thrown off here and there.

Lennox, Nina noticed, stayed resolutely on the side of the dance floor. She tried smiling at him and was about to ask him how the lambs were getting on when he hailed a man he knew across the floor, an older gentleman wearing unflattering tartan trews. They immediately plunged deep into conversation.

The boys had begun talking about feed compounds, and slightly emboldened by the very strong gin and tonics, Nina wandered over to join them.

'Hi!' she said. 'I wanted to ask how the lambs were getting on.'

Both men stared at her, quite rudely.

'Yes, fine,' said Lennox dismissively, then turned back to his friend. Nina felt stung. She'd been up all night helping this guy, and first he didn't want them to come to the dance, and now he was completely ignoring her.

'Not dancing?' she asked, rather cheekily. His brow furrowed.

'No thanks,' he said shortly. The other man stared into the distance.

'I wasn't asking,' said Nina, annoyed and embarrassed. 'I just wondered, that's all.'

'No,' said Lennox shortly. 'Not for me.'

The silence became embarrassing and Nina was thinking about beating a retreat when, thankfully, a young man came up and asked her rather nervously if she would like to dance. She was about to politely refuse when, to her surprise, she spotted Surinder waltzing towards the dance floor in another chap's arms.

'What. Are. You. Doing?' Nina hissed after her.

'Come on!' shouted Surinder. 'For goodness' sake. We're not here for long! Might as well have a shot.'

Nina shook her head. 'You're mad,' she said, before realising that the young chap who'd asked her, whose name was Archie, was looking crestfallen and obviously feeling a bit of an idiot. She was conscious that all his mates were lined up watching them from the other side of the room, so with a glance to her left, where Lennox had dived back into conversation with his friend, she extended her hand.

'Of course, I'd love to,' she said loudly, while Archie flushed the same colour as his hair. As he led her to the floor – or what felt to Nina a bit like a gladiatorial arena – she whispered, 'You're going to have to tell me what to do. I don't know what's going on.'

At this Archie looked less terrified, and puffed up his chest a little bit.

'Don't you worry yourself,' he said. 'You're with me now! Just follow me.'

To begin with, Nina couldn't follow anyone. It was a little like being on a waltzer at a fairground, where you had to scream if you wanted to go faster. There was a lot of yelling and shouting, and some competitive arm-swinging from the men, and at first it seemed to be nothing but a melee: a game of rugby on a dance floor.

Then, as Archie patiently showed her the repeated moves, she gradually came to recognise the sequence of dips, twirls and claps, and before she knew it, he was flying her around as she twisted and turned. She found herself caught up in the music and laughing with excitement, but just as she had figured it out, the band stopped playing and she had to finish, breathless and disappointed.

The second dance, she got the hang of it straight away, as the entire room danced in a circle for eight counts and back. Archie grinned at her widely as he spun her away from the circle, and when she came back, she found he had moved down one, and now a heavily bearded young chap was grinning at her just as brightly and preparing to twirl her around.

Emboldened by the heady atmosphere, the alcohol, the sense of being unimaginably far from home, of being somebody else, Nina threw herself into dancing with a will. She had always been dainty, but never quite confident enough to dance where anyone might see. Here, though, nobody cared or noticed. The emphasis wasn't on looking good or being sexy or standing out; it was about hurling yourself into it and dancing as if you didn't have a care in the world, or a worry, or even a thought; it was dancing as catharsis, and Nina very quickly found that she absolutely loved it.

The atmosphere in the barn was making her dizzy; she could hear Surinder laughing loudly and bouncing off tables several couples away, but she felt as if she was moving in and out of the dance as a piece of something larger, barely an individual at all, as the music burned louder and hotter in her ears.

She joined in the huge round of applause as the dance ended, then curtsied deeply and drank, greedily, from the fresh bottle of local cider Archie passed to her.

'And now,' said the caller from the band, 'it's time for the Dashing White Sergeant.'

Nina raised her eyebrows at Archie, who nodded enthusiastically. All around them a massive land grab was going on as people broke up other couples and partnerships.

'What's going on?'

'This one's in threes. We need another girl. Or another boy,' said Archie.

They glanced around. Everyone was divvied up already, and all the girls were gone. A row of large chaps were standing at the back, obviously not wanting to dance and instead concentrating very hard on drinking their pints. Their faces were bright red.

Nina glanced around. There was no one else. Except ... She looked for Lennox, but he was busy. Fine. She wasn't looking for him anyway, she told herself. Archie managed to round up Fat Tam, who'd been in the Land Rover with them, and they joined up with another lot who had two girls, to make a mixed group of six.

Archie briefly explained the dance to Nina. First of all they went round in a circle, then back in a circle. Then Nina, in the middle, had to dance with each of the boys beside her, and with the boy in the middle of the other group. They had to perform a courtly sidestep, then whirl each other round by their waists, then move back and forward. Finally they moved under the raised hands of the other group and started again with the next three they met.

Nina frowned. It seemed complicated. But as she got started, she began to see the pattern, the simple beauty of the circles coming together, bowing to one another, then coming apart again. From above it would look like the petals of a flower opening.

Her light floral dress was ideal for twirling as she was whizzed round by the men, and her ballet pumps were perfect. Her cheeks were pink, giving colour to her normally pale face, and her hair bounced and spun around her head as she danced, completely unselfconscious for the first time in what felt like so long.

(Surinder, catching sight of her when they danced in the same circle, thought that if Scotland could do shy little Nina this much good, it might have rather more going for it than she'd thought.)

Near the end of the dance, Nina ducked under some other arms and came up to their new group, only to be confronted by the figure of Lennox straight ahead. The two girls dancing by his side – he was the figure in the middle, just as she was – were rather drunk, giggling and flirting with him, but he was completely oblivious, and, Nina noticed, he was a fine dancer, slipping in and out exactly on the beat; effortlessly swinging and catching the squealing girls. Controlled.

When it was her turn to dance towards him, she looked at him crossly.

'Thought you weren't dancing,' she said, although she regretted it almost immediately, annoyed with herself for looking like she cared even the tiniest bit that this grumpy, stupid old farmer would happily dance with some blonde floozy but not with her. Then, suddenly, he caught her by the waist and spun her round, and she realised that her feet had lifted quite off the ground. She felt like thistledown as she flew through the air, her hair a sheet behind her, her dress flowing; and she looked up at him as she landed, but he just picked her up again as if she was nothing, and she flew once more and landed back perfectly in the exact same spot, and there was nothing to do except smile, and curtsy, and move on; although Nina found she hesitated, just a tad, and tried to hold his eye, but he was gone, and she didn't see him again for the rest of the night.

Nina and Surinder sat in the back of the truck that some-one had commandeered to drive them home. It trundled through the morning mist towards the village, pink and gold alighting on the fields, the dew turning everything to a glistening web. It was, Nina was astonished to see, after four by the time the last of the fiddles was packed away, and girls everywhere were looking through the hay for their shoes. She was exhausted, but happily, wonderfully, down-to-the-bone dancing-and-laughing exhausted.

She realised quite quickly that Surinder wanted to sit next to Fat Tam, so she moved into the body of the cab, where there was a pile of three hairy men all fast asleep.

'They're going straight back to work,' said Archie, who was still awake, his shirt unbuttoned, his friendly freckled face beaming at her. 'Me too.'

'Really?'

'Aye. No lie-ins for farmers.'

They were approaching the cobbled road down to Lennox's farm. Archie looked at her.

'This is my stop,' said Nina. 'Thank you. Thank you so much for a wonderful evening. I really, really needed it.'

Archie leaned forward. 'Can I ... could I maybe ...'

'No,' said Nina. 'Thank you. Tonight was exactly what I needed. But I think ... I think that was maybe all. Though you are a wonderful dance teacher.'

He smiled. 'Thanks.' He looked at her. 'You're not from round here.'

'You just noticed?'

'No, no. I just meant ... I know you're not from round here. But it feels like you've fitted in really well. And not everybody does.'

Nina beamed with pleasure. 'Thank you,' she said.

Archie banged on the side of the van and it stopped. Nina banged on the side of Surinder, and she stopped too.

'Aww,' said Fat Tam.

'Another time,' said Nina, jumping down and giving Surinder a hand. Surinder had drunk more cider than Nina had.

'This is a great place,' she was saying. 'This is just ... this is good. I like Fat Tam.'

'He liked you too,' said Nina. 'He was going at you like you were breakfast.'

'Oh yeah?' said Surinder, who was carrying her shoes. 'Do you think he was maybe just hungry? And can you make me more breakfast now, please?'

Chapter Sixteen

Both the girls slept long and late the next day. Nina sat up about eleven as Surinder made coffee, and they both looked at something Nina had bought called 'potato scones'. In the end they decided to toast them and slather them with butter, which turned out to be a better solution than either of them could have imagined possible, as they ate them looking out into the windy sunlight.

'What a beautiful day,' Nina exclaimed.

'Lots of wind,' pointed out Surinder.

'Yes,' explained Nina patiently. 'It stops you getting too hot.'

'You have gone totally native,' said Surinder.

'Not as much as you have,' said Nina. 'I haven't swapped DNA with anyone.'

'When did you get so cheeky?' said Surinder, wolfing another potato scone. 'Oh my God, these are good.'

'I don't know,' said Nina, genuinely musing on it. She'd noticed it in herself. She opened the door and stood enjoying the warmth of the sun and the cool breeze beneath it. 'I think . . . I think it was when we moved the books out. Found them a home.'

Surinder nodded. 'I think you're right. A psychological weight has been lifted.'

'And also an actual weight,' pointed out Nina. 'But yeah. It's like we can just be normal friends again without you tutting at me all the time.'

'Because you were about to bring my ceiling down,' said Surinder.

'Yes. Exactly. Weight. Lifted.'

'I've noticed something else,' said Surinder.

'What?'

'You haven't got a book in your hands.'

'Well . . . I'm just about to go to the book van. With all my lovely books. And then I'm going to go out and sell some books.'

'I know. But you didn't read a book over breakfast.'

'I was talking to you.'

'You didn't take a book to bed.'

'We were drunk and it was four o'clock in the morning.'

'You've stopped clutching one everywhere like a security blanket.'

'I didn't do that.'

'Mm,' said Surinder.

'Anyway, what's wrong with reading?'

'Nothing is wrong with reading,' said Surinder, 'as I have told you a million billion times before. But it finally seems you're doing both. Read/live/read/live. And proceed, etc.'

Nina looked out at the wild flowers growing in the

meadow to the left of the lower field. They rippled gently in the breeze. Over in the woods she could smell the faintest drift of bluebells on the wind.

'Mm hmm,' she said.

'You know I'm right,' said Surinder. 'You're getting happy. I can tell.'

'It's not that,' said Nina. 'I just want another one of those potato scones.'

'You're also hungrier,' said Surinder. 'Also, I can tell you, a very, very good sign.'

'Shut up! And oh LORD, I am going to work. Yes I am. You can lie here and hang out.'

'I totally intend to,' said Surinder. 'Got anything to read?'

'Shut up! Again. And if Mr Farmer Grumpy Pants comes round?'

'Mmm?'

'No, don't say anything. He's an arse.'

'Roger.'

Chapter Seventeen

It was blowy but bright, and Nina pulled a jumper on over a grey dress and leggings. The Little Shop of Happy-Ever-After, minus its Second World War hardbacks, still looked as tremendous in the light of a new day as she remembered it. She made sure that all the canvas straps were pulled tight to stop the books from falling out, then got behind the wheel, treble-checking, as she always did now, that the handbrake was on and the gearstick was in neutral before she even thought about pulling away. She took a deep breath and started the van.

It was market day in neighbouring Auchterdub – she'd checked everything out before she started, and planned to follow the crowds around – so she headed straight there. Sure enough, there was a throng around the stalls where people had gathered to sell their hand-made cheeses (and occasionally a little unpasteurised milk under the counter if you asked nicely), straw dollies, warm eggs and enormous big splurges of cakes, vast, soft pillowy things chock-full of sensational ingredients. Nina kept her eye on a large ginger sponge for later.

There were hand-made sausages: venison, beef and even ostrich. There were early harvests of artichokes and potatoes, still marked with the dark earth; vast deep green cabbages and fresh young sweet lettuces; some forced tomatoes, which were still small and awkward-looking, but the cauliflowers and carrots were already gorgeous. Nina had also been told about the strawberry season, where the fruit threatened to pour over the sides of the baskets, there were just so many.

Land Rovers, jeeps and all forms of mud-splattered cars were parked along the little narrow cobbled streets and pale grey stone walls, but Nina found her booked slot easily enough and pulled up happily. Even before she had put out the big illuminated letters, shoppers were circling around. As she pulled the doors wide, the women in particular were practically jumping inside to have a look.

Nina looked behind her proudly. The stock looked neat and tidy and enticing; some of the particularly beautiful covers were turned out to face the room. In a moment of madness that morning, she had hung a chandelier from the light connector on the ceiling, but she was pleased now, as it swung prettily in the breeze.

A woman looked round. 'Goodness,' she said, smiling. 'I don't know where to start.'

'I know what you mean,' said Nina.

The woman glanced down at her rambunctious toddler in reins, who even now was cheerfully gumming the bean bags. 'I kind of . . . I only read baby books when I was pregnant, and now I've totally got out of the habit.'

Nina's heart leapt, and she jumped into action.

'Well,' she said. 'Maybe you need this.' And she brought out a beautiful book translated from Russian called *We Are All Big Girls Now*. It was a series of very short chapters about the experience of early motherhood, illustrated in glorious colours like a medieval book of hours, ranging from the deeply profound – the passing-on of the female bloodline – to the scary tales of Baba Yaga that the author's own grandmother used to terrify her with, to the simple logistical difficulties of a toddler who wouldn't keep his snowsuit on in St Petersburg in January. It was a book that had made Nina herself feel entirely and deeply maternal without ever having given a thought to motherhood, and she had never met a new mother who hadn't adored it.

The woman's face lit up as she looked at the beautiful illustrations.

'Perfect,' she said. 'Thomas, stop that! Stop that at once!'

But Thomas was not for stopping; he had spied, and retrieved, the biggest, shiniest book about buses and trucks and diggers and forklifts that Nina had on the shelves.

Nina looked away, feeling awkward; she wasn't at all used to people having to actually pay for books, unless they were late, in which case, if they looked suitably poor and/or distressed, she always waived the fine anyway.

The woman looked at it, then said, 'Do you know what, this might even keep him quiet whilst I'm trying to do the shopping, instead of grabbing at the sticky buns.'

And she took that one too, and Nina found that actually taking the money and handing over change wasn't a problem at all.

An old lady came in next and sighed and said she hadn't

realised the books were all so new, because nobody was writing the old-fashioned style of books any more, did Nina know what she meant, and what a shame that was, because all she wanted was a modern book with old-fashioned values. As it turned out, Nina did know exactly what she meant, and pulled out a rather charming series called *St Swithin's*, about a young nurse starting work in a hospital, but instead of lots of paperwork and reorganisations, this nurse – whose name was, pleasingly, Margaret – managed to exist in a contemporary multiracial world by simply loving and caring for all her patients wherever they were from, whilst regularly taking time out to go and perform daring deeds of rescue. She was also in the early throes of an exciting, but also excitingly chaste, love affair with the gorgeous, sensationally brave and daring surgeon Dr Rachel Melchitt.

'Try this,' Nina said with a smile. 'If you don't like it, you can swap it, and if you do like it, there's about another forty-seven to read.'

The woman had already lit up reading the back blurb. 'No, I think this might do nicely,' she said. 'Do you have a large-print edition?'

Nina cursed to herself. The problem was that the large-print copies were so in demand and well borrowed, there hadn't been anything in good enough condition to liberate.

'No,' she said. 'But I promise I'll source the large print for the next lot.'

After that, there was a steady stream, some people just wanting a look around, some with specific titles in mind. If they didn't know what they were after, Nina tried to get a grip on the kind of thing they liked and steered them towards the appropriate item. As she bagged up and took money – and credit cards, on an incredibly clever little device Surinder had taught her to stick on to her iPhone – she spotted a young girl hovering outside. She appeared to be about sixteen, awkward-looking, glasses, a little puppy fat still. She was wearing a long-sleeved cardigan with the sleeves pulled right down over her fists, with big holes through which her thumbs poked.

'Hey,' Nina said, gently. The girl looked at her, startled, and backed away.

'It's okay,' said Nina. She gave the girl her best smile. 'You can just come in,' she said. 'I don't mind. Just come and have a look, you don't have to buy anything.'

'Neh, it's okay,' said the girl, and walked away with her head down.

It had been a more successful launch than Nina could possibly have imagined, and she drove back later that afternoon full of the joys, and with a bottle of Prosecco, which they used to toast their enormous (relative) success ('Well, I did do the painting,' said Surinder). Then they sat in the sitting room while Nina got down to doing the books and checking what she needed to order next.

'This is the less glamorous side of running your own business,' pointed out Surinder.

'Wait till I get a puncture,' said Nina. 'Oh Lord, I'm so tired.'

'Go to bed, then.'

'I was going to ... I was going to maybe pop down to the level crossing. Wave to Marek.'

'Seriously?' said Surinder. 'What is this, *The Railway Children*?'

'No. I was ... I looked out a book he might like.'

It was a very old but mint-condition edition of *I Am David*. She had no idea if he'd read it or not, but she thought he would like it. After all, he knew a little bit about what it was like to roam.

Surinder gave her a stern look. 'Are you sure about this?'

Nina flushed. She didn't want to admit how much she had thought about him, his gentle, melancholic, poetic nature. He seemed so exotic, so sad.

'Just a thought,' she said.

'Well maybe have that thought when you've had a little more sleep,' said Surinder.

Chapter Eighteen

After several days busier than she'd have thought possible, Nina decided it was time to start story hour. The sky was overcast and grey, so she didn't have to keep the blackboard outside for very long before lots of families started to crowd in to the van.

She read the children the story of the nine tumbling princes who wove the sky, and they sat, snot encrusting noses, missing teeth whistling occasionally, utterly rapt, and she sold lots and lots of books afterwards, but my goodness they left the most dreadful mess, particularly if they had small, clambering siblings. She was just looking up with a cloth in her hand, and trying to deal with other customers, when she saw the girl again.

This girl had a look that Nina recognised. She looked avaricious; hungry for books, desperate to get her hands on something.

'You again!' said Nina cheerily. 'I'll have to start charging you rent. Come on in. Have a look.'

Lumpily – her posture was terrible – the girl mounted the two little steps into the van. Inside, her face lit up. It changed her completely; she had the loveliest smile.

'It's nice,' she said, speaking so quietly Nina could barely hear her. She moved towards the shelves, entranced, running her fingers across the spines, smiling at certain books as if they were good friends.

'What kind of thing are you looking for?'

'Oh.' The girl's face dropped. 'I can't really afford to buy books. Hey, this is misfiled.' She took out a Daniel Clowes that had slipped between two Frank Darabonts.

'Thanks,' said Nina in surprise. The girl handed her the book and expertly continued scanning the stacks.

'You like books?'

The girl nodded. 'More than anything. It was shite when they shut the library. I don't . . . There aren't any books in my house.'

'None at all?'

'Neh. My mum would sell them. If she knew what they were.' She didn't say it in a self-pitying way, simply as a statement of fact.

Nina noticed that the girl's clothes were cheap and not heavy enough for the breezy weather. She glanced thoughtfully around the post-story-time mess.

'Well,' she said thoughtfully. 'You know, I could do with an occasional helping hand around here. I can't afford to pay you very much to begin with.' She couldn't afford to pay herself at this point, by the time she'd bought a bit of petrol and put something aside for stock and the occasional sandwich. 'It would only be half an hour here and there, and you could take a book at the end of it. Would that work?'

The girl's face lit up. 'Seriously?'

'It's not a job,' said Nina, hurriedly. 'I don't want to exploit you or anything like that. It's literally just a quick tidy-up.'

But the girl had already started neatly arranging the children's books in height order, so the little ones could easily pick out the brightest colours and jolliest creatures.

'Um, what's your name?'

'Ainslee.' The girl didn't even turn round.

'Right, thanks, Ainslee,' said Nina, and went back to the steps of the van, where she sold a full set of Regency potboilers to a local lady with an enormous Labrador, a woolly tweed dress and a completely bizarre accent. It was only when she took out a large chequebook (Nina would have said that they didn't take cheques, but the woman was buying an awful lot of books, plus she was quite frightening) that Nina saw she was Lady Kinross. Then she didn't know where to look.

'That's the posh woman from up the road,' said Ainslee when she'd gone. 'Her house has got a hundred rooms. She hasn't even been in some of them.'

After twenty minutes, Ainslee had straightened everything perfectly and had made a start on sweeping the floor. Nina was embarrassed and insisted on buying her a coffee, then looked round to choose a book for her.

Eventually she realised exactly what it should be, even though it was outrageously expensive: *Fore Girl*, a graphic novel written by a young South American girl about a female superhero in Rio, taking from the absurdly rich and giving to the poor in the favelas. It was funny, glamorous and completely and utterly kickass, and Ainslee's face lit up like a light bulb. Her distressed, downtrodden look had lifted completely.

'Can I come again?' she whispered.

'Yes,' said Nina. 'Come again on Saturday, it's market day.'

Ainslee almost shook with pleasure. Nina noticed that she stashed her book away incredibly carefully, tucked right at the bottom of her bag amongst scruffy papers and dog-eared homework. Nina worried that this was to keep it away from prying eyes. Ainslee caught her looking, and blushed deeply and scurried away. Nina watched her go, wondering.

'I need to get a message to Marek,' said Nina. 'Seriously, I do. No messing this time. Work stuff.'

'You mean, start a major smuggling exercise?' said Surinder, who was kindly doing the accounts in return for food, as they explored with alacrity the excellent fresh fish, cheese and fruit and veg of the region. 'You know, I'm not sure this is right.'

Nina sighed. 'But I didn't know ... I didn't know we'd be this busy.'

It was true. Everywhere they'd gone in the Little Shop of Happy-Ever-After, every market they'd stopped at, they'd been overwhelmed by people who hadn't had a bookshop or a library in their community for the longest time.

'I know,' said Surinder. 'Remember when they used to let you out of work at four p.m.?'

'On WEDNESDAYS,' protested Nina. 'Not every day. Just one day. Anyway, when are *you* going back to work?'

Surinder shrugged. 'Oh, I have a ton of holiday stored up.'

'Yes, but I thought you were going to Vegas or LA or Miami; somewhere more suitable for how fabulous you are,' said Nina. 'Those are exactly the words you used. You didn't say, "I'm just off to rural Scotland to do some accounts".'

'I know, but . . . ' Surinder looked slightly embarrassed and gazed at her feet. She was wearing . . .

'Are those new wellies?'

She was indeed sporting a pair of very fancy new floral wellingtons.

'Because, you know, there isn't much call for new wellingtons in Las Vegas.'

'And how would you know?'

Nina conceded this was a fair point, but even so she narrowed her eyes at Surinder.

'Have you been calling Fat Tam?' she said.

'None of your business.'

They were at a stand-off. Nina knew from long experience that it was best to change the subject.

'So anyway, I was wondering,' she began, nervously. 'What would you think if maybe I asked Marek—'

'You'll get him in trouble,' said Surinder, with a warning glint in her eye.

'It's just that Griffin has told me about another library that's trying to offload a lot of stock before it closes, and they'll sell it to me pretty cheaply.' Nina had given Marek's email address to Griffin in preparation for moving the stock but hadn't discussed it with Marek yet. 'They keep on shutting libraries,' Nina said sadly.

'Oof, that's harsh,' said Surinder.

'I know!' said Nina.

'But you can't risk getting Marek into trouble! I thought you liked him.'

'I like to think of it as evacuating the books to safety,' said Nina. 'Letting them fly free into the world, don't you see? It's a good thing.'

'Only it's against the law. What if Marek was secretly transporting dynamite?'

'Books aren't dynamite.'

'What about *Mein Kampf*?'

'Surinder!'

'What? I'm just saying. You're asking him to do something bad.'

'I don't think he'd mind.'

'He wouldn't mind because of you asking him. Which is worse.'

'Okay,' said Nina. 'I suppose you're right.'

'I am right!'

'I just wanted to ask him. I thought he wanted to do it.'

'I'm sure he does. You still can't ask him. Neens! I know you're a major successful businesswoman now, but I'm telling you, this is wrong.'

Nina paused.

'All right. Okay. I won't. I'll try and figure out another way.'

'Fine.'

'What are we doing tonight?'

Surinder turned away looking slightly embarrassed. 'Actually,' she said. 'Actually, I'm going out. Kind of. I kind of have a date.'

Nina stood up. 'No way! I knew it! No way.'

'What? No one would ask me on a date?'

'Of course they'd ask you on a date, you idiot,' said Nina. 'Who is it? Fat Tam, I hope.'

'No. He was really a highland gateway drug. Angus. Or Fergus. One of the Gusses, anyway.'

'You don't even remember which one?'

'Big sturdy forearms. Broad manly chest. Thick curly hair.'

'You sound like you're dating a tree! What was wrong with Fat Tam?'

'Oh, I was just warming up,' said Surinder. 'No. It's another lovely boy from the ceilidh. I can't understand a word he says, up to and including his name, so it barely matters.'

'Where are you going to go?'

'A Michelin-starred restaurant followed by a top West End show,' said Surinder. 'JOKE! We're going to the pub, of course. Where else would we go?'

Surinder got ready whilst Nina felt mildly jealous. She would have gone and tidied the books up, but Ainslee had already done that for her, and the stock was looking decidedly low anyway. Instead, she decided to heat up some soup and reread something – anything – set in a boarding school, which rarely failed to cheer her up.

'I mean it. Don't go and see Marek. Don't do anything bad,' Surinder said once she had finished getting ready.

'I wasn't going to! And don't you do anything bad with someone WHOSE NAME YOU DON'T EVEN KNOW.'

'I don't mean that. I mean the delivery thing. Just because you're quite good at losing jobs doesn't mean everyone else is.'

'I won't.'

Then there were lights on the gravel driveway and a large car drew up.

'Ooh!' said Surinder excitedly. 'It's the Hogwarts Express.' She kissed Nina on both cheeks and danced out of the door, even as a tall outline stepped down from the SUV to open the door for her, and they drove away into the misty evening, not the slightest bit dark at 8 p.m.

Nina tried to read, but for once she couldn't concentrate. The words swam in front of her eyes as she was distracted by the baaing of lambs in the fields and wondered if any of them were her own personal lambs. Then she thought about stock for the shop, but there wasn't anywhere in Scotland that could provide what she needed; she'd checked online, almost falling down a rabbit hole of beautiful first editions and ancient manuscripts for sale in Edinburgh.

No. She knew where there was a source of great and saleable and almost free books that would be greeted with joy and really enable her to get the business moving. And she knew how to get at them. All she needed to do was . . .

She decided to make some shortbread to take her mind off it. Just butter, sugar and flour, all creamed together, simple and delicious and easily done. She made far too much. She looked at it sitting there and decided to wrap some up in a pretty bag she happened to have. And a gift box Surinder had bought her. It was only 9.15, and still light outside. She would just take a walk. She wouldn't run into the train, it wasn't due for hours yet. Just a walk.

She put her wellies on and walked up the side of the field,

looking at the wind turbines spinning slowly far away and the lambs bouncing along beside the fence, playing and prancing with one another.

She took a handful of sweet meadow grass and held it out to a lazy-looking ewe, who came over and munched on it calmly as the little ones underneath her sucked milk steadily. It was a tranquil scene, and she smiled. Then she trudged onwards. She needed the exercise after sitting in the van all day; the air was fresh, and she pulled her jacket closer.

She was amazed, truly, how much she wanted the Little Shop of Happy-Ever-After to work now that she had seen it could, now she knew that there were people – people everywhere – who cared about and loved books as much as she did. How on earth would she get her stock up?

She saw it on the tree before she got to it. It was high up; if you weren't specifically looking for it and didn't already know the exact – and slightly sickly – tree, you might never have seen it, even if your feet had led you almost without your knowledge all the way to the level crossing.

It was a stone-coloured worsted bag, rough, with a square bottom, carefully thrown over a branch with a counter-weighted rope; the train would barely have had to slow down.

She shinned carefully up the tree, mindful of what Lennox had said about it, and peered inside the bag. It was utterly overflowing with wild flowers: sharp yellow gorse; bluebells and daffodils; lily of the valley and baby's breath. It was glorious. Without allowing herself to think about what she was doing, she tied the bag with the shortbread and a book around the tip of the branch. If they slowed the train, they ought to be able to simply lift it down, or fish it off.

She slipped back down the tree again. It was definitely getting darker now. She plunged her face into the bag of flowers and inhaled. There was plenty of lavender deep down in there, and rich thick heather, as well as the lighter, sweeter tinkling smells of the bluebells. It was heaven, and she swung the bag all the way back home.

Lennox was sitting on a bench outside the farmhouse in the nearly faded light. She didn't quite catch what he was doing at first, and merely nodded at him. He grunted back in response. She focused closer. He appeared to be ... She smiled, unable to help herself.

'He looks just like you,' she said.

Lennox looked up again from where he was feeding the tiny lamb with a baby's bottle.

'Think dead lambs are funny, do you?' he grunted back.

Nina rolled her eyes. 'You're the one always telling me to wake up to the realities of farming,' she said. 'What's up with him, then?'

Lennox looked down, an uncharacteristically gentle look on his face. 'His mam didn't want him. Happens sometimes.'

'Why not? Did she have another lamb?'

'No, just him. They get rejected. Not all mothers want their bairns.'

'So you've adopted him?' she said.

Lennox shrugged. 'Naw, just doing the night shift when the boys have gone home.'

180

'Work never ends as a farmer,' said Nina, genuinely impressed.

'Neh,' said Lennox. 'It don't. So you been off seeing someone?'

Nina allowed herself just for a moment to think about the long tinge of Marek's eyelashes on his high cheekbones. 'And no. Too early.'

Lennox put down the lamb, who scampered back into the kennel where he was obviously sleeping with Parsley.

'Not for me,' he said shortly. 'Think I'll turn in. Goodnight.'

And Nina carried on towards the barn, and barely woke even when Surinder came in, extremely late and rather inebriated, giggling loudly and telling someone to be quiet.

Chapter Nineteen

'You've got your head in the clouds,' said Surinder.

Nina gave her a look. 'Well, you've got your bum in the bed, so I have to look somewhere.'

Somewhere along the line, Surinder's mini-break had turned into a massive leave of absence. The weather, completely unusually for Scotland – if the jackets people carried nervously everywhere were anything to go by – had turned unutterably beautiful: clear blue skies, with the occasional high white clouds scudding along like galloping lambs.

Nina had, true to her word, not done anything; hadn't contacted Marek or asked him any favours at all.

The books had arrived regardless.

Griffin had independently arranged with Marek to send up stock from the latest library to close, adding an invoice for the small fee and a slightly poignant note saying that if she was short of staff at any point to get in touch as the overgrown children he had to work with were all driving him absolutely crackers. He really wanted to be working with books again rather than trying to stop kids from getting round the library security system to access large amounts of pornography, which appeared to be something of a full-time job.

Marek had simply placed the books by the side of the railway line, Jim had alerted her by email, and she'd picked them up in the morning.

'You're a book-smuggling operation,' Surinder observed. 'This isn't right at all. If the police track him down ... What about when the railway realises he's stopping all the time? If he loses his job? Will it all be fun and games then?'

Every single box had come with a little something from Marek on it: a joke, a poem, even a lovely drawing of a dog. And every day, when Nina had finished tending to the book-hungry of Lanchish Down or Felbright Water or Louwithness or Cardenbie or Braefoot or Tewkes or Donibristle or Balwearie – where she would park the van and serve up the hottest romances, the grimmest crimefests or the latest, goriest Japanese serial-killer series (as always, going to the mildest-mannered-looking of people; in Nina's experience, the more sensibly dressed the person, the more unutterably depraved they liked their fiction; no doubt there was a cosmic balance in it somewhere) – she would unpack some more.

She also sold a lot of copies of *The Hamlet Cookbook*, written by a woman who had moved to a tiny island in the Hebrides and who ate nothing except what she could digest of the local grasses. There was a lot of boiling involved. But you did get thin pretty fast. Surinder could tut all she liked, but she couldn't deny that Nina was beginning to make a success of it.

Ainslee was looking as shy as ever as she unpacked the latest box, then gasped in delight.

'What?' said Nina, leaning over.

'It's a whole box of *Up on the Rooftops*,' said Ainslee. 'An entire box! It's like gold!'

'Not the originals?'

'I haven't ... I mean, there was one in my old school, but I wasn't allowed to touch it.'

'Oh goodness,' said Nina. 'Oh goodness, they can't have known what they had. Otherwise they could have sold them.'

'But you bought them,' said Ainslee.

'I bought a hundred boxes, sight unseen, library closure clearance,' said Nina. 'You don't really know what you're going to get. But this ... this is treasure.'

It was a clutch of hardback first editions of the famous book about three children who had to cross London without touching the ground; the books had inlaid binding, golden covers and numerous exquisite line drawings.

'Oh my word,' said Nina, bending down. 'Shall we just close the doors and sit down and read our favourite bits to each other all afternoon?'

'AINSLEE?' came a voice outside the van. They both looked round.

'Who's that?'

'No one,' said Ainslee, scowling. 'Can we shut the doors?'

'Not really,' said Nina, going forward.

'AINSLEE!'

'NOT NOW, BEN!' yelled back Ainslee suddenly, louder than Nina had expected. 'I'M BUSY. GO AWAY.'

Nina hurried down the steps. Standing at the bottom was possibly the dirtiest little boy she had ever seen. His hair had obviously been cut with kitchen scissors. His cheeks were sticky, his fingernails black.

'Hello,' Nina said. The child, who looked to be around eight, scowled back at her.

'AINSLEE! I WANT BREAKFAST!'

Ainslee came out, scowling. 'I told you not to come here.'

'There's no breakfast!'

'I left some custard creams in the side cupboard.'

'I ate them yesterday.'

'Well that's your fault, isn't it?'

The boy screwed up his face as if he was going to cry.

'Is this your ... brother?' said Nina, not wanting to sound nosy or interfering.

Ainslee had started coming in mornings before school and Nina had started to pay her a small wage.

'Aye,' said Ainslee. She reluctantly took out the wages Nina had given her the day before.

'Can I go to the bakers?'

'Aye, but don't come back.'

Nina didn't say anything, in case what she said was wrong, but she didn't like the look of this at all.

'Where's your mum?' she said gently.

Ben looked at her rudely. 'Shut up,' he said, and snatched the money out of Ainslee's hand.

Ainslee turned back to unpacking the books, her face closed up and inscrutable, daring Nina to say something, so Nina didn't, and instead concentrated on serving one of her regulars, who only read books that took place in a

185

post-apocalyptic universe. He didn't care if it was zombies, flu or a nuclear bomb that had taken everyone out; he only cared that there was almost nobody left to get in the way.

Nina let her eyes stray out of the van. The boy was still loitering in the square – they were back in Kirrinfief where Ainslee lived – chowing down on a sausage roll and staring at them. She smiled encouragingly. When the customer left, she went back to helping Ainslee with the beautiful golden editions of *Up on the Rooftops*.

Suddenly he was there again, looking over Ainslee's shoulder.

'What's that?'

'Go away,' hissed Ainslee. 'I told you not to come here.'

'You can come here,' said Nina, even as Ainslee shot her a look.

'Looks boring,' said Ben. He was still staring at the cover, though: the three children, and Robert Carrier the pigeon, in his top hat, silhouetted against the dome of St Paul's Cathedral.

'Off to Galleon's Reach ... to meet the Queen of the Nethers,' said Ainslee dreamily. 'Oh how I would love to be reading this for the first time.'

Nina nodded emphatically. 'Every time I stopped reading it, I couldn't believe I couldn't fly.'

Ainslee nodded. 'You're going to have a whole village full of kids who haven't read it.'

'Everyone still reads it, don't they?' said Nina. 'Otherwise how do they know what it's like to fly?'

'No one can fly,' said Ben scornfully. He'd now taken out a packet of crisps and was eating them messily, crumbs falling on to the floor of the van. Ainslee scowled at him.

186

'They can in this book,' she said. 'That's what you don't understand about reading, idiot.'

'What, that it's a bunch of made-up stuff?'

'You can look at it if you like,' said Nina, although she was nervous of his sticky fingers. These books were valuable.

Ben shrugged and turned his face away. 'Sounds rubbish.'

'Well it doesn't matter to you, does it? He won't go to school,' said Ainslee.

'Can't you make him?' said Nina. 'Or your mum?'

'Ha! He won't listen to us!'

'Reading's for babies,' burst out Ben suddenly, his ears bright red. 'It's stupid. I don't care.' And he suddenly hurled his crisp packet on the floor and disappeared out of the van, running across the square.

Ainslee sighed and shrugged. 'That's all he does,' she said. 'I can't help.'

Nina looked after him. 'But can't the school help? That's not right.'

'They've washed their hands of him,' said Ainslee. 'He won't go. My mum doesn't care. The school doesn't care; he's a "disruptive influence".' She hung her head. This was a long speech for her. 'And there isn't another school for five miles. I don't think anyone cares.'

'Do you want me to ring social services?'

Ainslee jumped up, her face a picture of dismay. 'No! Please no! You can't! They'll separate us!'

'They're very good these days,' said Nina, who'd come up against them a lot in the library service. 'They're really kind and helpful. Honestly.'

Ainslee shook her head, tears gleaming in the corners of

her eyes. 'Please no,' she said. 'Please. Please don't. Please. We're fine, really. We're okay. We're all right.' And she looked so heartbroken, Nina didn't know what to do.

Another child came in, nicely dressed and cared for, with her mother.

'Oh look!' said the mother. 'I haven't seen this for years! *Up on the Rooftops*! Wow!' Her rather tight face softened suddenly. 'I loved this book so much. It made me feel like I could fly.'

The little girl looked up curiously. 'Can I have it?'

'Of course, darling. We'll read it together. I think you're going to love it!'

Ainslee's face was stony as Nina took the money, the most she'd ever made in one sale.

Chapter Twenty

The days began to take on a pattern. After Nina had finished work, she would cash up, then start planning what she was going to leave for Marek on their tree. It had developed into a full-blown flirtation. Some days she wanted to be funny; some days more serious. Some days she just wrote to him what was on her mind, and he'd write back. She realised that she hadn't written a letter for years and years; actually sat down and committed her thoughts to paper rather than pinging them off in an email. She wrote more slowly; felt more deeply.

Always she remembered Marek's big puppy-dog eyes; his sweet concern for her. He wrote to her about things he missed from home, about funny things he'd seen through people's back windows. His English was broken and his spelling could be hit and miss, but he had a lovely, often curious way of expressing himself, and she understood him perfectly.

No matter how much Surinder told her it wasn't real, that she was living through a fantasy, she couldn't help it. For even with Surinder there, and the new people she met every day at the van, she still felt rather lonely; brand new, alone up here in this little green corner at the tip of the world. Daydreaming about Marek was something to keep her warm; a lovely idea she kept in her heart all day long, thinking of things he would like, what would make him laugh, what would make a pretty parcel in a bag. One night it was a little sculpture of a bear she found for pennies in a market; another time a book of woodcut art nobody wanted; a miniature of whisky she'd been handed as part of a promotion in one of the larger towns; some deep-scented heather. And he would drop off packets of sweeties from his home country; a carved pencil she thought he might have made himself; some new hand-made notepaper, which she treasured.

And then, one day, as she was wondering to herself, wandering down the lane by the meadow, how on earth it could possibly still be light at 10.30 in the evening, she opened his latest note in his familiar dark hand, written as if the pen was too small for his large paw.

Saturday, it said, simply. *No sleeper*.

Her heart began to beat faster immediately. What had been delicate, a little courtship played out in an unusual way, had suddenly changed into something far more real.

Every night, she'd gone to bed thinking about Marek, about his gentle, strange foreign ways; his unflappability. And this unexpected relationship that had somehow sprung up between them. She knew that the railway tree, ailing as it was, was just as important to him as it was to her. His notes, filled with poetry and the occasional snatches of his own language, felt to her deeply rich and romantic, and she had saved them, every one.

Nights when he was not working or there was nothing on the tree were wholly disappointing. Nights when a bag rocked gently in the wind filled her utterly with delight.

But now ... to meet. To be with one another in person once again. Her heart sped up in her chest with excitement.

Surinder, predictably, was unimpressed.

'What are you going to do, snog on a train? What if you get covered in coal?'

Nina swallowed hard. 'Of course not. It'll just be ... it'll just be a chance to stop and chat, that's all.'

Surinder snorted.

'Oh come ON, Soors. It's just ... it's been so long.'

'What about Ferdie?'

'Ferdie doesn't count.'

Technically Nina's last boyfriend, Ferdie had been a faintly cadaverous poet who'd hung around the library in Birmingham after an event because she was the only person who would listen to him. They'd ended up kind of dating, although he got very upset if he didn't feel she was listening properly to his poetry, which was convincingly awful and squarely of the dead crow/I hate you Daddy school. On the other hand, this had made it far easier to break up with him; Nina had simply indicated that she hadn't really understood the metaphors in his most recent work, entitled 'All is Black (17)', and he had flown into a rage and declared her a philistine. She'd heard that after that he'd given up the poetry, cut his hair and taken a job in a bank in Aston, but she didn't know if that was true.

'Well he certainly hung around my kitchen for long enough.'

'That's not a real relationship, is it? And Damien, in university.'

'Yes, you told him you were leaving him so that you could take on the world and go out and do lots of different things, then you sat upstairs in your bedroom reading for the next eight years.'

'Well exactly. And now I'm here, and it's all exciting and full of possibilities! You're the one always telling me to get out there and do more.'

'Yes, but not with some guy you met on a train.'

'Why not? People meet each other in all sorts of places. You met the Gus in a barn!'

'Yes, and then we hung out together and got on.'

'You use my luxury pad to screw in!'

'That's hanging out! We don't moon about and leave poetry on treetops and behave like funny little people in a story or teenagers or something.'

'Well that's what this is about. We're going to spend some time together. Get to know one another.'

'Why doesn't he just come up during daylight hours?' said Surinder.

Nina couldn't answer that.

'See? It's because he's as hooked on the entire thing as you are. This little fantasy life you've got going where he sends you pretty flowers, which he can do as long as he likes because it's all in your heads. I'm sure it's fun and everything, but it isn't real. And neither is meeting at midnight in a goods shed.'

'It's not a goods shed. It's a level crossing. It's . . . romantic.'

Surinder rolled her eyes. 'Well good for you. The Gus is coming round and we're making a takeaway – which would be like getting a takeaway if there was anywhere to get a takeaway, which there isn't – and watching a movie.'

192

'Hang on, have you moved in here? With the Gus?'

'I'm on holiday,' said Surinder severely, in the same tone of voice she used every morning when the office rang to ask politely if she was considering coming back at any point.

'Are you going to find out the first part of his name?' said Nina.

'I don't feel it's very important at this juncture.'

'Okay, well try and learn it before you get married.'

They were now coming to the very height of summer. Although you still needed a jacket after the sun went down, the fields were ridiculously awash with glory: wild flowers, ripening crops; waving long grass, soaked during the long winter, and now sprouting profusely in every hedgerow and space it could find; an orgy of blooms and growth everywhere, the entire countryside spilling over.

It was how Nina felt herself; that after a long, long winter she too was ready to emerge, proudly casting off her old clothes; her protective coating of books and high-denier tights and a downcast head. She was nervous to absolute distraction, couldn't help it. And she was cross with Surinder too; wasn't she always saying she had to live more? Stop burying herself away? Well, here she was. Going out. Into life. And a big life too, not takeaway and telly. Not listening to someone complain about the lack of opportunity for poets in Birmingham, and how misunderstood they were. This was great buckets of flowers; of poetry, real poetry; of, she truly believed, deeply held feelings. She was catching the night train.

Chapter Twenty-One

It was, unusually, warm enough for Nina to sit, swinging on a gate, and she did so, enjoying the gentle creak against the other sounds of the wood at night. She felt as if she were in the Magic Faraway Tree, with the forest saying *wisha-wisha-wisha*.

She closed her eyes and wished very hard, a smile playing around her lips, her heart beating nervously in her chest, the countryside alive around her; and when she awoke from what had in reality been half a dream, the lights of the great train, with its groaning axles and heavy trundle, were suddenly there in the distance.

Nina's heart sped up as the train slowed down. She checked. Make-up on. Matching underwear . . . The fact that she'd come prepared felt a bit strange. But on the other hand. Well. This was a date. A peculiar type of date. But a date nonetheless. It was finally happening. She wasn't just reading about it: she was doing it. She wiped her hands on her skirt. It was a wide fifties-style one, with a belt, and she was wearing a plain top with a cardigan over it.

The train slowed even more, cranking gradually further and further down the line, its brakes giving out that odd sharp smell of asbestos, which she'd never liked but which now reminded her of the night she and Marek had met. At last it juddered to a tremendous halt. It sounded like it was exhaling, slowly.

Then the night and the air were suddenly very still and Nina felt adrenalin shoot through her. Her hand strayed to her mouth. The train was very quiet. Nobody came.

She had worked out from learning their shift patterns that Jim wouldn't be on the train tonight; it would just be Marek. No sleeper. No timetable; or none they looked at too closely. Just the two of them in the middle of the Highlands, all by themselves.

The cab door opened quietly, and Nina took a step forward. Then another. She was breathing heavily now, a mixture of nerves and extreme excitement.

Marek didn't emerge, and she had a momentary panic that maybe he wasn't there after all; it was someone else, coming to tell her how dangerous it was to mess about on the railway track . . .

Still no one. Steeling herself, she slipped through the closed barrier. There was never anyone along at night; surely there wouldn't be this evening either. That would be the cruellest of luck. But the roads, as ever, were silent; the farmers and the workers finally fast asleep in their well-earned beds.

She moved towards the engine, the enormously long train snaking behind it. She kept her focus on little steps. And then she was there, looking up.

Marek was leaning against the cab door. His hooded black eyes were slightly tentative; his curly hair wild as usual. When he saw her, he broke into a wide smile.

'I didn't ... I not sure you would come,' he said, blinking. He still looked amazed to see her standing there, as if she'd appeared from a dream.

'You invited me,' said Nina.

'I did, yes.'

They looked at each for one second more. Then, in the stillness of the great night, Marek carefully, slowly put his hand out to help her up, and Nina took it.

In the tiny space of the cab, neither of them knew quite what to do or say. 'I have ... I have picnic,' said Marek, blinking heavily. Nina smiled. She hadn't brought anything tonight, knowing she would see him after all.

'That sounds lovely,' she said. 'Do we have time?'

Marek shrugged. 'I think ... I think she will be fine.' He patted the console fondly. 'You will be fine. I have informed control of technical stop. They are okay.'

'Okay, wow. That's great.'

They clambered down again and found a patch of soft grass, the great train blotting out the landscape behind them and keeping the wind away, and they sat on a blanket Marek unfurled with some ceremony.

'Wow,' said Nina, smiling. 'A midnight picnic.'

Solemnly Marek opened up a wicker basket and brought out food Nina had never seen before: little meat dumplings, and blintzes and pickles. She tried a few things, including the

196

tart fresh radishes. He also produced a tiny bottle of champagne with its own straw. Nina exclaimed.

'I cannot drink on train,' he said shyly. 'But I thought you might ...'

He popped it for her with great care and she giggled over something so silly and so wonderful. He took a sip too, and made a face, then insisted she try something else from the little boxes he had unpacked, and she thought it was all wonderful and they chatted inconsequentially of this and that.

After they'd eaten, they both fell silent, and Nina found herself focusing quite strongly on his large, well-worn hands, covered in dark hair, and thinking of the little notes, the poems, the overspilling wild flowers. He was suddenly so close, and she wondered what would happen if she simply reached out and took his hand ...

She glanced at Marek. He was looking at her with a dreamy, hopeful, dark-eyed gaze. He was attempting to appear casual, but clearly he wasn't feeling that way at all. He looked intense and, suddenly, overwhelmingly attractive. Nina let her hand stray a little, almost casually, towards his.

And now his hand moved forward, and suddenly it was on hers, covering it completely, caressing and stroking it. She moved towards him, just inching, and he took her wrist and drew her steadily closer until she was practically on his lap; then he turned her face towards his, his wide soft mouth and huge dark eyes, and she found they were kissing, and suddenly Nina realised that what she had imagined and built up in her head was here; was actually happening. That was the last thing she thought of before his strong arms went around her and she lost herself utterly; pressed up against him, his mouth on hers, the rest of the world simply melted away.

Suddenly, shockingly, out of the blue, a bright light shone over the top of the hill, and a Land Rover roared towards the level crossing. When it saw the gates were shut, it honked its horn loudly, in frustration. Nina and Marek leapt apart, both of them startled, breathing heavily. Nina stared towards the vehicle. The voice that came out of it was loud and familiar and cut across the quiet landscape.

'What the bloody hell is going on? Move this effing train.'

Marek leapt up and went to the barrier, where Lennox was standing in front of the Land Rover, looking typically furious.

'Sorry, we're doing technical—'

'MOVE THE SODDING TRAIN!'

Nina joined Marek at the gate. Lennox gave a sigh of exasperation.

'Oh, I might have known you'd be caught up in this. What the hell?'

'Why are you so cross?' said Nina boldly. 'It's the middle of the night. Where do you have to get to in such a hurry?'

It was then she saw that he was holding the lamb in his arms. There was blood on his jacket.

'What's wrong with him?' she said in horror.

'Stray dog,' muttered Lennox. 'Bastards. They must have let him off the leash. Should have shot the bloody thing.'

'You'd shoot a dog?'

'If it worries my sheep I will. Move the damn train.'

Marek had already leapt up into the driver's seat and turned on the engine. He looked down at Nina desperately.

'Come with me,' he said.

Nina stared back at him. Lennox was glaring at her. She felt completely torn. Marek's big dark eyes were pleading. Lennox was growling in impatience.

'I . . . I can't,' she said. Marek blinked and nodded. They stared at each other for a long time.

'And I have to . . . '

'I know,' said Nina, not breaking his gaze. She could feel Lennox humming in frustration next to her as the train started, very slowly, to move.

Suddenly, barely knowing what she was doing, and completely surprised at herself, Nina made a run for the steps, and jumped up on to the footplate of the engine, where she kissed a very surprised Marek firmly on the lips through the window, caressing his face; his mouth was soft and warm and she wanted nothing more than to stay with him, but she knew she could not, and as he took his hand off the dead man's handle to slow the train down, she jumped lightly back down to the ground again.

Lennox had gone back to the Land Rover, and was watching as the train steadily gathered speed, chugging faster and faster. When it was beyond the crossing, he looked at Nina contemptuously and opened the car door.

Nina found herself running after him.

'I can't take you with me,' he said crossly. 'I'm off to Kyle's, remember.'

The lamb, she could now see, had a great tear in its flank and was whimpering.

'Oh,' she said. 'Can I hold him? Poor little thing.'

'No,' said Lennox curtly. 'Haven't you got a railway to get yourself killed on?'

'Why are you so mean all the time?'

'Because I'm trying to save an animal's life. So sorry if that interferes with your utterly ridiculous love life.'

'There's just no need for that,' said Nina, white hot with anger. 'You're my landlord, not a policeman.'

Lennox fired up the Land Rover angrily.

'Whilst you're parking trains up willy-nilly and doing God knows what at all hours in public, I think I'm allowed an opinion.'

The lights of the Land Rover lit up the remains of their picnic, the champagne bottle lying sadly on its side in the damp grass. They both stared at it.

Lennox turned round one last time to look at Nina, who was shaking with fury and cold in the night air.

'Do you know anything about him?' he said. 'Because I know men who travel far and work the longest, the hardest shifts. And it's always . . . it's always for their families.'

And with a lurch, the Land Rover was gone, leaving Nina alone and furious in its wake.

Nina watched the red lights disappearing into the distance. Hateful bloody horribly embittered old divorcé. How dare he? How the hell was it his business? And what the hell did he know?

So she hadn't asked Marek much about his background, but it had been so lovely and delicious, just falling into it, the whole romance of it. He never spoke about Latvia, so she never asked, it was that simple. She didn't . . . she didn't want to think of it: that somewhere on a cold and snowy plain, in a little village, or a Soviet apartment block, there were people waiting for him. People relying on him.

She was turning round to stomp back towards the village when the Land Rover returned and the door opened.

'So I can't leave you here on your own in the dark, although he apparently can.'

'I'm fine.'

'Yes, but you think climbing dying trees and dancing about on railway lines is also fine, so excuse me if I'm not sure I trust your judgement.'

Lennox drove her rapidly home in silence, then headed off again still with the lamb in his jacket. She barely thanked him.

Nina couldn't sleep. She was thinking back to the feel of Marek's mouth against hers. His beautiful soft mouth; his big, solid hands. She knew there was a poet in there. She was sure of it. They couldn't communicate much, but she was sure she could feel him inside. Couldn't she?

Around 4 a.m., she saw the lights of the Land Rover scrape the roof and knew Lennox must be back, but that merely made her cross again. She heard a soft baaing as the car door opened, and a gentle murmuring, which annoyed her even more, seeing as he patently had it in him to be perfectly kind and sweet, as long as you had four fricking legs.

She was still cross when she heard the chickens start squawking two hours later as Lennox set off for work and she realised she'd barely slept a wink. Her shoulders were up round her ears; she was so stressed, it was worse than being back in the city. She pulled herself out of bed and stood in the shower for ages, but it only made her long for bed more than ever. No. She had a job now. That was how it was.

Only Surinder was sleeping peacefully on the sofa as Nina wandered over to fiddle with the expensive coffee machine in the kitchen, then stomped crossly out to the van. The weather steadfastly refused to reflect her mood and the sun beamed down in a most uncharacteristic fashion. Nina blinked and put her sunglasses on for practically the first time since she'd arrived.

Chapter Twenty-Two

A Book for the Furious: Nina almost laughed when she saw it because it was so precisely what she was looking for; an enormous tome of revenge stories, ranging from pouring molten silver into the eyes of a thief, to launching a pirate fleet.

I don't care, she thought. I don't care about him. But she did want to see Marek again; to kiss him again under the moon.

She sighed and glanced at her watch. Edwin and Hugh were crossing the cobbled square to sit and have a pint in the sunshine, and Nina waved to them. They waved back cheerily and asked her if she wanted to join them, and she didn't know how to explain to them that she couldn't drink because a) she was driving a van and b) it was just past eight o'clock in the morning. But she knew what they wanted really, and dug it out: the newest labyrinthine saga from the subcontinent; Hugh had developed a real taste for them. It was a thank-you, really, for everything they had done for her, helping her buy the van. Hugh would always insist on paying, and Nina would make sure there was no price written on it and purse her lips and say, I'm terribly sorry, Hugh, that one is one pound fifty, and he would look pained and she would offer to discount it even further and he would gallantly refuse. So they got tremendously cheap books and she got to say thank you, so everyone was happy.

Ainslee was usually sidling up at this time; even though Nina welcomed her wholeheartedly every single day, the girl still acted like she wasn't wanted, mooching towards the van bent over as though trying to hide. But today she was nowhere to be seen.

There was, however, someone else. A grubby, cheeky figure dressed in a ragged T-shirt and shorts displaying very scabbed knees: Ainslee's little brother.

'Ben?'

The child sniffed. There was snot crusted round his nose, as well as long lines on his dirty sweatshirt. He marched up to her defiantly.

'Ainslee's no' coming today.'

'Why not?'

'She's got ... dunno.'

Nina frowned. 'Well, is it something to do with school?'

'Aye.'

'Has she got exams?'

Ben shook his head. 'No,' he said. 'No. She's been told she can't take her exams. She's all sad and stuff. Exams sound rubbish.'

Nina looked around. The market wasn't busy yet; in her bad mood, she'd got up far too early after her rough night. She yawned. There were just a few old men walking their dogs, and some women sniffing the produce.

'Why can't she take her exams?' she said. 'That's awful. She's such a smart girl.'

Ben shrugged his shoulders. 'Dunno,' he said.

Nina blinked. 'Okay,' she said finally, remembering Ainslee's horror when she'd tried to find out more about her home life. 'Okay. Thanks so much for coming to tell me.'

Ben lingered. She could see he was peering inside, looking at the red and yellow bean bags. She waited a moment.

'Would you like to come in?'

'Naw.'

She paused. 'Okay.'

Ben still didn't seem keen to leave.

'I think I'm going to sit out on this step,' said Nina gently. 'Enjoy the sunshine. And maybe just read for a bit.'

Ben sniffed. 'Hmm,' he said.

Nina was going to ask whether he had school that day, but she figured that was probably something he heard quite a lot, so she didn't. Instead, she picked up a copy of *Up on the Rooftops* – they'd sold all but two of them, including one she'd kept behind for herself – and took it out to the step, remembering as she did so how reading this book as a child had made her feel utterly and without a doubt that if she only met the right magic pigeon, kept St Paul's as her compass and didn't forget 'North for truth; West for fresh; South for source, but East, ever East', then everything would work out all right in the end.

'East, ever East,' she said out loud, eyeing Ben carefully. He was affecting an unconcerned look but still hadn't moved away.

Hattie, a local woman she'd got to know with four children

205

under five and a look that occasionally said 'kill me, kill me now', came bounding up.

'Oh my God, you're here early!' she said in delight.

'So are you,' observed Nina.

'Are you joking? It's nearly eight thirty; I've been up for four hours. As far as I'm concerned, it's lunchtime ... Euan! Stop that! Leave that dog alone! Tildie! Tildie!'

In their buggy, the twins set up a cacophonous roar. Hattie didn't go anywhere without a halo of crumbs around her, and outside the van was no exception.

'Are you doing story hour?'

Hattie was constantly trying to persuade Nina to do a story session that involved her leaving all the children there, but Nina strenuously refused, muttering 'Health and Safety' as a warding-off spell, to which Hattie had once sadly responded, 'Well I don't mind if you lose *one* of them, I've got loads of others,' and then laughed it off a little too shrilly.

Nina blinked. 'I'll do it if you like, but you have to stay.'

'Just one tiny spa break?' said Hattie. 'That's all I ask. Just one teensy-weensy forty-eight-hour break in New York?'

'I wish that was within my magical book powers,' said Nina. 'Actually, I can recommend some globetrotting glitzbuster stuff if you like. Might help.'

'Yes!' said Hattie. 'I'll read it in the two seconds a day I have spare. Normally just before they discover I've locked myself in the bathroom.'

Nina sat back down and started reading aloud from *Up on the Rooftops*, and the twins quietened down immediately – not because they could follow the story, but because the soothing cadence of somebody reading always had a transformative effect on babies; Griffin's theory was that children were evolutionarily engineered to listen to stories, because it stopped them wandering off into the woods and getting eaten by hairy mammoths.

And as the three children in the story found themselves stranded on the top of their building, after climbing the thousand steps, she couldn't help but notice scruffy little Ben edging closer and closer, until he was sitting cross-legged right in front of her at the foot of the steps.

At the end of the chapter, she closed the book to great sighs, particularly from Hattie. 'I love that book,' she said. 'Thank you. Ten minutes of peace and quiet. That is my record this decade.'

Nina smiled. The children started clamouring for more.

'Oh good,' said Hattie. 'The bakery's open. I'm going to go and get them all sticky. Then we can have a bath. Surely that will take me up to nine thirty. Just out of interest, and absolutely nothing to do with anything, what time do you open a bottle of wine of an evening stroke afternoon stroke lunchtime?'

'See you later,' said Nina, smiling and tactfully prising a set of very sticky fingers off the book.

'I'll take one,' said Hattie.

There was only one copy left after this. Nina looked at Hattie.

'I need it,' said Hattie.

'Okay,' said Nina, rather regretfully selling it.

She watched them all clattering noisily over the cobbles, somebody wailing.

'What happened, though?' said a little voice by her feet. 'What happened next?'

Nina looked down. 'Well, lots of things,' she said.

Ben pouted. 'I would like to know,' he said. 'Have they made it into a film?'

'Yes,' said Nina. 'But the film is terrible.'

'Why is the film terrible?'

'It's not really the film's fault,' said Nina. 'But you know when you're watching a film you feel like you can see what's happening?'

Ben nodded.

'Well, that's one thing. But when you read a book, you feel like you're in it.'

'Like a computer game?'

'No. Not like a computer game. Computer games are fun, but you're still just looking at stuff and pressing buttons. Reading is being in stuff.'

Ben squinted. 'Like actually being there?'

'Like actually being there. You plug straight into the writer's brain. It's just you and them. You experience what they experience.'

Ben looked at her for a while, then scuffed his trainer on the pavement. There was a long pause.

'That sounds no' bad.'

Nina figured she needed more coffee, and poured some from her flask. Then she brought out *We're Going on a Bear Hunt* and looked at Ben.

'Want to have a look?'

Ben glanced all round the square to make sure nobody was looking at him and there weren't any other boys around. Then he shrugged.

'All right.'

'Well come and sit down here.'

And the two of them sat on the steps in the morning sunshine and painfully, slowly, and with much grunting from Ben, made their way through it.

Finally they got up. Ben looked like he might almost say thank you.

'Where are you going now?' Nina asked carefully. 'Are you going back home?'

Ben shrugged. 'Maybe.'

Oh Lord. Nina thought again that she really needed to call social services. Or someone. But Ainslee had begged her so hard.

'You could go to school,' she said, as gently as she was able, feeling as if Ben was a timid animal that might bolt at her touch. 'You know. If you liked.'

'The other kids are mean,' said Ben. 'They call me dirty.'

He was, undeniably, dirty. Nina sighed. She would slip a little more money to Ainslee, suggest she bought him a new shirt.

'You could wash in the coffee shop,' she said. 'They wouldn't mind. And just go to school. Ignore those other kids. Who cares about them?'

'I hate it,' said Ben. 'It's just stupid people saying stupid things and telling you to eat vegetables and stuff.'

'I know,' said Nina.

She watched the little figure pad across the square – he did go into the coffee shop, she noticed – and then the next of her customers arrived. Farmer McNab came in once a week and bought four space westerns – fortunately there'd been a lot of them in the boxes, because it was a narrow interest

209

that wasn't getting any new input any time soon. She'd tried to move him over to either real westerns or space opera, but he was having absolutely none of it, so now she'd emailed Griffin and was desperately trying to source anything online that had a picture on the cover of a cowboy wearing a space helmet. By the time she'd dealt with Mr McNab's queries about how one tamed a Martian horse (neutron reins), she'd lost sight of Ben.

She worried all morning, serving a long line of people, many, she was pleased to see, absolute regulars.

'This is your fault,' said Mrs Gardiner, brandishing a huge saga about a Native American woman who'd been magically sent back in time to the court of Henry VIII, who had promptly set about attempting to make her his seventh wife, with pulse-racing results. 'You've got me hooked on these book things.'

'Good,' said Nina, but she was still thinking about Ben when Surinder turned up to whisk her off to lunch.

'The lucky thing about you . . .' began Surinder, watching Nina's eyelids droop as they sat in the little pub garden and ate cullen skink, a fishy, creamy soup with which they'd both become horribly obsessed, accompanied by rough brown bread and locally smoked salmon, which tasted so different to the oily, rubbery stuff that Nina was used to on the rare occasions she could afford it from the supermarket that it might as well have been a different food altogether.

In the sunlight, with half a lager shandy in front of her, Nina felt her horrible mood start to lift a little.

'What's lucky about me?' she said. 'Because I don't feel very lucky.'

'Well, you can just finish for the day now, can't you?' said Surinder. 'You've sold a bunch of stuff. You can go home and take a nap.'

This hadn't occurred to Nina, who tended to work a full day from force of habit, not to mention being unable to shut the shop if there was even the slightest chance of another sale. After years of working in public service, it had come as a bit of a surprise to her how genuinely interested she was in running a business; seeing what worked, looking at stock and, of course, matching the right book to the right person. It was the same joy she had always felt at the library, but somehow, watching people leaving with books they could keep for ever was even more profound.

'Oh yeah,' she said.

'Well, can't you? You're making enough, aren't you?'

Frowning, Nina explained about Ainslee and Ben.

'Oh God,' said Surinder. 'You should just report it.'

'But Ainslee begged me not to.'

'Yes, but you don't know what's going on,' said Surinder. 'It could be really, really awful at home. There could be some evil stepdad doing horrible things. She might have Stockholm syndrome or something. Kids are weird like that: they'll defend their family even it's completely messed up.'

'Yeah,' said Nina. 'Yeah.'

'So, last night . . . ' said Surinder, leaving it hanging.

'Argh,' said Nina, dropping her head. 'Oh GOD.' And she told Surinder everything.

'Oh,' said Surinder. 'Well, Lennox might be right. I mean, why hasn't Marek invited you anywhere normal?'

'Lennox's a judgemental arsehole.'

'Or Marek's sending all his money back to his family.'

Nina didn't reply.

'Oh come on,' said Surinder. 'What did you think would happen? Marek was going to take you boldly in his strong and manly arms?'

Nina didn't want to answer that either.

'What, he was going to lay you down and give you a doing on the floor of the cab?'

'You don't need to be so explicit.'

'It's what you were thinking, though.'

'It's been AGES! AGES!'

Surinder laughed and shook her head. 'Your fantasy life is out of control, man.'

Nina felt herself going pink. 'I know.'

'I mean, it's not real, is it?'

Nina thought back to his soft lips on hers, the surprise on his face.

'Yes,' she said. 'Yes it is. And I just want some romance in my life. Is that so wrong?'

Surinder shrugged. 'There's plenty of romance around here. Boys outnumber girls five to one. There's a million blokes to choose from. Only you could get yourself hopelessly hooked on one who passes through at midnight and can't stop. It's not about Marek. It's about you.'

Nina felt her face make a defiant expression.

'Ha,' said Surinder. 'You like to appear a pushover, but inside you're as tough as old boots.'

'Everyone's different to how they look on the outside,' said Nina.

'Not me,' said Surinder, and Nina was forced to concede that she might well be right.

'Listen,' said Surinder. The tone of her voice made Nina lift her head. She knew almost before Surinder said it. 'Look. I have to go. They're really going to fire me this time.'

They were meandering back from the pub, heading for the van. Nina suddenly felt overcome with exhaustion. She stopped suddenly in the road.

'No!' she said. 'Do you have to?'

'Uh, all I've done since I've been here is eat toast and give you a hard time,' pointed out Surinder, not inaccurately. 'I have to get back to work. Plus watching how hard you work makes me feel guilty.'

'It's been great having you here. What about the Gus?'

Surinder let a smile play about her lips.

'Well,' she said. 'It's nice to know he's here. But also that I can do it, you know? It's just nice to attract men I actually like.'

As they crested the hill in the van, the farm came into sight below them, its old stone walls golden in the light.

'I'm really going to miss this place,' said Surinder. 'You're so lucky, you know.'

'Do you think?'

'I do think,' said Surinder. 'I think you've found what you should be doing, where you should be doing it. And most people don't get that. They don't get anything like that.'

'But I'm lonely,' said Nina.

'You're making friends every day,' said Surinder. 'Don't

rely on fantasy guys, okay? Meet real ones. There's no shortage.'

They watched Lennox striding across the fields not far from where they were passing.

'You could even try getting it on with your hot landlord,' said Surinder.

'He's not hot!' said Nina.

'Let me see. Six foot two, curly hair, long, lean body of the kind I totally know you like, muscles, blue eyes, jaw like an Action Man . . . ' Surinder was counting off on her fingers. 'Saves baby animals, strides about in a manly fashion, has a posh barn. No, absolutely nothing hot about that at all.'

'He's not hot because he's a dick,' said Nina.

'Well so's that boy you fancied at school,' Surinder reminded her.

'One, that was school, and two, he's in prison.'

'Proves my point.'

Back at the house, Nina watched Surinder packing.

'Are you . . . is Marek giving you a lift down?' she couldn't help asking eventually.

'Take your nap! And no, because I, for one, know when to leave well alone. I'm flying out of Inverness.'

'Invernish,' corrected Nina absent-mindedly. A clutch of islanders had been passing through and had bought all her commercial fiction, and she'd picked up their pronunciation. 'Do you need a lift?'

There was a honk in the farmyard. It was the Gus. Surinder ran outside and jumped up on to him, wrapping herself around his waist as he kissed her deeply. Nina sighed; she couldn't help it. That was what she wanted. Just some lovely romance. Someone happy to see her. Why couldn't it be Marek?

'Don't go!' the Gus was saying.

'Come down to Birmingham,' Surinder said, throwing her bag in the back of his SUV.

'Oh, I'm not sure. I don't do well in cities,' said the Gus. 'They won't let me bring my dog.'

'Entire cities?' said Surinder.

'Entire cities. And I can't walk there. Too many people in the way.'

They kissed again as Nina went over to say goodbye.

'Get her to come back,' said the Gus, his freckles more comically visible than ever after all the sunshine. 'Soon! For ever!'

'I can't get her to do anything,' said Nina, smiling.

'Uh, excuse me, right back at you,' said Surinder, leaning out of the window. She touched Nina on the arm. 'This is the place for you. Genuinely. I think you belong here.'

'So I'm never to darken your doors again?' said Nina, grinning.

'Oh God, yes, you have to do that. We're still not quite finished with ALL THOSE BLOODY BOOKS!'

Chapter Twenty-Three

Summer holiday time meant masses of children's books, and big fat summer novels; romances, but also a lot of serious fiction, as people carved out time for themselves to read books they'd been putting off for years. Nina found herself getting through a load of classics.

As she toured the little towns, everyone came to tell her where they were going on holiday, and what they were thinking of reading, and she passed on her recommendations and tips. She was asked so often if she was going to the midsummer festival that she almost considered it. She had also called social services about Ainslee and Ben – feeling quite horribly guilty as she did so – and they had sighed and said they would add them to the list but they were quite backed up so it wouldn't be straight away. Nina had tried to ask Ainslee about her exams in a roundabout way, and that sullen teenage mask had come clanging down and she hadn't been back to the van for four days. Nina hated the idea of her losing that too, so she didn't say anything else; just snuck her as much money as she could spare.

She had other things on her mind too. More specifically, a little note left in a beautiful carved wooden box on a branch of the old tree that said, simply, 'Please come.'

She was torn. She didn't want to miss her regulars; miss her busy selling days.

On the other hand she wanted to visit her old home to see if she felt different or if it had changed at all; and to see Surinder, obviously – everyone in the village had been asking after her; she'd obviously made quite an impression, and the Gus was quite lovesick with sadness and buying lots of books about lonely mavericks who lived lonely lives solving crimes on the road. Also, Griffin had tipped her off about some stock that was going up for auction in Birmingham, and she finally felt brave enough to do the long-haul journey in the van.

But more than anything, she wanted to see Marek again. She wanted to see him so much. He was all she thought about.

So she made herself go for it. She was going to tell Lennox she was leaving for a few days, but she hadn't seen him so reckoned there was absolutely no point, not that he'd give the smallest rat's arse. She did buy Parsley a bone, though, so he'd know she'd miss him.

It was strange being back in the city. Nina realised she'd got used to everyone in the village recognising her and knowing everything about her and her business. The speed with which it had happened had been both surprising and actually very touching; it was lovely being greeted by name at the post office, or in the bank, and being able to help out here and there.

217

Surinder, after flinging her arms around her, was frowning.

'It's awful,' she said. 'It's sticky and too hot and every patch of grass has horrible fat men lolling on their horrible fat arms, looking like they've dressed in toddler's clothes. Three-quarter-length trousers. Sandals! Hairy toes! It's gross. I miss Scotland SO MUCH. At least you can sleep at night.'

'It smells weird here,' said Nina. 'Did I really never notice before?'

'No, I noticed it too,' said Surinder. 'When I got back. It's bins and rotting food and unfresh air.'

Soon they were walking down the road. The tarmac was sticky and shimmered in the heat. The air was hot and still. People were sitting aimlessly on their front steps. The pub at the corner of the road was overflowing with outdoor drinkers, shouting and talking noisily. Everywhere was mobbed and hot and full. Nina frowned.

'I've just lost the habit of so many people. There's too many people here.'

'Yeah, all right, all right,' said Surinder. 'Could you get them to open a Kirrinfief branch of my business, please? I don't think I can commute that far.'

Nina smiled. 'Yes, that's right, all we need up there is a great big city dumped right in the middle of it. You could move to Perth.'

Surinder sighed. 'I don't think so,' she said. Her tone of voice changed. 'I'm not brave like you, Nina. I couldn't toss my life up like you did. What about my mother?'

'Encouraged by you,' Nina pointed out.

'Yes, but I didn't think you'd actually do it! I thought it was just leverage so I could get my hallway back.'

Griffin hailed them from across the horribly crowded bar, waving furiously. He looked strange without his beard, and was wearing a ridiculous T-shirt with a picture of a raccoon on it, and a weird beanie hat.

'Griffin?'

He came up with three bottles of cider and hugged them both.

'Oh thank God. Grown-ups. Thank God.'

'What's up with you?'

Griffin held Nina at arm's length and looked at her.

'What's up with YOU? You've changed.'

'No I haven't,' said Nina. 'Apart from being out of direct sunlight.'

Griffin shook his head. 'No. It's not that. You look … you've got roses in your cheeks.'

'Does that mean fat?'

'No! But you do look … sturdier.'

'Fuck off, Griffin!'

'That sounds wrong, but I don't mean it like that. You look … stronger. More substantial. Less wispy.'

'I'm not a photograph from *Back to the Future*!'

'I don't know what I'm saying. Ignore me. My head is being done in by my job. Take it from me, you look good. Better than good.' And Nina could see in the way he looked at her that he meant it.

'So do you,' she said, even though he looked a bit daft. He was obviously trying to fit in with his cool young team. He'd even had his ears pierced.

'How's work?'

Griffin made a face and took a huge swallow of his drink.

'Don't start,' he said. 'It is so lovely to see you, but if you start going on about how wonderful your life is now and how you choose your own hours and have a lovely bookshop tootling around the country, I'm going to have to kill myself.'

'Okay,' said Nina. 'It's awful.'

'It isn't,' said Griffin. 'Surinder told me all about it. She says it's awesome and gorgeous and she's going back up next time she gets some holiday.'

'Or I might just pull a sickie,' added Surinder.

'Why don't you come up too?' said Nina.

Griffin shook his head. 'No. I couldn't bear it if it's nice. I really couldn't. I have to go in every morning at seven and start ploughing through all the human resources paperwork, then go to county meetings about development access, then come back and fix all the computers that have broken down because they break down every day, then I have to show ninety-year-olds how to use them because they've shut all the rural banks down so they can't do their banking. It's like an entire generation has been thrown into a world they don't understand and where nothing makes sense, and they've just been told, tough luck, learn how to type or you can just starve to death.'

He took another swig of his cider.

'Do you remember how nice it used to be when the kids came in?'

'You hated it when the kids came in!' said Nina, outraged. 'They got sticky fingermarks on all your Frank Millers.'

'Yes, I said I hated it,' said Griffin.

'You did! You hated it!'

'Well, it was paradise compared to this. It was lovely. People coming in to share stories or books or things they

220

liked. Now, it's people coming in because they're desperate. They're cut off from the world because they don't have the internet or their benefits have been taken away and they can't make ends meet, and nobody is left out there to care because they cut and they cut and they cut. I'm a librarian, and now I'm an IT support worker with a side order of psychology, addiction counselling and social work. Plus I generally have a nineteen-year-old member of staff crying in the toilet because they're not feeling self-actualised enough.'

Nina fell silent. She wasn't sure what to say.

'You should move there,' said Surinder.

'So should you!' shot back Griffin. 'We're not all as cool as Nina.'

Nina wasn't in the least bit cool but didn't feel up to pointing it out. They all moved outside the pub. Over the side wall, a fight was brewing, and a girl with very blonde extensions was hovering about it, excited to be in the middle.

A clutch of teenagers were boasting loudly and cheerily in the corner, not listening to one another, looking lairy and anxious. People were pushing and shoving to get to the bar. Nina realised she was feeling stressed. Her heart rate was raised and she was overwhelmed by the sheer amount of people around her; the smell of exhaust; the noise of honking cars and clinking glasses and noisy squeals and all the general Friday-night sense of a summer city weekend in full swing.

She thought how the evening would end – girls without shoes, lots of hollering in the street, ambulance sirens wailing – and wondered, rather traitorously, how soon Surinder would want to go home.

In the end, she didn't have to wait that long. Griffin got

drunk and maudlin and looked like he was about to cry, and then suddenly a whole clutch of lovely young people, noisy and expectant and giggly, arrived and it turned out one of them worked with Griffin and yelled his name.

He immediately transformed and became bouncy and cheerful and started using phrases like 'reverse reem' and 'that's so basic', and Surinder and Nina looked at each other and by mutual agreement sidled away.

They walked home together slowly through the muggy evening, the dark settling around them.

'It's still light up at . . . ' Nina realised she had been about to say 'home'. 'Up north,' she finished quickly.

They passed two cats having a fight on a wall as someone hollered at them from on high to shut the eff up. From the next building came loud banging EDM. Someone was yelling at them to shut up too. A car with its top down and music blaring out of it came squealing up the road, far too fast. The girls both started. The occupants of the car laughed loudly, then started catcalling a hen party that was marching in the opposite direction.

Surinder sighed. 'So. Desperate to move back?'

Nina shook her head. 'I'm going to fill the van once and for all, and then that's it. I think . . . I think I'm done here. I've just bought a whole load of stock at auction.'

Surinder nodded. 'I didn't . . . I don't know why. I thought it was just going to be some kind of freezing no-man's-land; I thought I'd kind of come and visit you and laugh at men in skirts and ask what haggis was and sing some Proclaimers songs.'

'The Proclaimers are great!' said Nina.

'Oh my God, you have gone so native,' said Surinder. 'It's ridiculous.'

'They ARE great, though.'

It was clear that Surinder hadn't finished.

'But it's not ... it's not like that at all,' she said slowly, as a police helicopter lit up the night and filled the air with noise. 'It's ... it's special up there. A kind of place of the heart. I mean, it just gets to you. Those long fields, and the sun that never goes down, and the way people look out for each other.'

'Well, we have to,' pointed out Nina. 'There isn't an Accident and Emergency for sixty miles.'

'It just feels like you can breathe up there; like these silly day-to-day problems and worries don't matter so much any more. That there's actually time to think about your life and what you want to do, instead of just racing from work to bar to dates to the gym to stupid stuff.'

'Also, all the hot men,' smiled Nina.

'That too,' said Surinder, smiling. 'If you like freckles. Which I do.'

'Come back with me. There's plenty of space.'

Surinder shook her head emphatically as they went in the gate of the little terraced house. Someone had left a bag of poo neatly tied up on top of the low wall. They both looked at it and sighed.

'Speaking of which, have you made a date with your dark-eyed stranger?'

Nina shrugged anxiously. 'I've left him a note. Hopefully I'll see him tomorrow night.' She pulled out her phone. 'I'm waiting for him to contact me the modern way.'

Surinder grinned. 'Ha! Look at you, you can't deal with stuff that's not on parchment!'

'It's not like that,' said Nina, but in actual fact it had been difficult for her to give up their secret message place; the thrill and romance of the tree. 'Plus, he hasn't texted me.'

'Maybe he has, and you're too medieval to work your phone any more.'

Nina stuck out her tongue. 'Just come back and live with me.'

'I can't,' said Surinder. 'I'm too cowardly. I couldn't leave my job; couldn't leave my mortgage and everything. Plus, what would I do? Being an admin genius isn't enough, you know!'

'I'm sure you'd find something.'

'But what if I didn't? And I'd be stuck making no money at a job I hated. I hate my job now, but the money's good. What do you make?'

Nina winced. 'Yeah, it's not a lot.'

'No,' said Surinder. 'You'll never be able to buy a property or take a holiday or get a new car.'

'I've got the van!'

'Yeah, whatever. But you love it. You're good at it. I wouldn't be able to do that.'

Surinder stared at the tiny scrubby square of garden, the fumes roaring down the road.

'Cup of tea?'

Nina had begged for their help, and once more her faithful friends had sweetly heeded her call. Griffin turned up the next morning looking incredibly hung-over and a little ashamed, and, as both girls noticed, wearing the same T-shirt he'd had on the night before. He had, it turned out, ended up pulling one of the young girls who had been out with the gang and was half embarrassed, half unbelievably proud of himself. Nina was half disapproving, half pleased that he seemed to have perked up a little bit.

'I don't know how to get in touch with her now, though,' he said, pretending to look shamefaced as Nina ordered coffee and slap-up breakfasts for everyone. 'I mean, is it Tinder, is it texting, what is it?'

Nina reflected that she still hadn't had a message from Marek. Maybe he'd changed his mind. Forgotten all about her. Figured they'd taken it far enough. She tried to stop her itchy fingers picking up her phone every two seconds.

'Send her an Instagram of a cup of coffee,' suggested Surinder. 'Even she ought to be able to interpret that.'

Griffin looked pleased. 'I will.'

The auction house was an old dank place underneath the arches of an abandoned railway station.

The large man in charge grunted briefly and nodded when Nina showed him her paperwork. Inside were great piles of books from a house contents sale. There were boxes upon boxes. Nina would have liked to have settled down and gone through them all there and then, but there simply wasn't enough time; she had to get back to work. But, after Griffin had mentioned it, she'd perused the list fairly thoroughly online before she made her commission bid, and it suited her purposes perfectly; many estate book buyers were looking for rare first editions, but she wanted good copies of contemporary books to sell on, and this collection didn't disappoint: loads of recent fiction and non-fiction from a careful, non-spine-bending reader. She'd definitely got lucky.

It was another hot, sticky day; the tar was practically melting on the roads. It was strange to go out without her jacket. She hadn't done that for so long, it felt like she was missing something.

She got a sense on the back of her neck, something prickling before she saw him. She turned her head as Surinder and Griffin happily bickered in the gloom of the arches. At first he was just a dark figure shambling up the road. Gradually he resolved himself and she jumped up.

'Marek?' she said.

He smiled his slow, lazy puppy-dog smile and held out his hands.

'I am here.'

'But how did you ... ?'

'Your friend Surinder, she say you need help today. She find me.' His voice softened. 'Whenever Nina needs help, I am here.'

Nina blinked. She remembered kissing him; how soft his full lips were on hers; how much she had yearned to move closer to his large, bear-like body. She found herself blushing.

'It's so good to see you ... '

He went to kiss her, but they missed and he gently kissed her ear, which wasn't ideal, by which time Griffin and Surinder had emerged into the sunlight and Surinder was clapping Marek on the back and Griffin was saying hello to him in a slightly suspicious way that, had Nina been paying attention, would have helped her to realise that regardless of the young ladies he met in bars, he still had a fairly vested interest in who Nina was seeing.

'How's Jim?' asked Nina, but Marek just shrugged and smiled and they started lugging great tea chests full of novels out to the van, into which Surinder and Nina had already loaded the last of the books stored at Surinder's house.

Nina was thrilled to see inside them, noticing old volumes of children's stories with thin tissue-paper protecting the inside plates, and hand-tooled gold leaf on the covers, along with all the pristine hardbacks – it looked, from the state of things, as if the owner, whoever he or she was, had simply bought everything, without regard to whether they would read it or not. Nina wondered what on earth it would be like to have that much money; to buy that many books without worrying.

Every so often she would notice a volume that she wanted to dive into straight away, but she managed to control herself until most of the work was done. Driving back to Scotland with all the books in the back was going to be a true long-distance-lorry-driver job, but once she had them up there, she'd be good for months.

They drifted afterwards to a little park, and found, with some difficulty, a free spot, clearing away other people's rubbish and cigarette ends so they could sit down and eat ice creams from the van at the entrance that was blaring its radio noisily to attract attention. Men were bare-chested everywhere, and space was at such a premium that Nina could smell their aftershave. The sun beat down uncomfortably on her head and she wished there was even the tiniest draught.

Griffin was lying on his front, exchanging messages on his phone with the new girl and laughing hysterically and possibly a bit too loudly, Nina thought. Eventually he jumped up and said, with a mock eye roll, 'Sorry, duty calls ... or rather, *Judi* calls,' and the others smiled politely. Then Surinder looked at Nina and said, 'Have you still got your key?' When Nina nodded, she said, 'Right, I'm getting out of gooseberry land ... see you later. NOT TOO MUCH LATER.'

Nina kissed her on the cheek and watched as she moved gracefully through the crowds in the park and the great mounds of litter that followed any nice day, as the sun started to sink a little in the sky. She felt her heart beat even harder and glanced over at Marek, who had his head down, not looking at her. The back of his neck was pink. Silence fell.

'Um,' she said finally, feeling she absolutely had to say something. 'How ... how have you been?'

Marek turned to her, his dark eyes intense. 'Nina,' he said. 'Come walk with me.'

Nina stood up. She could tell he was as nervous as she was, but she didn't find this any more reassuring a thought, not really. They walked through the lengthening shadows of the park and out of the gates towards the canal. Slow narrowboats drifted up and down in the early evening sunshine, people sat outside bars and restaurants talking loudly; others were walking dogs, or yelling into phones and not looking where they were going; all the normal business of the city on a hot summer's day.

But Nina was concentrating on Marek's hand, swinging casually by his side, wondering if she should take it. It felt strange, the two of them together, in daylight, like a normal boy and girl on a date. She snuck a peek at him. He glanced at her too, and she smiled back.

'Through here,' he said quietly, and, surprised, she followed him. They stepped off the road and up a side street. Nina suddenly felt a bit nervous, but Marek smiled at her and she felt reassured. Then she gasped as the street opened out into the most beautiful little garden square. Nina had never seen it before. In fact, there was absolutely no way you could ever find it unless you knew it was there. It had railings all around it and a little gate beneath a bower with a small sign: Craighart Community Garden, painted rather charmingly in the handwriting of several different children, decorated with butterflies and flowers.

Inside were rows and rows of cabbages and carrots. A grandma and a couple of children were hoeing in tidy lines, the chatter of their voices sounding sweet in the evening air, but apart from that, there were very few people about. Bumble bees buzzed in the air, up and around, and there was the scent of late honeysuckle from a tranche that someone had planted in the flower beds at the side.

'Oh,' said Nina. 'I didn't even know this was here! It's gorgeous! So beautiful.'

'Like you,' said Marek simply, drawing her into a secluded corner away from where the family was working. Nina looked into his dark eyes. It was the loveliest evening after all.

'Oh Nina,' he said, holding her hand. 'Since I came to this country . . . I came here, so far away, and everything is so strange. And I meet you and you are so kind and sweet and clever, my Nina. And how I love to get your message and send things to you.'

She found herself moving closer to him.

'I almost . . . I live in room with many other men. It is so hard. I work all night and I cannot sleep in the day because I can't find it quiet, and I am sad and I miss, oh I miss my home so much, and I miss my little boy so, so much. It is hard here, and nobody is friendly, and everything is so expensive, and Nina, you have done more than you know; you have done so much to make me happy . . . '

He pulled her close. Nina froze suddenly. She grabbed her hand away as if it had been bitten.

'You have a little boy?' she said, thinking immediately back to snotty bloody Lennox suggesting it as a possibility.

'Oh yes,' sighed Marek, clearly unable to read the tone of her voice. 'Let me show you photo.'

'And he lives with his mother?' she said, still reaching tentatively for the possibility that he was divorced, separated. That was normal, yes?

He pulled out a tatty old wallet. 'Here,' he said, taking out a photograph.

The little boy was Marek's absolute double, big puppy-dog eyes threatening to overspill his long dark lashes. Beside him sat a beautiful, slender blonde girl, smiling shyly at the camera.

'Who's that?' Nina could feel her heart thumping in her chest.

'Well that's my son, Aras,' said Marek, obviously close to tears. 'And that's Bronia.'

Nina squinted at the picture. 'Your wife?'

'No, no, no . . . my girlfriend. She is Aras's mother. She live with my mother.' Marek's eyes were downcast for an instant.

'So you're still together?'

He looked puzzled. 'What do you mean?'

'You're a couple?'

'Yes. But I work here for a year. So far from home. And I am so lonely, Nina. So lonely. And I meet you and suddenly ... it is like sun coming out! And I have someone to talk to and to write to and to think of ...'

'But you write home?'

'Yes, I call home every day. But what to say? I make money. I am sad. They are sad. My mother and my girlfriend fight. Aras does things and I am not there. He starts to say words and I am not there. I call and everyone is there and everyone is sad and angry with Marek and I am in my room with all the other men and they say, oh Marek, are you out in bars all the time, you are away all the nights, oh Marek, are you having all the fun, oh Marek, we are stuck here and we need more money ...' His voice trailed off. 'It is so hard, Nina.'

Nina swallowed. Her emotions had shifted 180 degrees, from anger and bewilderment to enormous pity.

'But didn't you know ... didn't you think that maybe I wouldn't want a man with a girlfriend and a baby? You have a family, Marek. How could I step in the way of that?'

Marek shrugged. 'I don't know. It is different here maybe? Things are different here?' His voice was cracking with hope.

Nina shook her head, close to tears. 'No. Not that different. I wouldn't ... I'm not that kind of—'

'But I did not think that about you!' he interjected. 'I never thought that about you! You to me were always special, Nina! So special! Not like other girls!'

His cheeks were pink now, the wallet still open in his

hand. Nina touched his arm gently under the lush green tree.

'Oh Marek.'

He looked at her for a long time, the hope gradually dying in his eyes.

'I am so sorry,' he said. 'I am sorry. I should not have thought . . .'

'Oh no,' Nina said, trying not to cry. 'Oh no. You could have thought. You could absolutely have thought.'

Marek looked at her. 'When you kissed me on the train, I was so happy.'

Nina shook her head. 'I think you need to go home, Marek. Make yourself happy there. At home.'

'When I have made more money. When I can look after my family and get a good job and have my qualifications . . . I have to do what I need to do. That is it, to be good man.'

Nina took him in her arms and hugged him, carefully.

'I think you're a very good man,' she said. 'And I think you're going to be fine.'

'I am not good man,' said Marek sadly.

'But think about Aras,' said Nina. 'Think how much he needs you and needs you to see him.'

Marek nodded. 'I know. And soon I will be able to drive trains in Latvia too and I can go home . . .'

They had started to walk again, aimlessly, past the old woman playing with her grandchildren and back out into the sticky, noisy streets.

'But I will miss it,' he added. 'Not here. Birmingham I do not miss. The men and the room and . . . no. Not that at all. But I will miss Scotland. Where it smells like home; rain on the air and wind in the grasses and the stars overhead. I miss it. And I will miss you.'

His face was such a picture of misery that Nina wanted to slip her arm through his. But they were approaching where she had parked the van full of books.

'I have to go,' she said.

Marek nodded. His face hung; his entire body looked heavy and sad.

'Do you want me still to bring books for you?'

'No,' said Nina. 'I have to . . . It helped so much. But it could get you into trouble. You risked so much for me. Too much. And I was selfish and wrong not to see it, and I was selfish and wrong not to ask about your family before. I was told I should, but I didn't listen. It's my fault.'

Marek shrugged. 'Was not your fault. Was my privilege.'

Surinder was lying on the sofa when Nina got in, tears tumbling down her face.

'I did warn you.'

'I know. I know you did. I just . . . I built him up in my mind so much.'

'Too much reading.'

'In my head, he was this kind of lost romantic hero.'

'He can't get lost, he drives a train.'

'You know what I mean. I just . . . I just wanted. For once. Things to happen. Things to be nice.'

Surinder sat up. 'I am genuinely sorry, you know. I know you liked him. I liked him too.'

'I liked what I thought he was.'

'And he definitely liked you. Honestly. People very rarely risk great big gigantic goods trains for no reason if they don't really like you.'

'I think he'd have clung on to anyone who was nice to him.'

'I don't. He's perfectly handsome you know. He could walk into any bar and come out with women clinging to him like burrs. I think he had a romantic soul too. I think you were two dreamers.'

Nina sighed. 'Well, too late now. He's got a kid and a girl-friend and all the rest of it going on.'

Surinder gave her a huge hug.

'I'm sorry. I really am. It would have been nice if it could have worked.'

'I know,' said Nina. 'I know.'

'But look at it this way: someone else fancied you! That makes Griffin AND Marek. You are giving off good Nina vibes.'

'Griffin just fancied me because there was nobody else about. Default. And I think Marek thought I was easy and would drop my knickers for him.'

'No he didn't. Even though you would have.'

'Yeah, well, shut up.'

Surinder looked at the clock. 'Do you really have to leave tonight? Come on, you're your own boss now.'

'I have to go because it'll be light traffic and I have to drive a billion miles. Plus I need to get back to work and actually earn some money so I can pay for petrol and the occasional bottle of Pinot Grigio. SO.'

Surinder looked at her.

'No. There's no point in staying here and throwing a pity party for myself.'

'I'll buy the snacks!'

Nina shook her head. 'No,' she said again. 'I don't want to think about it. I want to go home and play the radio loud and never see another train for the rest of my life.'

She kissed Surinder and gave her a long hug, telling her to get back up north pronto, and Surinder hugged her back and said she would be coming up when it stopped being warm in Birmingham, because then she could be cold in either place, and told Nina to stop being daft if she ever could.

'And just look for something real,' she whispered. 'Something real.'

As Nina drove past the railway station in the noisy Saturday night, she looked at the long trains in the sidings and, despite herself, started to cry. Would it never happen to her? Everyone else got to meet someone, but when she finally did, she ended up with someone else's boyfriend, or just an idea for a person rather than the person themselves.

Look for something real, Surinder had said, but how could she when she didn't even know what that was?

Chapter Twenty-Four

'Are you ready?' said Lesley, the woman from the local grocer's. She'd been very sniffy about the bookshop to begin with, and disliked Nina's recommendations, as well as expressing general doubt about the entire enterprise. Even though it was becoming obvious that her prophecies of doom weren't being fulfilled, she still liked to come in and poke through the stacks, making disappointed sounds at everything. Nina was determined, somehow, to find something she'd like.

So far historical, romance, comedy, and one of those novelists who specialised in child abduction had failed to hit the spot. True crime had raised a flicker of interest, but nothing had made Lesley rush into going 'Yes! This is the book I've been looking for that will change my life.' Very little seemed to make her happy.

'Am I ready for what?' said Nina. In the back of the arches at the auction house in Birmingham, where the books had been deposited, there'd been a great roll of brown paper. She had asked the man there about it, and he'd said it was nothing to do with him, so they had taken it on board too. Now she was becoming expert at wrapping the books up – for gifts, or just to take home, tied with the cheap farmer's twine that was plentiful around town.

Lesley squinted at her. 'Sunday, of course!'

'Nope,' said Nina. 'Still none the wiser.'

'How long have you lived in the village?'

'Ten minutes.'

'Well it's midsummer, you Sassenach. It's the midsummer night. The festival.'

'Everyone keeps going on about this festival!'

'Are you a heathen, or what? Every year on the longest day there's a festival, as everybody knows. If we're not rained off, there's dancing and a party and a celebration. And if we are rained off, there's all of those things but it'll take place in Lennox's barn.'

'Well I'd better come then,' said Nina. 'I live up there.'

'Aye, I know that,' sniffed Lesley. 'Everyone knows that. How's he doing, the poor man?'

'Poor man?' spluttered Nina. 'He's ... well, he's very rude and a bit obnoxious, if you must know.'

'Aye,' said Lesley. 'But he went through such an awful time of it with that Kate.'

'What was she like?'

'Hoity-toity,' said the woman. 'Posh. Not like you.'

'Well thanks very much,' said Nina.

'Things around here were never good enough. She complained about the pub and all the old men hanging about outside it all the time.'

Nina thought she might have a point about that.

'She complained about the town, about how there was nothing to do.'

'There's loads to do!' said Nina. It was true. You could barely walk down the street without being corralled into something or other. There were festivals and choirs and school fairs and shinty matches. It was astonishingly busy for such a small place. Nina had grown to understand the longer she stayed there that because they were so far away from big-city attractions, and because the weather was so often not their friend, they had to rely on each other through the long winter evenings and difficult days. It was an actual community, not just a long terrace full of people who happened to live next to one another. There was a difference, and she had simply never realised it before.

'Aye, well,' said Lesley. 'You probably wouldn't enjoy the party anyway. I don't think there's anything here for me.'

Nina unpacked a book she knew well and straightened up. She looked at Lesley, who worked crazy hours, who lived above the shop, seemingly on her own, who always seemed angry about how life had turned out. She wondered.

'Try this,' she said gently, handing over a copy of *The Heart Shattered Glass*.

The woman looked at the cover suspiciously. 'I don't think so.'

'Just give it a shot and let me know what you think.' Nina lowered her voice in case anyone else heard her. 'If you don't like it, no charge.'

It had become a matter of professional pride now to find something that would suit Lesley. She just seemed to be a woman absolutely in need of the right book. There was, Nina was fervently convinced, one out there for everyone. If only that went for everything in life.

'I hate the longest day,' said Ainslee, who had fallen on the new book boxes with alacrity and was unpacking them with utter reverence, exclaiming over every shiny new hardback; every precious early edition or unbroken spine. It was a marvellous collection. Nina had promised she could borrow some as long as she treated them well.

'Why, what happens?'

Ainslee sighed. 'Oh, everyone dresses up in stupid clothes and runs about singing and dancing and being idiotic all night,' she said. 'It's rubbish.'

'Seriously? Because that sounds quite nice.'

'Well it isn't. I don't know why people can't just stay inside by themselves if they want to and listen to their own music rather than stupid horns and jingly-jangly stuff.'

'Horns?'

'Yeah, great big horns. And drummers and stuff. And they light a big fire. It's totally stupid.'

'You'd better be coming,' said Dr MacFarlane, the GP, who was standing by practically licking his lips as Ainslee unpacked the big boxes, in case there were any obscure 1920s American gangster novels he hadn't yet read. 'Everyone does.'

'Oh, that's a great reason to do things,' said Ainslee, rolling her eyes.

Nina noticed from the corner of her eye that Ben had crept in. She was keeping her last copy of *Up on the Rooftops* by the cash desk, so he could help himself, and she noticed him picking it up, sitting carefully, sounding out the words on the back jacket, moving his lips as he slowly moved his finger. She smiled, and decided not to approach him quite yet.

'What clothes?' she said.

'Oh, you know, the boys in their kilts right enough, but the lassies, they do look braw,' Dr MacFarlane replied.

Nina had been in Scotland long enough to understand that was a compliment. Since she'd started working for the shop, her plain way of dressing had changed. She looked at Ainslee, whose eyeliner today was a startling purple, clashing with her green hair. She looked like Wimbledon. Nina figured it was a good sign she was beginning to express herself and decided not to mention it. She had attempted to talk to Ainslee about her exams again, but the girl had clammed up straight away and it had not been a success.

'It'll be grand,' said Dr MacFarlane, surprisingly turning up trumps with a book, the cover of which showed a flapper being held up by a space alien with a ray gun. 'Ach, this'll do.'

'Wow, I haven't even priced those yet,' said Nina. 'You are fast.'

He handed over some cash anyway and said, 'Look forward to seeing you at the party tonight.'

'Can I go too?' Ben was whining as Ainslee dragged him away.

'No,' she said.

Work was easy to deal with, but coming back to the empty barn, with no Surinder to cheer her up, no midnight strolls to look forward to, no thinking of poetry or little jokes or

240

drawings to scribble down to go in the tree: that really was hard.

During the day, she got to see lots and lots of people, but as the endless white nights stretched on and on, and you had to tell yourself to go to bed at 10.30 whether it was daylight outside or not, she felt the hours drag heavy on her hands.

She hadn't heard from Marek at all, and hadn't been down to the level crossing to check. She didn't want to know. But she sensed too that he himself knew how far they had got, and how close they had been to making a terrible mistake.

Or maybe he didn't, she thought with a particularly self-pitying sniff one evening, halfway down a tub of Mackie's ice cream. Perhaps he just thought she was some easy British girl who had turned him down, and now he was on to the next one. Perhaps he never thought of her at all. She sighed. It was even harder with Griffin and Surinder thinking she was doing so tremendously well up here, that she had it easy. It felt like there was no way back, even if she wanted one. Which she didn't. But oh, she felt so lonely.

Sighing, she switched on her very slow internet connection and turned to her Facebook page. Surinder had made her start one up for the bookshop, which she had thought was a stupid idea, but actually it had been very useful; for starters, it meant that everyone knew where she would be on particular days, so that people could find her.

In addition to this, she'd received a message from someone whose name appeared to be Orkney Library – this couldn't be their real name, she decided – suggesting that if she wanted to expand or relocate, their rural visitors would also love a mobile bookshop to complement the lovely independent in Kirkwall.

She had looked at the message, smiling. She already felt remote from the rest of the world; Orkney would surely be the ends of the earth. If she ever found the Highlands too dramatic and fast-moving ... she thought, and filed it away just in case.

There was a knock on the barn door. She looked round, bemused. She didn't get a lot of visitors, except sometimes local children in a complete and utter desperate state of need for the next Harry Potter/Malory Towers/Narnia, whom she generally managed to oblige, remembering the feeling so well.

She opened the door expectantly. To her surprise, it was Lesley from the grocer's.

'Hello,' she said. 'Um. Hi. Can I help you? The van isn't really open just now, but if you need something ... '

'No,' said the woman. 'Look, I just wanted to say ... I finished that book you recommended.' There were tears streaming down her face.

Nina glanced at her watch. 'Wow, that was fast.'

The Heart Shattered Glass was a courageous scream from the abyss from an abandoned woman, written in four days from the side of a precipice down which she was hurling all her worldly goods, one at a time, meditating on their meaning. It had taken the world by storm with its candour and wit. The fact that the author had subsequently fallen madly in love with and married the book's publicist had only prolonged its popularity, but it was truly a book that deserved its worldwide fame.

'It was ... She got it exactly. Exactly what it feels like.'

Nina looked at the tightly buttoned-up woman she had struggled to connect with and marvelled, not for the first time, at the astonishing amount of seething emotion that could exist beneath the most restrained exterior. To look at

Lesley you would think she was just a middle-aged shop-keeper quietly going about her business.

The fact that she completely and utterly empathised with an American woman who had let her own blood drip down a mountainside in anguish, who had changed sexuality and howled at the moon with a wolf pack, just went to show. There was a universe inside every human being every bit as big as the universe outside them. Books were the best way Nina knew – apart from, sometimes, music – to breach the barrier; to connect the internal universe with the external, the words acting merely as a conduit between the two worlds.

She smiled warmly. 'That's fantastic. I'm so pleased. Do you want to come in and have a cup of tea?'

The woman shook her head. 'No, no, I have to get on. It's just after what I said earlier . . . '

'About what?'

'About you not liking the summer festival. I think I was wrong. I think you have to go.'

Nina shook her head. 'No, I really need a good night's sleep! I find it hard when it's so light all the time.'

Lesley looked at her sternly. 'Don't be ridiculous. It's once a year. You're a young single girl. All the single people have to go, it's the rule.'

'Is it?' said Nina. 'Honestly?'

She still felt so bruised after the Marek episode, she certainly didn't feel ready to be out and about and interacting with people again. 'I'm not sure I'm up to it.'

Lesley frowned. 'You know,' she said, 'I wasted my youth on that man. We were married at twenty-one, together since school. All the way till I was fifty. I never even thought about another man. Oh, Bob was a pig, but I just assumed everyone was like that. I didn't even think about it, I just thought that was the way things were. And guess what: he left anyway. And it was too late for me.'

'It's not too late for you!' protested Nina.

Lesley rolled her eyes. 'I have wrinkles from the crown of my head to my hairy old toes, and I work all the hours God sends,' she said. 'It was almost the cruellest thing he did, not to leave me when I still had the chance of meeting someone else, when I still had a bit of juice left in me. Me and the woman who wrote that book – we both know we're better than that. But even I don't think I'm going to be crowned queen of midsummer in a silly dress. You, on the other hand . . .'

She brought out a plastic-covered clothes bag from behind her.

'Here,' she said. 'It should fit you. I was a scrawny little thing too.'

'I'm not scrawny!' protested Nina.

'Lennox said if you were one of his lambs, he'd leave you on the hillside,' said Lesley.

'He said WHAT?' said Nina, outraged, but Lesley was still shoving the bag in her direction and not listening.

Nina looked at the crinkled plastic.

'Honestly, I don't think . . . I don't think I can.'

Lesley frowned. 'Now,' she said. 'You've come to this town. It's worked out better than I thought it would, I'll admit that. But you're not just here for us to give you money for books. You're in the Highlands now. We have to pull together. It's what we do. You can't just take, you have to give back. There's a lot of people who've worked incredibly hard to make tonight a success, and you owe it to them to go and support them.'

'I hadn't thought of it like that,' said Nina, truthfully. Lesley waggled the bag at her one more time.

'Take it. It's going to be the most wonderful evening. Enjoy every second of it. Show everyone that you belong here.'

'I can't believe I'm being blackmailed into a party,' grumbled Nina, but she couldn't help feeling slightly excited nonetheless.

After Lesley had left, Nina carefully slipped off the plastic clothes bag, and caught her breath.

The dress was white, but it didn't look like a wedding dress. It was a very plain chiffon, high-necked, tight-waisted, with a full skirt falling to knee length. To pin to it at the shoulder and the hip was a fine tartan sash in pale greens. What really gave Nina pause, though, was the corset in deep green velvet, which laced up the front and was clearly meant to go over the top of the dress.

It was actually rather beautiful; Nina couldn't think what it reminded her of, until she remembered the illustrations of Snow White and Rose Red in her old-fashioned Ladybird books. She smiled and spread the dress on the bed.

She wished like anything that Surinder was there. She'd have found it unutterably hilarious. She looked at her watch. It was 7 p.m. The party started at eight. She bit her lip. Well, if she was going to have to go – and she could tell straight away that now that Lesley had given her the dress, she, and probably her business, would be in huge trouble if she didn't – she was going to have to think about getting ready.

Lesley, it turned out, had been absolutely spot on about the size. Nina had a quick shower and washed her hair, letting it fall rather than tying it back as she normally did. It was going to be quite big and bushy, but there wasn't much she could do about that. Then she slipped the white dress over her head. It settled on her hips as though it had been made for her; it was lighter and stretchier than she'd expected. Obviously made for dancing. Then she wriggled into the corset. It covered her waist and her ribcage; her breasts, however, spilled over the top.

She looked at herself in the mirror in some astonishment. She normally preferred shapeless clothes that meant she could be comfortable. This dress, teamed with her flat ballet slippers, was incredibly comfortable. But it was also extremely provocative compared to what she wore every day.

She had a sudden panic that nobody else would be dressed like this, that it was some cruel prank to embarrass the new girl. Then she remembered Dr MacFarlane talking about all the lovely girls, and decided it couldn't possibly be that. Could it?

Her face flushed pink as she admired herself in the mirror. The corset pulled her waist in to nothing, and her bosom, normally small and unimpressive, swelled up and over in a pleasing fashion. No wonder they used to always wear them like that in the old days, thought Nina. She tried an experimental twirl and was smiling at herself when suddenly she became aware of someone standing in the doorway.

She whisked round, gasping, horrified, realising belatedly that it was Lennox.

For a split second, he stared straight at her, unabashed. Then he recovered himself.

'Sorry! Sorry!' he said fiercely, putting his hands up and backing away. 'The door was open . . . ' Nina had left it open after Lesley had left, to let the soft summer breeze in through the sitting room.

'You gave me such a fright!'

'I'm sorry, I'm sorry, I'm not that type of landlord . . . Christ, is that the time?'

Nina smiled. 'It's all right. I'm just embarrassed I got caught preening.'

He looked at her again, but rather nervously, as if he shouldn't.

'So you're going to the festival?'

'No,' snapped Nina. 'This is what I wear when I need to relax.'

Lennox laughed suddenly, as if despite himself. 'Actually,' he said, 'I think it rather suits you.'

'Don't talk daft.'

'I'm not. You look nice. As if you've taken off your cardigan for once.'

'I don't wear a cardigan!'

'Your metaphorical cardigan. Your librarian's cardigan. It's as if . . . ' This was a long speech from Lennox, and he seemed to be flailing a little bit. 'It's as if you pull something around yourself, make yourself look smaller and more insignificant. Than you really are.'

Nina blinked.

'Like you don't want anyone to notice you.'

'In case they want to leave me on a hillside.'

Lennox looked puzzled. 'Sorry?'

'Never mind.'

He immediately turned to go. He got halfway down the path, stopped at the van, then turned round again.

'You can't drive that deathtrap up there. Want a lift?'

'You're going?' said Nina in surprise.

'I am if I want people in this town to buy my wool again,' snorted Lennox. 'No bloody choice, have I?'

Nina smiled. 'Well then. Maybe this time you'll start dancing a bit earlier.'

His forehead creased in confusion; he had obviously forgotten the barn dance completely.

'Wouldnae have thought so,' he said, heading towards the house. 'See you in twenty minutes.'

'You have two kilts?' said Nina in astonishment, looking at him twenty minutes later. She had attempted to tame her hair, without success, and had ended up simply twisting two strands from the front to the back, in the style of a coronet. She had given up completely on the tartan sash, not having the faintest idea what to do with it. She noticed now that it was the same tartan as Lennox's kilt; a soft green grey.

'Have you got two pairs of jeans?' growled Lennox. He had washed his hair, and it fell in soft curls, not hidden as it usually was beneath a flat cap. Likewise, without the waxed jacket on, Nina noticed once again the breadth of the shoulders; his slim but muscular build. He wasn't over worked out – she couldn't imagine him ever working out, as if farmers ever needed artificial exercise – nor skinny; just nicely

248

proportioned. The grey-green of the tartan made his eyes seem even stronger blue.

'Yes, but . . . ' Nina decided this line of conversation was pointless.

'Where's your sash?'

'Um, I didn't know what to do with it.'

'So you didn't even try? Bring it here.'

He stood by the Land Rover and gravely, and with care, pinned the sash to her hip and her shoulder. As he straightened it, they were suddenly standing uncomfortably close to one another, and Nina realised she was holding her breath. She immediately gave herself a stiff telling-off and jumped into the front seat, then out again when she saw that Parsley was already in there.

'Does Parsley dance a lot?'

Lennox shrugged. 'He likes a party. More than I do, at any rate.'

'Will I sit in the back?'

'Don't be ridiculous. On boy, on.' The dog immediately moved to the back.

Nina turned and rubbed Parsley's ears affectionately. 'You gorgeous boy, you.'

Parsley licked her hand. Lennox glanced over.

'You're very soppy about that dog.'

'Because he is so very lovely.' Lovelier than you deserve, she thought, but didn't say.

'Kate always said he was too nice for me,' said Lennox, reading her thoughts.

They bounced down the rutted track in silence. There were more cars on the road than usual, partly because normally there weren't any cars on the road at all, and most were heading up the hill towards Coran Mhor, full of jolly and excitable people including, thank goodness, lots of white dresses and girls spilling out of them. Nina looked out of the window, as Lennox seemed typically unwilling to get involved in a conversation. The evening was dreamy and clear, puffs of cloud settling; the sun looked unwilling to shift anywhere.

'How's the train driver?' said Lennox awkwardly, out of the blue.

Nina looked at him in shock. 'Excuse me?'

'I mean, is he coming or what?'

'Um. No. NO, of course not. No. It wasn't . . . it didn't . . .'

Lennox cut his eyes towards her. 'Not quite what you'd thought?'

There was a long silence in the car.

'He had . . . it turned out he already had a family.' Nina hated having to admit it, to say it out loud. 'Not that it's any of your business.'

Lennox paused and patted the dog, who'd stuck his head in between the two of them in the front.

'Sorry,' he said finally. 'I shouldn't have asked. I did have a bad feeling about him. Something about the way he wouldn't meet my eyes.'

'Maybe he just thought you were grumpy and scary,' said Nina.

Lennox looked surprised. 'I'm not like that at all.'

Nina harrumphed. 'Yeah, right, okay.'

'I just work hard, that's all. People think there's nothing to keeping a big farm going, but it's a hell of a job . . . '

He caught the look on Nina's face.

'What?'

'Nothing.'

'What?'

'Well, who doesn't think farming is an incredibly hard job? But I see Fat Tam out having fun at the pub all the time, and other farmers have a right laugh. Loads of people have tough jobs, but it doesn't make them miserable all the time.'

Lennox went quiet for a moment.

'No,' he said finally. 'I suppose not. I suppose . . . for the last few years . . . '

He paused again, and looked at the bright green hills rolling past the windscreen.

'The last few years . . . have been difficult. And it's as if . . . I don't know if you'll know what I mean, but it's as if somehow being low has . . . it feels like it's become rather a habit.'

He looked down at his kilt.

'But I'm out now, aren't I?'

Nina looked at him playfully. 'I don't know. Are you going to hug the bar looking angry all night?'

'I don't do that.'

'You did at the barn dance! You spent most of the night talking with that guy and totally ignoring everyone.'

Lennox sighed. 'Oh aye, *that* night.'

'Oh aye, *that* night,' mimicked Nina. 'You know, given all the social events that go on around here, I don't know how anyone keeps up with the whirl of it all.'

251

Lennox narrowed his eyes and kept his focus on the road ahead.

'Aye, I remember.'

Nina looked at him, waiting for him to elaborate. Eventually he did so.

'That ... that was my lawyer, Ranald,' he sighed. 'He wanted to talk to me face to face.'

He tightened his grip on the steering wheel. 'Oh Lord. Sorry, Nina. I didn't want to tell you yet ... not until I knew for sure. I've been trying to sort it, but I don't think I can. I'm sorry to have to tell you this, especially tonight, but I was ... I mean, before. I was actually coming over to tell you ...'

Nina looked at him. His face was pink.

'I ... Kate wants the farm. Or she wants me to sell the farm.'

'What?' said Nina. She thought of the expensive lined curtains, the beautiful objects so carefully chosen, the care that had been taken over everything. Surely someone with such good taste, with such an eye for the nice things; surely they wouldn't march in and destroy everything?

She realised how selfish she was being. This was only where she was renting a space. It was absolutely nothing compared with what was going to happen to Lennox.

'Oh my God,' she said. 'She can't take your farm!'

'She's trying,' said Lennox.

'But isn't it a family farm?'

'Doesn't really matter,' said Lennox. 'I mean, she was my family. For a while.' He fell silent.

'But doesn't she have a job?'

Lennox shrugged. 'Doesn't seem to matter.'

252

'Didn't she leave you?'

'That neither.'

'What will you do if you don't have a farm?'

Lennox blinked rapidly. 'I don't know,' he said slowly. 'Start over, I suppose. Go and work on somebody else's farm.'

Nina couldn't see Lennox as a labourer somehow.

'That can't happen,' she said fiercely. 'I've seen how hard you work on your place.'

'Well the lawyers don't seem to think that matters.'

They bumped slowly up the rutted track, Nina aware that they were even less in the mood for a party than ever. But she had to ask.

'Why did you break up?' she asked quietly. 'Did she really just fall for someone else, or was that an excuse?'

There was a very long silence in the car.

'Well, isn't it obvious?' said Lennox.

'You're a grumpy old sod?' said Nina.

'Uh no, that wasn't what I was going to say at all,' said Lennox, clearly hurt.

'Oh. Um.'

There was another long pause.

'She felt buried away,' said Lennox. 'Felt that I'd promised her something different, something more. No, that's not it. I hadn't. I hadn't offered her anything. She knew what the deal was. And she thought that would be all right, that she'd be able to cope up here in the isolation. But she couldn't.'

He looked out over the golden hills.

'The winters are very long here, you know,' he said. 'It's hard; it's very hard to be a farmer's wife. It's not for everybody.'

'How did you meet?' said Nina.

'I was at the agricultural college in Edinburgh ... she was at the art school.' He smiled. 'Should have realised, huh?'

Nina tilted her head. 'So why did she agree to come out here? If she wanted to stay in town and be a cool artist?'

'She thought it would be good for her work. To give herself the solitude she needed to truly become a great painter.'

Nina thought of the contemplative canvas on the wall.

'Oh,' she said. 'That's hers! That picture! It never occurred to me.'

She thought again of the dark, gloomy layers, so at odds with the rest of the room.

'Oh yes,' said Lennox. 'She didn't want to hang it. I did it. I thought ... I thought it would cheer her up.'

'Did it?'

'Not really. But I did think it was beautiful.'

'It is,' said Nina fervently. 'It's really beautiful. But why ... why would she want to take your farm away from you, just because she hated it?'

'I think she's really hard up,' said Lennox. 'It's expensive for artists, trying to make it in the city. It's pricey down there. And I think she's been teaching a little bit, which ... I can't imagine she enjoys that in the slightest. Not really her type of thing. And she says it's for my benefit, that I need to get out of the rut she thinks I'm in, stop working so hard, take on a more relaxing job.'

'She might have a point about that.'

Lennox looked at her. 'Do you really think that?'

'I hear you up at all hours,' said Nina. 'I see you striding for miles around the hills.'

254

Lennox's brow creased in confusion. 'But that's what I do,' he said. 'It's not work, it's a way of life. *My* way of life. I know she didn't like it, but that's not really my problem. *I* like it. I couldn't . . . Man, I just couldn't be in an office all day. Doing things on the computer. That would be torture for me. I'm not an artist like she is, and I'm not clever like you, finding something the community needs and bringing it in. I can't do that at all.'

Nina was embarrassed at the compliment.

'I think,' she said. 'I think you could do all sorts of things. If there's one thing I've learned, it's that you never know what you can do till you try.'

'But I love what I do. I love this land.'

Nina looked at him. 'There must be a way. There must be a way to stay.'

Lennox shrugged, then extended a hand. They had crested the hill now, and the valley was laid out beneath them, the railway line running through it. Nina averted her eyes from that. Instead, at the top of the next hill was a great crowd of people; striped tents and brightly coloured stalls. There was a steady noise that sounded to Nina like the thrumming of rain on a roof, but as they drew closer, she realised it was in fact the sound of drums. She screwed up her eyes. A group of young men, in kilts but shirtless, with mud spread all over their chests and upper bodies, were banging on huge bodhráns and making a massive racket. Every so often one of them would throw back his head and howl.

'Gosh,' said Nina. 'Is there going to be much of this?'

For the first time, Lennox smiled properly. He had a lovely smile; it crinkled his blue eyes. 'Oh, and the rest,' he said.

Then his face fell again. 'Sorry I had to notify you about your potential eviction.'

Nina blinked. 'It's okay,' she said. 'I've had ... actually, I've had an offer elsewhere.'

Lennox's eyebrows went up. 'Really?' he said carefully.

Nina swallowed. She didn't want to leave Kirrinfief, she really didn't. But she didn't see any point in making Lennox feel worse about things than he already did.

'Just sort things out with Kate however you have to,' she said. 'Don't worry about me.'

The Land Rover came to a halt next to rows of other cars parked in a field. Lennox looked at her and nodded.

'Aye,' he said, but his face was worried.

'I mean it,' said Nina.

Lennox got out of the vehicle, then instinctively moved round the back to help her down; Nina had almost forgotten the dress she was wearing. It wasn't quite the thing for scrambling in and out of Land Rovers. He put out his long, rough hand and she took it.

'Where were you thinking of going?' he said, as she jumped lightly to the ground.

'Oh, Orkney,' she said breezily.

Lennox stood stock still. 'Artney?' he said, pronouncing it the local way. 'You're heading up to *Artney*? Is this really no' isolated enough for you?'

'If I don't have anywhere to live here, I might have to,' pointed out Nina.

'Oh,' said Lennox. 'Aye.'

They stood awkwardly. The drumming grew louder and louder, and with it on the breeze came the sound of skirling pipes. Clouds raced across the sky, little puffy things being chased across as if something was after them. Nina heard a crowd of children laughing.

'Are you *sure* I'm dressed for this?' she said, and Lennox looked her up and down.

'You're gor—' he seemed about to say, then stopped himself. 'Do you know what?' he said finally. 'I am in the mood to get drunk. Want to join me?'

'You? What about all the little baby lambs?'

'The little baby lambs are bouncing about eating my thistles. And it's midsummer, which means one is required to get drunk, didn't you know?'

As if on cue, a hugely fat man whom Nina recognised as the local postmaster, even though he was tremendously well disguised, covered in red make-up, and with great vines of fruit and flowers draped around his copious shoulders, ran up brandishing a large horn.

'BACCHUS! BACCHUS IS HERE!' he shouted broadly. 'Worship the god of the midsummer!'

'What is this?' said Nina suspiciously.

'It's midsummer night,' said the man. 'We make merry and we make magic. Water shall turn into wine and flowers shall show the way. Also, it's £5.'

'That's not answering the question,' said Nina, but she took a tentative sip anyway. The concoction tasted a little strange – like wine flavoured with raspberries – but it was fresh and fizzy and good, and she smiled and passed the horn to Lennox, who drank deeply and smiled in response and handed over ten pounds, whereupon Bacchus shouted, 'Come, come, join the revels! Also don't forget to support your local post office.' Then three of the young girls who normally hung around the village bus stop looking discontented with the world and complaining about things came bouncing up in their white dresses with big garlands of flowers and offered one to Nina.

'I don't think so,' said Nina.

'It's supporting the local girl guides,' said one of the girls, and Nina rolled her eyes.

'You need to bring deep pockets to the midsummer festival,' said Lennox. 'On you go, then.'

And Nina bowed her head and let them put the flowers around her hair.

It was, to be fair, the most wonderful party. Little children were running and skidding about, the girls with floral headdresses and their dresses blowing in the wind, flowers everywhere; the boys in kilts just like their fathers, with loose white shirts, and here and there brandishing the little swords that came in their socks.

At the gate where they bought their tickets was a great bower, bent around with summer peonies and roses, filling the air with their heavy scent. Lennox had to duck to get through it, and beyond it they emerged into the most extraordinary sight.

A vast bonfire shot into the air at the very top of the hill, crackling and sending sparks upwards. Dotted all around on the grass were musicians playing their fiddles to the noise of the heavy drums, and in the centre was what in England Nina would have called a maypole, though this strange arched object didn't seem anything like the twee Morris-dancing memories of her childhood.

This was larger, wilder, an entire caber on its end; its full green foliage promising forests and vines. Couples, she now saw, were going up to the twisted tree trunk, winding foliage around their wrists to bind them together, then unwinding themselves around the trunk until they met again, full of giggles and kisses, on the other side, whereupon the vines would be tied back on to the maying tree and the ceremony would begin again. They must have been building it for weeks.

A huge figure loomed into view, startling Nina and several of the children. It was, she realised gradually, a green man on stilts. He was completely covered in leaves and looked like he was made of the forest itself, and he was controlling the drumming, ordering and arranging the couples, in general being the master of ceremonies.

More horns came round now, brimming with the strange wine, and Nina sipped at it even as she realised that it was going straight to her head; that the music and the drumming and the noise of the wind in the trees was pumping in her bloodstream; and that although she knew it was just a fund-raiser for the village – an event, that was all – everything felt rich and wild and strange.

She found herself gradually separated from Lennox and borne off with the other women, all in white and some wearing masks; most with flowers and ribbons in their hair, which made it difficult to recognise anyone, and even when she did, there wasn't time for more than the briefest wave until she was cast off again in the tide of people, laughing and dancing as children shrieked and ran in and out of their feet. She

259

found herself making new friends and greeting old ones and being totally unable to tell the difference between the two; it was impossible, anyway, with the noise levels and the crackle of the bonfire, to make or hear a conversation, so there was nothing to do except follow the flow.

Then, bossed about by the green man, who wouldn't take no for an answer, they all had to take hands in two great rings, one clockwise, one anticlockwise, and, to the beat of the drummers and the skirl of the pipes and the fiddles, perform a strange stomping dance, around and around the bonfire, faster and faster, until Nina was utterly breathless and dizzy, overwhelmed with it all but still laughing wildly and feeling unable to stop.

'Behold the rites of midsummer,' boomed the green man through a megaphone. 'Behold the lads and lasses and the spirit of growth and renewal and the shortest night and the longest day, and we shall CELEBRATE it, Mother Earth, for the fruit and flowers of your bounty!'

And everyone yelled and clapped, and then the dance collapsed on the grass in heaps of giggles but the musicians played on, their music wild and eerie on the sweet night air, with its heavy scents of lavender and wild thyme, rippling foxgloves and honeysuckle and buttercups and maidenhair and baby's breath, for as someone had told Nina, with great seriousness and intent, she had to pick one of each type of flower, seven flowers for seven nights, and that would make her true love come. Once they'd all found them, the girls folded the flowers carefully into each other's hair as coronets, sipping from the horns that kept on being passed round, and as soon as they were done, the men came forward again, laughing, and grabbed their hands and made them dance.

Nina was having a great time. The evening passed in a blur, until finally, after 11.30, when the twilight started to deepen and the night grew chill, tartan blankets were passed out and people huddled together next to the fire to watch the stars come out.

As the sky lowered to a deep blue – not black, not up here at this time of year – suddenly the drumming stopped and the music faded away to a mere light dance on a pipe, as if the god Pan himself was playing a haunting low tune many miles away.

And then even that died away, and for an instant in the cool air there was a tremendous silence, as if the earth itself was holding its breath. Then, in the very far east of the night, over the sea, there was just the faintest glimmer in the dusky blue; a pale green and pink so light and subtle it was like fingers running delicately over piano keys.

There was a collective gasp from the crowd. Then suddenly everyone was stomping and cheering, people jumping up from their blankets and trying to take photographs, which rather spoiled the moment, but Nina barely noticed. She was entranced, looking at the faint shimmering colours of the Aurora Borealis against the night sky. She had never seen anything so beautiful, so awe-inspiring; had never read anything quite so lovely.

Then the MC shouted, and the drums and fiddles kicked off again, louder than ever, quite extraordinary; but she didn't hear them, or see everyone throw off their blankets and get up and start to dance once again round the bonfire; she was stuck still, gazing at the sky, as people celebrated around her.

Suddenly she felt a presence at her elbow, and whirled

round. Standing there, tall, silhouetted against the darkening sky, was Lennox. He said nothing; simply followed her gaze to the sky above and nodded. Then he reached out and gently touched her hand.

It felt to Nina as though it burned like fire, and she snatched it away instinctively. He looked at her for a short moment, then stepped back into the whirling crowd and was gone so quickly it felt like she'd dreamed it.

Hours later, Nina sat with a bunch of brand-new friends, watching the sun come up when it had barely gone down, still pondering furiously on what had happened, if anything had indeed happened, or if she'd misread it.

But her instincts had said: stay away. She'd been so recently burned; had thought she knew what was going on when she didn't. She couldn't get into that again. And despite the fact that that evening in the car was the first time they'd ever managed a civil conversation, she generally found him rude and curt, and she knew from what he'd told her that he was in the middle of something emotionally horrible.

She thought back to Marek's big, sad puppy-dog eyes and sighed. Wasn't there somewhere out there some available guy who wouldn't completely screw her over; who would be there just for her? Or was that something only for story books and fantasies?

Ainslee walked past. She was working there, Nina noticed, and she got up to say hello, after Ainslee helped serve the utterly splendid breakfast that was included in the ticket price: great thick jugs of fresh creamy milk to stir into huge vats of porridge, with salt, sugar or honey; slices of locally smoked bacon in rolls; square Lorne sausage; kedgeree or scrambled eggs with smoked salmon from the nearby loch; and enough tea and coffee to sober up even the midsummer crowd, although there were plenty still imbibing the pink fizzy mixture.

'This is great,' said Nina. 'It's an amazing party.'

'Aye,' said Ainslee.

'Is it fun working here?'

Ainslee shrugged. 'No' really. But I need the money.'

'Is everything all right at home?'

'Aye,' said Ainslee shortly, and Nina realised she'd had too much fizz and was going too far.

'Sorry,' she said.

Ainslee looked over her shoulder. 'Who's that grumpy guy over there?'

Nina glanced over. Lennox was standing by the bar, drinking whisky. He turned back to his friends when he noticed her looking at him.

'Oh, just my landlord,' she said. 'He's a miserable old bugger.'

'It's Lennox, isn't it? From Lennox Farm? He's dead old,' said Ainslee.

'He's in his early thirties!'

'Yeah. Really, really old.'

'Uh, all right,' said Nina.

'But he's pretty cute. For an older guy.' Ainslee had blushed bright pink.

'You think?'

She nodded. 'I mean, not that it matters what I think.'

'Ainslee,' said Nina, leaning forward. 'Never believe that. What you think always matters.'

Ainslee looked at her for a moment. Then they both heard her name being called by whoever was in charge of the waitresses.

'So you're going to go for it?' she said, attempting a conspiratorial smile.

'Um, no,' said Nina. 'But I value your opinion.'

Ainslee nodded, as if it was the way of the world for her to be roundly ignored, and lumbered off into the dawn.

A fleet of taxis, and cars that had been pressed into service as taxis, turned up to take the partygoers home. Several people were just flat out and would stay that way until they woke up, rather damply. Some well-prepared tents were dotted here and there. Nina felt very sobered up after about four pints of coffee and shared a cab with some of the villagers she'd met there, glad that she didn't catch sight of Lennox again on her way out. Her hair had got loose, and she didn't even want to think about her eyeliner.

'Did you have a good night?' asked their driver. 'I always used to go as a young man. Great place to meet the lasses, oh yes.'

'Did you meet any?' said a very drunk girl squashed into the back seat.

'Met my wife,' said the cabbie. 'She won't let me go any more, unless I'm working. It was fun, though. Did you get the lights tonight? I've never seen them in the summertime.'

'They were amazing,' said Nina, thinking back. If she forgot about that awkward moment with Lennox, it had been, in many ways, the most marvellous evening. She recalled nights out she'd had in the city. Yes, it was definitely true. There was no comparison. She might not go out as often here, but when she did, it really meant something. She wished Surinder had been there, she'd have loved it. And the Gus had been asking after her too. She didn't think he'd ended up with anyone either.

But now, as she sank gratefully into bed, after taking off the lovely dress and checking it for marks – fortunately she appeared to have got away relatively unscathed, just some mud here and there; she'd need to look out a lovely set of new books for Lesley to say thank you, especially now she knew what she liked – her memories weren't of the wild dancing or the sweet wine or the shimmering lights across the horizon.

They were, disagreeably, of the look on Lennox's face when she'd snatched her hand away; and a growing uncomfortable knowledge of what she'd felt wasn't dislike, or fear, or anything like that, which she suspected had shown on her face.

She had pulled her hand away because what she had felt, the very second he had touched her, even lightly, was heat; deep, instantaneous, burning heat. It had seared her.

She didn't want to – couldn't – think about that now, the trouble she could cause as she was on the point of losing her home, of losing everything she'd worked so hard to build.

(And she never cast a thought, never even considered that a couple of miles to the west, a train had stopped, sat idling on a level crossing, as the driver leaned his head out of the window beside an empty tree, and also gazed up at the astonishing lights in the sky, and thought that no one but he had ever felt so lonely.)

Chapter Twenty-Five

The morning sun fell across her bedspread as Nina woke late but arose feeling oddly better, considering how much she'd drunk and danced the evening before. After a long soak in the bath, using the incredibly expensive bubble bath and smellies that had been left out in a basket, like a posh hotel, and which she'd never dared use before (she cared less now, if she was en route to eviction), she even felt cleansed.

As long as she didn't think about Lennox.

She blinked as she sat down and combed out her hair. This was terrible. This was a truly awful idea. He was a vulnerable man. In wellingtons, for God's sake. Who had lowered his guard for one night; who had himself said he wanted to get drunk.

He was almost certainly every bit as embarrassed as she was this morning. Probably more so. The best, the only thing to do was to ignore him, because if he had to walk in here one day – soon – and tell her that she was being evicted and that Kate was getting the entire farm, well, she was going to have to deal with that. She looked at her computer, to see another friendly message from Orkney Library suggesting she go up and have a look around, and saying that the Northern Lights were particularly tremendous this year, which made her smile. Perhaps she ought. Anything to get out of the way for a few days.

To leave everything behind would be so hard, though. She thought back to the antics of the night before and smiled, couldn't help it. But then that was the Scots, wasn't it? Endlessly welcoming and hospitable, particularly up here. It didn't necessarily mean she belonged, did it?

But she didn't know what else to do. She didn't want to hang around, moping, on the farm. She really didn't want to see Lennox. No. She might feel strange, but she'd get out, make some money, stock up the van, make sure everything was in tip-top condition . . . try to see herself as a rolling stone, someone who liked moving on, who liked to travel and keep going.

Even though it was Sunday and none of the shops in the village were open, she decided to get out there anyway. The sooner the better. And also, she realised, the further away she was from Lennox and his stupid farm the better right now. The idea that he might pop over and apologise made her feel embarrassed and awkward. She remembered again the look on his face when he'd first seen her in her white dress.

No, she told herself. She was imagining things. Again. As she always did, as Surinder kept pointing out. It was nothing. Or at the very best it was a lonely, angry man wondering if she'd oblige because she only lived up the hill, and that wasn't at all what she was after either.

Then her traitorous thoughts strayed again to the feeling of his strong, large calloused hand on hers.

No. No no no no. Moving on. She was moving on. This wasn't her home, they wouldn't really notice. It was a stopping point, that was all, a way of getting her out of an unsatisfying career and into an interesting one. Life would go on here and she would go elsewhere, and no one would miss her.

Actually, it turned out, since the weather was still holding – almost unheard of for this part of the world – the little village was absolutely thronged, people everywhere exploring the historic cobbled streets. The pub had thrown open its doors, and Edwin and Hugh waved merrily to her, perched at wooden tables set up outside, both of them nursing their usual pint of 80 Shilling.

She stopped off for a chat, as she normally did, and presented them with her latest finds: a Cold War submarine thriller for Edwin, which he adored, no matter how similar they ended up to one another, and a contemporary rom com for Wullie, of all people, who had accidentally stumbled across one and now adored the entire genre, notably unfazed when teased about how many pink-jacketed books he was reading.

And as Nina looked around the little village in the sunshine, she couldn't help but notice something.

Everyone was reading. People out in their gardens. An old lady in her wheelchair by the war memorial. A little girl absent-mindedly swinging on the swings, her feet dangling, completely engrossed in *What Katy Did*.

In the bakery, someone was laughing at a book of cartoons;

at the coffee stand, the barista was trying to read and make someone a cappuccino at the same time.

Nina was amazed. It couldn't be – surely – that she had turned an entire town into readers. And yet, as she opened up the Little Shop of Happy-Ever-After, and more people came cheerfully out of their houses, exclaiming that she was open on a Sunday, it seemed that she had.

'The kids have almost stopped playing Minecraft!' said Hattie. 'Of course they just want to read books about Minecraft. But that's still a miracle as far as I'm concerned.'

'I don't even know when I stopped reading,' an elderly man confessed, picking up one of the most beautiful editions of Sherlock Holmes Nina had ever seen; she hated selling it and had stuck a huge price on it in the hopes that she wouldn't have to, but it appeared that she did. Still, it would help for her moving fund, she thought sadly.

'I think I just stopped seeing books around,' the man went on. 'You know, on the bus, everyone used to read books. But then they were fiddling with their phones or those big phones, I don't know what they're called.'

'They were probably reading on their tablets,' said Nina, loyally. She loved her e-reader too.

'Yes, I know,' said the man. 'But I couldn't see. I couldn't see what they were reading or ask them if it was good, or make a mental note to look for it later. It was as if suddenly, one day, all the books simply disappeared.'

Nina looked at him. 'I know what you mean,' she said. 'I do, I know how you feel.'

They both admired the Sherlock Holmes, with its hand-tooled leather cover and beautiful watered-silk endpapers.

'You don't want to let go of this, do you?' said the old man.

'Not really,' said Nina honestly.

'I'll look after it, I promise.'

'Okay,' said Nina, taking his cheque and putting it in her old tin cash box.

'You can come and visit it from time to time if you like,' said the old man, with a slightly flirtatious tone.

Nina grinned at him. 'Oh, I'm not sure how long I'll be around,' she said, and tried to make it sound careless and light-hearted, although she did not think she succeeded.

She was sitting trying to unobtrusively watch mucky little Ben sitting on her steps, quietly sounding out a book with his lips moving, his eyes shooting up every ten seconds in case anyone was passing or saw him, when Ainslee came up and scowled at him.

'Don't run out the house! I thought youse were lost.'

'I's no' lost.'

'Yeah, I can see that now, but you cannae just up and go and no' tell me.'

Nina frowned. Now Ainslee was hissing at him.

'If they see you . . . if they see you wandering the streets Benny . . .'

'I dinnae care.'

'You will.'

'I dinnae.'

He looked back down at his book, and Ainslee sighed in exasperation and turned her attention to Nina.

'I didn't know you were open today.'

270

'I'm not really,' said Nina. 'I just … I just came down to …'

She didn't know how to explain what was going on and changed the subject.

'Didn't you like the midsummer party? It was lovely.'

Ainslee shrugged. 'It was boring.'

'There were lots of nice boys there,' said Nina, trying to raise a smile but not succeeding.

Ainslee looked around grumpily. 'There's nothing to do.'

'I know,' said Nina, who'd had a flurry of anxiety-displacing tidying. 'Honestly, I don't need you today.'

Ainslee shrugged and set off again into the bright market square, her heavy black eye make-up and badly dyed hair looking strange in the morning sunlight.

'C'mon, Ben,' she snapped, and the little boy reluctantly put the book down – Nina would wipe it for fingerprints later – and trailed behind her, head down.

It was then that Nina made the decision. She had held off for long enough. And if she wasn't going to be here for long, it didn't matter if people thought she was a busybody. She waited an instant, then quietly closed and locked the doors of the van and slipped down the street, following the pair.

The village wound on through its cobbled central section and dribbled off into less attractive streets at the bottom: grey-built 1950s social housing, some of which was smart and lined with flowers and some of which was a little tattier, though it all overlooked beautiful green fields with long views across the countryside.

Even if you were skint, Nina couldn't help thinking, it was still obviously the loveliest place in the world to grow up.

271

Ainslee and Ben turned in at the most broken-down-looking house of all. Rubbish was scattered all over the front scrub, as well as an old armchair without legs and some broken toys. There was only dirt on the ground. The door was covered in scratches and dents; the glass in the windows was cracked. It was completely unloved and uncared for.

Nina swallowed. She realised suddenly that she was quite frightened. In her darkest scenarios, she imagined Ainslee kept in by some horrible stepfather, or a family on substances who couldn't be bothered to look after the children. She didn't know if she had the courage for this. She was used to having to deal with various social problems in the library; they would often have a quiet word with social services if the same people were coming in every day and falling asleep, obviously without anywhere else to go, or if their regulars were becoming increasingly unkempt. And many people used the library as a kind of informal citizens' advice bureau anyway, so they tried not to mind.

But this was different. She was poking her nose in, it was undeniable. She tried to comfort herself with the thought that it was about a child after all, a child who wasn't well looked after, who wasn't clean, who could barely read at the age of eight, who wasn't attending school; and Ainslee too, who only came alive when alone with her books; whose lack of interest in everything else in life seemed to indicate a real issue somewhere, more even than for normal teenage girls.

Nonetheless, Nina still felt like a busybody, someone inserting herself into other people's lives, making herself a nuisance; the city girl turning up where she wasn't wanted, poking about where she didn't belong. It had been different back in the library, where people asked for help or were gen-uinely grateful for it. However carefully she'd tried to probe, Ainslee clearly didn't want to discuss it. But there was a child involved.

She sighed, twisting in indecision. What was right? To stay or to go? Ainslee was functioning, wasn't she? Although Nina thought back to that awful conversation about her not sitting her exams. That wasn't right, a clever girl like her. She should be looking at universities, thinking about what fun she was going to have when she left home. Not slouching around the place, shouting at her brother and planning absolutely nothing for the future. Maybe Nina could just have a gentle conversation with the parents, try and convince them what a clever girl they had on their hands. Yes. That would do it. That would be it.

Boldly, she walked forward to the gate. The handle was broken, and the gate sat balanced gingerly on its hinges. She slipped through it carefully and walked up the cracked stones of the garden path. The road was eerily silent, empty of cars; a lone kestrel lazily circled the air above the trees. Nina watched him for a moment, in awe of his silent majesty, and slightly envious of his uncomplicated social obligations.

Then she stepped up to the door and knocked, briskly, before she had the chance to change her mind.

Chapter Twenty-Six

For a long while there was silence. There weren't any lights on inside the house; if Nina hadn't watched them both go in, she would have thought it was empty. Then at last there was a shout Nina recognised as Ainslee's, but it sounded something like 'Don't answer it!'

It was too late, however, as a small grubby hand was already drawing back what sounded like several bolts from the other side of the door.

'Nina!'

Ben's sticky face was unable to hide his delight, and the smile that cracked his face made him unrecognisable from the sullen little boy she'd met for the first time on the steps of the van.

'Hi, Ben.'

'Have you got some books for me?'

Nina cursed herself for not having thought of this.

'No, sorry, I didn't . . . I should have brought some. Yes, I do, but they're at the van,' she improvised quickly. 'Is your mum in?'

Ben's face immediately became evasive and he glanced to the left. Looking behind him, Nina could see an incredibly messy kitchen covered in rubbish and old milk containers. The house smelled of dust, neglect and something underneath it she couldn't quite identify.

'Ben! Who is that?' came Ainslee's voice. She appeared behind her brother and squinted at Nina standing out in the sun.

'What do you want?'

The normal quiet deference in Ainslee's voice had completely vanished. She sounded bolshie, cross and ready to throw Nina out. Suddenly Nina realised that Ainslee was substantially physically bigger than her, and quite capable of doing so if she fancied.

'Um ... I just wondered ... is your mum in?'

Ainslee and Ben looked at each other.

'What's it to you?' said Ainslee rudely.

'I just ... I just wanted to tell her how great I think you're doing, that's all. You left without your wages and I wanted to make sure you got them.'

'You didn't just come here for a sticky-beak?'

Nina didn't know how to answer this, so she looked down.

'Is she here?'

'We're fine,' said Ainslee. 'We don't need your charity.'

'It's not charity,' said Nina. 'It's your wages. You earned them.'

Ainslee looked torn.

'Please,' said Nina. 'Please, Ainslee. I don't mean any harm, I promise. I don't want to cause trouble. I just wanted to make sure ... everything was all right.'

Her eye was caught by a sudden movement behind the children; it was a mouse, a huge one. Either a mouse or a rat, she thought. And she knew straight away that she couldn't leave. She looked up at Ainslee, who had clearly come to the same conclusion; she let out a great sigh and heaved her shoulders.

'You can't tell anyone you've been here,' she said.

'Okay,' said Nina, not even bothering to cross her fingers. Something was clearly not working here, and she was determined to find out what it was. 'I'll just come in for a minute . . .'

'You can't.'

'Is your mother here or not?'

Suddenly there was a small noise. It was a tinkling bell. Everyone looked at each other. Ben was hopping up and down, unable to control himself.

'Ainse,' he was saying, tugging her jumper. 'Let her come in! She's NIIIICE!'

Ainslee stared straight back at Nina as if she'd never seen her before.

'I won't stay long,' said Nina, in a calm tone. She needed to be here. She stepped over the threshold.

'Mrs Clark?' she called out softly. 'Mrs Clark?'

And in response the bell tinkled once more.

The sitting room smelled, in the local parlance, foosty; dusty, old and tired. There were piles of papers and books everywhere. Nina looked at them. 'This looks like exam homework to me,' she said. Ainslee shrugged, unsmiling. The nervous, eager-to-please girl from the van had gone. In her place was someone far more truculent and intransigent, and she did not respond. Nina looked around and cleared her throat.

'Um,' she said. 'Where's your mum?'

The door was badly warped, and Nina had to push it quite hard to make it open. The room was at the back of the house, decorated in old pink textured wallpaper, heavy and ridged. There was a smell of talcum powder and, heavier, the scent Nina had detected before and now recognised: the smell of illness.

'Hello?'

As she stepped into the room, the figure in the bed turned its head, painfully slowly. Nina nearly gasped. It was an old woman – wizened and completely ancient. Then she looked closer and realised that the woman wasn't that old, but that her face was marked with deep lines of pain; her neck twisted at a strange angle.

'Hello,' she said in a very soft, gravelly voice, still with the Highland musicality, that sounded as if she was having trouble finding the breath for it. 'Excuse me for not getting up.'

'Are you Mrs Clark?'

'Are you from the social?'

'No,' said Nina.

'The school? I had a word with the school.'

'No, no, I'm not from the school . . . I'm from the book bus.'

'Oh, that van?' said the woman. Her breath rattled as she spoke. She looked intensely unwell. 'I heard about it. It sounds great.'

'I'll ... I'll bring you something to read,' said Nina. She risked a step closer. 'It's just ... it's just I was a bit worried about Ben.'

'Oh he's quite the tearaway,' said Mrs Clark slowly. Every word seemed to be torn from her throat. The room felt oppressive, and Nina's skin prickled. She forced herself to move closer to the bed.

'I'm sorry,' she said. 'But what's wrong with you?'

'MS,' said the woman. 'I have good days and bad days, you know.'

She didn't sound like she had good days. Nina moved closer.

'But you can ... you should be able to get up and about in a wheelchair with MS,' she said. 'Do you have someone coming in to help you?'

'Naw,' came a sharp voice behind Nina's back. She turned. It was Ainslee, eyes bright and burning. 'Naw. We don't need anything like that.'

Nina blinked. 'But some social services care ... someone to help look after you ...'

Ainslee shook her head sternly. 'What, have some interfering old busybody come in and tell me I can't look after my own mum? No chance.'

'That's not what they do,' said Nina. 'They help with the cleaning and—'

'I'm not sixteen,' said Ainslee fiercely. 'You know what they'd do? They'd pack us off to a children's home. Me and Ben, to separate homes. Have you heard what goes on in those types of places?'

Nina nodded. 'But it wouldn't ... it wouldn't be like that.

278

I'm sure they'd do everything they could to keep you at home with your mum, or to keep you together.'

'No they wouldn't,' said Ainslee. 'I can look after her. I can look after her just fine.' Her voice was tight.

'She's a great girl,' said the woman in the bed.

'I know,' said Nina. 'I know she's a great girl, she works for me too. But honestly, she should be sitting her exams. And Ben needs to go to school every day when they start back.'

'I DON'T WANT TO,' came a loud voice from outside.

'I know, I know,' said Mrs Clark, letting out a deep retching cough. 'But I need them so much. When we're all together, we just curl up on the bed, and we don't need anyone else, and we have a nice cosy time. We don't need to go anywhere, do we? They're not nice at that school anyway.'

Ainslee nodded. 'We're fine.'

Nina moved forward. 'There are definitely things that can be done. It can absolutely be better than this, I promise.'

'But I need them,' said the woman plaintively.

Nina shook her head. 'You need help,' she said. 'But not from them.'

'They're my family.'

'They are,' said Nina. 'But they have to have their own lives too.'

There was a silence, and Nina was horrified to see a tear start to steal down Mrs Clark's waxy cheek.

'I'm so sorry,' she said. 'I didn't mean to upset you.'

'No,' said the woman. 'It's all right for you. You're not ill. You haven't got kids who love you. You don't know what it's like.'

Nina shook her head. 'I don't,' she said. 'But there has to

279

be a better way than this. You deserve people who can look after you properly.'

She could feel Ainslee bristling behind her and stood stock still. Mrs Clark sighed.

'Ainslee used to be so good, didn't you, Ainslee? You was happy to do it all. Cleaned and changed the beds and made the dinner ... I don't know why you stopped.' She looked around as if seeing the horrible mess for the first time. 'I don't even know how it got so bad.'

Ainslee let out a sigh.

'Haven't you been making Ben go to school?' said the woman. 'He has to go to school, Ainslee. You used to be so good at it.'

'Aye,' said Ainslee. 'Aye. But that ... that was all I ever did. That was all I was ever going to do. Be your slave. Be stuck here for ever. Cleaning and washing and scrubbing. I don't ... I don't want to do that. I want to do other things.'

She looked angrily at Nina.

'I like working for her.'

Mrs Clark's tears were falling swiftly now. 'But I thought ... you always said you didn't mind.'

'Because I didn't want them to take me away. Or Benny. But I thought ... when I was little, I thought you were going to get better. I didn't realise you were always going to be the same. For ever. I didn't know that. That I was going to be here for ever.'

Both of them were crying now, and Mrs Clark reached out a hand. Ainslee took it, and grasped it, hard.

'We can fix it,' said the woman, looking at Nina. 'Can't we?'

Nina looked around. 'Well I think I know where we can get started,' she said.

She couldn't get Ben to stay in the house with his mother and sister; instead, he trailed after her, asking lots of questions in a frightened voice. Nina tried to placate him as best she could, then finally got him to keep quiet by letting him sit up front in the van, which he absolutely loved. Even better, he saw some of his school friends playing in the swing park, and Nina let him honk the horn so they all turned round and he waved furiously. Nina smiled, seeing how quickly the mood of an eight-year-old could turn.

At the farm, she jumped down and ran into the barn, gathering up all the heavy-duty cleaning materials she'd bought for mucking out the van, and a host of thick black bin bags for good measure. As she was loading them into the back, Lennox strode across the farmyard, Parsley at his heels. He stopped when he saw her, went slightly pink, then cleared his throat.

'Hey,' he said, drawing closer. 'What's all that for? Have you run someone over and are trying to get rid of the evidence?'

Nina flushed too, and told herself not to look at those long, strong, hard-working fingers. Not to think about them and wonder what they could do. No. She wouldn't. Nor his blue eyes, drilling into her.

'No,' she said. She didn't want to explain.

'Is that Ben Clark?' he said, nodding at the front of the van. 'Hey, Ben, how's your mum? Hang on ...'

He disappeared into the farmhouse and reappeared with a bowl of eggs. 'Want to take these to her?'

'You knew about his mum?' said Nina, suddenly enraged.

'What, Mrs Clark? I heard she'd been a bit poorly, but it's nothing too serious, is it?'

'She's completely bed-bound!' said Nina. 'Ainslee and Ben have been covering for her for months … maybe years. Ainslee's a child carer. Didn't you know?'

Lennox looked at her. 'I try and keep out of people's business,' he said. 'Hoped they'd keep out of mine.'

'Hmm,' said Nina.

'Are you do-gooding?'

'Well, you appear to be do-nothing, so I might as well.'

Lennox sniffed suddenly and marched off. Nina watched him go, wishing she hadn't flown off the handle with him. She didn't understand what on earth seemed to get her all riled up every time she saw him.

Ainslee complained bitterly, even when Nina took out her second bag and revealed two packets of chocolate digestives, bananas, tea, ice cream and a large bottle of Irn-Bru.

'The harder you work, the more treats you get,' she said, smiling.

'I'm not four.'

'I know,' said Nina. 'But I'll pay you your wage for this if you like.'

Ainslee immediately sparked up a little, and they rolled their sleeves up and got to it.

Ainslee lifted her mum out of bed whilst Nina stripped

the sheets and hurled everything she could find into the washing machine. Many of the clothes were badly mildewed, and she took away what couldn't be salvaged, or cut it up for rags. She'd find them other clothes somehow.

Once all the rubbish was removed, the house looked miles better already, and they washed, polished and scrubbed, filling bin bag after bin bag that Nina would then take to the dump. Little Ben, grubbier than ever, helped pick up and tidy away, and was even persuaded to put his broken bits of toys into a box when Nina promised him she would get him new ones. She wasn't entirely sure how she'd be able to afford that, but she'd think of something. She got him hoovering and washing windows, where a few streaks here and there weren't really going to matter.

Then she set about, with Ainslee, opening the exhausting forms and official letters that had been dumped and piled up haphazardly on the kitchen table.

'Oh Ainslee,' she said. 'No wonder things are so hard. Look! They're asking for proof of all sorts of things, and they're going to stop your money.'

She picked up one letter asking Janine Clark to attend a fitness-to-work assessment.

'Oh for crying out loud,' she said. 'This is nuts.'

'I didn't know what to do,' said Ainslee. 'I couldn't get her up, and it's two buses away, the assessment centre. I mean, you can't get there for ten o'clock in the morning even if you could walk, and she can't walk. I didn't know ...'

'Why on earth aren't social services more on to you?' wondered Nina. 'You guys have just fallen down a crack. You don't bother anyone and they don't bother you.'

'That's how we like it,' grunted Ainslee.

'But it isn't, though, is it? It hasn't been for a long time.'

Ainslee shook her head.

'It's going to get better,' vowed Nina.

'Don't …' Ainslee was furiously pink. 'I know you've helped us and that, and we are grateful and everything. Bu don't go telling people in the village. I don't want charity. don't want clothes from the charity shop and school uniform from the leftovers bin.'

Nina shook her head. 'I understand. Okay.'

'I don't want handouts. Please.'

'Okay,' said Nina. 'I'll see what I can do. But Ainslee you have to sit your exams. You're such a bright girl and you could do really well. If we manage to get you all se up here, you could go far. And make a much better life fo your mum.'

'Without me?'

Nina had to admit she had a point.

'Well,' she said, 'let's just take it as it comes.'

'It's all right for you to say. You just turned up out o nowhere. You'll probably move on again as well, won't you?'

Nina didn't have an answer to that.

The emergency social workers were tremendous; they breezed in and assessed the situation instantly, making a spe cial point of congratulating Ainslee on the wonderful job she' made of being a carer – and telling her repeatedly that tha was what she was – as well as somehow conjuring up a large box of new Lego for Ben. He sat on his mum's bed, happily putting it together with a skill and concentration Nina would not have expected of him.

She avoided Lennox when she got home, utterly exhausted, grubby to the bone but with a feeling of pleasant exhaustion; of deserving her hot bath. She wasn't going to consider him a bit, she decided. The man had been so wrapped up in his own problems, he hadn't even noticed those on his doorstep.

Chapter Twenty-Seven

The summer stretched on. There were great heaving stormy days, when the clouds lay on the very top of the van, and the rain poured down, leaving the meadow grass bent low under its weight. But equally there were glorious, bursting days, when the sun rose golden and pink ahead, and the wind blew soft and warm, tiny clouds scudding across the sky, rabbits everywhere, and the vast scent of hay rising from the fields and perfuming the air made the whole world feel fresh and washed clean. Most importantly, there wasn't a day when Nina could imagine being anywhere else.

The axe had not fallen yet. Because what had seemed an easy thing to say – of course I'll keep moving; of course I'll go to Orkney – was, she realised, in fact not at all easy. As she tracked down people's favourites, coped with the overspill of the now incredibly well-attended toddler story sessions (she could have done ten a week had she been so inclined) – and struggled to get down the main street without saying hello to about sixty people, in a way that made her think this must be a little what being famous was like, it struck her that it would be very hard to give this place up.

Because despite everything, she couldn't deny it. She was happy.

Ainslee was turning up regularly to work, amazed that social services had been so kind, so understanding and helpful; had actually sent someone round who could help them with the cleaning. Ainslee was so close to her sixteenth birthday, and her mum had made such an effort to be engaged and make sure Ben went to school – she had fervently promised to stop keeping them off and tucking them up in bed with her, although it did mean, Nina had noticed inadvertently, that Ben had the most tremendous in-depth knowledge of 1980s teen movies – that although there was a case conference coming up, it was highly likely that the whole family would be allowed to stay at home together.

Ben now was attending the local summer play scheme every day, more or less; occasionally, on a particularly beautiful day, Nina would notice him heading Tom Sawyer-like for the river and would tip Ainslee off, with a slight tinge of regret at having to curtail his freedom.

He had also caused her to break her most adamant rule; the one she had sworn never to be moved on: to never, ever lend a book. Occasionally she would offer to buy back particularly lovely editions if they were in great condition, but no, she was not a library service. She had to live and eat and pay people. Edwin and Hugh got preferential rates, and Ainslee her staff discount, but everyone else absolutely had to pay, otherwise she couldn't get by.

Except Ben. The child, once unleashed, could not be held

back. He tore through the Faraway Tree books, Harry Potter, the Adventure series, *Swallows and Amazons*; he read like a dam bursting, and Nina couldn't find it in her to deny him a word. He was an endlessly familiar sight that summer when the play scheme was out; running errands for his mum, then settling himself in the sun on the step like a cat.

With the help of the overworked local headmistress, who was just desperately relieved to be on her break and filling it with a selection of books called things like *Breaking out of Teaching* and *My Life as an Astronaut*, Nina was gently and discreetly talking to Ben about how much fun Primary 4 was, and how many people had moved into the village, so there'd be lots of new kids there who really didn't know who anyone was. She told him about the trips they would be going on, and how they did all sorts of amazing things like growing frog spawn into tadpoles and frogs. And when the book bus was quiet – which wasn't often that summer, as the village filled up with walkers and hikers and people who wanted local maps and local history and simply something to enjoy in the sunshine with a pint of local ale, or to keep them company whilst the rain hosed sideways on their tents all night and they decided to spend their next holidays in the Gobi desert – she made Ainslee take out her geography and history textbooks, and work away quietly in the corner of the bus, just a little bit.

Her effort was partly for the family, Nina knew, but more selfishly, and deep down, it was something for her. So that even if her romantic life was a disaster; even if her hopes of staying here turned to dust and she had to move to the islands; even with all of those things, she hadn't done nothing.

Chapter Twenty-Eight

Nina spent less and less time at the farm as the Little Shop of Happy-Ever-After became ever busier. After her first disastrous attempt, which involved quite a lot of thrown raisins and Akela hitting the roof, Reading Cubs had become intensely popular; the toddler group never went out of fashion; and book groups were springing up all over the place. Nina would try and find the best of the absolute best for the groups, rather than suggesting something new and expensive, while the little ones liked absolutely anything by Maurice Sendak.

Imagine, she direct messaged to Griffin one night, *going into a publishers these days and saying, 'I'm drawing this picture book of a young naked boy with his knob out getting baked into a cake – yes, sugar for breakfast – by four Oliver Hardys.'*

You sound weird, Griffin had replied.

I'm working a lot of overtime, she typed back. *I only think in books. So I'm working too hard and it's like* Hard Times, *then I go home and it's* Cold Comfort Farm.

I wish I could think in books, typed back Griffin glumly. *We're not allowed to think about books at all. It's all about social media presence.*

Microserfs?

Oh God, they're all too young even to have heard of it. Everyone is 23 and they keep trying to get me to come nightclubbing.

I thought you were loving all that.

I'm EXHAUSTED, he typed back. *And at risk of alcoholic liver disease. All they do is shout AWESOME at everything. I hope it keeps up till my appraisal. Of course you don't have anything like that to worry about any more.*

No, typed Nina. *No holiday pay either. Or sick pay. Or days off.*

Boo hoo hoo, James Herriot. I've got a ten-page confluence scheduling report to do. And I don't even know what that means!!!!

They'd logged off and Nina had sighed and tried to go back to reading and feel better that way, but all she could find were romantic heroes that reminded her of Lennox if they were gruff and uncommunicative, or Marek if they were sweet and cheerful, until she thought she was going completely mad. She was restless, not sleepy, and decided she could take a walk – she could, she could – down her old paths without getting too maudlin about it. He wouldn't be there, he wouldn't stop, and even if he did, there was nothing more to say. But the exercise might help her sleep; might even give her hope that one day there would be somebody else; that not all romance was dead; that sometimes, maybe, it was just bad timing.

Parsley barked hopefully as she left, but she passed him by and scattered the chickens to wander the lanes by herself. The hawthorn was in full bloom, its scent heavy on the fresh night air. Nina pulled her coat tighter around her and walked on. It was better, she felt, better to be out and about, pondering her future, than sitting indoors in a beautiful home that did not belong to her and soon wouldn't belong to Lennox either; that would be snatched away by a woman who did not want it; who did not want lovely Kirrinfief or the farm or the little mercat cross, or the bunting that festooned the town square in midsummer; who didn't want any of it; who would turn it into money and fritter it away.

Crossly she dug her hands into her pockets. She could look for somewhere else round here, she supposed. But nobody had anywhere apart from a spare room above the pub, which she really didn't want, and certainly it would be nothing like as nice. Meanwhile Orkney had said there was a lovely vacant farmhouse she could rent, all mod cons, super-cheap rent, and by the way if she could bring twenty to thirty thousand other young people to help repopulate the islands whilst she was at it, that would be great, thanks.

She sighed at the dilemma and stomped on. Before she knew it, she was approaching the level crossing, her heart full of regrets.

When she saw the tree, she stopped and gasped.

It was completely covered in books, all tied to the branches with shoelaces, cascading down like low-hanging fruit. It was strange and oddly beautiful, a tree full of books on a deep blue summer's night, in the back end of absolutely nowhere at all.

Nina stared at it. Oh Marek, what on earth have you done? she thought. There was history, fiction, poetry, many of the books in Russian or Latvian, but some in English; several were waterlogged, which meant they had been there for a little while, and some pages had come loose and plastered themselves to the trunk, which had the added effect of turning the tree itself into a huge book made of papier mâché.

As Nina stood back and gazed, entranced, a breeze passed by and the books spun and danced in the wind, paper back to pulp, back to the wood where it had once begun.

'Oh my,' she breathed to herself, and pulled out her phone.

Then she put it away again. No. No, she wouldn't. She couldn't.

She glanced at her watch. It wasn't long. Not long until the train was due. Maybe it couldn't hurt to see him once more before she left. Just to say thank you, maybe? His feelings, she saw now, were much stronger than she'd realised.

But weren't they too just the yearnings of a lonely, romantic heart? And shouldn't two hearts like that be together?

No, absolutely not. There was a little boy involved. There was a family. She wouldn't do that to anyone else's family, she couldn't.

She swallowed hard. SO. She would turn around. She would walk away.

In the distance, she heard the quiet note of the low whistle, the delicate rattling she'd come to know so well, and her heart started to beat in time with the rhythm of the rails.

Chapter Twenty-Nine

It was as if she was frozen to the spot. Slowly the train came up the line, trundling its precious trucks behind it, and throwing caution to the wind, she ducked under the barrier and waved her arms, hugely, flapping them as if she had no idea what she was doing, as the train slowed down and down.

Heart pounding, she tried to think what she was going to say: simply no, or it's not possible, or a proper goodbye, a sad look at chances missed and timing gone wrong . . .

She stood there, stock still now. Blinking. A million different things racing through her mind. Jim was up in the cabin, and she called his name. He didn't look round. He didn't even seem to be stopping. But at last he did, just further down the line, so that Nina was directly facing the very last truck, the one with the little balcony on the back.

Marek was sitting on it, his legs dangling. Not in his uniform: in plain clothes.

She looked up at him. 'Hey,' she said, unsure what to do. 'Hey,' she said again, stepping forward, as he still didn't meet her eye. 'The tree,' she said. 'The tree. It's so beautiful. But ... I mean, it's lovely, but ... '

He stood up. 'Nina,' he said, and his voice was sad and low. 'I came ... I came to say goodbye.'

'Why?' said Nina. 'Why? Where are you going?'

'Oh, I got in trouble. Slowed the sleeper too many times, yes?'

'No,' said Nina. 'They're not ... you didn't lose your job?'

Marek shrugged. 'No picnics on the railway,' he smiled. 'It was all my fault.'

'No!' Nina said. 'You can't! You can't get fired! Won't they go on strike for you?'

A thought struck her.

'Is that why Jim isn't talking to me?'

'He is very cross with you,' said Marek. 'He blame you for everything.'

'Oh God,' said Nina, in agony. 'I'm so sorry. I really, really am, so, so sorry.'

Marek shook his head. 'Was not your fault. Was not Nina.'

'I didn't help,' said Nina miserably, thinking of all the huge favours she'd let him do for her; how she'd encouraged him to play fast and loose with his job. 'Won't the men come out for you, though?'

'Of course,' said Marek. 'I am good train engineer. Who does naughty things sometimes. But ... '

There was a pause.

'Will you get another job?'

'Oh no,' said Marek. 'No, no. No job. I cannot stay in Britain, huh.'

Nina was horrified. 'Oh my God,' she said. 'You're being deported! You can't be deported!'

She swung on to the railway line and climbed up the steps.

'Even this is naughty,' said Marek.

'I don't care,' said Nina hotly. 'They can't deport you. Let me take the blame!'

'Maybe it is time,' said Marek sadly. 'I was fooling myself. Playing that I was in a romance with you, huh? A big story-book romance, like the poets write.'

Nina looked at his huge dark eyes and spiked lashes and felt her own eyes fill with tears.

'But you were right. It was not real. I have a life. Everybody does. And my life is Aras and Bronia. This is pretend life. I want real life.' His face was full of pain.

'You're ... you're going?' said Nina.

Marek nodded. 'Oh yes. I am going home. I will find a job. I can fix engines, many types of engines. There are always jobs for people who can fix engine.'

Nina blinked. 'But,' she said. 'But ...'

Without warning, there was a loud honk. Jim had started to move the engine.

'Goodbye,' said Marek.

Nina stared at him. The great train was starting to move.

'Get down, Nina,' said Marek. 'Get down, it's not safe.'

'But ...' said Nina. The train was starting to gather speed.

'Go!'

She looked at him one last time. Then she jumped, and landed safely by the side of the track, and watched the huge long rolling stock push its way through the valley and slowly slide on, until it was out of sight.

Standing by the railway line, she tried Marek's number with a pounding heart, but there was no answer. She hammered out a text message to him, but again no reply. She rang Surinder.

'I knew this was stupid,' she sobbed down the phone, and Surinder, to her eternal credit, didn't say 'I told you so' when she'd have been well within her rights to do so. 'I thought it was ... well, it was romantic. It was sweet. It was kind of a game.'

'He lost,' said Surinder simply, and Nina burst into sobs again.

She ran all the way back to the farmyard, where Lennox, hearing her footsteps, threw open the door. His tall frame was silhouetted in the doorway, the light glowing behind him in the farmhouse, Parsley at his heels.

'What's happened? What the hell is it?' he said, fear striking his face at her tears, his arms opening instinctively. 'Are you all right? Did something happen?'

He grabbed something from behind the door.

'What's that?' she said, stopping short and staring at it.

Lennox looked at her levelly as she took a step back. 'It's a shotgun. What's the matter with you? Did someone do something to you?'

Nina furiously wiped her tears away and resisted her principal urge, which was to run weeping into his arms, bury her head in his strong shoulder, get him to make everything all

296

right the same way he looked after those damn sheep of his. Instead she tried to pull herself together.

'No,' she said. 'No. Nothing like that.'

She followed his arm as he put the gun down, still slightly shocked that he had had it there.

'It's ... it's Marek ...' she stuttered, dissolving into tears again.

Lennox's face changed utterly: it closed up, like a door slamming shut. His arms slowly lowered to his sides.

'Oh,' he said. 'Girl stuff.'

He turned to go, and Nina wanted to throw something at his head.

'No!' she said. 'You don't understand. He's in trouble.'

'For stopping his train where he shouldn't,' said Lennox. 'Good.'

'But he's lost his job. He's being deported! They're sending him home!'

Lennox turned back and looked at her calmly.

'Maybe sometimes it is time to go home,' he said.

Nina could only stare at him; she couldn't think of anything else to do.

'Oh,' she said.

Lennox gazed at his feet. 'I didn't mean that,' he said finally and with effort. 'I'm sorry to hear about your boyfriend.'

'He's not ... he's not my boyfriend!' said Nina. 'He's just a man, okay? In trouble. For being friends with me. He made a mistake and so did I and we didn't even do anything, not that it's any of your business, and now he's being sent out of the country. Forgive me for thinking you'd give a shit about anything that isn't a fricking sheep.'

She turned away to go towards the barn.

'Wait,' said Lennox, still sounding annoyed. 'What did you think I could do?'

'I thought you might know a lawyer,' said Nina sullenly. 'But forget it. It doesn't matter. You don't care.'

He moved forward. 'I only know a Scottish divorce lawyer,' he said. 'I'm not sure how much use he'd be.'

'Don't worry about it,' said Nina bitterly. 'Sorry to trouble you.'

It took days, but an email finally came from Jim. Marek had gone; flown out on a deportees' flight, with goodness knows how many other unlucky refugees and travellers. Nina sat up long into the night when she got the message, cursing the name she had given her bookshop, wondering whether, in real life, anyone actually got a happy-ever-after.

Chapter Thirty

The clouds were scudding against a bright sun; now that they were past the very peak of midsummer, there was pink once more in the sky, the promise of a proper, protracted sunset rather than a simple fade. Nina was waiting for the axe to fall; for Lennox to lose his farm, the mean old git, and for her to be evicted. It was just a matter of time.

And the stupid thing was, even with everything that had happened, up here in the peace and the wilds of the great valleys and deep lochs of Scotland she had found something that suited her, that soothed her soul: a peace and quiet, a feel for the landscape that she'd never known before, for gentle husbanding and wild creatures, and a sense that things didn't have to change; that skyscrapers didn't have to be thrown up in minutes for foreign investors; that seasons would come and go with the clouds passing across the sky, but also that everything would come around again and find itself much as it had been generations ago, in the farms and the rivers and the towering cliffs and the gentle running valleys, where life did not move so fast that there wasn't time to settle down with a cup of tea and a piece of shortbread and a book.

It was horribly difficult, she reflected, to have finally found the place you thought of as home, only to realise you were going to have to move on again. Maybe she'd be just as happy in Orkney. She'd heard it was incredibly beautiful there, fish leaping from the sea straight to your plate, skies as big as the world, and people thirsty for books ... But every day she followed the familiar road winding down into the valley of Kirrinfief, and found her heart was missing it before she'd even left.

The sun was lying heavy and full, casting rays down the little valley; the cobbles looked warm, the town square was filled with tourists and people flocking around; Edwin and Hugh were outside the pub as usual, no doubt commenting on the world and everything in it.

Lesley was putting fruit out outside the shop, and waved a cheerful hand to see the book bus back again; as did other locals as they saw her drive past, used to her in their midst. Carmen the headmistress honked the horn of her Mini. Nina felt almost tearful at their welcome. A group of boys were playing shinty in the near field; she was surprised beyond belief to notice that Ben was amongst them.

She carried on past the dangling purple bells of the foxgloves that lined the roadway at this time of year and on upwards to the farm.

The sheep were turned out in the lower meadow, the cows in the upper, and the lambs that had been left to grow were almost big enough now as to be indistinguishable from the sheep. Half smiling, Nina recognised little Fluffy, always the runt, with his jagged scar, still lagging behind the rest, completely unable to grow up, trotting around behind Parsley when he could find him. It did her heart good to see him.

No sign of Lennox or Parsley today, though. She was so used to seeing them striding the sides of the hills – two little blobs, one tall and intent, one bounding in a flash – that she could generally spot them from miles away. Not today. She felt nervous. She was going to have to see him at some point. And try not to get angry with him. And wait, of course, for her eviction notice. And move on.

Professionally she had achieved more than she'd ever dreamed possible. Personally ... she had made a hash of it. She thought back to the good advice Surinder had given her before she'd left. No, it hadn't gone right. Things didn't always. But at least she'd put herself out there. At least she'd tried and given it a shot. As Surinder kept saying, everyone's love life went badly until the end. That was just how it was.

And now she'd learned a little, and she'd know what to do if she met any more puppy-dog-eyed men – or at least she'd find out their status before she started flirting with them and sending them poetry – and if she met another grumpy farmer, well, she'd know to run a mile and not let herself get sucked in to thinking about the touch of a hand, a strong masculine body pressing against hers ...

In the midst of her reverie, she was startled to realise that Lennox and Parsley were standing right in front of her.

'Dreaming about books?' said Lennox.

Nina looked around the farmyard. It was suddenly full of farmhands armed with tools and shovels.

'What's up?' she said.

'Thought you'd like to come,' grunted Lennox. 'We're off to the Clarks'.'

'Where?'

Lennox sighed and turned round to the boys. 'Sorry. I told you she was a bit glaikit.'

'I am not whatever that is you just said,' said Nina defiantly.

'Those kids. Ainslee and Ben,' said Lennox. 'I thought you said they needed help.'

Mrs Clark was overjoyed to see them; completely overwhelmed. Nina and Ainslee took down the dirty curtains and stuffed them in the washing machine, while Lennox directed his men, who fixed the broken doors and replaced the glass in the windows. Two of them even started painting the sitting room, whilst someone else went up on the roof to replace all the loose tiles. It was absolutely astounding how much a band of people could get done with a will when they set their minds to it. Nina tried to thank Lennox, who looked at her completely dumbfounded that she would even consider it something worthy of thanks. It needed doing, that was all.

Ben ran about in a fit of delight, trying to help the gardeners and plasterers in turn as they fixed up the tumbledown house, as well as mainlining biscuits and turning Radio 1 up far louder than his mother could normally bear it. The sun beat down – it was incredibly hot – as they worked through the day, barely taking breaks.

Nina glanced over from time to time. It was so hot, Lennox had taken off his shirt, and was splitting kindling for the winter on an old log.

302

'Why have you stopped?' asked Ainslee, as they rinsed the nets.

'Um, no reason,' said Nina.

'Is it that old bloke again?' said Ainslee. 'Oh aye, I see it is.'

'Yeah, all right,' said Nina.

They both watched him for a second.

'Okay, let's get on!' said Nina.

Pushing into the afternoon, Nina noticed with surprise an older gentleman she'd seen before. He was wearing a suit and tie, and she realised it was Lennox's lawyer. He spoke in a low and intent voice to Lennox, who had put the axe down. Lennox's face turned absolutely miserably cross, and he appeared to be swearing under his breath. The lawyer looked apologetic, and turned to go.

As he did so, he glanced up and caught sight of Nina through the window. He held up a hand and popped in through the new kitchen door.

'Ah, hello,' he said.

'Hello,' said Nina, fearing the worst.

'I just wanted to say ... to say I was sorry to hear about your ... your friend. I did speak to the Home Office, you know, but apparently it was voluntary, so there was nothing they could do.'

'You ... you called the Home Office about Marek?'

'Oh yes. Lennox asked if I wouldn't mind ...'

Nina didn't hear any more. She was staring out of the kitchen window. The lawyer took his leave, but she hardly noticed him go.

Lennox had hired Mrs Garsters from the village for when they all trooped back up to the farm, exhausted, at the end of the afternoon. (Mrs Garsters loved books about beetles and was practically an expert; Nina had to repeatedly apologise for her failure to source the most up-to-date *British Journal of Entomology*. She would huff and puff and ask what kind of a service she was, and Nina had to explain that she wasn't a service, she was a business, which didn't seem to placate her in the least.)

Set out on long tables in the courtyard were thick slabs of ham, with piccalilli and mustard on the side; fresh home-made bread, cut roughly, with salty local butter; sweating wheels of white and blue cheese; creamy potato salad, and a cool cucumber and green cabbage salad with fennel, orange and oats, which looked utterly delicious, followed by huge apple pies and warm frothing cream from the dairy.

Nina couldn't remember the last time she'd felt so hungry, but her hands were sore and cracked from all the bleach she'd been using, and before she ate, she nipped into the barn just behind her own conversion; she was sure she'd seen Lennox leave some lanolin there – he used it for softening his own hands and for the sheep's udders – and it was just, she felt, what she needed.

She rubbed the lanolin in, and was just refilling her bottle with water from the cold standpipe that fed directly from the well when she saw him.

She couldn't actually see him at all to begin with; he was silhouetted against the sunlight pouring in from outside the barn, nothing but a tall shape. He could have been anyone.

But he wasn't just anyone. And in a millisecond, everything changed.

She could leave it all behind. She could. She had before. She could do anything she wanted, like the travelling people, like everyone who moved around in the world. But she wanted to experience everything she could. She wasn't going to hide any longer.

She had started with a van. But somehow it had opened her up to so much more. And now she wanted that real life that she felt she had been missing out on; that she felt other people got a shot at while she sat quietly in a corner being nice.

She pressed herself against the wall of the barn, feeling the warmth of the ancient stone on her back. The sweet smell of freshly gathered hay was thick in the air, golden strands breaking off and drifting down from the loft above. Lennox's shirt was half unbuttoned in the tumultuous heat; his chest was hairless.

Nina blinked and realised she'd been wondering about it for weeks. Thinking about it. Dreaming about it. But she hadn't been able to admit it to herself; couldn't admit it to anyone; was scared that it was just her imagination running away with her again, a foolish fantasy about a man she barely knew.

But all she knew now, the one thing taking over her brain completely, was that she wanted – needed – to touch him, and soon. And that there was no one here to judge her or be patronising to quiet little bookish Nina.

'Do you want a drink of water?' she found herself saying, and her voice was breathless and lower than usual.

Lennox advanced into the barn and she held out the bottle of water, condensation running down the outside, and looked straight at him. She tried to smile, but she couldn't. She couldn't move.

His eyes gave nothing away as he advanced towards her; close enough that she could feel the heat of his body; smell the fresh, clean sweat. It made her dizzy. She swallowed hard. He took the bottle without a thank you, and drank from it without taking his gaze off her.

There was a split second to decide, she knew. The tiniest split second in which she could take the bottle, turn away, remove herself. Instead, she did something she wouldn't have known she was capable of: she pressed herself, defiantly, even further up against the wall and stared brazenly right back at him. Her heart was pounding and she couldn't trust herself to speak. She needed the wall to brace herself, in case her legs gave way. She looked at his outline against the brightness of the day, in the cool, quiet sanctuary of the barn, and realised she'd never wanted anything or anyone more in her life, and to hell with everything else: Kate, Marek, the consequences, what might happen next.

She held his gaze in a single timeless, endless moment; an instant trembling in the heat, as though the world had pressed pause; as though she were a shy ballerina waiting to take the stage.

Then Lennox took a brief step backwards and pushed the barn door closed behind him with a loud bang.

What happened next was so quick, it took her totally by surprise, even though she had decided; had clearly and deliberately chosen to be provocative; was thinking of nothing but the fact that this was what she wanted.

But even with that, the speed and ferocity of his kiss was overwhelming. He kissed her skilfully but hard, insistently, as if there was some biding fury in him that he had to work very, very hard to control.

It was by a vast margin the best kiss Nina had ever had. She kissed him back, furiously, realising that up to this point in her life, kisses had always been a prelude; a tease or an exploration; a precursor to what might or might not happen next.

This was not the case here. This kiss was several steps down the line from that; this was serious and purposeful; it was the real thing, and Nina felt the thrill go through her down to the bones.

And when they stopped, momentarily, with a huge rush of disappointment on her part, she felt sure he would apologise, like the gentleman she knew him to be; step back. Everything she knew about Lennox and his taciturn ways made her think that what came next would require discussion, negotiation, embarrassment, possibly; dinner, probably, and her heart sank.

Instead she simply whispered in his ear, 'More.'

'Oh God,' she heard him groan, and he pulled back, breathing heavily, looking at her. Outside, there was noise.

'I have to ... I have to see to the workers.'

Nina nodded, still staring at him.

'Later?' he said shortly, and she wondered why, all along, she had bothered about how little he spoke to her. It didn't feel to her like they needed words at all.

Chapter Thirty-One

The high tea was agony. Or rather, in other circumstances, it would have been entirely marvellous.

The early sunset went down slowly in a bright blaze of pink and gold, and many of the farmhands' wives turned up with extra plates of food to share – great shining pies and sides of ham – as the hungry men and women came in from all around for the party. Huge jugs of cider were filled to the brim and emptied equally quickly; hunks of thick home-made bread with farm butter and local cheese were consumed on the side. Ben and large numbers of other local children ran in and out of the house, chasing the farm cat, who was unimpressed, giving food to Parsley, who was delighted, and stealing nips of cider.

Someone had brought a fiddle, and couples danced up and down the courtyard; songs were sung and jokes were made. Nina and Lennox simply stared at each other, utterly oblivious to everything around them, clumsy and unfocused. Nina felt sure everyone could guess exactly what was going through her mind; she found herself blushing at regular intervals, utterly unable to concentrate, always aware of where he was standing and which way he was facing and how long she would have to wait until the instant they managed to steal themselves away.

At last the dishes started to be cleared away, and by mutual agreement, as soon as was even vaguely polite, they left the revellers and headed to her barn, with its windows facing away from the farmhouse and other prying eyes.

Nina wondered briefly if the sight of the flouncy curtains, the expensive kitchen, the immaculate Scandinavian bed might not make Lennox broody and sad, but still he said nothing; the second they were inside, he grabbed her again and kissed her breathless. Then he led her upstairs and took off her clothes, quickly, expertly, and when they were both naked, he laid her down on the bed.

'You,' she said in surprise, staring at him. 'It's you.'

He held her gaze and looked back at her, his hands caressing her body.

'I think it is,' he said wonderingly, almost as surprised as she was. 'I didn't ... I didn't mean this to happen. I just ... I can't stop thinking about you. Everything about you.'

He held off, his hands either side of her face.

'The look you get when you're reading in your van, and your feet are up and you sit so still, and your face is alight, and I don't know where you are; you could be anywhere, so far away, off in a part of your mind I'll never get to ... It drives me crazy. The way you just came here, just got up, changed your entire life ... I mean, my family's been here for four generations. It would never have occurred to me to do what you did, just to start over and do something different. Amazing. You're such a tiny thing ... you'd never think you had it in you. And that train driver ... that drove me crazy. I'm sorry. I was jealous.'

Nina's heart felt like it would burst.

'I couldn't ... I couldn't let myself ... I couldn't handle another stupid crush, another waste of everything that didn't go anywhere and just left me feeling stupid, and you did treat me like an idiot ...'

'Because *I* am an idiot.'

Nina closed her eyes. 'Kiss me, please. Right now. Hard. The way you do.'

His face darkened. 'Kate,' he said. Nina winced. 'Kate ... she didn't like how I was in bed. Said I was too rough.' His face took on an uncharacteristically vulnerable cast.

Nina looked at him, her eyes misting over slightly as she felt a slight cracking in him.

'Everyone is different,' she said, softly but clearly. 'Everyone is different in what they like. Which is okay. And what I like, I think ... is you. Very much.'

'You don't look the type,' he muttered, plainly embarrassed.

'You can't tell anything about anyone just by looking at them,' said Nina pertly, and stuck her tongue out, which finally elicited a smile from him.

'No,' he said. 'I suppose you can't. Can we stop talking now?'

And they did. Afterwards, there was no laughing or joking or small talk. They simply leaned against each other, out of breath, his head collapsed on the side of her neck, the bristles against her soft skin, a little overwhelmed, almost scared, by what they had done; Nina's heart still beating fast; the tension relieved momentarily but even now building up again, her chest stained a deep red.

That had been something else altogether; a surprise, something inside herself she didn't even know was there.

'Can I stay?' he whispered, finally.

'Yes,' said Nina abruptly, and she didn't say thank you and she didn't say please, because this was a very different Nina in a very different space, and she didn't know how long it would last.

His face, she realised as he tumbled into sleep for a brief interlude, did not relax in slumber as most people's did. She couldn't look at him and admire the prettiness, or the boy he once was, or see a deeper softness beyond his harsh interior, like one could imagine doing with a lover.

No, this was what he was: the steely jaw, the look of utter concentration, whether on the farm or on her. She stared at him in fascination, until he woke up, without a second of confusion, and pulled on her wrists.

'Nina,' he said, as if he was starving for her, and he was; he absolutely was, and as the fiddles and the partying went on late into the night, so did they.

Chapter Thirty-Two

By the fourth day after the party, it was getting ridiculous. They couldn't go on like this. For starters, she was going to end up in hospital, and bankrupt. And secondly, they hadn't spoken at all about what they were actually doing, and that couldn't go on indefinitely.

Because she couldn't help herself. She couldn't think of anything or anyone else at all. She couldn't handle money, she couldn't be trusted to work; she recommended nothing but Anaïs Nin, which raised the minister's wife's eyebrows (although she notably didn't return it).

There wasn't a time of day when he wasn't either working or coming back to find her, wherever she was, which once involved him walking in to the Women's Institute book swap and telling Nina with a completely straight face that his Land Rover required a tow from the van and could she come at once? Nina assumed, given the sensibleness of the nice ladies discussing Second World War novels, that they all thought this was perfectly normal and didn't notice for a second the raised eyebrows and titters as she left and he drove her the shortest distance possible out of town where they couldn't be seen and took her roughly and without preliminaries behind a tree, and she yelled so hard she thought she might die.

Nina found it extraordinary. For a man so closed up in himself, so uncommunicative, he was wildly inventive and varied as a lover, and extraordinarily passionate. It was as if everything he couldn't say he could express in other ways. This was how she was getting to know him, getting to the heart of him. Not through long chats or fancy poetry or shared interests, but through the physicality of him, the same way he worked at one with animals, or the landscape, and never felt the need to question why; he was simply a part of the earth, and so was this.

And she was falling in love with him, she realised anxiously, day by day; she was learning to speak his language, and she couldn't help it, or help herself; she was delirious with it, heady, desperate for him in a way that made her feel utterly vulnerable, and she knew that if he didn't feel the same way, she wouldn't be able to bear it.

'We're so different,' she said down the phone. 'Honestly, it's . . . I don't know. I don't know. It might just be sex.'

'Oh my God, that's everything,' breathed Surinder. 'Tell me more.'

'I don't want to tell you more,' said Nina. 'Firstly, you're disgusting, and secondly, it'll just make me miss it and go over there, and if I don't get some sleep, I'm going to crash the van.'

'I thought he'd be like that as soon as I saw him,' said Surinder.

'You didn't.'

'I totally did. He's the type. I could just tell. All buttoned up and devastatingly sexy underneath. All that repressed emotion.'

'Stop it!' said Nina. 'I can't bear it. I have absolutely no idea what he feels and it's driving me bananas.'

'Oh sweetie,' said Surinder, contrite. 'I'm sorry. I didn't realise ... I didn't realise you'd really fallen for him.'

'I haven't,' said Nina, panicking. 'I haven't. I can't. I won't.'

'Right, that's why you sound completely normal and unfussed when you talk about him. Come on. Did you feel like this about Marek?'

'No,' said Nina. 'But I didn't sleep with Marek.'

'Do you think it would have been like this?'

Nina paused before she spoke. 'Nothing has ever been remotely like this.'

'Well then.'

'We haven't even discussed his ex. He's probably still in love with her. We haven't discussed *anything*.'

'Are you absolutely a hundred per cent sure you're not overthinking this?'

'I might be homeless soon,' said Nina, looking around the lovely little barn, tears plopping on to the expensive sheets. 'Kate's probably awesome. I'm probably just a local distraction. Convenient, that's all. Maybe I've just rushed stuff.'

'It's not your fault. If he's a dick, you need to deal with that. If he's a nice guy going through a hard time, well. Maybe he's worth hanging on for.'

'I think he's ruined me,' said Nina in a small voice. She expected Surinder to tell her to stop being so melodramatic. But she didn't.

Chapter Thirty-Three

'Do you want to go for a walk?'

Lennox looked at her strangely. 'A what?'

It was 5.30 on a clear, blowy Sunday morning. Lennox was getting dressed. Nina was lying exhausted, happily weary, in bed.

'A walk. You know. Enjoy nature and the countryside?'

He blinked. 'By walking up and down it?'

'Uh huh!'

'But that's what I do all day.'

Nina sat up. 'Well let me come! It'll be, like, an outing.'

Lennox frowned. They hadn't, Nina was more than aware, *been* anywhere. Not to the pub, not to the bakery to get delicious sausage rolls and sit outside kicking their heels against the wall like the teenagers did, pastry flaking down for Parsley to grab. They hadn't jumped in the Land Rover and gone for a romantic picnic, or walked hand in hand along the beach …

She looked at Lennox shrugging into a clean twill shirt. It

had to be, she had figured out, several degrees below freezing before he added a jacket. At the door, he leaned down to lace himself into his heavy work boots. He poured coffee from the pot on the stove into an insulated cup; he'd eat breakfast later. Nina watched him as he prepared to leave in silence.

'Not coming then?' he grunted eventually.

Nina leapt up. 'Yes!' she said, piling her clothes on enthusiastically. She grabbed her coat from the peg and chased him outside.

Dawn was breaking, and it was bitterly cold outside. Parsley galloped cheerfully out of his kennel and Nina made a big fuss of him. Lennox disappeared back inside and reappeared with a second cup of hot, sweet black coffee that he passed to her wordlessly.

The waking birds chirruped in the hedgerows as they passed by. Early-morning mist hovered over the fields. Wrapped up snugly, with a steaming coffee cup warming her hands, Nina scampered to keep up with Lennox's long strides as he marched ahead, popping his head into the cows' barn to make sure milking was going ahead properly – Ruaridh nodded quickly when he saw him – then on up to the high fields to check on the sheep's grass and feed. The sun was rising pink in the mist over the far hills, and Nina gasped to see it, but Lennox was simply moving on through his morning: checking that one of the stone walls wasn't crumbling too much; examining a fence for deer damage. As he did so, Nina saw, a few metres away, a fawn, brown-spotted, its head lifting and nose twitching in excitement. It gazed at her for a second, its huge brown eyes luminous, then turned and bounded away.

'Whoa!' she said. 'Did you see that?'

'A deer?' said Lennox incredulously. 'Can't get rid of the buggers.'

'But did you see how lovely it was?'

'Bloody protected species,' said Lennox.

'You have no romantic soul,' said Nina, rather despairingly, watching as he carefully fixed a tiny hole in the fence with a spare piece of wire and some pliers he'd pulled out of a Swiss army knife in his pocket. He looked at her, and she realised she had made a mistake; that she might not have been the first person to say that to him.

'Mmm,' he said.

'I don't mean that,' said Nina. 'I just thought the deer was beautiful.'

Lennox crossly extended his arm. 'You know, the trees from here all the way up to Sutherland … they're centuries old. Go back to Mary, Queen of Scots, and even earlier. And they used to house grouse and hedgehogs and golden eagles and millions of midges and bugs. But oh no, the deer were the prettiest. Everyone watched the film and thought deer were cute and they were the ones that had to stay. So now they overrun everything. They eat the tree roots and they eat the seeds and they eat pretty much everything, which means there are fewer and fewer of those ancient forests left, because the deer destroy all the ancient habitats. So there are no robins and no cuckoos and no adders and no woodlice. But they're not as pretty as Bambi, right?'

Nina looked at him. 'I didn't realise,' she said.

'Didn't read it in one of those books o' yours?'

They headed back to the farm in silence, Nina desperately worried.

'I'm sorry,' she said, back at the farmyard gates.

'What about?' he said.

'Saying you weren't romantic.'

'Oh,' he said. 'I'm not. You coming in?'

'Yes,' Nina said. 'Yes. I want to ... Can we talk?'

Lennox sighed as she followed him into the pretty sitting room. 'You wouldn't rather ...'

'What don't you want to talk about?' said Nina. 'Is it ... is it your ex?'

Lennox looked weary. 'Nina, must we have this conversation?'

Nina looked at him for a long time. Then she shook her head.

'Obviously not,' she said. 'Sorry. I thought this meant something. But clearly it doesn't. When you still can't even say if I'm going to get my marching orders any minute.' She stood up to leave.

'Oh Lord, Nina. I'm not even a single man yet. You must know it's out of my hands.'

'So this isn't anything to you? Fine.'

He looked at her, shaking his head in amazement that she would even talk like this.

'Me neither,' said Nina, regretting the words before they were out of her mouth.

There was a very long pause. Lennox stood up slowly, went to the door and put his boots back on.

'Don't ... don't go,' said Nina, looking at his broad back in consternation. If there was one thing she knew about him,

318

one tiny thing he'd let slip about himself, it was how vulnerable he'd been after Kate had left him. And what had she done but go straight for the heart of that vulnerability; take what he had offered her and reject it for not being enough, just like Kate had done.

'I didn't . . . I didn't mean anything. I didn't.'

'I know,' said Lennox gruffly. 'It's all about the house. But really you want the hearts and flowers and everything like that. That's what you think is important.'

'It isn't! I don't think like that at all!' She looked at him. 'Will you . . . do you want to come round and eat later?'

'Ruaridh and I will probably eat at Alasdair's,' he said, not catching her eye.

She watched him go, and something rose in her, something that threatened to overwhelm her; a flood of emotion and pain. As he ducked through the doorway, she said his name briefly – his first name. She hadn't even known it until he'd told her.

'John,' she said, quietly.

But although he stiffened for a second, he did not turn back.

'You're an idiot.'

'Shut up, I know. He is too, though.'

'You were one first. Why did you have to push?'

'Maybe it's better I know now that he's a sullen bastard.'

'Oh for God's sake, you knew he was like that anyway. Neens, you wouldn't know the real thing if it came up and spat in your face.'

'I wouldn't put that past him either.'

'Nina, WAKE UP!' yelled Surinder, whom she'd woken up. 'It's not about fricking romantic picnics and moonlit walks and story-book stuff! This is real life. Yes, he's difficult and grouchy. He's going through a divorce. He's also sexy, solvent and nice, and until about half an hour ago, he seemed very into you.'

'Oh God.'

'I'm coming up.'

'You can't possibly have any more annual leave.'

'Mmm,' said Surinder.

'What?'

'Nothing,' said Surinder. 'They owe me, that's all.'

'Don't come up. What could you do by being here?'

'Hang out? Buy ice cream to cheer you up? Smack you on the head and tell you to stop being such an idiot?'

'Maybe he'll come over,' said Nina hopefully.

'He doesn't seem the type to beg forgiveness,' said Surinder.

And Surinder was right.

Chapter Thirty-Four

Nina found herself up on her tiptoes late at night, peeking through the kitchen window to see – just to see – if his light was on. They'd barely crossed paths. It seemed crazy that they could have spent the last three weeks utterly naked with one another, completely open; vulnerable and as close to each other as two people could possibly be, and now they were supposed to pass each other on the street and not mention a thing about it. It was completely nuts. Now that Nina had the chance to think about it, she could have beaten herself up for pushing so hard, so soon.

And she wanted him so badly. She missed him desperately. Not just, she realised, the sex, although she missed that like crazy – it was as if she'd never eaten chocolate in her life, then she'd got a taste and now wanted to eat it all the time.

Everything before this, she realised, had been mere fumbles, nice, nervous, gentle, pleasant. They had been black and white, and this had been colour; sex so intense she'd had headaches, or on one occasion burst out crying, and Lennox, not saying anything, had simply held her tight against his chest and wiped away her tears as they fell; had comforted her more than anything ever could, even if she hadn't quite known why she was crying in the first place. Oh Lord, she missed him.

She missed the half-dozen eggs placed on her doorstep from time to time; the home-brewed cider they had drunk in the kitchen. She missed Parsley sniffing around to welcome her home; more often than not now he was out in the high fields with his master, and on the rare occasions he was at the farmhouse, he was so tuckered out he couldn't do much more than cock an eye at the van when she came home. She missed that odd feeling she got with Lennox that whatever happened, whether it was to a lamb, a dog or herself, he would make it all right; he would sort it out. He made her feel more secure than she could ever have imagined.

She had one more look out of the little window, and was just about to draw the curtain and turn away when she caught, for a tiny instant, a reflection on the window across the way and realised that he was looking at her too.

The breath caught in her throat and she stared at him, frozen on her tiptoes, just gazing, feeling a longing, a desperate wanting that threatened to overwhelm all thoughts of sense or reasonableness, that made her want to run across the courtyard . . .

Something clattered suddenly, and glancing down, she realised that she had knocked a plate into the sink, startling herself. When she looked back, he had gone. And she still did not know how long she had left.

t was hard, she thought, this self-realisation business. She could barely read a word, and that was the final straw. He could take away her sex life, he could take away her peace of mind, her hopes for happiness, her home, her livelihood. But NOBODY was taking away her reading.

She should leave, she thought boldly. She should go to Orkney. Start over. She'd done it once, she could do it again. Start from the beginning, away from this whole town, away from the gossip and the prying eyes and the sheer hardship of being in such proximity to someone who had made her feel so much.

She told herself she absolutely was going to go. That it wasn't a case of throwing down her last card – leaving for ever – in the hope that it would force him to see sense, beg her not to go, make everything all right. She was going to stand up for herself. Again.

She threw on a dress it wasn't quite warm enough to wear, applied some lipstick with a trembling hand and, trying to fake a confidence she didn't feel, flung open her front door.

He was standing there, his huge hands on the door frame. She jumped.

'Oh!'

'Nina,' he said, and his face was drawn. 'I can't. I can't do without you. I can't ... I'm sorry. Please. I know I'm ... difficult. I know I am. Give me another chance. I just want another chance. Please ...'

He didn't need to say another word. Nina grabbed him tightly and went to pull him to her, knowing that whatever was happening, she couldn't let him go, couldn't get him ou of her system; he was in there, whether she wanted him to be or not, and she no longer had the slightest choice.

She crushed her body to his, and he held her so tightly i nearly knocked the breath out of her. Her heart was pound ing, and suddenly something in her crashed down, something she hadn't seen coming; something for once that wasn' comparable to anything she'd read in a book or dreamed o fantasised about.

He moved towards her achingly slowly, and she stretche up to him with longing, prolonging the delicious secono before she could feel him, taste him once more, and he smile at her, knowing exactly what she was feeling and exactly wha it meant.

Then all of a sudden he jerked back, and she heard it too tyre tracks on the farm road. She smiled ruefully, assuming it was a feed supplier or the vet, but he shook his head; he obviously recognised the sound of the car. He stepped back his face distraught.

'Oh Nina, I'm sorry,' he said, although she didn't realise what he meant straight away. 'I'm so sorry.'

And into the courtyard, scattering chickens as it went came a white Range Rover Evoque, skidding to an ungainly stop.

Chapter Thirty-Five

Nina watched from the shadows of the barn as the woman emerged.

She was, amazingly, pretty much exactly how Nina had thought she would be: blonde, with curly hair, slightly boho in style. Gorgeous, in fact. She didn't look like she fitted with Lennox at all, although when they were standing together, Nina could suddenly see it, his height and his lean, broad-shouldered physique showing off Kate's sleek curves very well. They made an attractive contrast.

Nina stiffened as Kate kissed him on both cheeks. She didn't know what to do. Hiding seemed ridiculous. Should she march out and demand to be introduced as Lennox's girlfriend? That was even worse; it wasn't at all what she was, and it felt like the most ridiculous word to describe what they were going through, a silly, childish term that came nowhere near describing what she felt when he was near her: like sunshine and a storm all at once, tearing through her. She swallowed, feeling her heart race.

Then Kate was marching towards her, smiling, showing very nice teeth. Nina felt incredibly awkward. In another life, in another world, she liked this woman, although she was nothing like her. Now all she could see was what she lacked next to her; not just the carefully mismatched style, or the barely there make-up, which even Nina knew took every bit as much effort as the more obvious look. No, it was the sense of shared history: Kate and Lennox striding the streets of Edinburgh together, arm in arm, building a world together, loving each other enough to get married. The idea of Lennox standing up in front of a crowd of people and saying 'I do' made her feel very strange, and deeply jealous and wrong-footed.

'Hi,' said Kate, disarmingly warm, but with calculation behind the greeting. Nina felt sized up, from the provenance of her shoes to her slightly bitten nails, a habit honed over hours of holding a book in one hand. 'Can I come in?'

She tried to remember that this woman was coming to take away what she had undeniably come to think of as her home; the only place she wanted to be, the only job she wanted to do, the only man she had ever wanted right down to the very bones of her soul.

Kate looked around dismissively at the piles of books Nina had managed to accumulate in the immaculate bookshelves; at the scatter cushions she'd bought for the minimalist sofa.

'Like what you've done with it,' she said, in a tone that seemed to indicate a joke but obviously meant anything but.

'Um ... I know ... I mean, I know I'm not on a long lease or anything,' said Nina, wondering why she was kowtowing to this person even as she had the power to ruin her.

e seen. Lennox was standing with his hands outstretched in gesture of supplication. Kate was red in the face, her beauful blonde curls bouncing everywhere. Nina didn't feel she uld drive through them, so she halted the van and got out.

'What's this?' Kate was screaming, gesticulating towards ne van. 'Did you buy it for your fancy woman? Who you've 1stalled in MY FUCKING BARN.'

Ah, thought Nina. What was meant to be the calm nd organised settling of things had obviously escalated nexpectedly.

'What the hell?' screamed Kate as Nina approached. 'Who ne hell are you? I thought you were a mouse. A quiet little 1ouse who doesn't cause any trouble, not someone who 1oves in on other people's husbands!'

Nina stood her ground. 'I thought you were getting a ivorce.'

Kate sniffed. 'Well, he's impossible. You must have seen it. Ie has absolutely no soul. No poetry. How could you bear it?'

She walked slowly round to the back of the van, snorting s she saw what was written on the side.

'Little Shop of Happy-Ever-After! Ha ha ha. Very fricking 1nny. There aren't very bloody many of those.'

Nina bit her lip. She didn't want to admit that she thought ate might well be right.

Kate moved on, walking through the farmyard as if she wned it. Nina didn't want to ask her whether she actually id. Lennox was standing stock still, watching fearfully.

'So what do you do, just drive around looking for vulnerble marriages?'

'Stop it, Kate.' Lennox's voice was curt.

329

'Why? I'm entitled to ask a few questions, aren't I? Thoug
I know you'd much rather I vanished for ever and lived in
hole in the ground and never bothered you again.'

'Kate, we've been through this.' His voice was weary
'This is my family farm. It's my birthright.'

'It's all you've ever done, blah blah blah. Yes. Which is wh
you're such a boring miserable old bastard who can't take
holiday or sit through a play or enjoy a night in a restaurant c
do anything even remotely fun, ever.'

'I'm just not that kind of person.'

'How would you even know, stuck here all the time? Ol
obviously with company. Seriously, Lennox, you couldn
even be bothered to go half a mile from your own front doo
I never had you down as lazy.'

'Don't talk about her like that.'

Kate rolled her eyes. 'I think that calculating madam ca
look after herself.'

'ENOUGH.'

Lennox strode forward, furious. Kate smiled back. Sh
obviously knew exactly how to push his buttons, Nin
thought. She was so beautiful and lovely and talented; s
confident – all the attributes Nina longed for, everything sh
had always envied in others – and yet here she was, screamin
and yelling in pained fury. It was truly strange.

Kate stepped right up to Nina.

'Let's have a look at your little hobby, shall we? It's all righ
for *her* to have a little hobby, I see, Lennox. It was just m
daubings you didn't like.'

'No,' said Lennox. 'It's that you wouldn't stick at any
thing. One day it was ceramics, then it was painting, then i

was pottery, then it was interior design. You never followed anything through.'

'That's because I didn't have any support at home. You were out all bloody hours, leaving me stranded here.'

Lennox looked sad. 'You used to dream of living here,' he said quietly.

'Yes, shows what an idiot I was.'

Kate opened the door of the van. Nina stood by and let her. She didn't want to get in front of anyone in a mood like this.

Kate stepped in and saw the soft grey walls, the lovely displays, the chandelier. She paused suddenly and turned back, looking enquiringly at Nina.

'Oh,' she said. 'Oh. This is ... ' She ran her hands along the shelves. 'This is lovely.'

The way she touched the books, Nina could tell she was a reader. She could always spot them, even the furious ones.

'Oh,' she said again. 'You run all this yourself?'

'I have some help,' shrugged Nina quietly. But Kate had stopped just next to the little cash box. Her mouth had fallen open.

Nina peered into the van to see what she was looking at.

'I haven't ... ' Kate started, and then stopped again. 'I haven't seen that for years.'

It was the last, very sticky copy of *Up on the Rooftops*. Kate's face softened, and suddenly Nina could see the child she must have been: pretty, petted, spoiled. She reached out a hand.

'May I?' she said, and Nina nodded.

'This is exactly the edition I had,' Kate breathed, carefully turning the pages.

331

'Yes, I was lucky to find them,' said Nina. 'It's beautiful isn't it?'

'Oh! Here's where the pigeon loses his leg and they make him a new one out of a lolly stick.'

Nina smiled.

'Here's the whispering gallery.'

'That always terrified me, that bit.'

Kate nodded. 'God, yes. And Galleon's Reach . . .'

'Every time I read it, I didn't think they'd make it.'

Kate held the book. 'Can . . . can I . . .'

'That's my last one,' said Nina. 'I can't part with it, I'm sorry.'

'Oh,' said Kate. 'Oh.'

'I kind of share it with . . . I share it with one of my other customers.'

'But I want it,' said Kate, pouting prettily.

Nina looked at her. She was obviously used to getting what she wanted. Always.

'You can't have it,' she said gently. 'It belongs to somebody else.'

They looked at one another for a long time.

'Oh God,' said Kate, sinking into one of the bean bags. 'I am SO SICK of all this. So sick of it.'

Nina nodded. 'I understand. I really do. What's the sticking point?'

Kate sighed. 'My lawyer said to push for the whole farm. Then we'd come to a settlement in the middle.'

'Do you really want a farm?'

'Fuck no, what would I do with it? But he just keeps saying no, you can't have the farm. No discussion. So fricking stubborn.'

Nina half smiled. 'Oh, I can see that happening. Doesn't he make you a counter-offer?'

'He says he's waiting for one from us. But my lawyer is adamant. And meanwhile, everything will just get swallowed up in costs.'

'Oh for goodness' sake,' said Nina. 'Just ask him ...'

She suddenly realised what she was about to say. But they had to end this, didn't they?

'Why don't you ask him for the barn? I bet you could sell that, or rent it, and then you could live wherever you liked.'

Kate frowned. 'But if he said no to that, I really would be losing.'

'He wouldn't,' protested Nina. Lennox was, it was becoming increasingly clear to her, taciturn, stubborn, bloody-minded ... but more than anything, underneath his crusty exterior, he was kind. Fundamentally and deeply. She believed that. She liked it more than anything else about him.

Kate looked at her. 'Do you think?'

I think you two need your heads knocked together, Nina thought but thankfully managed not to say.

She went back outside to where Lennox was pacing the yard furiously, Parsley trying to get his attention to cheer him up, but failing.

Lennox looked at her gloomily. 'Do you think I should just give her the farm?' he said. 'I know I can do something else ... probably.'

'Don't be silly! She doesn't want the farm. She was just starting from that standpoint to negotiate.'

'That's why Ranald said to play hardball.'

'Well you've been playing stupidball. Why don't you just offer her the barn?'

Lennox frowned. 'I don't want her living next door.'

'She isn't going to live next door, you moron. She'll sell it or rent it as a holiday cottage for loads of money.'

Lennox looked at her. 'But where will you go?'

'Can we manage one problem at a time, please?'

Lennox sighed. 'Seriously? You think that might work?'

'Go into the van and sort it out,' said Nina. 'Now. Quickly, before those evil lawyers ruin everything.'

Nina sat on top of a low sun-warmed stone wall in the courtyard. Parsley came over and put his head in her lap.

'I know,' she said, stroking his ears. 'Me too, Parse. Me too.'

Everything inside the van was quiet, and they were in there for a long time. Nina let out a great sigh. What on earth were they doing? Getting back together? Talking about their future? Had Lennox just signed everything over to her the second he saw her? Oh Lord. It was getting cold, too.

Eventually, Lennox emerged, pale-faced. He glanced at Nina and nodded.

'Well?' said Nina.

'I said ... I hope you don't mind, but I said she could have the barn. I'm so sorry, Nina.'

Nina sighed. She left a little space for him to say, 'So would you like to move into the farmhouse?' but of course he didn't, and why would he? They'd only been together a few weeks, and they hadn't even managed to have a conversation about what they were doing. So. Of course not. She thought once again of the Orkneys, and felt her throat go dry.

'Oh,' said Lennox casually. 'Also, there was one of your books she wanted.'

She looked up at him, startled. 'Did you give it to her?'

He looked at her. There was a long pause.

'Of course not,' he said shortly. 'I told her she'd have to kill me to get one of your books.'

She gazed at him, and then smiled, the tension broken.

'Um ... tea?'

At that exact instant, her lovely last remaining copy of *Up on the Rooftops* came soaring through the air, thrown with tremendous force; hit the damp wall and fell straight into the muddy horse trough. Lennox and Nina turned in shock to look at it as Kate came storming out of the van, a malicious look on her face.

'You don't get everything you want. Not bloody everything.'

And she jumped into her car and drove away.

They tried to retrieve the book, but it was irredeemably ruined.

'I'm so sorry,' Lennox said. 'I'll get you another.'

'They're like hen's teeth,' said Nina. 'Oh well. Maybe it was better in my memory anyway.'

They looked at one another.

'Can you come in?'

Lennox shook his head. 'I'm not finished. There's something else I have to do today; I promised Nige. His chainsaw's broken.'

'What is it?'

He shook his head. 'You won't like it. It was thinking about the job that made me ... made me want to see you.'

'Can I come with you?'

'If you like.'

They sat in silence on the way. Parsley rested his head on Nina's knees, his big eyes looking up at her. Nina didn't know where they were going until they turned down a familiar wild-flower-lined lane.

'What?' she said, her heart beating dangerously fast.

'It's ... it's that tree,' said Lennox, looking at her carefully. 'It's diseased. It has to come down. It's a hazard. I did warn you.'

Nina bit her lip. 'I see,' she said. She prodded her heart to see how she felt. Sad, she realised, but not heartbroken.

While Lennox took an axe and a chainsaw from the back of the Land Rover, Nina walked down the track towards the tree. Marek's books were piled up against the trunk, but as she got closer, she noticed something else. Little plastic models of books; book key rings; book icons hanging from every branch, with names on them: Elspeth and Jim for ever. Callie loves Donal. Kyle+Pete 4EVA.

'Where did all these come from?' she said, amazed.

Lennox stared at it, shaking his head. 'People are mad,' he said. 'Honestly. Who does this?'

But Nina was walking around the tree, exclaiming in delight.

'It's ... Lovers come here,' she said. 'Like the bridge of padlocks in Paris. Look! They leave little books! And models of books! And poems! But how did they even hear about it?'

336

The tree jangled gently in the wind.

'Someone must have spread it about. Oh, wow . . .' She smiled. 'I think Marek would have liked it.'

'Do you think about him a lot?' Lennox said gruffly.

'No,' said Nina. 'And I won't talk about it any more. But no.'

Lennox was standing there with his chainsaw.

'You can't!' she said. 'You can't cut it down now! Look at it!'

'I have to. It's sick.'

'But it's beautiful.'

'Nina,' said Lennox. 'This tree is dying. It needs to be removed. It's eaten itself up from the inside. It could fall on the road. It could fall on the tracks. It has to go.'

'But . . .'

He shook his head. 'Not everything in the countryside is lovely. Beautiful things can be dangerous too.'

Nina nodded. 'But all the books . . .'

'I swear you think books are alive,' said Lennox.

'Because they are,' said Nina.

Lennox strode forward and grasped her round the waist. He pushed her against the side of the tree and kissed her fiercely and deeply.

'As real as this?' he said.

Nina looked up into his eyes and smiled wickedly.

'In a different way,' she said.

Lennox kissed her again.

'What about now?'

'You know, I think people can love more than one thing.'

Lennox pulled back.

337

'What did you say?'

Nina realised instantly what she had said. Her hand flew to her mouth and she went bright pink.

'Oh, I didn't . . .'

Lennox looked at her seriously underneath the book tree.

'Do you mean that?'

Nina felt so embarrassed she could hardly speak.

'I don't . . . I mean . . .'

He paused.

'I mean . . . could you?'

Nina looked up into his deep blue eyes.

'I . . . I'd like to,' she whispered softly, and he leaned down and kissed her again, and his soul was in it.

Later, she moved away from the tree.

'You're not going to cut it down now, are you?'

He grinned. 'Yes! Do you never listen?'

'I never listen.'

'Okay, well, it's a good thing I don't talk much then, isn't it?'

Nina turned to look at the tree.

'I'll be in the car. I can't watch.'

'It'll burn nicely for us. In the wintertime,' said Lennox. Nina glanced up enquiringly, but he didn't elaborate.

As the chainsaw roared, she hugged Parsley in the car, rocking him back and forth and occasionally going 'oh my God, oh my God' in his ears. She watched Lennox's broad back as he worked, content to do nothing but look at him, even if her heart was saddened when she saw the beautiful tree come down.

Lennox loaded the Land Rover up with logs as the day faded.

'It looks all bare there now,' she said.

'Yeah, but they'll have the new one there in a couple of days.'

'The what?'

'The new tree ... You didn't think we'd just leave a hole in the earth?'

'I don't know,' said Nina, whose head felt jumbled up like a washing machine.

'Well you don't know much about farming, then. There'll be a new tree planted, a sapling probably. Or maybe a bit older. Anyway. Something nice that isn't utterly riddled with disease.'

'Wow.'

'Maybe your idiots can come and stick their books on that.'

'Maybe they will.' Nina smiled.

'You look happy,' said Lennox.

'I am, very,' said Nina, looking at him. 'Are you all right?'

Lennox nodded. 'I'm happy too.' Then he said something very surprising. 'I was thinking of taking some time off.'

'You?' said Nina in utter surprise.

'Aye. I never do normally. And it hasn't worked out very well for me.' He looked awkward. 'Anyway. Ruaridh can run this place just as well as I can; it's time he stepped up a bit more. And I was thinking, well. I've always wanted to take a look at Orkney.'

Nina shot him a sharp look.

'Or. I mean. Doesn't have to be Orkney. Just a little trip. But if you were going to be in Orkney, well. I might come up.

Because … Christ, Nina. I … I don't think I can do without you.'

Nina smiled. 'I don't necessarily have to go.'

He looked at her. 'I thought you said you had an offer of work there.'

She shook her head. 'I was hoping … I was hoping for a last-minute reprieve.'

'But I let Kate take the barn … your home.'

'If only there was somewhere else I could live,' said Nina.

He looked at her. 'You mean the farmhouse?'

'It's a bit early … I mean, we barely know each other.'

Lennox frowned. 'Aye, we do.'

Nina laughed.

As they pulled into the driveway, chickens scattered everywhere. Lennox parked carefully and they both got out of the car.

'What do you think?' he said cautiously.

Parsley jumped down, ran to Nina and then to Lennox. Nina glanced at the van.

'I'd need to bring it down. Park it outside the house.'

Chapter Thirty-Six

The winters were colder and darker than Nina could ever have imagined. Out here there were no street lights, nothing between her and the thick dark blanket of sky that had rolled in during October and showed no signs of going anywhere until the springtime. Some days it barely got light at all; the trees were hung with sharp fingers of frost, the roads thick with snow, impassable to all but the Land Rover; the livestock blew out thick puffs of steam; the storms drove the hail hard against the windows. There was almost nothing to do except hunker down, conserve your energy, waiting for the darkest months to pass.

She absolutely loved it.

She lay in front of the wood-burning stove, soup warming on the Aga, thinking happily of Ainslee, who had rushed in to work for an hour that morning, then rushed off again, explaining that she was earning extra money tutoring in her spare time and it paid a lot better than Nina did, which was true. Nina was waiting for Lennox's tread in the hallway, the careful way he took off his boots.

They had indeed gone to Orkney and had the most wonderful time stuffing themselves with scallops and black pudding and oysters, and sleeping in a creaking fisherman's cottage and sailing in the great bays and making love through the night. There wasn't a day when Nina didn't want to know this quiet, thoughtful man more and more, and when they finally decided to return to the home they both loved so much, it was the easiest thing in the world to move in to the lovely austere farmhouse, start to make it cosier and softer, as Kate put the barn on the market. Nina sent Surinder the spec every day. Just in case. She was coming up to have a look at the weekend. Just in case.

There was a different tread to Lennox coming in tonight; she and Parsley both sat up in anticipation. He came in looking slightly shamefaced.

'What?' said Nina, watching him with a smile on her lips as he came over and kissed her.

'Nothing,' he said guiltily.

'What?!'

'I've been thinking ... well, if there's maybe something in all this reading business.' And he unpacked an absolutely pristine copy of *Up on the Rooftops*.

'Where on earth did you get that?' said Nina in delight.

Lennox grinned. 'I have my methods,' he said.

They ate supper and he poured them both a peaty-tasting whisky, then she sat in front of the fire and he lay on the floor with his curly head in her lap and smiled up at her, and Parsley came and lay alongside, and Nina felt the warmth and contentment and happiness roll up and crest over her like a wave.

'Well,' she said. 'Once upon a time there were three children. And their names were Wallace, Francis and Delphine ...'

Exam Board

Results 2016/Torthaí scrúduithe 2016

Name/Ainm: CLARK, Ainslee Aurora

Date of birth/Latha breith: 14/9/2000

District/Céarn: Highland

Examination Results National 5

ENGLISH   A band 1
HISTORY   A band 3
MATHEMATICS   C
ART AND DESIGN   B
GEOGRAPHY   B

Acknowledgements

n my career, I have been lucky and unlucky in my editors; ucky because throughout my career they've been some of the most inspiring, amazing women I've ever met, and nlucky because the second I get them they immediately get romoted to become head of the world and leave. I'm never ure whether to feel pleased or paranoid about this. Anyway, Maddie West, my new editor, is utterly jolly brilliant, and I m feeling very lucky right now.

Thanks also at Little, Brown to: Charlie King, Jo Wickham, Emma Williams, Thalia Proctor, David Shelley, Ursula MacKenzie, Amanda Keats, Felice, Jen and the sales team, nd the whole team; the indispensable, irrepressible and wholly xtraordinary Jo Unwin, and thanks also to Orbit and LBYR or being so holistic. I absolutely hate the word holistic, I don't now why I used it. But you know what I mean.

Ben Morris, whose beautiful and much-missed dog arsley's name I borrowed here, and Alison Jack for Nat 5 nfo.

A very special thank you to everyone in Scotland who welcomed us home this year with such kindness. It has been so appreciated. Could you turn the rain off now please? That'd be great. Thanks!

Also Mr B: there's a lot of you in this one. So glad you won't read it ;)

Read on to enter the charming
Bookshop on the Shore . . .

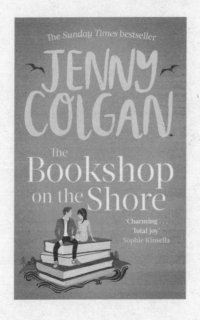

PART ONE

'The view from up here is different,' said Robert Carrier, extending his wing. 'When you look at things the same way you've always done, nothing changes. When you change perspective, everything changes.'

'But this doesn't look like the city at all,' said Wallace in amazement. 'It's all sky.'

'Quite,' said Robert Carrier, fixing his beady eyes on the slightly grubby boy. 'There are many different types of sky.'

From *Up on the Rooftops*

Chapter One

So, tell me about the crying?'

The woman sat, kind but formal, behind the tatty scuffed old NHS desk. A poster on the wall suggested a confusing acronym that you would have to remember if you thought you were having a stroke.

The idea that you would have to remember an acronym while also having a stroke was making Zoe very anxious, even more than being there in the first place. There was a dirty Venetian blind just about covering a bunker window that only looked out onto another red brick wall, and coffee-stained rough carpet tiles.

'Well, mostly Mondays,' Zoe said, taking in the woman's lovely shiny dark hair. Her own was long and dark too, but currently tied roughly with something she hoped was a hair tie and not, for example, an elastic band dropped by the postman. 'And, you know. When the tube is late or I can't get the buggy in the carriage. Or someone tuts because I'm trying to get the buggy in because if I don't take the buggy I'll be an hour late even though he's too big for it and I know that, thanks, so you can probably stop with the judgemental looks.

'Or when I'm caught up at work and I can count every minute of how much it's going to cost me by the time I've picked him up and it makes the entire day's work worthless. Or when I think maybe we'll take the bus and we just arrive at the stop and he shuts the doors, even though he's seen me, because he can't be arsed with the buggy. Or when we run out of cheese and I can't afford to get more. Have you seen the price of cheese? Or ...'

The woman smiled kindly while also looking slightly anxious.

'I meant your son, Mrs O'Connell. When does *he* cry?'

'Oh!' said Zoe, startled.

They both looked at the dark-haired little boy, who was cautiously playing with a farm set in the corner of the room. He looked up at them warily.

'I ... I didn't realise,' said Zoe, suddenly thinking she was about to cry again. Kind Dr Baqri pushed over the box of tissues she kept on the desk, which did the opposite of helping.

'... and it's "miss",' said Zoe, her voice wobbling. 'Well, he's fine ... I mean, a few tears but he doesn't ...' Now she knew she really was going to go. 'He doesn't ... make a sound.'

At least, thought Zoe, after she'd cleaned herself up, slightly gone again, then pulled herself back from the brink as she realised to her horror that the NHS appointment they had waited so many months for was nearly up and she had spent most of it in tears and looking full of hope and despair at Dr Baqri, Hari now squirming cheerfully in her lap. At least Dr Baqri hadn't said what people always said ...

'Einstein, you know ...' began Dr Baqri, and Zoe groaned internally. Here it came: '... didn't talk till he was five.'

Zoe half-smiled. 'I know that, thanks,' she said through gritted teeth.

'Selective mutism ... has he suffered any trauma?'

Zoe bit her lip. God, she hoped not.

'Well, his dad ... comes and goes a bit,' she said, and then slightly pleadingly, as if wanting the doctor to approve of her, added, 'Th-that's not unusual though, is it? You like seeing Daddy, don't you?'

At the mention of his father, Hari's little face lit up as it always did, and he poked a chubby finger enquiringly into her cheek.

'Soon,' she said to him.

'When's the last time you saw him?' asked the doctor.

'Um ... three ... six ...'

Zoe tried to think back. Jaz been gone all summer, truth be told. She constantly told herself to stop following his Instagram feed, but it was like a nasty addiction. He'd been to about four festivals. There were lots of shots of him in different multicoloured hats.

'Well,' said the doctor, who had played a sharing card game with Hari, taught him how to click his fingers, played peekaboo with him and got him to find things she'd hidden around the place, all of which the four-year-old had tried to do, nervously and constantly tearing back to clamber in his mummy's lap, his dark eyes round and scared.

'It's a social anxiety disorder.'

'I know.'

'It's very unusual –' The doctor examined her notes. ' – for a child not to speak even to a parent. Is there anything about the home he finds unsettling?'

They lived on the ground floor of a horrible Victorian conversion on a main road in Wembley. The pipes clanged; the upstairs neighbour often came home drunk and blared music deep into the night. Sometimes he brought friends home who would bang on the door and laugh loudly. Getting the money together for a deposit on a new place – not to mention paying the rent – was a pipe dream. The council had offered her a B&B which she thought might be even worse. Her mum couldn't help – she'd moved to Spain years ago and was finding it more expensive day by day, eking out a pension in sterling and working in a horrible bar with pictures of fried eggs in the window.

Also, since she'd accidentally got pregnant with Hari, Zoe had spent a lot of time pretending she was fine, that everything was okay to her family and friends. She couldn't bear facing up to how serious everything really was. But it was having dramatic consequences.

Dr Baqri saw Zoe's face.

'I'm not . . . I'm not blaming you.'

Zoe's lip started to wobble again.

'You know,' said Dr Baqri. 'You seem well bonded. He's timid but I don't think he's traumatised. Sometimes – sometimes it really is just one of those things.'

There was a very long pause.

'That,' said Zoe, in a low voice, 'is about the nicest thing anyone's said to me for ages.'

'We normally start on a system of rewards for effort,' said Dr Baqri, handing her wads of charts and lists of goals. 'Nothing but encouragement, of course. Something nice for a whisper . . . a treat for a song.'

Zoe blinked, trying to figure out where money for treats would come from when she was already terrified of what they'd do when it got too cold for Hari to wear his summer sandals every day.

'We could try medication if this doesn't work.'

Zoe just stared at her. Drugging her beautiful boy. This was the end of the line – literally: it had taken them two hours to traipse across London on a boiling day to see a consultant-level speech therapist, the waiting list they'd been on having taken eight months to get them there.

'Do you talk lots to him?' said Dr Baqri.

'Uh-huh,' Zoe said, finally glad there was something that didn't appear to be her fault. 'Yes! I do do that! All the time!'

'Well, make sure you're not talking too much. If you understand everything he needs and wants, there's no motivation. And that's what we need.'

Dr Baqri stood up. Seeing Zoe's stricken face, she smiled.

'I realise it's hard that there's not a magic bullet,' she said, gathering up the booklets.

Zoe felt the lump in her throat again.

'It is,' she said.

It was.

Zoe tried to smile encouragingly at her little boy. But as she sat on those two crowded, noisy buses, schoolchildren shouting and screaming and watching videos loudly on their phones and kicking off, and too many people crammed on, and the bus moving painfully slowly, and Hari having to sit on her lap to make room for other people and giving her a dead leg, and trying to count up what it had cost, her missing another shift, and how her boss Xania was really at the end of her tether, because she kept taking time off, but she couldn't lose this job – everything just seemed so overwhelming. And even when they finally got home, closing the grubby woodchip internal door behind them, Hari stumbling with tiredness, there was a letter lying on the mat in the post that was about to make everything substantially worse.

Chapter Two

'Who did you rent the barn out to? Can't they help?'

Surinder Mehta was sitting in the kitchen of her little house in Birmingham on the phone trying to give constructive advice to her friend Nina, who was doing that usual thing people do when you give them constructive advice – rebutting all of it point by point.

Nina ran a mobile bookshop in the Highlands of Scotland. This was about to become temporarily tricky given that she had also fallen in love with a very attractive farmer, and it had been a particularly long, dark and cosy winter and frankly, these things happen. Up in Scotland, she stroked her large bump crossly. They hadn't got round to putting it on the market.

'They're farmhands! They're busy!'

'There must be someone who can help. What about that girl who used to tidy up for you??'

'Ainslee's at college now. There's just ... Everyone around here already has three jobs. That's what it's like here. There's just not enough people.'

Nina looked out of the farm window. It was harvest and all hands were on deck. She could make out distant figures in the fields, bent low. The light was golden, the wind rippling through fields of barley.

She'd been spared harvesting this year but was still going to have to cater for quite a lot And so she'd come back to the farm to make soup for everyone working late.

'Well,' she said finally. 'Think about it.'

'I'm not giving up my job to cover your maternity leave!' said Surinder. 'That doesn't mean I don't love you, so don't twist it.'

Nina sat in the kitchen after they hung up, sighing. It had all started out so well. She remembered the day: Lennox had been up overseeing the lambing in the upper field; spring had been late and a lot of the lambs had had to show up in harsh conditions, born into lashing sidewinds and in many cases snow. She wasn't absolutely certain of how Lennox would react. He'd been married before and she didn't want him to think she was demanding anything – she was perfectly happy how they were. And he wouldn't want a fuss; bells and whistles were absolutely not his style.

She was so distracted at the book van that day she tried to resell Mrs McGleachin the same Dorothy Whipple novel twice, which would have caused a minor diplomatic incident. She also gave out the wrong mock exam workbooks, likewise, and found herself scrambling *What to Expect When You're Expecting* behind her back every time someone came up the steps to the little book bus, with its swinging chandelier and pale blue shelves, the beanbag corner for children and the tiny desk, which now had a contactless point of which Nina was incredibly proud (when it worked, if the Wi-Fi was blowing in the right direction) and many of the older residents of Kirrinfief denounced as witchcraft.

Finally, Nina had driven the van over the hill, checked the stew she'd left in the slow cooker that morning and greeted the weary Lennox with a soft smile and a deep kiss. 'Book?' she said after supper.

'Och, Nina. I had a bit of a run-in with the coos, you know,' he said. But then he saw her face.

'Aye, all right, just a wee bit,' he said, pulling Parsley the sheepdog over to sit under his arm.

Heart beating wildly, Nina took from the little recycled paper bag she'd used to keep the cover clean the book she'd chosen. It was called simply *Hello* and was beautifully illustrated with a series of slightly impressionistic paintings that tracked the way a baby learned to see, starting in black and white, endlessly fuzzy at the edges, and as the pages turned, coming more and more into focus and going into colour – from the motion of clouds, to the sense of a wind – until the very last page, which was a beautiful executed, very detailed picture of a baby and a mother staring each other in the eye, with just one word: 'Hello'.

Instead of falling off to sleep as he usually did, Lennox stayed stock-still and rigid throughout as Nina's voice quavered, turning every new page. He stared at her as if he'd never seen her before. Even Parsley stayed awake, sensing an atmosphere in the room.

When she'd finished, her hands trembling slightly, Nina closed the little board book with a determined air, casting her eyes down. There was a long pause; nothing could be heard but the ticking of the ancient clock, which still needed winding once a week, on the old wooden sideboard. Tick, tick, tick.

Nina couldn't bear it. Slowly she glanced upwards. Lennox was staring at her with an expression of incredulity on his face.

'You should probably tell me if you're happy,' said Nina quickly.

'Oh!' he said. And in his non-effusive way he said, 'Well, noo.'

Nina looked anxiously at his face.

'I know we didn't discuss it,' she said. 'On the other hand, we didn't *anti*-discuss it ...'

He nodded.

'So,' he said.

'This is going to have to be one of those occasions we discussed,' said Nina, 'where you have to do that talking thing. I mean, are you pleased? Are you happy?'

He looked at her in consternation.

'Of course,' he said, as if he was amazed she could possibly have thought he'd feel any differently, as indeed he was.

'I mean, we do do it a lot,' mumbled Nina. 'It does kind of follow on.'

'Thank you, yes. I am a farmer.'

She beamed up at him as he reached over for her and pulled her onto his lap, kissing her gently. His hands moved to her tummy.

'That's just me,' said Nina. 'I think it's only a tiny pea.'

'Well, I like this too. So. When?'

'November? I figured nice to have a birthday in a really dull, wet month when there's not much to do.'

He heaved a long sigh and rested his large head on her small one.

'Well,' he said. 'That will be ... that will be ... '

Nina laughed. 'Say *something*.'

There was a long pause as he held her tighter.

'Perfect,' he said eventually, very quietly. 'That will be perfect.'

And they had stayed like that for a very long time.

So, that was fine. Everything else – not so much.

Escape with
JENNY COLGAN

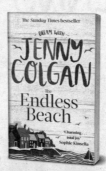

Escape to a remote little Scottish island and meet the charmingly eccentric residents of Mure...

'Charming, made me long to escape to Mure. Total joy'
SOPHIE KINSELLA

Escape with
JENNY COLGAN

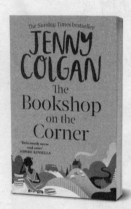
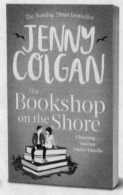

Nestled amidst the gorgeous Scottish Highlands lies
a magical world of books and romance…

**'Gorgeous location, dancing dialogue and
characters you'll fall in love with. Irresistible!**
JILL MANSELL

Escape with
JENNY COLGAN

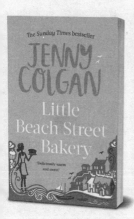

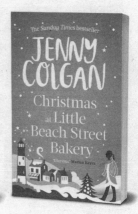

In a quaint seaside resort, where the air is rich with the smell of fresh buns and bread, a charming bakery holds the key to another world…

'Deliciously warm and sweet'
SOPHIE KINSELLA

Escape with
JENNY COLGAN

In a delightful little sweet shop, pocket money jangles, paper bags rustle and, behind the many rows of jars, secret dreams lie in wait…

'An evocative sweet treat'
JOJO MOYES

Escape with
JENNY COLGAN

Escape to a remote little Scottish island and meet the charmingly eccentric residents of Mure…

'Charming, made me long to escape to Mure. Total joy'
SOPHIE KINSELLA

WATCH OUT FOR
Jenny COLGAN

writing as Jane Beaton in

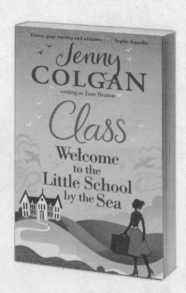

Escape to a beautiful Cornish boarding school by the sea with the wonderfully warm and funny *Class* and *Rules*.

'Funny, page-turning and addictive ... just like Malory Towers for grown-ups' SOPHIE KINSELLA

'A brilliant boarding school book, stuffed full of unforgettable characters, thrilling adventures and angst ...' LISA JEWELL

Jenny Colgan is the author of numerous *Sunday Times* bestselling novels and has won various awards for her writing, including the Melissa Nathan Award for Comedy Romance, the RNA Romantic Novel of the Year Award and the RNA Romantic Comedy Novel of the Year Award. Her books have sold more than five million copies worldwide and in 2015 she was inducted into the Love Stories Hall of Fame. Jenny is married with three children and lives in Scotland.

For more about Jenny, visit her website and her Facebook page, or follow her on Twitter and Instagram.
Twitter: @jennycolgan
Facebook: jennycolganbooks
Instagram: jennycolganbooks

~ DREAM WITH ~

JENNY COLGAN

Keep in touch with Jenny and her readers:

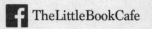 JennyColganBooks   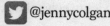 @jennycolgan

 JennyColganBooks

Check out Jenny's website and sign up to her newsletter for all the latest book news plus mouth-watering recipes.

www.jennycolgan.com

LOVE TO READ?

Join **The Little Book Café** for competitions,
sneak peeks and more.

TheLittleBookCafe   @littlebookcafe